Last Castle in the Sky

Pelham Pugh

For All My Teachers, Classmates and Alumni of Louisville High School. Red Devils Forever.

Chapter 1

Vernon Frank Bruce wasn't listening to the gavel banging on the judge's desk. He wasn't even looking in that direction. He just lay his head down upon the cold wood of the table. As the judge's booming voice handed down his sentence, he couldn't hear the words. Vern could feel the emotions pouring from his nephew, Cliff Bruce, however. He could feel the teenager's rage radiating from behind him, but there was nothing he could do. He had never felt so helpless in his life.

Cliff couldn't contain himself as the judge pronounced the sentence of death for the murders. Murders that Cliff knew in his heart, that his uncle didn't commit. He couldn't have. In his fourteen years, since his father went missing and was presumed dead in Vietnam, Unc, as Cliff called him, was his life. He took him in, treated him like his own son. Now he was going to death row for someone else' crimes.

The teenager jumped to his feet, screaming at the judge, "He didn't do it! You can't kill him!"

The judge pointed in his direction while banging his gavel. A husky bailiff sprinted to catch Cliff before he jumped over the waist-high railing separating the audience from the trial participants. Cliff wasn't going to give up easily, so the bailiff grabbed him from behind, forcing him to the floor. The entire courtroom fell silent as a sharp gasp escaped Cliff's lips, crushed beneath the weight of the bailiff.

During the commotion, Vern's own biological son, Casey Bruce, sat stoically. As the judge sentenced his father to death, his face didn't change but for a small smirk that appeared but faded quickly. The boy's mother, murdered about the same time as his father's crimes, consumed him. He didn't know how or why, but Casey, three years younger than his cousin at twelve, felt his father must've had something to do with it. He didn't show it but deep inside he didn't care if Vern lived or died. In fact, the boy felt his father had died along with his mother.

Vern kept his head buried within his cupped hands as the bailiff drug Cliff away. He couldn't look his own son in the face. He may not be guilty of the murders, but he was certainly guilty of not taking care of his family the way a husband and father should. His wife, Patty Lee, died mysteriously at sea while running away with a South American drug smuggler. He may not have been the one to take her life in the literal sense, but he certainly pushed her into the position that extinguished it.

Vern rose, his head still low, and stood perfectly still as chains were attached to his arms and legs. He felt the cold steel on his skin and the pinch when they clicked shut. The feeling inside him wasn't anger or sadness, but regret. Regret over how his actions led to this moment.

Only a few short years ago he had a wonderful family, a business that was growing, money flowing in and a home on the emerald waters of the northern Gulf of Mexico. Hell, he had even held aspirations of becoming a congressman. As the thoughts of his short-lived political career entered his mind, he shook his head.

One of the crimes he was now convicted of was murdering his campaign manager, Lucky Clay. Clay, a silent member of a loose group of criminals roaming the Southeast United States known as the Dixie Mafia, was found dead in a Georgia swamp. Lucky worked with candidates that would help, or at least not hinder, the sinister organization's interests and Vern meant to become one of the candidates that would not hinder their operations along the Gulf Coast, didn't play along as the organization wanted. He held his own ideas and convictions, and it cost him the election by a landslide. Lucky Clay had paid with his life when he tried escaping with their money.

Lucky, already afraid his ties to the Dixie Mafia were wearing thin after his failure, tried to loot the campaign and make off for a Caribbean Island before they caught up with him. He didn't make it, but his body wasn't the only one found in that Georgia swamp.

Dumped beside Clay was the dirty cop who performed the hit on the corrupt campaign manager. They both ended up next to each other on the bank next to the swamp's black, stagnant water. Vern ended up taking the fall for both, as the gun used in both ended up in his hands, set up by the man who now took care of his nephew and his son, but, at this moment, he couldn't focus on Burt Williams. He did what he had to in order to keep his boys safe and alive.

Now, Vern sat alone in a small holding cell outside the courtroom. His chains were still attached, and he strained against them, but he couldn't reach his eyes. He felt tears forming and wanted desperately to hold them back. Bruce men didn't cry, but lately, he found himself surrendering to his emotions more often.

He didn't want to think about his fate. He didn't want to think about prison, death row, or any of that. His tears flowed faster when he thought about Patty Lee, Cliff, and Casey. His mind drifted back. He thought about the years he was happiest. The years before his quest for power took over his life. Over the years that were the happiest for them. The days they ate breakfast at the little café over in Port St. Joe and spending the rest of the day on the beach with the boys. He closed his tear-stained eyes and thought about the white sand and wiggled his toes, pretending his feet were buried in the powdery grains. He could see his wife sitting beside him, smiling, and he reached for her but felt nothing but air. His mind turned dark and in the distance he could see her father, staring at the him with that look. The look of disappointment with his daughter's choice of a husband.

When his ties to the Colombian cartels became more than he could handle, he took his own life, leaving his only daughter to deal with the aftermath. Patty Lee, growing tired of Vern's timidness and obsession with his dead brother, ended up falling in love with one of them, ending with her murder beside the smuggler.

Vern jolted back to reality as the door opened and Cliff stood in the doorway. Instinctively, Vern lunged towards him, only to be jerked back to the cold steel of the desk by his chains. He winced as the steel cut into flesh. Despite the pain, he smiled at his nephew. Cliff stepped slowly forward, alarmed by the sight of his uncle bound like an animal, his feet and hands secured to the floor and table. His escort, a county deputy, followed him closely, his hand on the teenager's shoulder.

Cliff broke free, racing to his uncle. "Unc, what are we going to do?" Cliff asked, vitriol dripping from his words. Vern tried to keep a smile on his face, but inside he wanted to die.

"First off, you are going to take care of your cousin. I know how he feels about me, blamed me for his mother, but I love him," Vern said, his voice surprisingly strong, "I love you, Cliff and you gotta know I didn't do this."

Cliff straightened beside his uncle, reached down, and put his hand on his shoulder. "We also got to find my father."

Vern froze. Cliff had told him about the letter from his father on an earlier visit. His brother, Ronald Frank Bruce, didn't die in the plane crash taking him to fight in Vietnam. There was no doubt now that the words of Rafael Demingo were true, for the most part.

Demingo was a dirty FBI agent that tried to get Vern's cooperation. Dangling hazy information about Rof, his brother's nickname, and warnings of his wife's involvement with Christian Lopez. The agent claimed to have pictures, even showed them to

Vern, but still he doubted his brother's survival. Then came the letter.

The letter, in Rof's handwriting, came from a former Vietnamese Colonel that worked in the prisoner of war camp that held his brother. That was a while back and Vern tried to remain hopeful, but with every day that passed, his hope faded. He couldn't hold the fake smile any longer and touched Cliff's hand with his head.

"Cliff, he's got to be..." Vern paused and considered his words, "gone." The words left a bitter taste in his mouth—he didn't truly believe them, but he knew his nephew couldn't spend his youth clinging solely to hope.

Cliff shook his head, and his anger began to reconstitute as sorrow with tears forming in his bright blue eyes. "I can't believe that. I just can't. But I've got to get you out of this, and *we* will find him."

Vern picked his head up, "Don't worry about me, son. You gotta live your own life. My life is done and so is your father's. You and Casey have your lives in front of you."

"Time's up, Bruce," the cop barked and pulled Cliff away from him. "I love you Cliff," Vern said with tears as Cliff muttered the same as the deputy grabbed Cliff by the arm and escorted him from the room. The slamming door echoed throughout the room and once again Vern was alone with his thoughts.

A couple of days later, Vern found himself shackled in a bus. The state of Georgia had extradited Vern to stand trial and now he was on his way to the state's death row just south of Atlanta. He savored each mile as the pines and swamps of the extreme southern part of the state gave way to seemingly endless open fields.

As the van made its way through countryside and endless fields of red clay northward to Atlanta, Vern thought back to his father and his love of the Atlanta Braves. He could often be found watching them night after night. The night his heart gave out on him he sat on a barstool watching them lose again. The official cause of death was a heart attack, but Vern knew his heart stopped beating because it was broken and he and his brother caused it. After Rof's plane went down in the South China Sea, Pops was never the same. He often thought about how disappointed his father would be with the family now. As the fields passed, he wished he could talk to him one more time and seek his advice. The driver opened his window, and Vern took a deep breath, as the smell of the red clay filled the bus. He closed his eyes and, in his mind, thought this might be the last time he breathed in the outside air.

The joy was fleeting and the trip shorter than he had hoped. The sight of the prison, sitting on a hill, surrounded by two rows of razor tipped wires, sapped what little was left of the happiness he felt watching the scenery from his seat in the van. He was stripped, processed, and led to his cell.

It seemed smaller than the holding cell in the courthouse. He sat on the hard bed and held his feet straight in front of him. His feet touched the opposite wall. There were no windows, and the flaking grey paint seemed to match his mood. There were so many chips in the paint that it seemed there was more bare concrete showing than paint covering the wall.

The door slammed shut and the when the lock engaged, Vern felt a shroud of darkness fall upon him. He wasn't dead yet, but he might as well be. It would be more humane to kill him now than enduing years of being left alone with his thoughts that lay in front of him. He leaned back and placed his head against the wall. His lawyer gave him little hope on appeals and Vern knew that Georgia meant business when it came to executions. He reached his hands outward and ran his fingers along each wrist, following the scratches left by the handcuffs. He put his head into his hands and sighed. About that time, he heard someone yell, "Lights out!" and the room fell dark.

In the days following his entrance into death row, Vern had nothing else but time to think. He wondered if Burt Williams, the Dixie Mafia gangster married to Cliff's mother, Susie, indeed set him up. Was Burt the killer, or did he hire it done? Was it Miguel Demingo the FBI agent that tried to coerce him with information about his brother? Was it his wife and her Columbian lover, Christian Lopez? How in the hell did all this spiral out of control so quickly? Even if his life *was* over, he wanted answers for Casey's sake. With Cliff convinced of his uncle's innocence and

Casey certain his father was a cold-blooded killer, the two of them would soon be at odds. If they weren't already.

Susie Williams, Casey's mother, had driven the two boys to the trial in Georgia and now they were headed back to West Palm where the Williams family had taken residence in Casey's grandfather, Old Man Clark's, mansion. Casey sat in the front seat with his mother and Cliff stared out the window from the back seat. Neither was in the mood to talk. She tried making conversation with the boys, but it never amounted to much, so she gave up the effort as they passed through Jacksonville and turned south. When they finally arrived back in West Palm and the two were alone, however, that quickly changed.

"I hope the bastard gets what's coming to him," Casey said without a hint of emotion in his voice. They had walked out on the beach, away from everyone in the house, including Burt Williams, the Dixie Mafia enforcer who had set Vern up and stepped into his life.

Burt, ever mindful of the precarious grip he kept on the family, walked out onto the back deck of the enormous home, and sat in a wooden chair. He chewed on a fat cigar and watched the pair as they talked. He didn't know their words, but he could read their body language, even from a distance.

Cliff pointed his finger at Casey, "You don't mean that Casey. He's your father."

Casey kicked at the brown sand and turned away from his cousin, "Not anymore," was his only reply. He didn't want to talk about how Cliff *knew* his father was innocent or how he was a victim of circumstance. Casey loved his mother dearly, and her death affected him severely.

Casey thought about the past few months, and he whirled around to face Cliff. His cousin didn't know what it was like to be dragged off a boat. He didn't understand how not knowing what happened to his mother was a nightmare that he couldn't shake. He had no clue how it felt to be thrown in a boy's home and left to fend for himself. He didn't know the embarrassment of his father's mug shot plastered on the television every night. Cliff, sheltered from it all by his mother, just didn't know. He used to look up to Cliff, but it had gotten to the point where he hated to hear his voice, much less look at him.

Cliff held up his hands in despair, "Look, I know you can't see it right now, but we *will* find out the truth. How could he do that to your mother, Cliff? He was in jail, and you know that is a fact!" Cliff's voice rose as he spoke.

Casey pointed past the dunes where Burt was perched, "Burt told me he could've hired it done."

Cliff pointed up to Burt also, countering, "Unc told me not to trust him."

Casey laughed, "Of course he did."

The conversation ended there. Casey walked back towards the house defiantly, and Cliff went in the opposite direction, walking along the beach. Burt watched as the two parted and chuckled to himself. He rolled the cigar around in his mouth, but he didn't light it, he just rolled it around his fleshy mouth, chewing endlessly. He flashed a toothy grin as Casey walked up the steps and pulled the chair beside him closer and patted the seat. Casey flopped down, frowning.

Burt didn't look over at the boy but leaned his head closer to him, "He still got the idea your daddy is a saint who did nothing wrong?"

Casey looked out over the Atlantic and reached his hand toward a distant gull, floating in the breeze. "Hell yeah, bastard killed two people and my mother. Still thinks it was pinned on him by somebody else," he replied.

Burt held the cigar between his teeth. "Every killer I ever knew always told anyone they could about their innocence and counted on weak minded people to believe that shit," Burt sneered, "And don't you forget that." He rolled the cigar to the other side of his mouth and motioned around him. "World's full of crooks, Case. Your daddy just happened to be one." He looked at Casey from the corner of his eye and saw the hurt in the young boy's face. "He was always jealous of your momma. The money, the power, and he wanted every single bit of it for himself. Why he had her wacked. He wanted it all. But you listen here kid, stick with me and I'll make sure all of this is yours."

Burt tried to fake a grimace, but the grin just wouldn't leave his face. *When these two boys go at it*, he thought, *they will take each other out and I'll be the one who comes out on top.* He laughed. He didn't mean to and it caught Casey off guard. All he could picture was Vern, alone on death row and crying uncontrollably. The man is weak. If he wasn't he'd be in this very seat right now talking to his son. Yet, here *he* was, chewing on a cigar, enjoying the ocean breeze, and feeding lies into Vern's son's ear.

The door opened and Susie stepped outside. She took a deep breath. She loved the salty air and these days she was always smiling. Her early days, after Rof's death and the birth of their son, were hard for her. The young girl, still a teenager, fell on hard times. During one of her lowest times, she left Cliff with his uncle and asked him to take care of him. Susie missed most of his childhood while she struggled to get her life on track. Now, she enjoyed every moment she had with her son, and felt she gained another son in Casey.

She motioned for Casey to come in for dinner and looked around for Cliff. She held her hand over her eyes and could barely see him in the distance. She sat down in the chair vacated by Casey when he went inside to wash up for supper.

She reached out and put her hand on top of her husband's. "I'm so worried about these boys," she told Burt, "They've been through too much. You know it's got to be rough on them."

Burt shrugged his shoulders, "I had a rough time coming up and I turned out just fine." He pointed to the ocean and around the Clark Mansion.

Susie was not in a sympathetic mood and replied, "This, all of this, is all because of their suffering." The tears started flowing and deep down somewhere Burt felt sorry for her. She had been used far more than she knew and for that Burt felt for her, but he could never let her know the truth behind it all. He'd take that to his grave.

Originally, he didn't want to be associated with Vern Bruce more than he had to. He knew the plan and stuck with it. He looked around, admiring his new home, and thought to himself that it was worth a few tears. He reached over, put his arm around his wife and told her he would take care of it. It wasn't the first lie he ever told.

Chapter 2

Veck Baxter, perched on the edge of his bed in the dimly lit room of the Fairmont Hotel in the heart of New Orleans, staring at the only light in the room. The lights were off, but the television glow brightened the room. His scarred face locked in and his attention unwavering, he watched the story of Vernon Bruce on the national news. Beside him lay a wooden cane and on the table, a medicine bottle, and a fifth of whiskey. A knock on the door aroused him from his intense gaze and he slowly lifted himself up from the bed, moaning slightly as he did. Little by little he made his way to the door and unlocked it.

Veck looked to be in his mid-forties, his jet-black hair showing no signs of graying just yet with piercing blue eyes and a heavy tan on his rough skin. He opened the door, transferring his weight to the cane, revealing a taller man, thin and slightly Hispanic in appearance. "Come in Jeff," Veck told him as he motioned towards the empty room, still holding on to the door.

"Thank you," he replied, his accent distinctly South American but with a Southern United States twang noticeably mixed in. Antonio Jefferson Black stepped into the room and took one of the empty chairs at the small table. Veck eased into the chair next to him, groaning once again as he eased his slender frame into the seat.

"I've been watching the news," Veck said in a heavy southern drawl, "very interesting television."

"I take it then, you know about Vernon Bruce," he replied.

"Yes," Veck said, reaching for the bottle of pills, "I saw where he got the death penalty," as he turned his attention to a window facing surrounding buildings and the muddy water of the Mississippi River in the distance.

"That they did," Black said flatly.

Veck turned back to face Black. With a slight grin that tried vainly to mask the pain, he asked him, "Burt Williams playing along?" Black smiled and replied that Williams now enjoyed the life they had laid at his feet.

"Good. We are going to need him happy to get what we need," Veck said and popped a small pill into his mouth. He didn't wash it down with water, he chewed and quickly swallowed it, "We need him feeding us money from the Clark Family. You can't go to war without that money."

Black's neutral expression gave way to a scowl and his mood turned somber at the mention of money. The money wasn't flowing as it should. The death of Christian Lopez, or officially, the *disappearance* of Christian Lopez caused the importation of the lucrative white powder from Columbia to drop drastically in South Florida.

Burt Williams was merely a foot soldier in the Dixie Mafia, nothing else. A simple hoodlum that both men knew didn't have the brainpower to smuggle and even less capability to run Old Man Clark's business. He was simply a tool.

Black stood and ran his fingers through his dark hair and stared out the window, "Maybe he is *too* happy in his present situation," he said, "perhaps we should remind him of who he *really* works for."

Veck knew exactly what that meant. These Brazilians were cold. They had to be. Black held no qualms about hurting those closest to Burt Williams, and if not for him, the family would probably already be dead.

He also knew Black had other reasons he wanted Williams out of the picture. The Brazilian and Williams had murdered Lopez and Vernon Bruce's wife. If Burt Willaims exited the situation, there would be no eyewitness. After all, Black was a ghost. One that didn't exist in this country. He slipped in and out of the Gulf Coast undetected. He had performed the trick for years and quickly became an expert at slipping over borders.

"No, I think we should handle this differently," Veck told him, holding up a finger, "I'm not cold-blooded, Jeff and I'm not going to hurt innocents in this. The Dixie Mafia would, the Columbians would, hell I know *you* would, but I won't. There are other ways to coerce people into compliance. The mind is more of a tool to exploit than physical pain." He tapped his leg with the cane, "And I would know."

Black walked over and placed his hand on Veck's shoulder and glanced back at the bright glow of sunlight streaming through the window, "I'll leave that to you, my friend," he replied as he stood up to leave. He helped Veck to his feet and the two men embraced.

Black chewed back questions he wanted to ask about how Veck would handle Burt Williams, but he knew the time wasn't right. What he already knew was that Burt Williams wouldn't survive if Veck Baxter infiltrated his mind. The Brazilian was accustomed to murder, but to wreck a man's mind, that was worse than death.

Black left and Veck eased back into his chair. He felt the warmth from the sun on his face, longing to be outside in the fresh air, but his injuries often caught up with him and today was no exception. He reached for the bottle of pills on the table next to him and popped open the lid. He threw two into his mouth, following them with a swig of whiskey to wash them down. It was the only way he held the pain at bay. When the pain drove him to the pills, his mind dulled—but for now, he could afford the haze.

When the time came and he finally had to deal with Burt Williams, this affordance would have to stop. *No stone left unturned*, he thought to himself. Once Williams was out of the way, he would turn his attention to the Bruce Family and the promise he made to a dying friend. Business and vengeance consumed the Brazilians, but to Veck his purpose in life was righting a wrong. A wrong that festered for years and would soon be ready to either heal or be cut away like a leprous appendage. It was up to Vern Bruce to decide.

While Veck Baxter contemplated the future, Jeff Black found a bench overlooking the rolling waters of the Mississippi River. In contrast to Baxter, thoughts about the past consumed his mind. As the stained water rushed by on its inevitable collision with the emerald waters of the Gulf of Mexico, it reminded him of his family's adopted homeland and the mighty river that flowed through it.

He admired the walls holding the massive river out of the city and thought about how his ancestors had built this city. *Hell,* he thought, *they built this country only to be exiled and cast aside.* He envisioned the area as it was before the war. He had heard legends passed down from family to family. The Black Family was not the only one forced from their homeland after Lee surrendered.

Some families that made the long voyage went back quickly. Back into subservience to their Northern masters. Some trod along, forcing survival in the heart of the Amazonian Jungle. Each exiled family that survived the jungle held the hope of one day returning, even if they pretended to love their new country.

They had adapted as well as they could to their new homes and over the many years they blended into a strange and foreign culture, but still, it was not home. It wasn't Dixie. This land was home, he thought as he took a deep breath. It smelled different, as a pungent smell filled his nostrils, but it *felt* like home. He wanted the others to feel as he did in this moment. The sense of history and belonging that didn't accompany them to their new home over a century ago.

A police officer strode by and Black tipped his cap. The cop's appearance snapped his thoughts back to the present. He watched as the officer walked into the crowded distance. To make his people's dreams into reality, he must do terrible things. He must become terror itself. His face hardened and his thoughts stiffened. He was prepared and ready to do what he must. Nobody, not even Veck Baxter, would get in his way.

The expansive office that once housed Daniel Clark, and later his daughter Patty Lee, now belonged to Dixie Mafia gangster Burt Williams. Old Man Clark, as he was known—just like his father before him—built a business empire from the ground up in the heart of Florida. First it was cattle, then oranges, and finally real estate and other, not always completely legal, arrangements.

The conglomerate was completely legitimate until Old Man Clark brought the family into dealings with people like Christian Lopez and his organization of cocaine smugglers from Columbia. The old man, over his head in his dealings, took his own life and left his daughter in the arms of Christian Lopez. A romance that blossomed quickly and ended with the same ferocity as their brief affair. Now, one of the very men responsible stood at the controls and the legitimate parts of the business shrank exponentially while the shady side grew healthy.

As usual, Burt, and his ever-growing bulk, sat in the plush leather chair once occupied by Old Man Clark. He propped his shiny new cowboy boots on the antique wooded desk, scuffing the treasure with every movement. He didn't care that the desk was probably worth more than the brand-new Oldsmobile he drove, he wasn't into things like that. The once pristine desk now bore scratch marks from the heel of his boots.

The phone on the edge of the desk rang and he rolled his ever-present cigar to the other side of his mouth, answering it on the third ring. Old Dixie Mafia habits die hard, and the three rings were one of the signals the organization used to send the all clear to the other person on the line.

"Burt Williams," he spoke into the receiver trying to sound as businesslike as possible.

The strange accent of Jeff Black came from the other end, "Mr. Williams, it has been a while. How are *operations* going on the coastal project?" Black never wasted pleasantries on a man like Burt.

Feeling slighted, Burt responded, "No, hello, how's the wife and kids?"

If he recognized the sarcastic dig, the Brazilian didn't change his demeanor or at least his voice didn't betray his thoughts.

"*Business*, Mr. Williams. How are things going?" he demanded once again.

"We are making progress," Burt said. Knowing there could be people listening to their conversation, they communicated in code. *Progress* indicated that money continued flowing in. However, in reality, the money was slowing down and both men knew it.

"That is not the way I understand it, Mr. Williams. Progress has slowed significantly since you picked up the project," Black said coldly.

Burt took the cigar from his mouth, slammed it on the desk, completely missing the ashtray, scattering tobacco. He defended himself, "the *contractors* have made things harder. Since their foreman left, they don't feel the need to play ball as they should."

Burt pulled another cigar from his shirt pocket and wiped the remnants of the demolished one onto the floor. He contemplated lighting this one but didn't feel like dealing with the smoke. The few employees left were all health nuts and complained just loud enough to hear when he lit one. Sometimes he missed his dirty Biloxi bar that often doubled as a makeshift office. He made a mental note to fire every last one of them and bring on some of *his* kind of people.

The response from the South American took longer than Burt thought it should, making him a little nervous. When Black finally spoke, he spoke slowly, "Your job is to smooth things over with them. They have their directives from me and *my* organization. Seems they don't respect you. Seems they feel as though you are a common redneck. It is *your* responsibility, I remind you, to convince them otherwise." Black paused and Burt could hear Black's breath through the phone. "We put you in this position, Mr. Williams, and we can take you out."

Black understood that Veck Baxter had no intention of bringing physical harm to Williams or his family—but a well-placed threat now and then didn't hurt. For now, he would abide by his friend's wishes; they needed Veck to see their larger plan through. But despite his loyalty and genuine fondness for Baxter, Black's patience was wearing thin. He was tired of waiting for the American to handle Williams on his own terms.

Burt didn't let the silence linger long, responding, "Sometimes it takes some force to deal with contractors like these. Maybe I get some of my associates together and go *reason* with them."

Black shook his head in disbelief and wanted to shout through the line but held his composure. "That is precisely what they expect. That is why they think of you the way they do. These people don't respond well to *force*. Perhaps you should try and show them some hospitality. You should already know respect goes a long way."

Burt didn't want to show these animals any respect. He knew the way they operated, and his philosophy was that steel always sharpens steel. He didn't want to be friends with them. He didn't want to invite them into his house and have dinner with them. The Dixie Mafia didn't work like that and neither did he. He was taught to deal with problems by brute force. But he didn't want to die either.

He had heard stories about Christian Lopez and how he dealt with unfaithful people. Lopez' fascination with butchery caused his own people to want him dead. That's why it had been so easy to do away with him and his mistress, Patrica Lee Clark, with no retribution from Colombia. Burt didn't fear the cartels but he damn sure respected the way they did business.

"I'll do what I have to Mr. Black, you can count on that," Burt assured him. The line clicked on the other end of the line and the resulting high-pitched tone from the receiver screamed in Burt's ear.

He had put off meeting the replacement the Colombians sent in place of Lopez, but after that phone call, he could postpone it no longer. He lit his cigar and blew the smoke in the air. A couple of people walking by the office glanced at him in disapproval and Burt blew the next puff of smoke in their direction. He hated these people and for a split second it crossed his mind to stand up and fire them all. He was the boss, but right now, he had another problem.

He dreaded calling home and informing his wife they would have company for dinner. Again, he wished he was back in Biloxi, but he looked out of the large window in *his* office and saw the Oldsmobile parked in *his* reserved spot. The next puff of smoke floated away, taking those feelings with it.

The car rolled into the driveway of the Clark Mansion precisely at seven, just as planned. The car, old and decrepit, looked out of place in the affluent neighborhood. Several spots along the jalopy's body were nearly rusted through. Burt thought he saw a small amount of smoke oozing from the tailpipe as it pulled to a stop. *Damn*, he thought, *when did I get back to Mississippi?*

Only one person occupied the battered vehicle and Burt thought that highly unusual. Every time he had met with Christian Lopez there had been a driver and he figured that's the way these Colombians rolled, yet this guy was alone. Burt figured the greaseball was either showing bravado or he was just stupid. He considered himself a superior judge of people and reminded himself to watch the guy closely. He needed to know tonight who he was dealing with.

The car had pulled right up to the front door of the residence and an average height man emerged. He wasn't skinny nor was he fat. Burt judged him as *portly*. His dark hair slicked back, and shining, and dark complexion indicated his Columbian heritage. When he spoke, his accent was thick, each word heavy with its origin.. Even more so than Lopez Burt thought, and the native Mississippian had trouble understanding him at first.

The Columbian extended his hand first and with his thick accent asked, "Mr. Burt Williams?"

Burt nodded and as he did so took the half-chewed cigar from his mouth and grabbed the extended hand of his guest with his free hand. "Yes, sir," was his reply. The two men shook hands, and each tightened their grip with each movement. *Bravado it is* Burt thought.

"Perhaps I should introduce myself. My name is Mateo Diaz," he said. Burt noticed how he pronounced his last name as Dee-az instead of the local Die-az, "It is a pleasure to come into your home tonight." Burt peered at him intently, trying to size him up.

"Come on in," Burt replied as he motioned for Diaz to follow him inside. Diaz glanced around and shook his head in approval.

"Certainly, this is such a beautiful home," he admired. They made their way into the house and Diaz looked out across the beach and whistled. He looked back at Burt with a wide smile and winked as he added, "with a most beautiful view."

Burt raised an eyebrow and shifted his cigar, "It'll do," and the two men walked out onto the back deck overlooking the beach.

"Cigar?" Burt asked him as they sat down. Diaz nodded and Burt took one of his plump cigars out of his pocket and handed it to him.

"A light, please?" Diaz asked and Burt obliged.

Susie appeared from the doorway and held a couple of open beers. Diaz rose at once when he saw her and introduced himself, reaching for her hand and placed his lips to her smooth skin. *These cats have some kind of charm,* Burt thought, and he peered at the Columbian from the side of his eye making a mental note to convey to his guest that his wife was not Patty Lee Bruce.

As soon as they were alone again, Burt pushed his personal thoughts to the back of his mind, wasting no time getting to business.

"Mr. Diaz," Burt started but Diaz cut him off, "Mateo, please". Burt thought for a moment and carefully responded, "*Mr. Diaz*, this is a business relationship and gonna stay that way. This is the only time I'll invite you to my home and there are some things I want to make clear." If Diaz was offended by Burt's forward language, he didn't show it. He merely nodded in agreement without speaking and let Burt continue.

"First, no meetings unless *I* call them. This is my turf and you gotta respect that. If you can't we are done right here and now," Burt's voice didn't crack nor show any weakness. He had been in these type meetings before, back home, and it didn't matter if it was rednecks or Columbian trash, you dealt with all types of gangsters in one way. Force.

"Second," he hardly missed a beat, "The only thing that matters is money. We make money, we are *all* happy. The most important thing is that you don't go over my head. Don't ever. Black and his goons think they are in charge since they got rid of...." he paused and considered his words, "your predecessor. I'll deal with them. You don't. We handle our business on our own. Too many hands in the cookie jar are a dangerous thing." Burt let his counterpart absorb his words and waited for a reply.

Diaz nodded in agreement, "Yes, I understand completely, *Mr. Williams* and I will work within your demands." The Colombian placed his untouched beer on the table between them and took off his sunglasses. "But let me say this, so we both know where we stand. You screw me over, cookie jar or no and I'll kill your entire family." Burt turned to him, meeting his gaze. At that moment, he realized there was no *Bravado* in this man. His eyes were like death, burning as an intense fire. His face, like a piece of steel, froze Burt for just a second. This man was all business. Burt struggled in regaining his composure and pulled his cigar from the corner of his mouth, replacing the stogie with a broad grin.

"We understand each other, then," Burt said and once again the men shook hands. This time neither tried to outgrip the other.

Chapter 3

Cliff clutched the stained piece of paper holding the only words he ever received from his father. His earlier tears stained the page, and he held it gingerly in his hands. He read it over and over. Even though the letter was written a few years ago from his father's prison camp in Vietnam, he didn't lose hope that Rof Bruce, his father, was still alive. He couldn't lose that hope. Cliff didn't know how he was going to find his father, but he knew it would take his uncle's help. He couldn't do it alone.

He carefully folded the letter and placed it in its hiding place in the corner of his sock drawer. Over it, he placed a couple of pairs of socks to protect it from any lurking eyes. His cousin was notorious for snooping and Cliff didn't want Casey's prying eyes in his business. Casey may hate his own father right now and wish him dead, but to Cliff, Unc was his world. His uncle was innocent and the only other person on the planet sharing his hope that Rof Bruce was still alive.

Vern didn't want Cliff visiting him on death row. He didn't even want him to send him letters. He had told Cliff this in the only letter he received from his uncle since the sentencing. Still Cliff wrote. He wrote at least several times a week and he wasn't about to give up.

As he closed the drawer, Casey burst through the door without knocking. Cliff didn't notice the loud music from his cousin's next-door room had stopped.

"Wanna go down to the shop?" Casey asked. The shop was a hangout in West Palm. The Atlantic Coast of Florida didn't have the giant waves that somewhere like Hawaii boasted but some days the surf was high enough to grab a board and ride the crest to shore. Casey loved hanging out at the shop, but Cliff didn't care anything about it.

"Hell no, I don't want to go hang around those bums," Cliff shot back.

Casey frowned, "You never want to go hang out."

Cliff spun around in his chair facing Casey. "Those guys down there are bad news, Case. They smoke, drink and God knows what else."

Casey's frown immediately turned into a smile, and he nodded his head, "Yeah, that's why I wanna go," he said leaving the room and slamming the door behind him.

Cliff turned back to his desk and outside the window, a Cardinal stood on the windowsill. Susie hurriedly came through the door and asked Cliff what was going on. She heard the door slamming from downstairs and Casey sped by her as they met in the stairwell. She stopped in her tracks when she heard the Cardinal sing and slowly peeked around her son to see the redbird perched just outside the window. Tears filled her eyes and she fell to her knees.

"Mom! What's wrong?" Cliff asked as he fell beside his mother, wrapping his arms around her.

Susie couldn't control her emotions, her eyes trained on the bird, "Cliff, it's a cardinal!"

Cliff's confusion was evident on his face, and his mother gently cupped his cheeks, her voice soft as she whispered, "Baby, it's your father."

He shook his head, "What are you talking about?"

She pointed a shaky finger at the bird, her tears streaming, "The cardinal. Haven't you heard about them?"

"No, mom, what?"

She stood up, Cliff with her, and eased her way to the window. Suddenly the bird lunged from the windowsill and with a few flaps of its wings, took off towards the ocean, gaining altitude with each motion. Susie rushed to the window and threw it open, salty air filling the room.

"Your father is gone! That was him!" she exclaimed.

Cliff took his mother's hand. In the distance he thought he heard the cardinal's song. He squeezed her hand, "Mom, you're scaring me."

Susie dried her eyes with her fingers, "Cardinals are dead loved ones, baby. I've always heard that when one shows up like that, they are visiting from heaven.," she looked back but couldn't find the bird any longer, "That was Rof. I know it."

Cliff pursed his lips and put his hands on the windowsill and leaned so he could see. The cardinal was nowhere to be found. "Mom," he said tenderly, "That's got to be just an old wife's tale."

"He's gone," she said under her breath, "He's gone." Susie slowly left the room and eased the door shut behind her.

Cliff left the window open as the breeze flowed over his body and calmed him. He didn't believe his mother's words. He couldn't, not now, so he tried to concentrate on other things. He fell back onto the edge of his bed and his thoughts returned to his cousin.

He eased back and put his head on a pillow and let out a deep breath. He worried about his cousin. Casey had taken to Burt too much. Unc warned him about trusting him. He told him to show respect but don't trust him until he earns it. Cliff took it to heart. He treated Burt as an authority figure but not as a father.

Cliff noticed the things going on around his stepfather and the people he associated with. Sure, on the surface, he seemed like a normal guy, and he played the part, so far, as a humble family man. He assumed a lead role in the Clark family business. Cliff, however, kept a close eye on the real Burt Williams. He felt it was his duty not only for himself, but for Casey and especially his mother.

Cliff grabbed a baseball cap and set out to bring his cousin home from the Surf Shop. When he stepped off the last step, he found his mother standing over the cooktop preparing eggs for breakfast. Susie caught him as he tried to sneak through the side door and although protesting, he sat down to eat before leaving.

"Have a seat," she directed Cliff to the seat beside Casey. Cliff followed the command and Casey grinned at him as he did.

She had already stopped him in his tracks as he tried to run out the door himself. Her eyes were still moist from their encounter upstairs, but she had regained her composure and actually held a smile on her face as she stirred the eggs.

Without looking up from her work she asked, "Where are ya'll off to this morning?" Cliff told her he was going to the library to look through the old newspapers. Casey lied and told her he was just going to the beach for a while. Cliff shot him with a look of disapproval, but Casey just smiled and kept up the charade.

Susie gave Cliff a worried look, "a fourteen-year-old living on this beautiful beach and in this beautiful house, you should enjoy it for once." She waved her hand in front of the window as she spoke. Cliff nodded but she knew he was more interested in his helping his uncle than frolicking on the beach. Susie realized a long time ago that he was more like Vern than his father. Rof was a beach bum to the core but Cliff was a bookworm like his uncle.

She looked over at Casey. He didn't look like Vern nor Rof, but she could see Rof developing in his personality, even at twelve despite never knowing his uncle. She smiled at both and told them both how much she loved them as she put their plates in front of them. Casey inhaled the aroma of the eggs and raised an eyebrow.

"No bacon?" he asked playfully. Susie smirked and said just a second as she walked over the refrigerator and pulled out the package.

The strips sizzled in the frying pan when the door connecting the kitchen to the back deck swung open and Burt stomped through. He held his nose in the air and said, "I knew I smelt bacon!"

As it was Saturday, he dressed in his now customary Hawaiian style shirt, shorts, and flip-flops. He reached for a cigar, but Susie made a "no" motion with her finger. She didn't like those things, lit or not, in her house. He grinned and slowly put his hand into the pocket of his shorts. "Yes ma'am," he said in the sweetest voice a man like him could muster and turned his attention to Cliff and Casey.

"Boys, what kind of hell are y'all getting into today?" he asked with a crooked grin. Cliff shook his head and Casey smiled and said, "You know, Uncle Burt." It bothered Cliff that he called him that. Burt let out a slight laugh, opened the refrigerator and removed a bottled beer.

"Little early?" Susie asked, biting her bottom lip.

Burt grimaced, "Can't have my cigar, I gotta have something," he retorted.

Susie didn't want to push the issue and just let it go with no more argument. Casey asked Burt to drive him to the shop. "Sure will," he replied, "those are my kinda folks down there. You going too Cliff?" Cliff shook his head. Burt's grin instantly changed into a scowl, and he growled, "Library again?" Cliff didn't answer. He didn't need to.

Susie, sensing the tension, broke into the conversation, "I'll drop you. It's on the way to the store I'm going to this morning."

Burt rubbed his thumb and forefinger together as he asked her "How much?" She didn't reply.

She thought about telling Burt about the cardinal, but let the notion evaporate quickly. Not only did he not believe in such things, but he also hated the mere mention of Rof Bruce. He was a jealous man, and a jealous man can be a very dangerous man. She discovered that fact quickly during her years on the streets.

Susie and Cliff climbed into the red Monte Carlo that once belonged to Patty Lee Bruce and began their trip to town. The meandering road leaving the secluded subdivision was lined with old, majestic oaks. Each time he passed them, Cliff marveled at their sheer size and flowing branches. He wondered how they survived so many storms and hurricanes. Susie noticed him admiring the centuries old trees and she smiled at him. He was too distracted to notice for a while, but when he turned his attention towards her he laughed at her "goofy smile" as he called it.

Susie, happy for the time alone with her son spoke quietly, as if she was afraid someone might hear her words besides Cliff, "You know, Burt feels like this is a fool's errand, all of this with your uncle," she told him, pausing for a couple seconds, "I'm concerned too Cliff. You are a kid, be a kid." Cliff noticed the concern etched in the premature wrinkles at the corners of her eyes.

He didn't want to worry her, but he couldn't give up on his uncle. "Mom, you know he didn't do what they say he did. I know him and I know he isn't that kind of person." Cliff ran his fingers through his hair, "Plus, all of the evidence they had was," he paused looking for the right word, "*circumstance. Nobody saw* him do it. All they had was the gun and fingerprints."

Susie looked at her son and this time she had to force a smile, "You're smarter than the lawyers, son, but..."

Cliff cut her off, "That ain't saying much." They both laughed at this but as the laughter died down, she turned serious once again.

She pulled the car over to the side of the road and eased the transmission into park. She grabbed her son by the hand and pulled him in as close as she could. "Burt wants to be a father to you. Casey has taken to him, why can't you give him a chance?" She lifted one eyebrow inquisitively as she spoke.

Cliff put his forehead on hers and said quietly, "Mom, I love you and I *trust* you. I don't trust *him*," Cliff refrained from telling her that his uncle had warned him not to trust Burt Williams. He didn't want to give her anything else to hold against Unc. "You know the type of people he runs with." He wanted to say "*the kind of person he is*" but didn't push the issue.

Susie's eyebrow smoothed back to a neutral position as she replied, "Used to run with."

Cliff just glanced back at his mother in disbelief and released a long sigh, "I'll trust him when he gives me *reason* to," Cliff said coldly.

While Susie and Cliff held their conversation beside the road, Burt and Casey were just pulling up at the surf shop. The ride had been mostly silent as Casey enjoyed just hanging around with Burt and he liked the gangster's style of music. It wasn't country and it sure wasn't the beachy music most people played around West Palm. Burt enjoyed the guitar-oriented groups of the seventies and in turn, so did Casey. They had been blasting Black Sabbath as loud as the speakers could handle before reaching their breaking point. Casey loved the banging drums and the super-loud guitars, but what he loved most was the singer. He had never heard a voice like his anywhere before and tried to sing just like him, but never could reach the same notes. Before he jumped out at the surf shop, Burt slid him one of his slender cigars.

"Enjoy it kid," he said as Casey shut the door and shot a wave back at him. Burt gassed the engine, and the tires screamed as he pulled back onto the road. Casey's stride was bold and swaggering as he approached the group of teenage boys.

Casey, one of the youngest to hang out around the surf shop, but also one of the most respected. Most of the others were high schoolers that often-skipped school to hang out, but a few were dropouts. With the shop directly across the street from the beach, they congregated there watching the bikini clad girls and pelt them with cat calls. He walked up to the group hanging near the rear of the shop and popped the cigar in his mouth. Without asking or hesitation one of the older kids lit it for him. He coughed when he inhaled, and the group all laughed. "Just wait until we let you try the *other* stuff kid," a tanned, skinny guy with long red hair told him.

Casey laughed as he coughed, "*Let* me? You don't *let* me do shit." He pointed to the sign above the door, "You know who owns this place."

"Yeah, yeah," the red-headed kid laughed as he lit a cigarette.

The guy that ran the surf shop slipped through the back door and joined the group. He worked for Burt and knew extraordinarily little about surfing. He was more interested in selling other products than those related to riding waves. He wasn't from West Palm and hadn't been in town long. Burt had called, offering him the opportunity to move to paradise and get rich and he jumped at the opportunity. The most important part of his job was making sure the kid, Casey, did the *right* things. The right things according to the Dixie Mafia.

Delano "Dell" Phillips, born to a poor family in Memphis, Tennessee, moved with his family down to the Gulf Coast of Mississippi right after he turned thirteen. Dell's name came from FDR himself. His father, a child of The Depression, wanted his son to do important things and thought naming him after such a great man would insure this from birth.

Dell's old man wanted so badly to be thought of as more than just another bum from Memphis that he told people he was related to Sam Phillips to get odd jobs. The same Sam Phillips that discovered Elvis Presley. They were not related, and most people caught on to the ruse quickly.

His high hopes for his only son faded quicky as Dell became a petty criminal and eventually, through Burt Williams, a low-ranking member of the Dixie Mafia. In fact, his only ally in the entire organization was Burt.

Burt felt sorry for the guy one night after a cop beat him to the ground for stealing something to eat from a gas station and took him under his wing. If something arose that he didn't want to personally get his hands dirty with, he sent Dell. His friendship with Burt was the most important thing in his life, and he would do anything for his mentor, no matter the cost. With Burt giving him this assignment, he felt special, or more importantly to Dell, felt like family.

"What's up kid?" Dell asked Casey as the pre-teen puffed away at the cigar, coughing each time he inhaled. The others in the group had no idea that Dell's job, other than selling weed, was to watch over Casey. They knew better than to ask any questions as Burt's reputation and position had gotten out on the streets of West Palm.

"Not much, Dell. Burt said hello," he responded with a grin. Dell loved it when Casey dropped Burt's name around the group.

"Good deal," was his only response as he walked back into the surf shop. He pretended to check on the guys working away, shaping a couple of boards in the workshop, but they just nodded and continued on with their work. They knew he was the boss, but not when it came to boards. They ran the shop.

Dell walked back into the office, nestled in the corner of the workshop, and kicked back in his chair. He opened the desk drawer beside him and admired the bundle of marijuana resting inside. Selling this stuff was his forte but he wanted to branch out and work with the *other* things Burt was involved with.

Burt had never told him outright what or who he was tangled up with in Florida, but Dell could figure some things out on his own. Handling Casey was the first step to a bigger world for him and he wasn't going to screw that up. He ran his fingers through his greasy black hair and popped his bony legs up on the desk and lit a joint. He held the smoke for a few seconds and exhaled, the earthy aroma engulfing the room, and filtering throughout the shop. The two guys shaping boards shook their heads. If the cops ever came, they were throwing the redneck from Mississippi under the bus. Quickly.

Chapter 4

Rolling through the microfilm for days on end revealed the other murders occurring around the same time of Vern Bruce's suspected crimes. Two deaths, within days of each other, caught Cliff's attention and he asked the librarian to help him print out the newspaper articles.

One that he found specifically interesting, but really didn't think it connected to his uncle, was a local kid found floating in a bay, but it was within the timeframe, so he kept it. The wrong place at the wrong time was the wording the journalist used. Another one, about a week before, however, caught his full attention.

Miguel Chatom, found floating in the bay, didn't drown, but died of a gunshot to the head. Reading further, he found out Chatom was Brazilian, and the police suspected his involvement with the Colombian cartels but could prove nothing. There was something about the name. Miguel Chatom.

Cliff leaned back in his chair and stared into the wall. From his research, he had learned Colombians ran the drug trade. So, a Brazilian working with them didn't sound just right. It felt like one of the Hardy Boy's Mysteries he loved to read, though murder and drugs were a little out of the fictional teen detective brothers' league. He read the article and wrote the name in the little white spiral notebook he kept in his pocket. It may be nothing, but he wrote down anything that sounded like it could be connected in some way to his family's predicament. Right below the Brazilian's name, he wrote the fisherman's name. Marcus Kendrick, placing a question mark beside both.

He flipped through the microfilm once more, finding only a single article that mentioned the fisherman's name in both cases. The reporter hadn't deemed it necessary to identify the man who discovered Chatom's bloated corpse, leaving Cliff with no reason to suspect a connection to Marcus Kendrick's murder.

Cliff caught a glimpse of his mother from the corner of his eye as she peeked through the library door. Most times she just waited outside for him to finish up but, for some reason, today was different. She pulled out the chair beside him, eased into it and focused on the screen, all the while her soft smile shining towards her son.

"Solve the whole thing yet?" she joked.

Cliff shook his head. He wanted to tell her about the two names he dug up but didn't. He trusted his mom with everything, but she wouldn't lie. If Burt asked, she told. She didn't believe in secrets in her marriage.

"Just a bunch of nothing," he lied, even though it was a minor lie, it bothered him to speak any untruth to his mother. She frowned and put her arm around him. She could feel his broad shoulders and thought even if he didn't act like his father, he was built just like him. She looked him over and thought he was Rof Bruce mixed with Vern's face and demeanor. She pulled him close, and she kissed him on the cheek. Most fourteen-year-olds wouldn't want their mother kissing them in public, but Cliff didn't mind. They spent so much time apart that he cherished the moments they spent alone. He reached over and hugged his mother, holding their tight embrace for several seconds.

When he finally let her go, Cliff noticed a tear had fallen down her cheek. He ran his finger up the side of her face, wiping it away and telling her he loved her once again. She put her forehead to his and told him the same. "Let's go get some ice cream," she said, standing up and turning the machine off. Cliff smiled, grabbed the microfilm, and started walking with her. He snapped his fingers, realizing he left his little while notebook and reached back to grab it. "Don't want to leave your notes behind," she said. Cliff stuffed it into this pocket and when he pulled his hand free, interlaced his fingers with his mother's.

Death Row was a quiet, desolate place for Vern. With no windows, every day blurred into a relentless cycle of darkness and monotony. Once, he had found comfort in stormy skies, but now he longed for more than the fleeting minutes of sunlight he was granted each day. His only view was the cold, unyielding block wall beyond the rusted bars of his cell. He could take only a few steps in either direction before meeting the concrete barriers that confined him, a constant reminder of the freedom forever out of reach.

The walls themselves were devoid of any kind of decoration beside the flaking dull paint. Some of the inmates on death row kept posters on the wall, mostly of scantily clad women. The guards allowed it, trying to maintain peace on the row. Vern didn't. He kept his walls bare and stared at them. Most times he let his thoughts wonder and the bare wall was his theater. He envisioned his dead wife, his boys, and sometimes, Pops. Each day he woke with the stench of mold invading his nostrils. Some mornings, he tried to hold his breath, but nature and the will to live intervened. He didn't keep a calendar and didn't want to.

He had welcomed no visitors since the first day the bars slammed behind him. Only one letter had come from Cliff, but after that one, he sent word for Cliff to send no more and, so far, he complied.

This existence was worse than death. The wait to die. The days turned into weeks. Before long, he lost count of the months. Some days he just lay upon his bed, staring at the ceiling, his mind consumed with images of his brother. He often thought of how his situation might match some of Rof's struggles. He read all he could about the POW camps over there and each time his mind turned to his brother, he ended up with the same guilt consuming him as it did when he first heard of the plane crash, leaving him in anguish. It made him hate this place more every day.

Without warning, the monotony of those days finally broke. One day, without notice, the guard called his name and informed Vern he had a visitor. He didn't even know what day it was, but he figured it was his lawyer.

When the guard led him into the small meeting room, Vern new it had to be *a* lawyer, but he didn't recognize the man sitting there. Dressed to the hilt, the figure seated at the small table looked like a lawyer, but it wasn't his. His three-piece suit was perfectly ironed, not one wrinkle. His hair was slicked back, almost appearing greasy. He was thin and lanky and when he spoke, Vern knew he wasn't from the Panhandle of Florida.

The lawyer jumped to his feet and stuck his hand in Vern's direction. Vern's raised his shackled hands as far as he could, and the man met him with his. He introduced himself with a scratchy voice, devoid of any discernable accent. His voice certainly didn't match his body as it sounded like a pubescent boy. As Vern struggled to shake his hand, he inhaled the strong cologne he wore, burning his nose but it was a nice respite from the mold.

He sat back down in his chair, pointing to the seat across the small steel table. "Good morning, Mr. Bruce. My name is Ryan Calley and I've been selected to represent you during your appeal process," he said matter-of-factly.

Vern glared at Calley with suspicion, "I have a lawyer, Mr. Calley. It's not you."

Calley nodded, "No. That is correct. *You* didn't hire me, but you have an interested party. A benefactor so to say and *he* hired me," he replied, and Vern still couldn't catch any kind of accent in his voice.

"Mr. Highland, out of Panama City. He *is* my lawyer. Isn't this unethical to solicit clients?" Vern asked, still unconvinced.

Calley didn't flinch when he responded, "Mr. Highland recommended me to represent you. Your *benefactor* approved the switch and here I am. Frankly, Mr. Bruce, you are lucky to have me. I am licensed in Florida but most of my work is centered among "big name" clients in New York and California."

Vern relaxed in his chair as much as he could with his shackles fixed to the floor and table. "Burt Williams hire you?" Vern asked. It could be nobody but Burt. Cliff must have put him up to this.

Calley shot a perplexed look towards Vern, "I'm afraid I haven't met Mr. Williams, and the answer is, simply, no. Your benefactor chooses to remain undisclosed. This benefactor is providing the funding for your appeals, including my retainer and hourly charges. Your estate is indeed controlled by Mr. Williams and his wife," Calley paused to look through his notes, "a Susie Williams in lieu of your son and nephew. Do I have everything correct?"

Vern nodded in agreement and Calley asked him to repeat his side of things. He told the lawyer everything he knew concerning the murders and Calley furiously scribbled it all down. Finally, Calley presented a contract allowing him to represent the death row inmate. He slid it over slowly and Vern studied it for several minutes. "What the hell," Vern said, maneuvering his hand to sign. *What do I have to lose*, he asked himself as he scribbled his name.

After the meeting, the guard led Vern down the dank corridor and back to his cell. The smell of mold once again penetrated his nose, replacing the pungent cologne. The bars slid shut with a deafening thud and Vern, once again, was left to his thoughts.

Isolated in his cell once again, Vern had time to think. He stared into the block wall once more but this time his thoughts didn't center on his family or freedom. He wondered about his benefactor. Who in the world would care about his appeals if it weren't Cliff and himself? Burt Williams certainly didn't care as Vern suspected he was probably the one of the people who helped put him here. Susie had Cliff and he was her entire world. Casey didn't care if his father lived or died. That was it. Those few people were the only ones on Earth who might care if he lived or died but none really wanted him free besides Cliff and he didn't have the means. A benefactor that wanted to remain nameless? Vern banged his fist on the hard concrete blocks. Something wasn't adding up and there was absolutely nothing he could do to solve it locked away in his tiny cell. He closed his eyes, but sleep wouldn't find him.

As soon as Calley arrived at the busy airport in Atlanta, he called the hotel room of Veck Baxter in New Orleans. Baxter answered on the first ring. He anticipated the call and sat patiently for an hour before it finally came through.

"Mr. Baxter. Just wanted to let you know everything went smoothly," he said, "No problems. Bruce is curious about who pays the bills, but we can keep that away from him."

"Thank you, Mr. Calley. Please keep me informed. I want him off death row with the first appeal," Baxter spoke softly into the phone, accustomed to keeping his conversations quiet and only for those intended. They both hung up the phone without exchanging goodbyes.

Baxter sat back in his chair and eased his aching legs onto a stool. This was the first step in order to reach the end. His journey had taken him nearly all over the world. He was tired. Most of the time, his head ached along with the rest of his body. His hair fell out in clumps, and he knew he aged differently than other people. A body can only take so much and his had been taken to the brink of death, only to be yanked back at the last second. Only a chance encounter with Jefferson Black allowed him to make it to this point in his life.

When he arrived on the docks of Porta de Santos, stowed away on a large container ship, Black's was the first face he saw. Discovered by the crew in the middle of the journey, they arrested him and put him in one of the empty containers that served as a brig. He feared the worst as the crew turned him over to the authorities at the port, but once Black heard his accent, a smile covered the Brazilian's face.

He had nothing. No money, no personal effects other than the ragged clothes he wore. He didn't even have a pair of shoes.

He remembered Black looking at his dirty, scarred feet and shaking his head in either disgust or pity. He didn't know which. Veck eased back into his chair. He had unconsciously sat forward as he remembered his arrival in South America and his bones ached in response. He perched his feet on a stool in front of the chair and admired the slippers that covered his withered feet. He didn't feel like moving around, aggravating his body any further. He sighed and closed his eyes. He needed to sleep. The last vision entering his mind before drifting into darkness was that of Vernon Bruce, staring into the distance in his cell on death row. Veck Baxter smiled.

Chapter 5

The assignation of Rodrigo Lara shook the country of Columbia to its foundations. The real power in the country had flexed its muscles and the result was felt all over the world, especially in South Florida. The bosses back home called Mateo Diaz to Colombia for a discussion, and he readily complied.

To slip across borders, the American more than Colombian, he traveled on private boats, and this time on Old Man Clark's, controlled by Burt Williams. The call to use the luxurious yacht wasn't made by Diaz but by Jeff Black. The tense meeting between the Colombian smuggler and the Dixie Mafia gangster didn't lend to the two men working together so Jeff Williams approached Burt. He reluctantly agreed, but he had a back-up plan just in case. Burt planned to claim it was stolen if things went wrong and went ahead and sent it along the appropriate channels, mostly the West Palm Police who he had already in his pocket.

The voyage was seamless and Diaz arrived in his home country unscathed. The mountains beyond the coast near Santa Marta rose in the distance, and the longing for home grew within him. He leaned on the railing surrounding the bow of the yacht, not knowing he leaned on the very spot where Old Man Clark plunged to his death and thought about life. A life behind him and a life that lay before him. *Once again*, he thought to himself, *they will intersect.*

The captain dropped anchor just outside the barrio between international waters and Brazilian jurisdiction. Diaz made his way ashore on a much smaller craft. The boat leapt over towering waves and each time it did, he thought this could be his last moment on Earth, but the craft ventured on. Finally, his clothes dripping wet from the spray generated from the bow crashing into waves, he eased the small boat onto the beach.

From the dense vegetation, a single person appeared, bathed in camouflage from head to toe. He motioned for Diaz and whisked him into a waiting jeep and the duo sped towards the heart of Santa Marta where the heads of the various cartels awaited them.

The meeting was held for basically one reason and for that very reason the bosses wanted it to be face to face. They informed Diaz that the flow of product from Columbia was going to slow down drastically. The organization's reliance on the Brazilian and his people would increase to compensate. They had made a drastic error in Lara's assassination, and they felt the pinch from not only the Colombian Government but also from the United States.

Jeff Black, if his network was as extensive as he bragged, assured the Colombians the slow down would only be temporary. To make money flow and the fight against the virtuous leaders in Columbia resume, Diaz would be counted on more than ever. In fact, one of the first warnings the bosses gave him was reiterated in the meeting. *Do not get involved with anyone in the United States on a personal level.* He knew what that meant.

Christian Lopez fell in love with the wrong person and at the wrong time. He began paying more attention to her than to business and his focus waned. It wasn't his first infraction with the bosses, and they made sure he paid with his life. You didn't steal from these men, nor did you come up slack in business. That was the second warning they issued, and Mateo Diaz took it to heart. After the meeting and he was safely back enroute to the American Coast, he laughed to himself. They wouldn't have to worry about him falling in love with an American woman.

But before the meeting concluded, Diaz made sure to speak to each man, look him in the eye, and shake their sweaty hands. He had never met all of them before, so he wanted each man to know he was their guy. Most took his hand, looked him back in the eye and smiled. All accept Don Vaquero, the leader of one of the most ruthless gangs. He tightened his grip on Diaz' hand and pulled him in until he felt the warmth of his breath and the garlicy stink of his breath.

"You fuck me on this, maricon, I won't only kill you, but those *special* to you," he whispered in English into Diaz' ear. The Don released his grip and leaned back in his seat, a wide smile appearing on his chubby, pock-marked face. Diaz only nodded, showing no emotion, only respect.

This time, the twenty-four-mile journey to international waters felt a lot calmer. The waves were just as high, but the spray didn't douse him when the bow sliced through. The journey gave him time to think about Don Vaquero's words. He thought he had hidden his past so deep that the cartels wouldn't find it. But he was only being naïve. That ended now. His new *friends* promised him they would ensure not only his safety but the one person the Don knew he could threaten him with. He was betting more than his own life on their word.

When he eased the small craft into position so it could be lifted to the yacht, he saw Jeff Black's slender frame peeking over the side. Black had gone with him on the trip, but he didn't leave the boat. As the boat began to lift, Diaz jumped over to a ladder hanging from the side and made his way up. Black extended his hand and pulled Diaz across the railing.

Black wasted no time, "Everything went well?" he asked as Diaz stepped onto the deck of the boat.

One of the crewmembers handed Diaz a towel and he ran it across his face, "Very well, my friend," he replied. Black smiled and motioned for Diaz to join him inside when he had dried and changed clothes. Even though the ride back had been fairly dry, the voyage to shore left his clothes dingy and smelling of foul seawater. Diaz offered no resistance to indulging in a hot shower and fresh clothes.

Black held a bottle of American beer to Diaz when he walked into the expansive entertaining room. Diaz whistled when he entered. "That old man had some kind of style," he admired. Black shrugged his shoulders and allowed the Colombian to admire their surroundings without interruption for a moment.

"The American? His plan? Will it work?" Diaz asked as he sat down on a leather couch, running his fingers along the material in admiration as he did.

"We made the American a part of this, because in fact, he *is* American. He knows how they think in the States, and he knows how we should play this. The plan is flawless. The *so-called* Dixie Mafia will soon come under our control and the people in Florida will be yours," he said tipping his head in salute. "You will control almost every single kilo of product coming into that part of the country..." He pointed his finger in Diaz' direction and took a sip of his beer, "We want nothing to do with it. To us, this entire business is merely a means to an end." Diaz smiled and flexed his hand, remembering Don Vaquero's bone crushing grip. Nothing was ever just *handed* over. When things change there was always blood to be spilled.

"Just like that," Diaz said as more a statement than a question and waved his hand around the room.

Black stood up, walked slowly over to a window, and watched the waves gently rolling beside the yacht. The ocean breathed as if it were living creature. Each wave gave the impression as a breath and as they rolled away, the air released.

He focused on the water as he spoke, "We have *other* ambitions. If they don't conflict with yours, it will in fact be *just like that,"* he responded, snapping his fingers.

Diaz tightened his lips, "In my country, nothing ever ends. Conflict breeds conflict and eventually blood is spilled." He stood up joining Black at the window.

Black turned his attention from the ocean slowly and looked Diaz in the eye, "I promise you that we want nothing of *this* business but what it takes for us to come home. The plan is for us to gain income and influence in ways other than importation. I promise you, Mr. Diaz, nothing further will we need from you."

Diaz knew exactly when to end a conversation, and that moment had arrived. He smiled, as well as he could, and asked his counterpart what the chef prepared for dinner. The day had been long, and his stomach growled. The two men made their way to the dining room and once again Diaz was taken aback by the beauty of the boat. He couldn't wait until he had one of his own.

Jeff Black didn't like being out of the loop for this long. Since the yacht had set sail and returned, he hadn't been in contact with Veck Baxter. The first meeting between Vern Bruce and Calley took place a few hours before they set sail for Columbia, and he wondered how things had gone. As soon as he was ashore, he found a payphone near the docks and called New Orleans.

The first attempt rang continuously for a good minute and concern swept over him. He wiped the sweat from his brow and exhaled the breath he had been holding. He dialed the number again and Baxter picked up on the first ring.

"Veck, my friend, it's good to hear your voice," he said before Baxter could say anything other than hello.

Baxter paused and offered, "Yours too and I hope you are calling with good news." He sensed no anxiety in Black's voice, so he already knew the answer. Baxter had gotten to know Black well and could sense the Brazilian's emotions even as he tried to hide them in his voice. It was a skill he had picked up from his Vietnamese captors.

"Splendid," Black replied, "We have been given a greater share of product to move. The Columbians are stupid beyond measure. They unleashed hell upon themselves when they killed Lara, but that is extremely good news for us. They need us now more than ever." Black allowed the words to hang in silence. Over the silence, Black heard ice clanking against glass.

"We just don't need to get *so* involved that we can't get out. Remind everyone of the goal, even those back in Brazil. We can't take our eyes off the ball," he finally replied.

Black thought for a moment as he didn't really know what that expression meant. It was part of a language that he grew up using, but at that moment, he realized that he barely understood its nuances. He did recognize the rest and responded, "Of course. I just reminded our Columbian friend of that very fact," Black noticed a woman standing near the booth, awaiting her turn. He smiled at her and eased the folding door closed before finishing, "I told him on the return voyage."

"How did he respond?" Baxter asked as the response would give him a clue to the true intentions of the man.

"How do I say.... skeptical. I don't think he put much trust in my words."

"Well, if you had grown up in a cutthroat world like the one he did, you might hesitate to believe people too. Remember where he comes from, Jeff. I've seen barbarity like that. I've lived it. It took me a while to trust *you*, remember?" Baxter said, his voice quivering slightly, but noticeably, even over the phone.

"Yes, I remember, my friend. I remember the cold stares you gave me, and I remember your stories and the reluctance to accept that I was indeed a friend. Trust takes time," Black responded.

"Time is something that we don't have a lot of," Baxter replied, "Take care of yourself, Jeff. We will see this thing through, no matter what." They said their goodbyes and each man hung up the phone.

Black eased the door open and waved the waiting lady inside the booth, bowing his head as she brushed past him. He loved Florida. New Orleans, despite how the Mississippi reminded him of home, was different, unwelcoming. He found a bench overlooking the Indian River and across the wide body of water stood the massive building where Americans built the missile that took them to the moon. *How remarkable*, he thought.

The sidewalk was crowded with people, most enjoying a leisurely stroll beside the river, unaware of his presence. A little boy, his mouth sticky from the lollipop he feverishly worked at devouring, sat next to him, the child and Brazilian almost touching. His father, in a heavy southern accent, asked Black to excuse his young son. He smiled at the father and son and motioned for him to have a seat.

The three sat in silence for a moment before the father pointed to the towering building in the distance and said, "Hell of a thing, huh?"

Black nodded, "Indeed it is. Wonderous." The father glanced over at the Brazilian and cocked his head to the side.

"Your accent," he said, "Interesting. You must've been in the South for a long time to pick it up."

Black, confused, shot him an inquisitive look, "My friend, what do you mean?"

"I can hear a little *country* in what has to be a foreign accent," the father replied. The child, between the two men, continued licking his lollipop, offering Black a lick. The Brazilian smiled but he held up a hand, politely declining.

"Indeed," Black said carefully, "I come from a country in South America, but my family, many, many years ago hailed from Alabama."

"No kidding, that's where we're from, Mobile," he said and stuck his hand in Black's direction. Black readily shook it. This was the first time since he came here that he met someone from Alabama.

"Mobile," Black replied, "What is it like. I've been through there, but never have I stopped."

The man ran his finger along his mustache, "Well, beautiful city, but the area around the bay is spectacular. If you go through it again, take a look at the *Alabama*, WW2 ship. It's a museum now, but damn, its impressive."

Black, stood, and once again shook the father's hand and patted the child on top of his head, "Indeed. I shall." He waved and said goodbye. He wanted to see Mobile and the *Alabama*.

Chapter 6

Mac Tate's best days were, by far, way behind the old politician. Over ninety now and nearly blind, he didn't expect visitors at his home. He spent most of his time, even in the sweltering Panhandle heat, in his wheelchair covered with a blanket. Most of his days were spent overlooking the sparkling waters of Grand Lagoon. One Saturday, as he sat watching the boats float by, his housekeeper touched him on the shoulder. The frail old man jolted awake from his doze; his curiosity piqued as he eagerly sought to see who had come calling. He couldn't hear too well and missed the name as the housekeeper mumbled something and went back to show the visitor the way to the deck.

When he saw her step out onto his perch, he recognized her face but couldn't remember Susie's name. He knew everyone in the district and even though names had faded, he was still adept at recognizing faces. He studied her round face as best he could through failing eyes, and another name surfaced in his mind—Rof Bruce. No matter how much he tried, he could never forget that name. Yet, for the life of him, he couldn't remember what connected the two.

Susie eased beside him and took the old man by the hand. She introduced herself as Susie Brannon instead of Williams. Tate looked out over the lagoon his mind falling into deep thought for a couple of seconds and then in a little over a slight whisper asked her, "Parents used to own a motel down on the beach, right?"

Susie smiled and responded that they had indeed once owned the Crystal Beach Motel. The old man squeezed her hand and said, "Rof Bruce."

Susie couldn't hold back her tears when Tate said his name. The old man patted her hand and tried to console her best he could. When she was able to contain her emotions enough, Susie told him about the pictures and Rof's letter. His mind once again drifted to long ago and a meeting of the local draft board. His feeble mind couldn't recall details, but he remembered the day that group of men selected Rof instead of his brother.

"Rof in place of Vern," he whispered just loud enough for Susie to hear. She leaned down but he said nothing more about the meeting, only low mumbles.

His mind cleared, as it often did, just as quickly as it faded. He couldn't remember the details, but he remembered the brothers, both of their young faces clear in his mind now and he wanted to know more.

Susie recited the story of Colonel Duy and the letter he delivered. She told him that since that day she hadn't seen the Colonel nor had any other information from him. There had been no further letters and the government would tell them nothing. Not knowing, she confided in him, was driving her crazy.

Mac ran his wrinkled hands across his face and held them in front of his eyes for a second before pointing across the lagoon at a pelican resting on a round post at the end of a boat dock,

"That was me," he said, his voice louder than before, carrying a newfound certainty.

Susie looked around, thinking he pointed to something else, but he shook his finger at the bird, reinforcing his intention.

"Sitting there day after day," he said, his voice becoming agitated, "day after day" he said again.

"Mr. Tate, I don't understand," Susie said, putting her hand back on top of the old man's. Tate shook his head, his mind clouding once again as he stared at the brackish water below. A passing boat blew its horn and instinctively he took his hand from Susie and stuck it in the air, greeting the captain. He looked back at Susie with confused eyes but once he focused on her face, his thoughts flooded back once again.

"Rof Bruce," he said again, his voice now quivering.

"Yes, Mr. Tate, Rof Bruce. Can you help me?" she pleaded.

Tears formed in his tired, old eyes and he leaned over as far as his archaic body would allow and whispered in her ear, "The camp is empty. If Rof was alive a few years ago," he paused and caught his breath for a second, "I'm sorry... but he isn't now."

What little hope she held evaporated in an instant. The cardinal. Rof had already come to her, letting her know he was gone. Susie placed her head on Tate's shoulder and began crying uncontrollably. A tear rolled down Mac Tate's cheek as the old man, finally wanting to tell the truth and at least give this young girl some closure, put a trembling hand on her cheek.

"I killed him," he said, "I killed him."

Susie put her hands on Tate's face and kissed his forehead, "No, Mr. Tate, you didn't."

He pushed her hand away, his regret giving way to anger, "No, no, no. Not him."

Susie stood up, confused, and leaned against the railing. His voice grew louder as he said again, "No, no, no...". The housekeeper, hearing his voice growing louder, rushed out the door with a cup of water and quickly shoved a pill into his mouth and put the cup to his lips.

"I'm afraid it's time for you go," she commanded and pointed to the door. Susie stood for a second, watching the old man squirm in his chair until the medication took hold. Then she nodded, but before she walked away, she hugged Tate, who was starting to calm down. He put his lips to her ear and said, "Ryan Talley." Susie gently pulled away from him, her eyes locking onto him. She could see the sorrow etched in his now hollow gaze, the emptiness searing itself into her memory.

"I'm sorry," the old man said several times as she walked away, and her heart melted for the sad figure she left behind with each step, repeating the name he had uttered repeatedly as she did.

Susie made the short drive to the parking lot of the new super store that replaced an amusement park she loved as a child and parked in a space as far away from the building as she could. She wasn't there to shop. A few gulls perched on a streetlight above her car, and she listened to their cries floating on air above the noise from traffic flowing in the intersection in front of her. She turned off the engine, and turned the handle, lowering the window. She took a deep breath and felt disgusted. This place, her home, looked nothing as it did when she left. The salty air replaced by exhaust fumes from the throngs of vacationers filling the slowly moving streets. Even the quiet street, or what used to be the quiet street, splitting the area between the "strip" and the main highway following the coast, roared with traffic.

She thought back about the very spot she was parked. Susie could see the lights from the old amusement park in her mind and for a moment she thought she could smell popcorn. She remembered as a child, riding a real steam driven train to an old west show. "This place just ain't the same," she said aloud.

She hadn't forgotten the name whispered by the old man as she left but all she could think about, other than how much Panama City had changed, was Rof. He was truly gone. If there was any doubt in her mind, it died today with Tate's feeble words. Through her mind's eye, over and over, she saw the cardinal flying out over the Atlantic. She dreaded telling Cliff even though she knew he would never believe it.

Susie started the engine, put the transmission into gear but hesitated. She needed to make her way north to the interstate but before leaving Panama City to return to West Palm, she decided to ride along strip once more. There was one more part of her past she needed to confront. Maybe for the last time.

She followed the long line of cars as they crept along at a snail's pace. Most of the motels she remembered from her youth had either disappeared or were closed. Plywood covered windows and signs of things to come greeted her as she inched along.

It took quite a while to make it to the spot but, finally, she pulled to the side of the two-lane road in front of a vacant lot. Where her parents' motel once stood, nothing remained, only a sign indicating the coming of a new high-rise building. Surprisingly, she felt no emotion as she opened the door and stared at the vacant lot for a few minutes. The gulf pulsated just beyond the dunes, the glittering emerald colored water rising and falling slowly, but her focus remained on the dirt at her feet. She felt no resentment toward her parents, but, at the same time, she felt no love for them either. They abandoned her, their own daughter, in her time of need. She never felt the need to contact them again. She figured they were long dead but never found out for sure and deep in her mind, she didn't care.

Susie picked up a pebble resting near her foot. She looked at it for a long time, rolling it around in her hand. Oddly enough, she saw no more laying around. She held rock in her fingers, kissed it gently and threw it as far as she could. She didn't see it land but instantly felt better and promised herself to never come here again.

The second place she visited also stirred memories deep with emotion from the start, unlike her parents' old place. The now dilapidated county pier stood but the boards that once sat firmly in place were broken and tattered. Their edges sharp appeared dangerous and foreboding to anyone brave enough to venture out. Its only visitors were a row of birds perched on its old, rotting rails, surveying the beach for crumbs left behind by the multitude of people resting under small umbrellas. Years of hurricanes and summer storms tore at the decaying wood foundations and people no longer enjoyed walks over the Gulf on its crumbling old boards. An iron gate barred entry, but she noticed a small hole to the side where the more adventurous defied the "no trespassing" sign.

She stepped over a low hanging rope and took off her shoes. She made her way through the sea oats that were gently waving in the wind, finding the spot where she and Rof spent their last night together. No matter how much things changed with the times, she would always be able to find that one special spot. She sat down and sank slightly in the warm sand. The proximity to the ocean overrode the horrid smells of progress. She inhaled the salt-tinged air, closing her eyes. She could see Rof's blue eyes vibrantly in her mind.

She just sat there. Her eyes remaining closed, feeling warm air flowing through her hair and her toes digging into the sugar-white, seemingly bottomless sand. Rof's soft blue eyes disappeared, and she heard Mac Tate's words once again. They forced finality upon her thoughts of a life with Rof. He was gone, and at last, she was ready to accept that truth.

Vern's face flashed in her mind, and she grimaced, the vision of his face reminded her how much she despised him. The only reason he had allowed her to visit Cliff in the first place was his own selfish interests. It turned out that not only was he a selfish bastard but also a cold-blooded killer. Burt may be a lot of things, but in her eyes and naivety, he was no killer. She knew he often did certain things to survive, but that was different. It was business. Every act of Vern's was selfish, and she never forgave him for Rof's death. She never would.

Her eyes furrowed as a dark thought emerged. There was one way she could return the hurt upon Vernon Bruce. One way that she could make his last days even worse. She wasn't the type of person who thought of revenge or spite often, but now, she wanted it so desperately that her whole body began trembling.

She decided that she wouldn't drive straight back to West Palm. Susie climbed into her car and peeled away, sending small pebbles ricocheting off the dilapidated pier. She didn't drive back down the strip. Instead, she headed east on the main highway towards the quickest route to Atlanta. Once she passed over St. Andrew Bay she turned north towards Alabama. "Here I come you bastard," she yelled from the open window, her words dissipating in the wind.

It just so happened that Burt was in his office, kicked back, enjoying a rare lit cigar when his secretary stuck her head in the door and told him he had a call from Biloxi. She wasn't Old Man

Clark's nosy secretary but a young, beautiful blonde that he hired without even finding out if she was qualified for the job. Her reluctance in using the intercom for announcements like this made him skeptical that she had been a secretary before, but she sure was fun to look at.

He winked at her and she let out a slight giggle. Burt watched as she turned around very deliberately, slowly walking back to her desk. Each movement of her perfectly shaped body laced with purpose. Burt grinned and thought it was sure fun to watch her walk away too.

He picked up the phone and a familiar voice greeted him. A voice that he hadn't heard in quite a while and his grin gave way to a toothy smile.

"You a millionaire yet?" came the deep voice of Ramsay Brown, or RB as he was known in Biloxi. One of the few detectives in Mississippi in those days that happened to be black, he made his way up the chain of command at a time when his race proved a roadblock to a career in law enforcement in the state, much less detective. But he earned every promotion he received and wasn't afraid to stand up to anybody, cops, Dixie Mafia or the red necks that gave him a hard time, to keep it. There was no better detective in the state, maybe the southeast, regardless of color. RB kept the peace down on the coast, often dealing with certain members of the Dixie Mafia to maintain that peace. Burt Williams was the only member of the notorious gang of outlaws that he not only respected but also considered a friend.

"You ought to see my office, bud," Burt pushed the end of his cigar on the antique wooden desk to put it out, "I'm looking out over the ocean right now." He could hear RB chuckle on the other end and added, "and my secretary ain't bad scenery either."

Even though he was happy to hear his old friend's voice, Burt knew that RB wasn't calling to catch up on old times. That wasn't something the detective did on a regular basis. Being friendly was part of their act, both men knew it and respected it.

"What can I do for you, RB?" Burt got right to the point.

"Just a little courtesy call, Burt. I know you done left Biloxi behind, but I'm hearing some things about a new guy over in New Orleans who is making some moves. Some of the guys in your *old* hang outs are getting a little nervous. This guy ain't no little fish. He's organized," RB told him, and Burt could sense the concern in his voice. He reached into his pocket for a fresh cigar.

"What's that got to do with me? I'm straight as an arrow now. To hell with Biloxi," he lied. Burt still considered Biloxi his town and nobody was going to just waltz in there and take it.

"Just thought you might want to know..." he paused, and Burt heard him clear his throat, "One more thing, you ever heard of a *Confederado*?"

Burt popped the unlit cigar in the corner of his mouth and rolled it around a couple of times. "Maybe," he answered. He knew Jefferson Black had called himself a Confederado a couple of times. He didn't know exactly what the term meant, and he had no intention of finding out. He had heard stories growing up about southerners leaving the United States, fleeing to South America. The stories went that some came home but most didn't. They just disappeared and that was that. They were just stories as far as he was concerned until Jeff Black.

RB popped his gum into the phone, "Well, I keep hearing that term pop up and it's got me curious. If you hear anything, you'll let me know. Right old bud?" RB didn't expect to hear anything further from Burt. He already knew his old friend knew more than he was telling. Burt got awfully quiet when he didn't want to lie to his detective friend.

They ended the conversation and both men hung up the phone. RB put his elbows on his desk and rubbed the whiskers on his chin. Maybe it was time for a vacation.

The conversation finished, Burt walked outside and found a concrete bench under a swaying palm tree facing the ocean. He lit the rest of the cigar that had been flopping around his mouth and slowly inhaled the smoke. He loved the ocean and South Florida in general, but it really didn't feel like home. The water was *too* beautiful, and the beach was *too* clean. He missed the Gulf Coast of Mississippi and its discolored water and muddy sand. The old, ragged motels and beer joints were fading away from the strip, but still, it was home. Even as the sun was at his back, he placed sunglasses on his thick face and still his eyes squinted from the glare coming off the ocean.

Burt knew that Black wanted something from the old town. He just didn't know what that something was just yet. Was

Jeff Black the leader of the pack of Brazilians calling themselves Confederados or maybe he was mistaken, and Black was only the front man. Why would these people even want Biloxi?

The Dixie Mafia was in decline. Burt knew it all too well and that was one of the reasons he was getting out. But still, he didn't want to just hand it over. Not to Black or to anyone else. He took another long drag from the cigar and held the smoke long enough for it to become bothersome and exhaled. He had to find answers.

He waddled back into the building and told his secretary to get his wife on the phone. When she asked him her phone or his, he just smiled and told her he would take care of it. She bent over to pick up a pencil she had dropped on purpose and the slit in her shirt reminded Burt why she was there.

He called home and the housekeeper told him she hadn't heard from Mrs. Williams. The old gangster inside him became nervous when family members didn't check in when they should. Susie should've been home from Panama City a while ago, but he had no reliable contacts up in the beaches of the Panhandle. There was only one person he trusted up there, but his mind was gone, if the old man was still alive. He felt helpless. A feeling he wasn't used to and hated it. It was time to push aside the old guard up there, he thought to himself.

Susie's reason for going, she had told him, was to check on some old family business but she didn't say where exactly she was going or who she was seeing. He knew better than to trust her as he didn't trust anyone, but his wife had never given him a reason to doubt before.

About the time he was going to get in his car and drive north, blondie stuck her head in the door. Burt smelled her perfume before he saw her. Damn, she smelt great too and he congratulated himself on the hire once again.

"Wife on one," she cooed and slowly shut the door.

Burt snatched to his ear, "Where the hell are you?" His voice sounded more panicky than angry.

"Little detour," she responded at once, "I found out a little bit more about Rof." That admission surprised Burt. He thought she had given up on him and hoped her son would do the same.

"So that's the family business, huh?"

She hesitated for a second or two before responding, her voice as stiff as she could manage. "Yes. I had to find out what old Mac Tate knew—for Cliff, if nothing else. You know he's not handling all this well. He spends too much time trying to piece it together, and it ain't good for him. So I came up here to talk to the old man before he dies."

That bastard still breathing? He's probably still trying to control the entire state."

Susie was surprised Burt knew Tate but didn't push it, not while she had even more to tell him.

"What did he have to say?" Burt grumbled.

"Rof's dead, or at least the camp is gone and there's no sign of him. He probably died right after he wrote that letter," she told him.

Burt hadn't realized his muscles had tightened up until began to calm down and involuntarily released tension. *Good*, he thought, *maybe that bastard will stay dead this time.* He lied as he said, "That's too bad. Hoped for Cliff, they would find him." He couldn't hide his smile. It was a good thing Susie wasn't there to see it. He remembered why he had tensed in the first place and asked again where she was.

She looked around and watched the cars zoom past on the four-lane highway before answering, "I'm at a rest area just outside Eufaula, Alabama."

Burt squinted his eyes trying to remember where he heard the town's name before, and suddenly he remembered the dark water of the lake. He had been to Eufaula to fish in the new lake, formed by damming the mighty Chattahoochee River, back in the seventies. He also remembered that just north of the sleepy little lake town lay Columbus, Georgia and across the river from the then booming Georgia town was the notorious Phenix City, Alabama.

Phenix City was a haven for the Dixie Mafia back in the fifties. The whole county was corrupt. Even the sheriff and the elected officials were in on it. The Machine, as it was called in the town, ran gambling, liquor, weed, and girls. It was the "sin city" of Alabama and southeast corner of the United States. That was until they killed the only man to stand up fighting the Machine's corruption.

The people of Alabama elected the guy as their Attorney General, mainly because of his stand against the corruption, and the Dixie Mafia gunned him down in the streets. Burt loved to tell the story to his cronies as a warning to never "get too big for your britches." It was one of the reasons he befriended RB. You had to make concessions to survive.

"Eufaula? Where are you headed, Atlanta?" he said in jest, not knowing that it was in fact her destination.

"Yes," she replied, startling Burt, but only for a second, before realizing where she was going.

"Vern Bruce?" he asked.

"He needs to know about Rof and I'm the one that's going to tell him." she said, and Burt heard her sweet voice change to a much harsher tone.

Burt shook his head. Even though he was locked away in a cell somewhere, Vern Bruce kept popping up in his business. He threw the last little bit of cigar into a trashcan and sighed over the phone. "Vern Bruce is like a bad penny; he keeps coming back."

Susie reverted to the best "Little Susie" version of her voice, but Burt knew her too well. It was the voice she used when she really wanted to get Burt to agree with something. "Baby, he needs to know. It's his brother. Even if Rof hated him, he needs this *thing* to end. Not for his sake, for Cliff's. If *he* believes that

Rof is gone," she paused and tried not to cry, "Cliff will have to believe it."

"Yeah," Burt responded, "Then he'll devote his time to Vern and getting him out of there."

"He ain't got long to worry about it. The D.A. in Georgia told me that they expect to put him to death quickly. The appeals should all go quickly and be denied and then he's *done*," Susie replied, still using her helpless voice.

"Let me send the plane to get you in Atlanta, at least. I'll send somebody to get the car. I need you home."

Susie felt that was a good compromise and she quickly agreed.

"The big airport or the little airport?" she asked, and Burt told her they would use the little airport outside of Atlanta. It was more like a field with a dragstrip than an airport and it held fewer prying eyes. He couldn't stamp out his old Dixie Mafia mentality. Smaller airports led to fewer questions. There were records kept in Atlanta's international airport. Out in the country, people didn't care what or who flew in or out.

They made their arrangements and said their goodbyes to each other. One last thing he mentioned to Susie was that *he* was not going to be the one to tell Cliff about Rof. There was no way he was going to try and console Cliff. He wasn't the type of person to be gentle. If he had his way, he'd kick the boy's ass until he got this dead dad thing out of his head.

Cliff held all these ideas and fantasies about reuniting with his father and to Burt it was bull. However, he wasn't about to be the one that burnt all that down. Cliff already didn't trust him and that caused Burt to grin. *Damn,* he thought, *the boy was smarter than his uncle.*

Chapter 7

Even though he had been out of the political circles for a long time, Mac Tate still held a good bit of sway throughout the southeast. In his years of political wrangling, he gained a vast number of friends, but he gained a lot of enemies too. Most of them had long since been placed in the ground, both friend and foe alike, but there were a few that still listened to the old man.

Usually, a request to visit a death row inmate took a long time to clear and then it was supposed to be only the closest of family. One phone call and Tate had Susie approved for a visit with Vern with very little persuasion needed. It turned out to be his last favor. A couple of days later, he joined his late enemies and friends.

Susie had never been inside of a real prison before. In her younger, wilder days she spent a couple of nights in the Bay County jail, but those stays were short and not like the place she just walked into. She was uncomfortable in the small room containing only two chairs and a small steel table in the middle. She noticed the looped steel in front of the other chair and the same type of shackle on the floor. She rubbed her wrists, imagining what it felt like to be strapped down like an animal to the cold steel.

The door slowly creaked open and a muscular officer led Vern into the room. He stopped in his tracks when he saw Susie sitting there in the dim room and the officer pushed him in the back. Vern avoided eye contact with her as he sat down. The officer snapped his restraints into place. He closed his eyes and enjoyed the sweet smell of her perfume. It reminded him of Patty Lee.

With his eyes still closed he said, "Not expecting to see you." He took another deep breath. The intoxicating smell engulfed him once more and he couldn't help it when a small grin appeared on his lips.

"Don't really want to be here, Vernon, and I don't know what you find amusing about it," she said sternly, noticing his grin. She leaned closer to Vern, made a grunting noise and slammed her foot on the floor. He finally opened his eyes but did not dare look into hers,

"I won't be long. Just got some news I thought you should know." Susie hesitated, took a deep breath, summoning the strength to get the words out, "Rof is dead. I went to Mac Tate, and he told me the camp was gone. Been gone for years. If Rof was alive a few years ago, there's no way he survived this long."

Vern's head dropped and his shoulder's sagged. With a quivering voice he responded, "I know. I've had a lot of time to think about it." He nodded his head to the four walls surrounding them, "More than likely he died right after the letter. I've read that the Vietnamese burned those camps to the ground and..." His voice trailed off and he couldn't finish the sentence as tears filled his eyes.

Susie reached out and put her hands on Vern's, the cold steel of the shackles and the thought of touching Vern Bruce sent a shiver along her spine, "Please, write to Cliff. Tell him the truth. He's so focused on Rof and *you*. You need to tell him to move on. Move on from all his hopes about you and Rof. You know I've never asked or wanted much from you, but please, *please* do this one thing, if not for me, for Cliff," her voice pleading.

Vern lifted his head, his eyes finally meeting hers. He felt the warmth of her hands on top of his. He had forgotten a woman's delicate touch.

"What do you mean he's focused on *me*?"

Susie's face reddened and she snatched her hands back from his, "Every moment he can be, he's in that damned library looking for clues. He's wasting his youth, Vernon." She paused and pointed her finger nearly touching his face, "You killed two people in cold blood. He thinks you didn't and says he's going to prove it. Tell him to stop!" The burly officer in the hallway stuck his face in the door's small window, alarmed by her rising voice.

She stood to leave, and Vern reached for her hand, but the cold steel of his restraints stopped him short.

"I'll write to him. You have my word."

Susie looked in his eyes for a second and slowly nodded. She then motioned to the guard. Vern watched as she slowly walked from the room. There were no goodbyes exchanged. She was gone.

The guard pushed Vern into his cell, almost making him fall but he caught his balance without looking back. The door slammed closed. As it slid into place and locked, the guard whistled and said, "Hell of a girl there Bruce. Maybe next time she comes, I'll have to search her *thoroughly*." He laughed as he walked back down the hall and Vern shook his head. There wouldn't be any more visits from her.

Vern fell onto his bed, staring at the ceiling, gathering his words for Cliff. He grabbed a pencil, one of his precious few sheets of paper the state of Georgia afforded him and the largest book he had for a makeshift writing table. He sat for a few moments and listened to the deafening silence. Death row was a strange place. If *you* didn't make a sound, most times there was nothing to hear. Sometimes other inmates would let the four walls invade their sanity and you would hear a scream, cry, or sometimes even a laugh. When that happened, the echo lasted longer than the original sound and Vern hated it. He would try to cover his ears, but the sound filtered through his attempts and echoed within his own mind. The only other sounds were steel sliding against steel or the guards' muted conversations. They wanted it quiet and for the most part they got it.

Vern put pencil to paper, but no words came. He had carefully considered his words and believed he was ready, but the pencil remained frozen in his grip, refusing to move. Cliff was the only person in the world that still believed in him, and he found it difficult to tell him that he must give up. He put the pencil behind his ear and leaned back on the wall. He rolled his head back and forth and a small flake of paint settled in his hair. He picked it out, examining it closely. He started to flick it away, but kept it between his fingers, careful not to destroy it. He laid it carefully on the small shelf beside his bed.

Susie was right. Cliff was only fifteen and with his sixteenth birthday on the horizon, he needed to be a kid. Vern didn't want the boy to waste valuable years in which he was supposed to be exploring the world, learning new things and becoming a man. Not embroiled in a fool's errand.

Vern wondered how Cliff would take the news about his father. The trial and conviction had distracted his focus from Rof, but now, if he told the kid to drop his search for justice, Vern knew what Cliff would do. He couldn't let him toss away these years.

Vern's thoughts turned to his own son. The look on his face when the judge passed down sentence was etched in his memory. Casey's hollow eyes haunted him. When he looked back at his only child, those cold brown eyes held only contempt for his father. His boys needed him, and *he* had to clear his name. He couldn't push the responsibility to Cliff. Maybe Calley was legitimate and really wanted to help, but he couldn't put all his faith in strangers, however. If he could at least get off death row, that would give him a fighting chance and Ryan Calley promised that it would happen.

He pressed the pencil to the paper once more, and at last, the words began to flow onto the starched brown sheet:

Cliff,

By now, your mother told you about your father. I wish I could be there for you. I want to be there for you, but I can't. I want to tell you that you are so much like your father, but I can't do that either. You are more like me, better or worse. You always have been. Rof was "go-lucky." He went with the flow. He never cared about much and never took things seriously. But I miss him. A day doesn't go by that guilt doesn't consume me. It should've been me. I know that. Know that your father would've been proud of you. I know it in my heart.

I know how it is eating away at you to help me. I know how stubborn you are, like me, but you must let the fantasy go. You have a long life to live. Don't waste it building castles in the sky. Don't dream and hope your life away. Be a kid. I want you to do something for me that I can't. Casey needs you, Cliff. He needs you to be there for him. I fear he's lost. You can't help him thinking about me all the time. I'll handle my own problems. Got a guy working on it now. A big-time lawyer took the case. I'm in good hands.

Remember your dad, love your dad, but don't waste your time hoping for something that ain't ever gonna happen. He's gone, you're not. Live.

I love you like a son. I forgot about what my dad told me about family, and you see where it got me. You can't. It's you and

Casey. Look out for each other. Don't let anything come between y'all like me and Rof. I'll write again soon.

Love you my boy,

Unc

Vern carefully folded the letter, slipping it into an envelope, but paused before he wrote the address on the outside. A vision of Burt Williams flashed into his mind. In the vision, the gangster stood on the back deck of the Clark Mansion, cigar dangling from a grinning mouth, looking out over the ocean. The back of Vern's throat began to burn as bile creeped up from his stomach. He felt physically sick but fought it back. It was the price he paid to keep his boys safe. He hated Burt to the gangster's core and the thought of him living in luxury, seeing his boys every day, while he rotted in this dismal tomb was too much for him. He couldn't fight it any longer. He rolled over and the contents of his stomach emptied onto the cold concrete floor. He almost cried out for help, but if the guards found the mess, there would be consequences. He scooped up the mess with his hands and placed it in the toilet, dry heaving as he did. When he cleaned it up as well as he could, he washed his hands and collapsed back onto his bed. He tried not to think about the stench. He couldn't do that a second time. He reached for the card from Ryan Calley and started another letter.

Susie flew into the West Palm airport and took a taxi home. She didn't want Burt to pick her up. He was sure to have questions that she was in no mood to answer. She stared out of the taxi's dirty window, ignoring the driver's attempts at conversation. She ran the words she wanted to say to Cliff over in her mind several times and hoped by the time she got home they would be perfect. She hated that she had to do this.

When she arrived home, she found Cliff alone in his room. Susie tried to turn the doorknob, but he had the door locked. He didn't want Casey, or more importantly, Burt's prying eyes in his room.

Knocking gently on the old wooden door she asked, "Baby, can I come in for a second?" Most of the doors and decorations in the century old house were hand crafted and she heard Cliff snap the lock on the antique square mechanism and the door slowly opened. She noticed the stacks of books piled on his desk and, by the titles on their spines, realized he had been reading about POW experiences.

"What's up mom?" he asked. She hurried to him, hugging him tightly. Cliff didn't think much of the embrace as she always felt the need to hug him. He figured she was still trying to make up for lost time, so he put his arms around her and squeezed back.

She pulled away, gently placing her hand under his chin. Taking a deep breath, her voice cracked as she said, "I spoke with someone about your dad and the news isn't good, baby."

His face sharpened with concern, and she tried to reassure him with a smile but one didn't materialize. "There's no way he's still alive, baby, the camp was destroyed, burned to the ground.

The word coming out of Washington is all POWS were murdered by their captors to hide their tracks..." She paused for a second, biting her lip, but she couldn't hold back a flood of tears, "He's gone. He's *really* gone."

Cliff stumbled backward, as if putting space between them could somehow erase the words he had just heard. He fell to the edge of his bed, "Can't be true," he mumbled and started shaking his head. "I just read they probably moved all survivors to a real prison in Hanoi. Guy in the book saw it." Cliff felt more anger than sadness or disbelief, the heat of it rising faster than he could contain.

"Wherever you got this mom, they lied."

Susie fell to her knees, "Baby, the man I talked to knows. I trust him. He's gone and you gotta let him go."

Cliff jumped to his feet and walked to the other side of the room, "I'll never do that, mom." He reached for the unfolded letter from his father laying on the edge of his desk. He didn't cry but cast a blank stare at the stained paper and continued shaking his head, "I owe that to him."

Susie, still on the floor, shook her finger in his direction, "No!" she said louder than intended, "You don't *owe* him son. You didn't even *know* him."

Cliff, no longer able to hold back his tears, lowered *his* head into his hands, "That's why I owe him," he sobbed.

Susie, in nearly one motion, leapt toward her son, covering him with her arms. As Cliff sobbed into her shoulder, she decided she wouldn't tell him that she had also talked with his uncle. That would be too much for her son right now. She kissed him on the cheek. "I'll be downstairs."

Susie closed the door with a loud click as she left the room. Cliff eased the bronze lever to the locked position. He didn't want to deal with Casey when he came home and he damn sure didn't want to talk to Burt. He just wanted to be left alone. He read the letter slowly, twice more, folded it gently and put it back into his sock drawer. Until he was shown definitive proof his father didn't make it out of Vietnam, he wasn't going to believe it. Before sliding the drawer shut, he reached in and took the letter out and unfolded it once again. He took a pencil from his shirt pocket and wrote in bold letters "NEVER" on the outside before returning it and slamming it shut.

The doorknob shook but the lock prevented whoever was on the other side from entering the room. Cliff heard the person begin to pry the lock with what sounded like a piece of steel and suddenly the door popped open. Casey stood on the opposite side with a small knife in his hand and a smile on his face. "Can't keep me out, cuz," he said, stepping into the room and slamming the door behind him.

Frustration tightened Cliff's features, his expression betraying the storm brewing inside him. "Don't reckon so," he retorted through clenched teeth.

Casey plopped down on the bed next to his cousin. He looked sideways at Cliff, confessing he had been eavesdropping on the other side of the door. Cliff, even though a storm raged inside him, he kept his cool and just shrugged his shoulders.

"I really don't want to talk about it," he informed Casey, but his younger cousin was having none of it.

"Oh, come on. You knew he was dead, you had to have," Casey didn't show the first bit of sympathy with his words, and they dripped with sarcasm, "Your dad's dead, my dad's dead. What the hell does it matter? We got Burt."

Cliff eyes narrowed and he glared at Casey. "Your dad isn't dead. You just gave up on him," he put his finger in Casey's face, "Burt ain't my father and he damn sure ain't yours!" Cliff flew into a rage as his face turned red, and his hands began to shake.

Casey remained calm as well. He really didn't care. He held up his palms, "You defend his murdering ass if you want. If it wasn't for Burt I'd be up there in that place in Marianna. He saved my ass."

Cliff's flushed face inched closer to his cousin's, his frustration simmering just beneath the surface. "Case, your *dad* saved you from that place. He wanted us together. Burt had nothing to do with it. He just wanted the money, he don't care nothing about your dumb ass."

Cliff, at first, didn't notice the fist hurling towards him until it was too late to block the blow. Casey landed the punch right below Cliff's eye and followed it up by tackling him to the floor. Casey was smaller but he held the element of surprise. The two began to wrestle, arms and legs intertwining with each trying to overpower the other. Eventually Cliff's larger frame pinned Casey to the floor. He held Casey to the floor with one hand as he drew his other to a fist, returning the blow thrown by his cousin. But before he could land his punch, the door flew open, and Burt stormed into the room. His bulky frame moved with unusual speed and a split second later the hard heel of his boot caught Cliff in the chest, hurling him backwards towards the wall. As his slender body bounced off the wall, all the oxygen in his lungs released, and he felt lightheaded. His ears rang like church bells, but he could still hear Casey's piercing laughter. Burt, not accustomed to physical exertion, fell across the bed, out of breath and sweating liberally.

When he finally caught his breath, he managed to say, "Boy, I ought to knock the hell out of you." He caught another breath, "Jumping on someone smaller than you!" Cliff didn't argue as the bells subsided, and his vision slowly came back into focus. He just stared at Casey as the kid rolled with laughter.

"You, shut the hell up!" Burt snapped at Casey and the young boy immediately complied, a confused look sweeping across his face. Burt ran his fat fingers through his sweat soaked hair and sighed. "What the hell is all this anyway?" Neither boy answered. They just continued staring at each other. Their faces revealed an unspoken resolve—the fight was far from over.

Burt held up his hands, "All right, I don't give a shit," he mumbled, still winded, "I ain't gonna tell your momma." Burt whistled, looking disappointedly at Casey, "Boy, I gotta teach you how to fight." Burt struggled to his feet, grabbing Casey by the collar and drug him out of the room.

Cliff didn't move. He hadn't moved since Burt's kick landed him against the wall. He wanted to cry but he wouldn't give his stepfather the satisfaction. He felt alone. It was as though he was the last person on Earth. Unc and his mom were the only two people in the world that cared about him. Unc was in prison and his mother was married to a monster.

He felt the weight of responsibility crash over him, heavy and inescapable. It was up to him to free both his uncle and his mother from the prisons that held them—one made of steel and stone. The other forged from pain and regret.

He finally turned himself over and sat on the floor. His stomach felt as if Burt's boot had carved a hollow pit inside him, raw and unrelenting. He rubbed it to make sure there wasn't a real hole. He pulled up his shirt and saw the imprint of Burt's boot still bruised into his abdomen. There was no way his mother could love a monster like Burt Williams. She was too good and kindhearted of a person to love someone that enjoyed hurting people.

Even though he was gasping for air and seemed on the verge of collapse, Cliff saw the glow in Burt's eye. The gangster enjoyed the pain he caused his stepson. Cliff stood to his feet and leaned on the side of the window. He lifted it until he felt the breeze filter past him and took a deep breath, hoping it would cause the pain to ease. It didn't.

He gazed out the window, his mind already shaping the plans that would set everything in motion. Proving his uncle's innocence had to come first, but simply scouring old newspaper articles at the library wouldn't be enough. He needed to dig deeper, to follow the trail no matter where it led. Giving up wasn't an option—not on his dad, not on his uncle, and not on his mother. They were all he had, and he wasn't about to let them go without a fight.

Casey sat on the couch with his leg dangling over the side right next to Burt, who nearly took up the remainder of the couch himself. The television was on and they pretended to watch, but neither was really interested in what was playing on the screen.

"So, what was that about?" Burt finally asked him without taking his eyes of the television.

"He said something about you," Casey told him, both still staring blankly at the television. Burt smiled and leaned over towards Casey. *This kid*, he thought, *was going to be all right.*

Casey already knew one of the first rules of the Dixie Mafia. Do not bite the hands that feed you. That was the kid's first step. Burt was taking the kid under his wing as not only a "son" but as a member of the rough band of outlaws. He rubbed Casey on the head while popped a cigar in the corner of his mouth with his other hand. He thought about offering one to Casey, but right then, Susie walked in the room, and he thought better of it. She smiled at them, sitting down in the chair next to them opening a magazine, unaware of everything that had just happened. Casey and Burt looked at each other, smiling.

Chapter 8

The day his flight was to leave for sunny South Florida, RB was tidying up his office at the police station when someone stuck their head in the door and told him the chief wanted to see him. That wasn't unusual before someone left for the amount of time that he intended so he took his time getting there.

When he finally made it to the chief's office, his boss ushered him in quickly and motioned to the couch where two middle-aged men in suits waited patiently. One had unkempt, long oily hair and the other's was trimmed neatly, military style. As RB took a seat across the desk from the Chief's chair, he wondered who they were. FBI was his first guess; DEA was his second. RB eased his chair around so that he could see everyone in the room. That was something he picked up from Burt.

The Chief grabbed his hat and turned to walk out, "RB, I'm not going to sit in on this meeting," he told him, "These men are DEA. They want to talk with you about a friend of yours." The chief nodded slightly, walking out of the room, shutting the door behind him and RB heard him tug on it to make sure it shut completely. The shades had already been drawn.

The agents didn't move. The one with the buzz cut's eyes stared through the Biloxi detective. "Detective Brown, your reputation precedes you," the agent with the military cut said in a cold, dry voice, "How do you know Mr. Burt Williams?"

RB guessed who the *friend* was the agents wanted to discuss, and he had guessed correctly. A crooked smile formed in the corner of his lips as he stared back at the agents. The shaggy agent said nothing. He just stared into the distance, not even looking in RB's direction.

"Introductions?" RB asked, still smirking in their directions.

"DEA, Mr. Williams. All you need to know at this moment, now, again, Mr. Burt Williams? A friend?"

RB nodded. He had dealt with men like this before, and he knew exactly what they were capable of.

"I *work* with Mr. Williams from time to time, keeping Biloxi from becoming Chicago or Detroit," RB's voice remained steady, unfazed. He felt no shame in working with undesirables if it meant keeping the peace, "He's pretty plugged into the Dixie Mafia, if you ever heard of that bunch."

Shaggy laughed slightly, catching RB's attention, and tilted his head towards him and with a sly grin replied, "Dixie Mafia is bullshit. Small time. Mr. Williams has graduated to a..." he paused to consider his words, "*higher* class of criminals."

RB rubbed the stubble on his chin, "Well if he's graduated, me and him ain't really attending the same school anymore then."

The buzz cut agent stood up and paced back in forth in front of RB a couple of times. He looked at Shaggy and tilted his head to one side and made a clicking sound with his mouth as if he were calling a dog. Shaggy mimicked his actions, and the decision was made.

The agent stopped in front of RB and extended his hand, "Well, Mr. Brown, or may I call you Ramsay?" he asked politely.

RB leaned forward in his chair to shake the agent's hand, "Most folks around here just call me RB."

"Well, RB, my name is Boston and this," he pointed towards the other agent, "is Randy, known as *Shaggy*."

"RB, I'd like to offer you a chance to work with *us* and I'll be very blunt with you. Particularly, your friendship with Burt Williams is what we need. Your dedication and experience are a huge bonus, no doubt, but this relationship can help us out," Boston told him. RB's crooked grin evaporated replaced by a worried frown and he listened intently. "You will remain associated with the Biloxi Police, but you travel to West Palm to visit your friend, just as planned but you'll like it there and want to stay. That's it for now. We'll cover the rest in the weeks to come."

RB thought about it for a second, "You *want* Burt Williams?" he asked with a hint of disbelief.

Shaggy, still in his seat, leaned forward and told him, "Williams is just a pawn. We are after *bigger* prizes than him. He's just our way in."

RB glanced over at Shaggy and asked pointedly, "If I do this, what's in it for me?"

Shaggy smiled and replied, "I wondered when you were going to ask that. Don't you have a plane to catch?"

RB annoyed replied, "That wasn't an answer."

Shaggy stood to his feet, his tall frame almost touching the ceiling panels, "We have a lot of *openings*." Those words elicited both excitement and apprehension within RB. He knew there was a reason the DEA always had job openings.

The agents told him to expect contact within a week and the three men shook hands. The two agents left. RB leaned back in his chair, feverously rubbing his chin, and staring at the shades covering the office window. His friendship with Burt had provided a lot of useful information in the past but if he did this, even though it could possibly further his career, their friendship would be essentially over. *But*, he thought, *Burt wouldn't hesitate to do it to him.*

RB made it to the airport just in time to board. He had to flash his badge a couple times. A Black man didn't just run through an airport in Mississippi without attracting attention. The plane was a small twin engine and there wasn't much room, even average in height, RB's head almost touched the top of the passenger cabin.

A couple of passengers gave him a side eye stare, looking at each other shaking their heads. RB was used to it. It didn't mean he liked it; he just knew how things *were* in the South. *Hell,* he thought, *people were pretty much the same everywhere, it ain't just Mississippi.*

He settled into his seat, closed his eyes, and thought they could look at him all they wanted to. He was a secret agent who was headed down to Florida to take on some bad guys slinging dope throughout the country. They'd thank him if they only knew. As he drifted off to sleep, he kept saying *you're welcome* to himself instead of counting sheep. It worked like a charm. The sleep he managed on the flight was the deepest and most restful he'd had in months.

"Mr. Williams, things that are happening in my country necessitate changes to our arrangements," Diaz told Burt as they sat under a large umbrella on the back deck of a riverside burger joint. It wasn't much of a place to eat but the view of the gigantic NASA building across the Indian River more than made up for it. Burt didn't get the chance to eat at places like this much anymore and he enjoyed watching the families that gathered to watch the shuttle launch in a couple of days.

Not taking his eyes from a small family seated at the table across the deck from them, Burt asked "What kind of changes?" Burt took another enormous bite of his burger and ketchup oozed slowly down his chin, catching on his new beard. Diaz motioned for Burt to wipe it off, but he ignored it and continued scarfing down his burger.

"Changes we will discuss in a more private setting, no?" Diaz asked, looking around at the people surrounding them.

Burt laughed, ketchup still smeared on his chin, now joined by a trail of dripping grease. "I love these things," he said, taking another hearty bite.

Diaz, ready for him to finish so they could hold a conversation without Burt slinging parts of his lunch in every direction, sighed.

Burt motioned around, "You think they care one bit about what we say? Best place to have a conversation, out in the open." Burt thought back to all the meetings he held in Biloxi on the playground of fast-food joints. "Just get to it," the old gangster commanded.

Diaz wasn't flustered easily, happily ignoring the command from such a man. "You're done helping us with *product*," the Columbian informed him, "We need help in another area. Moving the profits." Burt shoved the last chunk of his burger into his mouth, chewing as confusion flickered across his face. Diaz noticed and lifted his palms toward Burt, a silent plea for patience, "My boss doesn't want to cut in the American bankers anymore. We would rather pay you and your fleet of fishing boats to simply transport certain *packages* out to international waters. I was thinking this could be done even when you take tourists out to fish. Drop a couple of packages here and there. Quite simple." Diaz put his hands back on top of the table and waited for Burt's response.

Burt snickered, nothing in their business was ever *simple*. "Let me get this right. You want me to take packages of money out, on charters, and nobody finds out?" Burt laughed so hard, the last chunk of burger landed on the wooden table and the family sitting next to them looked at him in disgust.

Diaz grimaced at Burt, then turned and looked apologetically at the family before turning a scowl back to Burt, "Nobody finds out if you do it *right*."

"Our cut stays the same?" Burt asked, pushing the half-chewed piece of burger to the side.

"Of course," Diaz replied, still scowling, "Plenty of money to spread around. However, I warn you, if you go about this carelessly," he leaned in closer to Burt, "You know what happens."

Burt rolled his eyes, "Don't you guys ever get tired of threatening your friends?"

This time Diaz snickered, raised an eyebrow, and with a tone mixed with both annoyance and amusement, asked "Wasn't it you who said we *weren't* friends?" Burt's face turned ghostly pale. He had been in this life long enough to know when enough was enough. He stood to leave, but Diaz grabbed his arm, "Understanding?" he asked casting a steely gaze up at Burt.

Burt looked down at him disgustingly, snatching his arm away from the Columbian's grip. He hated these people and couldn't wait for the moment he would put a bullet in this man's head. Burt nodded and squeezed his bulk through the maze of tables.

Diaz peered out over the slowly flowing river and his mind flashed back to the swift, deadly rivers of his youth. This was a river in name only. It was more of a brackish inlet from the Atlantic that barely moved. He squinched his eyes and thought he could see the space shuttle in the distance. He couldn't make out a whole lot, but it matched what he'd seen on television.

Columbia was his home, but he liked America. It was indeed a land of opportunity. He looked around at the happy families enjoying their food, the sunshine and each other. The fate of his predecessor burst into his mind. Christian Lopez failed not only because of his choices, both here and back home, but also because he didn't understand these Americans. He didn't observe them. He didn't learn their ways, their customs. He only cared about money, power, and that *woman*. He looked toward the heavens, squinting from the bright sunshine and silently thanked Lopez for his mistakes. Diaz assured himself that his fate would be different.

Keeping a low profile in Florida was his main priority. He didn't want a fancy house, nor did he want a large entourage that attracted attention like the one Lopez had kept. The more people you surround yourself with, the more people you must worry about betraying you. Mateo Diaz was a loner.

He left what little family he had behind long ago in the jungles of Columbia. His *tastes* also made being a loner a necessity. When people got to really know him, they usually ended up disliking him. Deep down he knew the reason, but here in America little of that mattered.

A family brushed past him, finished with their meal, and the little girl of the family gave him a smile when she asked him to excuse her. He returned the smile and nodded eagerly. Diaz loved children and often thought of fatherhood, but it was never to be. Nature would not allow it.

Burt, nearly out of breath from the lengthy walk to his car, said aloud as he shut the car door, "He's got one more time to put his hands on me." He started the engine and cranked the air conditioning. It was January, but in this part of Florida, winter rarely flexed its muscles. The temperature was a sweltering ninety degrees. The air, cooled by the car's condenser, sent chills over him as it hit his sweat soaked shirt. He opened the glove compartment and pulled out a small bag filled with white powder. He looked around, saw nobody near his car, and took a small amount on the end of his finger and held it up to his nose. The rush was instant, and he immediately felt better.

He had started using the stuff only recently and told himself that he only needed the powder for an occasional helping hand. Before, he never needed anything but maybe a beer or shot of whiskey, but down here, with all these unfamiliar problems and headaches, it helped a lot more than alcohol. Burt, always in control, feared nothing and the powder was no different. Nothing could conquer Burt Williams. Not even these damned

Columbians. At least Jefferson Black and his friends were kindred of sort. These Colombians were nothing but animals, following their beastly instincts. He stuck his finger back in the bag and snorted one more time. "Damn," he said under his breath as he put the car into gear.

When he arrived back to the Clark Building, a familiar face waited patiently outside his office. RB, busy making small talk with the blonde secretary, pretended he didn't notice Burt walk up. The old gangster couldn't hide the surprise on his face as he shook his friend by the shoulders, thinking he had gotten the drop on the detective.

"What in the hell are you doing here?" Burt asked.

RB tilted his head, and his face held the look of disappointment, "Hello to you too, bud."

Burt tried to backstep his surprised greeting, "You just surprised me, that's all. It is good to see you," Burt raised an eyebrow, "But still, what's up?"

RB stuck his hand out and Burt shook it vigorously, still wanting to pry RB's purpose from his stubborn lips. Burt, realizing his friend wasn't talking in the presence of his secretary, motioned for RB to follow him to his office.

RB gently placed his hand under hers, softly placing a delicate kiss on her soft skin.

"Good to meet you. I'm RB."

"Jaqueline," she cooed, her accent thick with the unmistakable cadence of the Mid-Atlantic. RB guessed—probably

New Jersey. She continued, her voice low, seductive. Her eyes flashing in Burt's direction, "I was named after Jackie Kennedy, her husband was president when I was born." RB slowly released her hand, letting his fingers drag over hers and followed Burt through the doorway.

RB closed the door behind him, throwing one last wink at his new friend before turning his attention to Burt. "New Jersey and young," he laughed as he eyed Burt to gain his reaction. When Burt turned back to him, RB recognized the look and threw his hands in the air, "Off limits right?"

Burt smiled, slightly, and said, "Damn right." RB just shook his head as he fell into an old leather chair. Burt, his mind still floating, eased into his chair behind the desk.

"Nice," his guest told him as he gestured around the room.

"Like it huh? A lot of this is *my* style. The old bastard loved the ocean and boats, but I like *old* style."

RB nodded a couple times, "Old gangster style? Godfather style?" Burt shrugged his shoulders and smiled.

Burt pulled a cigar from his pocket, ran it under his nose and offered one to RB. RB wagged his finger at his friend, "Those things will kill you." Burt laughed and reminded RB that people in his profession didn't have a long shelf life anyway.

"That may be true, but I'm not going to chance it," RB chuckled, "I'm going to be an old man one day."

Burt gathering his thoughts as well as he could with the cocaine still in his bloodstream, leaned towards RB and asked

"Well, once again, what brings you to Florida?" He tried to hide his annoyance, asking a third time, but the detective sensed it right away. He also sensed something different about his old friend but couldn't yet put his finger on it. If he didn't know Burt any better, he would've sworn he was high.

RB smiled and raised his hands in the air, "Can't an honest cop take a vacation without someone thinking they are up to something?"

Burt eyes narrowed and he once again tried to focus, "Vacation, huh?"

RB nodded in agreement and said, "Came down to watch the shuttle take off. I've been fascinated with space since Sputnik; back when I was a kid."

He launched into a story about his father, who had been terrified of the Russian satellite as it streaked across the night sky back home. Most folks believed its purpose was something sinister, a watchful eye from the other side of the world. But RB had been different. He needed to understand it, to uncover the truth for himself. That curiosity had set him on the path to becoming a detective. He always needed to know.

"Anyway, that ain't the only reason I wanted to come down here," RB confessed, "We need to talk about Biloxi and a guy named Baxter."

Burt raised an eyebrow and rolled the cigar around in his mouth searching his foggy brain, "Ain't nobody named Baxter around Biloxi that I know of. Nobody that counts anyway."

RB shook his head, "This cat is new. I don't know where he came from, but word is he's working out of a fancy hotel in New Orleans, and I hear he's making a move." RB leaned back towards Burt, glancing around to make sure the door was completely closed, "Veck Baxter. No prior, no record, just a name and a social. Guy named Jefferson Black, Brazilian dude has been seen coming in and out of the hotel." RB, watching for any sign, saw the look on Burt's face change. *Gotcha*, he said to himself.

Both men knew when the other lied, so Burt decided on the truth, or at least some of it, "I know Jeff Black. Brazilian. He and I had some *business* together once." The gangster waited for the detective's response, wondering if he had already told RB too much. He may be a friend, but he was still a badge. He wondered if it was the powder that was doing too much talking.

Damn, he thought, *I got to slow down my thinking.*

He took a big breath and RB sat back in his chair. Each squeak from the RB's leather felt like a dagger to Burt's head. The powder was finally wearing off, and the crash was beginning to set in.

"What kind of *business*?" RB asked, hoping to pry at least a little more. Burt, his head hurting but his thoughts becoming clearer, put his finger to his lips. Some things were off limits between the two men and that question crossed that border.

RB gave him a nod, understanding that he had pushed the conversation to a line they couldn't cross. "Well, just so as you know, he *is* connected to this Baxter guy. I don't know exactly what they are up to, but it damn sure ain't good. For you or for me."

Burt desperately wanted to change the subject and maybe get RB to leave so he could close all the blinds and have a meeting blondie with out there. He stood up, reached out his stubby hand to his friend and said "Understood. Anyway, my friend, let me and my *family* take you out to eat tonight. I know several elegant spots here in beautiful West Palm for my vacationing friend," his voice tried to mimic Robin Leach but failed terribly.

RB nearly fell out of his chair laughing. "You look *elegant*. It would be nice to meet your family, Burt...." RB scratched the side of his head, "Never thought I'd say that." Burt mimicked a laugh while RB shook his hand.

"See you tonight then." Burt smiled, "Oh yeah, send Ms. Jersey in here, I need to *dictate* some things."

Chapter 9

Inside the pitch-black room, Veck Baxter lay restless, struggling in vain to find sleep. The heavy blinds suffocated the midday sun, but no amount of darkness could quiet his mind. He had hoped the numbing mix of painkillers and alcohol would dull the aches that tormented him, and as the pain gradually faded, he felt himself slipping away.

Yet, as his body surrendered to exhaustion, his mind betrayed him. The very thoughts he had fought to bury clawed their way to the surface, twisting into dreams that felt just as vivid—just as relentless—as the memories he couldn't escape. Even in sleep, there was no refuge.

When the dreams came, they were as vivid as the days he lived them. His mind faded back to the jungles of Vietnam, but more, it faded back to that *place*. There were ten of them when he first arrived in the camp. Four South Vietnamese and six Americans.

They were all relatively healthy in the beginning. But, as the years passed, their numbers fell. Most died from disease. But some died when their bodies simply could take no more abuse, expiring prematurely. The rest died from hope—hope that one day their country would remember them, that someone would come for them. But that day never came. Not until Baxter decided he'd had enough.

That fateful day only two Americans remained. Himself and the very first guy to arrive in the camp. He was a very athletic type of guy, but like everyone else, he endured so much pain that at night Veck could hear him cry out, no matter how he tried to hide it during the day. He cried out not from the physical pain, but the psychological torture administered by the sadistic colonel that ruled over the camp. Both men, subjected to relentless torture, survived by sheer will as the others slowly died off. The fewer prisoners left to torture made the wicked man focus his wrath on the two remaining Americans. They nicknamed him Lucifer, not just for his ruthless cruelty, but for his short, pointed ears that only added to his demonic presence.

Lucifer played mind games with his prisoners. The men could see it in his wicked smile—these cruel games were his only true passion. He only smiled when inflicting pain, and a grin was always perched on his lips.

The night before Baxter accomplished his escape, he suffered one of those sessions with Lucifer. Veck knew tonight would be especially brutal when the guards dragged his friend from the cramped bamboo hut, his limp body leaving a dark trail of blood in the dirt behind his toes.

The guy that often told him how great of an athlete he was couldn't draw the physical nor mental strength to walk. His chin rested on his chest and his long blonde hair covering his eyes. Veck noticed the tears streaming down his sunken cheeks. Whatever Lucifer told him had broken what little spirit he had left. After seeing his friend in such a state, he knew the end for both drew near. The evil little man just wanted to torture them as much as possible before he actually killed them. When the thought of welcoming death crept into his mind after seeing his friend in such a state, Baxter knew their escape couldn't wait any longer. It had to be tomorrow. If they hesitated, they might not live to see the next sundown.

Lucifer was short, even by Vietnamese standards. His neatly trimmed gray hair exposed the sharp points of his ears, adding to his unsettling presence. He was the image of a career military man—his uniform pristine, without a single stain or wrinkle. A slow, satisfied smile spread across his face as Baxter's tattered body was hurled into a chair by a guard.

The guard reached down to tie his hands and feet to the chair with a grimy rope, but Lucifer waved him off. The guard saluted, leaving the two alone.

"Good evening, private," Lucifer said in his broken English, "I'm not going to beat around the bush, as you Americans love to say. Bad news from America, I'm afraid. I had to give your comrade the same news, as I'm afraid we always don't get everything, *on the head*?" he finished with that as a question. Lucifer loved to use American slang, but Veck could tell that he never really understood the exact meaning of his words.

Veck Baxter stared straight ahead, his body as rigid as possible. He was, after all, still an American soldier. He didn't flinch or respond and if that infuriated Lucifer, the crafty old

Vietnamese soldier didn't show it. "Again, apologies, but as I said, I just get what I get." Veck knew the old man was trying to evoke some kind of response with each word he uttered. The colonel drew closer to his chair. Baxter bit his bottom lip until he felt blood. He wouldn't give the bastard the satisfaction.

"Seems like either you or your friend's child," he motioned to the pit, was in some sort of terrible accident. I don't know details, again so sorry, but the child didn't survive." Lucifer's smile widened and by now his face was close enough that Baxter winced from his foul breath. He involuntarily pulled his nose back and in response, the colonel pressed the hard heel of his boot into Baxter's foot, drug it across the rest of his toes tearing toenails from flesh. Blood poured from the wounds, pooling on the floor.

When he finished, Lucifer went into the gory details of the child's death. Both surviving prisoners' children were nearly the same age, and both were sons. Neither had ever seen their sons as both deployed before their children's births. Lucifer had shown each pictures, claiming the images to be their sons but they never knew for sure.

This was, of course, Lucifer's plan. His prisoners were only beaten as *punishment* for stealing, fighting, or escape attempts and you felt those beatings deep in your bones. Baxter knew from experience. He endured more beatings than any other prisoner, his body a canvas of bruises and scars, because his escape attempts were frequent—and, unfortunately, always unsuccessful.

Playing mind games was Lucifer's true passion and he preferred his prisoners in relatively good health so he could invade their thoughts. Veck never flinched no matter what Lucifer told him and Lucifer never broke eye contact, studying each of his victim's slight movements. Each man probing the other's breaking point.

When he finished detailing the child's death, he stepped back and waited for a response that wouldn't come. He stood silent, staring into Baxter's face for a few minutes and when the prisoner didn't give him his pleasure, he grunted and motioned for the guard to take him away. Veck won this round but didn't smile. No emotion shown upon his face, but inside he was screaming.

The guard snatched him by the arm, expecting to drag him like the other prisoner, but he stood at attention and walked. When they reached the hole in the ground that served as their cell, Baxter braced. He expected the blow and absorbed it best he could, but he stumbled, falling into hole with his body thumping against the wooden ladder sending stabs of pain throughout his body. His back hit the cold, wet ground and the sponginess of the soil saved some of the impact, but his breath released when he hit, sending his mind spinning. When he gathered himself and caught his breath Baxter saw his friend standing towards the back of the pit, his head buried in his hands. There wasn't much light, and he could only make out a silhouette, but he heard his cries.

The broken soldier's arm stretched toward him, trembling. Baxter could barely see, but he noticed something clutched in the man's hand. He reached out, fingers brushing against it, and just as his grip closed around the object, darkness swallowed him. He recognized the rough texture of a piece of paper.

"Please, if my son is alive, get this to him," he said, each word a struggle, his breath ragged and weak.

Veck, focusing on the paper, didn't notice that in his friend's other hand he held a makeshift knife. A knife obviously fashioned and hidden over a lengthy period of time. They both agreed to keep it hidden and only use it if there was no hope left. Apparently, the other prisoner felt that his time had come. Before he could say or do anything, the shadow pulled the blade across his throat, smiled for the first time Baxter could remember and slowly fell on one knee.

The note fell from his hand as Baxter lurched forward and caught his friend in his arms before he hit the ground, but it was too late. Through the faint light he could see his friend's hollow, lifeless eyes and the metallic smell of blood filled his nostrils.

He didn't yell for help or make any sound at all. He held the lifeless body against his, carefully folding the stained paper, placing it gently inside his shirt. He held his friend's body for the rest of the night. He owed him that.

The next morning, Colonel Duy arrived. They may have the same rank, but Lucifer held sway over Duy for some reason unknown to anyone but the two old soldiers. But when Lucifer wasn't at the camp, Duy was in charge. He was sympathetic to the Americans and treated them with as much respect as not to attract attention to himself. Veck Baxter walked over to the officer, handed him the note, and motioned with his eyes back towards the lifeless body. Duy nodded and pain spread across his face. He truly felt for the fallen soldier, but deep in his mind, he rejoiced. It would be easier to get just one man out.

Baxter jolted upright in bed; his breath ragged as he wiped the sweat from his brow. His eyes darted in every direction, searching for the bamboo walls of his Vietnamese prison, but all he found was the dark, still hotel room. The shrill ring of the phone echoed through the space, yanking him back into the present.

He lifted his hands in front of his face, and in his drowsy haze, he swore he could still feel his friend's blood clinging to his skin. As the fog of sleep faded, reality took hold—but the regret remained. Staring into the darkness, he whispered a wish to no one but himself: that he could go back, back to that moment, back to the blade, and stop it before it stole his friend's life.

Baxter fumbled in the darkness for the lamp's switch, finally finding it and flipped the light on, almost blinding himself in the process. He always found it difficult to regain his bearings after those type of dreams. He had read somewhere that most people didn't remember their dreams and right now, he wished he was one of those people. The phone began to shriek once again and this time he answered it on the first ring.

"Yes, yes..." he said into the receiver instead of the customary hello, still somewhat groggy.

"Hello, irmão. I hope you slept well," the accented voice on the other end greeted him. Even though the day was almost over, he sensed drowsiness in his friend's voice.

Baxter smiled and his mood changed drastically, "Good morning to you, brother. What can I do for you so early?"

Black chuckled, "It's early in the afternoon, have you lost track?"

"Yes, The pain doesn't wait for dark most times."

"The black man, Ramsay Brown, has acted just as you said he would. He is in West Palm," Jeff Black told him, his voice holding its usual confidence, "The tip worked. He has been tasked by the *DEA* with getting information out of Burt Williams." The smile spread across Veck Baxter's face. Thoughts of his lucid dreams faded, and he cleared the remaining cobwebs from his mind.

"Great news, my friend. Williams' stupidity will finally come home to roost. The man is nothing but predictable," Baxter paused, "Everything hinges on his isolation and deterioration of his mind. The child is my only concern, but children are gullible, and we've got to be careful."

"What about the son of Vernon Bruce?" Black asked carefully.

"Vernon Bruce," Baxter repeated. Just saying the name burnt like acid in his mouth, "Just keep to the schedule. Calley visits Bruce again this week, right?"

"Yes, this week," Black responded, "I will keep you informed on Brown and Williams." Baxter thanked his friend and hung up the phone. The dream reminded him that he needed to contact his *savior*, Colonel Duy. He needed the old Vietnamese soldier's help one more time.

Cliff burst into the kitchen, spotting the mail placed on the counter by the housekeeper. Sometimes it would stay there for days before his mother finally looked through it and Burt never cared about the mail as nothing ever came for him. For some reason, today Cliff felt particularly nosy and decided to check if anything had arrived for him. He had subscribed to all sorts of newsletters about crimes and unsolved mysteries, and while they arrived sporadically, he always hoped one would show up when he checked the mail.

As he thumbed through the stack, it wasn't a newsletter that caught his attention but an envelope from the Georgia prison. His name was printed on the front. His pulse quickened as he took it in his hands, held it up to the light, and exclaimed, "Finally!"— his voice ringing through the empty house, met only by the hollow echo of his own excitement.

The envelope, he discovered, contained a letter from his uncle. He ran upstairs, locked his door, and put a chair under the pearly white doorknob to keep his cousin out. He opened it carefully and eased the paper from its sheath. As he read, he shook his head, holding back tears. He pulled the chair from underneath his desk, sat down and read the short letter over and over with anger replacing tears. He wasn't going to give up, no matter what anyone, including his uncle, told him.

Just as he began to fold the letter to put it in his pocket, he heard someone prying the locked door and suddenly the door swung open, sending the chair flying across the room. Burt and Casey bounded into the room.

"Why are you barricaded in here like this boy?" Burt snarled, snatching the letter from Cliff's hand. As he scanned the words, he began to laugh. Casey laughed too even though he had no idea why. He just loved to mimic everything Burt did.

When he read the last word, he turned his eyes to Cliff and through gritted teeth said, "Such a damn pansey," his laughter filling the room once more. He threw it back at Cliff, but it fell short, landing on the floor. As he walked by, Casey hovered his foot over the letter, mockingly. Cliff glared at Casey, lunged from his chair, pushing his cousin to the side, preventing him from smashing it with his foot.

"Watch it!" he yelled as he stumbled sideways, catching himself on the edge of the bed.

Burt pointed his stubby finger at Cliff, "Don't start no shit, boy," he grumbled. Casey once again giggled as the two left the room and Cliff heard the television come to life in the living room. Cliff, as angry and frustrated with his younger cousin as he was knew that he didn't hate him. All of Casey's attitude originated from Burt. All this attitude that Casey developed wasn't his but stemmed from *his* stepfather. He picked up the letter, brushed it off and vowed once again to free his uncle.

Cliff put the letter on top of his father's faded, stained letter in his sock drawer and hurriedly descended the stairs, yelling into the living room that he was going to take a walk on the beach. Neither Burt nor Casey responded because they didn't really care.

When he heard the door shut, Burt motioned to the kitchen and told Casey to get him a beer out of the fridge. With a sly grin, he also mentioned that he could *open* it for him. Casey knew what that meant. The thirteen-year-old could have a swig.

As Casey fetched the beer, Burt eased up the steps and into Cliff's room. The boy, in his haste to leave, left it unlocked. Burt noted how sloppy the kid was when he was flustered. Just like his uncle. Burt often snooped around the house when Cliff and his mother weren't there. It was just part of his nature to be suspicious of everyone and everything.

He fumbled around with some papers on Cliff's desk and looked under the bed and between the mattresses, thinking back to his teenage years and where he hid things from his grandfather. He expected to find some dirty magazines hiding there but there was nothing. *This kid needs a girlfriend*, he thought. The bed didn't rest completely against the wall, so Burt decided to look at the little bit of space between the bed and outside wall. He saw a small spiral notebook placed between the mattress and wall near the bed's headboard. His burgeoning girth prevented him from squeezing into the space so he slid the bed frame enough so he could fit through, although barely.

Grabbing a cigar from his pocket, he sat on the edge of the bed, his knees pressing against the wall in the cramped space. As he turned the object over in his hands, he realized it wasn't just any notebook—it was Cliff's. The boy carried it everywhere, filling its pages with notes, theories, and connections he believed tied back to his father, his uncle, or both.

The first few pages were nothing new, just a rehash of things already known to Burt and the rest of the world. When he turned to the last page and read Cliff's scribbled notes, he rolled the cigar to the opposite side of his mouth and took a deep breath. He ran his thick finger along the letters as he read the names Marcus Kendrick and Miguel Chatom. "Damn," he said aloud, but just above his breath.

He put the cigar between two of his fingers and peered out the window to the swaying palm trees. He saw the face of Marcus Kendrick staring back at him. He didn't know Chatom but knew what had happened to him. He was one of Black's men and Christian Lopez took him out. But Marcus Kendrick's face and name would forever remain burned into Burt's memory. It was his curse, he supposed, to remember the name and face of all the people he *terminated*. He didn't like the word *killed* as he didn't consider himself a cold-blooded killer. Every person he *terminated* was business and Kendrick was no exception, but the kid's last moments haunted him as he begged for his life. He shook his head and closed his eyes. When he reopened them, the image was gone.

Marcus Kendrick was a loose end. He was the one that stumbled into Chatom's body. He made his fatal mistake in calling the police. That act sealed the young man's fate. He was just a working stiff in the wrong place at the wrong time. Lopez always feared loose ends, and, in his mind, Kendrick was a loose end that could potentially lead back to him. It wasn't worth the risk, so one of Burt's first tasks, when he became involved with Lopez, was taking care of this particular loose end.

Burt intercepted him leaving work one afternoon and pretended to be a detective. He told Kendrick that he needed him to accompany him to the place where he found Chatom's body. Kendrick, in his naivety, was more than happy to help.

Burt tortured the poor kid until he was satisfied that he knew nothing. He then, without hesitation, ended Marcus' life. Now, the kid's name stared back at him from Cliff's notebook. Burt closed the book and placed it precisely where he found it and pushed the bed back into place, all the while making sure there were no wrinkles on the bed where his bulky frame had rested.

All he could think as he stumbled down the stairs and plopped back onto the couch was *Damn that kid.* He put the cold beer to his lips, noticing about a third of it missing. Casey grinned but Burt was in no mood to return the gesture. He just grunted. Susie was going to have to put her foot down with *her* son.

Burt took another sip of beer and thoughts of Cliff consumed him. The kid needed to go to the surf shop with Casey or he needed to do something other than stick his nose where it didn't belong. He was just about seventeen. Maybe it was time for him to get a job. Something to occupy his time. Burt grinned. *He* controlled the money, and he would cut the little son of a bitch off. Susie would just have to get over it. He finished what was left of his beer and motioned to the kitchen.

Chapter 10

"Well, no new trial, that motion was dismissed rather quickly," Ryan Calley informed Vern. Vern didn't expect the motion to succeed so he didn't respond to the lawyer's statement. In his limited excursions outside the tiny death row cell, he had asked about this Ryan Calley. He was well known among the guards and a lot of the prisoners. Vern got his information mostly from the guards who were as nosy as any prisoner. They did their research on prisoners and *lawyers* to find out which ones were susceptible to bribes and payoffs. Ryan Calley's reputation stood as one of a straight arrow. He followed the rules.

Calley shuffled some papers in his briefcase and spoke without looking up, "The appeal process begins now and I'm going to expedite it. If nothing else, we must get you off death row," Calley hesitated and looked at their surroundings, "and out into this paradise. Yes," he shook his head, "the first step is saving your life, then we can prove your innocence."

Vern took a deep breath, hoping the strong, musky cologne Calley wore would stick in his nose and he put a fake smile on his face and tried hard to believe the slick-haired lawyer's words. He didn't really put much hope in anything since Susie told him that his brother was truly dead. The hope of one day reuniting with Rof, hugging him, and telling him he was sorry had vanished with Susie's visit.

"That would be great—except for one thing," Vern said, his eyes fixed and unblinking, as if staring straight through the cold steel desk. "Whoever put me here could get to me then. And I'm sure I'd be dead within days."

Calley shrugged, pursing his lips in a gesture that was neither agreement nor disagreement—just quiet acknowledgment, "I'm not going to lie to you, Vern. It's a possibility, but if you tell me everything you know, and I mean *everything*, you might stand a chance of getting out of here." Calley stopped and tried to look Vern in the eye, but the prisoner's eyes didn't budge, "You are innocent right?"

Vern glanced at Calley from the corner of his eye, catching a slight smile on his attorney's face, receiving the statement as it stood, without the added sarcasm.

"That's right," Vern responded.

Calley raised his hands, "Well, now would be a good time to come clean, Vern. It stays between you and me. Attorney-client privilege."

Vern picked up his head, looking through the tiny window in the room. The slight rays of warmth shown through. He tried to move his hands into the rays, but his shackles prevented it. "What are you *confused* about?" he asked, "You have my statements, everything's there." Vern pointed to the stack of papers.

Calley sat back in his chair and pushed back his slick, dark hair. "Well, Burt Williams for one. Where does he fit in all of this? You *gave* him custody of your son. He's running your business.

The guy is Biloxi through and through, Dixie Mafia to the core. He comes down, makes off like a bandit. Why?" Calley snapped his fingers and Vern slowly turned his head towards him, finally making eye contact.

Vern shook his head, "I had to. My son was going to Dozier. You heard of that place?" Calley nodded that indeed he had, and Vern continued, "That place would've taken his life. Burt is my nephew's stepfather. It didn't matter about his past; he was Casey's only hope. His wife, Susie, is a good person. I put my trust in *her*."

Calley raised an eyebrow, "Do you think he had it all planned?" Vern looked at his lawyer for a second in silence before bursting out with laughter. It was the first time he laughed in a long time, so he didn't hold back. When he finally gathered himself, Vern said "Williams is a thug, an enforcer, that's it. A planner he is not. All of this fell into his lap, and I pretty much *let* it happen."

"What about the murders? Lucky Clay, Beck, your wife?" he asked, "You think he played a role?" He had finally broken Vern's silence and he fired away, hoping to hit a mark.

Vern, the shackles cutting into his flesh, shook them as vigorously as he could, "Lucky Clay and Beck? Sounds like him but Patty Lee pretty much got herself killed. Got involved with the wrong people," Vern responded, tears forming in the corners of his eyes. Images of his wife filling his mind.

Calley ran his tongue along his bottom lip, rehearsing before releasing them, "Her case hasn't been *solved*. You are not a suspect. You were already in custody, but you knew that," Calley responded. He wanted to ask more questions about Patty Lee but decided today was a win and didn't want to jeopardize progress, "Let's just focus on the murders they have you in here for. Lucky Clay was Dixie Mafia, did you know that before?"

Vern shook his head, "I didn't until Williams came into the picture. I barely knew the man. Mac Tate trusted him, so I did."

Calley's head titled a little, "Mac Tate?"

"Panhandle politician that helped me…" Vern closed his eyes, "My dad too. Doesn't matter." Calley nodded and Vern continued, "Why in the hell would I kill Lucky Clay? It's never made sense why anyone thought I had a *reason*."

Calley shuffled his papers once more before finding the one he searched for, holding it up in the faint light, "Motive played out in court was you were upset you lost the election and blamed him. Stranger things *have* happened."

Vern snickered, "I didn't care if I won or lost that damned election in the end," he responded angrily, "Old Man Clark and Patty Lee wanted that, not me." Vern knew he was lying, but there was a hint of truth hidden in his words. He wanted to win the election on his own and on his own ideas. If he had stuck to the plan, he would've won but he wouldn't have been able to live with himself.

Calley pointed to the paper again, "What about Beck? How did you know him?" Calley asked.

"Never met the guy, never even *heard* of the guy," Vern stated, "I wasn't even in Lake City the last time anyone saw him."

The lawyer flipped a couple more pages, reading for a second before looking up at Vern after he finished, "No real alibi here, Vern. Drunk in a motel room? Alone?"

Calley shook his head, but Vern protested, "The clerk testified I was there."

The lawyer kept shaking his head, "No, he testified he *thought* you were there. That's not exactly a sound alibi." Calley started putting the papers in order and tapped them on the table, making sure all the edges were even with each other.

"It is the truth," Vern said without emotion. Calley carefully placed the papers in his case and prepared to leave.

Vern held up his hand to stop him, "You asked me if I thought Burt Williams was involved? *Yes.* I don't think he *planned* all of it, that's not him, but I think he did have some kind of hand in it. He wanted Cliff for Susie. Casey and the money were just a bonus."

Calley put his hand on Vern's shoulder, "I think we should focus on Burt Williams." Vern nodded in agreement without looking at the lawyer as he motioned for the door to open.

"I'll see you in a couple weeks," he told Vern, patting him on the shoulder, and walked through the door.

Calley wasted little time getting through the prison checkpoints and to a phone. "Checking in," Calley said into the payphone. The little gas station down the road from the prison had become like a second office to him. There were very few customers and those around didn't even seem to notice him. He figured they were used to seeing lawyers using the payphone on the side of the building. He smiled as he looked up at the giant painted bulldog that seemed to peer at him through wrinkled eyes as he spoke.

"Good to hear from you, Mr. Calley," Veck Baxter responded on the other end, "You get anything out of him?"

Calley waited until a kid rode his bicycle past the phone. He didn't want to take any chances. "Finally managed to get him to admit Burt Williams probably played some part in the murders, that's about it. Vernon Bruce doesn't trust people and I can't say I blame him," Calley put his free hand into his pocket. He wished these booths were like the ones in New York, enclosed all the way to the bottom as the kid rolled past again. There was a cold northern wind blowing and Georgia cold felt even worse than the cold Big Apple days. "You want me to dig into the Williams thing?" he asked.

There was a silence over the phone. Calley hated long pauses in conversation and with the wind howling, he wished Baxter would just get on with it. Finally, Baxter told him not to pursue it. There were other things in play and Burt Williams would be *handled*.

"Just get him off death row. Get him into general population. That's where I want him," Baxter ordered.

"Yes sir," Calley responded as he hung up the phone and rubbed his hands together blowing warm air from his lungs into them. He was glad he left the car and the heater running. Veck Baxter wasn't telling him everything, but he didn't' want to know *everything*. His job was to simply get Vern off death row. That he would handle. What he couldn't figure out was why Baxter was so adamant about that. If he just wanted to kill him in general population, he could let him rot on death row and the state would do the dirty work. It didn't really make sense to him, but what the hell, he was being paid a king's ransom for such little work. He settled into the warm seat and headed for the airport. He smiled as he put the car in drive and said aloud, "Mac Tate."

Mateo Diaz stood on the grass and stared at the massive ship. He couldn't believe something made from so much steel could float, much less fight in battle. As he walked up the long entrance ramp, the huge guns of the USS Alabama intrigued him. He couldn't imagine anything withstanding a single shell from one of the steel cannons, much less a barrage from the massive weapons. The biting wind sent a shiver down his spine, but the deck of the old museum ship radiated heat in the brilliant sunshine despite the chill in the air. On this blustery day, without a cloud in the sky, he was surprised there were very few people visiting the ship. When he stood under the massive weaponry, he felt completely alone. He walked back over the landlocked side of the ship, leaned over the rusty railing, and stared towards downtown Mobile. The city looked so peaceful from a distance.

It wasn't the largest city he had seen since he'd been in America, but from this distance, it was beautiful. The tall buildings didn't seem real. There was a slight hue to them even in the crisp air. They looked like silhouettes instead of actual steel and concrete.

He didn't smell the salt air as much as fresh paint newly coated onto the ship's hull. He wondered, as he admired the city, how much paint it took to paint the entire ship. The tall, slender figure of Jeff Black ascending the long walkway from the shore to the ship caught his attention. As much as he enjoyed admiring the ancient ship, business beckoned.

"Thank you, Mr. Black," Diaz said as he tipped the bill of the baseball cap perched atop his head. It was white and blue with the letter "A" inscribed on the front in white. He had no idea what it stood for, but he felt like an American when he wore it.

"Thank you?" the Brazilian asked in his hybrid accent, confused.

Diaz waved his arms about and said, "Thank you for the opportunity to visit this magnificent relic. I wouldn't have known about it without your invitation, and the view," he pointed out towards the city. He motioned to other side of the ship, "the other side isn't a terrible view either." The muddy waters of Mobile Bay whitecapped in the strong, chilly wind and the reeds almost bent far enough for their tips to touch the water. Diaz smiled as he admired the scenery surrounding the old ship.

"You're certainly welcome, but I didn't choose the location. You can thank Mr. Baxter. He knows the Gulf Coast and offers suggestions such as these," Black returned the smile as he spoke.

Diaz tipped his cap once more, "Please, extend my thanks to Mr. Baxter."

Black acknowledged that with a slight tip of his head before his expression turned serious. "The wonderful views aside," he said, his tone sharpening, "I'm afraid this is business."

"Of course, my friend. Always," Diaz still wore the smile of a man on vacation rather than a man meeting his criminal counterpart.

"Is Mr. Williams holding up his end of the deal?" Black asked, his face stern, his tone leaving no room for evasion.

Diaz' smile faded quickly, concern covering his face, "Mr. Williams is no *businessman*. That fact is certain, and I'm concerned."

Black's expression didn't change, "Concerns?"

Diaz took a step towards the massive bow of the ship, admiring the enormous chains holding her at anchor. When they reached the very tip of the bow and there were assured of privacy he continued, "Burt Williams is quickly becoming a drunk and..." he paused to look around, "user of our product."

Black, unconcerned, shrugged his shoulders, "Do you expect anything else of such a man?"

Diaz couldn't hide his surprise, "You *knew* about this man and yet you chose to do business with him?" He pulled out a pair of sunglasses and perched them upon his nose, watching the interstate traffic speed by on the bridge above them.

Black, feeling the effects of frigid wind blowing over the water, pulled his trench coat closed, "Burt Williams is merely a pawn in our game, nothing else. But he is *needed* at this moment. Nothing happens to him until his *usefulness* is usado."

Diaz smirked, "We're in America, *amigo*, we should use American words."

Black, his face finally showing emotion, smiled, and pointed to the downtown buildings of Mobile, "*Amigo*, we are in the *Confederacy.*" Both men laughed and began walking back towards the stern.

Black walked with purpose while Diaz continued lazily strolling, gazing at the ship's guns. "Such power," he told Black, "If we had one of these, we wouldn't need anyone else to move our wares."

Black laughed, "You know this machine is nearly half a century old?" Diaz nodded and then he noticed for the first time the vessel tied up behind the battleship.

The submarine USS Drum, also a museum ship, was moored behind the Alabama. Diaz couldn't contain his excitement. He had loved tales of submarines since he was a child.

He picked up his pace and passed Black as the two men made their way down the ramp and to the old diesel submarine. As he admired the relic, thoughts ran through his mind.

Black was right. There was no way to smuggle on a ship the size of a battleship, but something like this, no matter how old, would work.

Black noticed the Columbian sizing up the boat and waved his finger back and forth. "I know what is on your mind, my friend. Some already use subs for our purpose. More than not, they fail one way or another."

Diaz, his face suddenly serious, stretched his arms as wide as he could, "The size! Do you know what would fit on this?" His voice was loud, and the few people gathered near the stern of the ship above them cast glances in their direction.

"Calmly," he scolded his friend.

Diaz, embarrassed, bit his bottom lip. He may have become overly excited, but he should always hold his emotions and show professionalism. The fate of Christian Lopez once more entered his mind. "My apologies," he told Black.

Black nodded his head gently and added jokingly, "perhaps we should not enter the submarine." Both men relaxed their guard for a moment, and they laughed quietly together.

They eased past the mighty submarine and entered a large box-type building. There they explored airplanes and vehicles that won the second great war for the Americans. They politely declined to have a picture taken, making their way out, parting ways with a handshake in the parking lot.

Black headed directly to New Orleans, but Diaz decided to drive along the eastern shore of the sprawling bay and explore a little. He drove along a winding road that took him around the edges of the bay and towards the coast. He admired the stately houses backing all the way to the water. Each house adorned with covered docks complete with a rocking boat, swaying with the rhythm of the water.

He didn't know how many miles he traveled and lost track of the time it took to do so. The road turned sharply to the left and suddenly the bay homes gave way to open pastures and grazing horses. *This country is so amazing*, he thought. This particular area reminded him, somewhat, of the Columbian valleys of his homeland. Not only did the landscape change, but the homes on this road weren't built of the same style as the ones lining the bay. Most were single stories and long instead of tall. Ranch homes, just like his father's.

"This is beautiful," he said to aloud as he drove along. When he was young, he read about America in school, but seeing this, if only a small part, often left him in awe. Columbia, a large, proud nation, wasn't nearly as diverse as this land. He longed to visit the great plains and perhaps the desert southwest. He tapped his fingers on the steering wheel to the rock and roll music streaming through the car's radio. There was no way he would go home when his work was complete. Every bit of money he earned, he stashed. On the dashboard, he noticed the fuel tank needle pointing towards empty. He needed gas.

He almost began to panic when he didn't find a gas station within a few miles, but it wasn't long until the small country road dead-ended onto a busy highway. Near the small town of Foley that he finally found one. Running out of gas in the countryside, especially as a foreigner, wasn't something he wanted to happen. He didn't want to meet anyone that could possibly remember him and begging for gasoline beside the road would be something people would definitely remember. When the gas station's sign came into view, he released a deep breath and made the sign of the cross across his chest.

After he began to pump the precious fuel into his car, he reached to take his wallet from his pants pocket, but before he did, he noticed the edge of a picture peeking from its plastic holder. He placed the photo between two fingers and stared at it for a few seconds and gently placed it back into the slot in which it belonged. "Soon, Phillipe', soon," he whispered.

An older, man with a solid white beard leaned on a stool behind the counter when Diaz entered the store. Hanging loosely on top of his white hair was an old greasy cap, with the word "CAT" on the bright yellow patch which held a few stains itself. He pulled his cap from his head and pursed his lips. It looked too neat and crisp and had no character. He wondered how long the old man had owned his.

The old man caught Diaz looking at his hat, glanced at his brand-new cap and asked in a slow southern drawl, "Braves fan?"

Diaz looked intensely at the old man, trying to figure out what he meant. The old man chuckled and pointed at the cap. Diaz laughed, "I bought this hat in Mobile. I don't know what this letter even means," he said trying to hide his accent, but he knew it was in vain.

The old man just smiled, "Tourist, huh? Where're you from friend?"

Diaz thought for a second and decided it wouldn't hurt to tell this man of his home. "Columbia, sir. Working on an oil rig out in the Gulf. Thought on my days off, I would explore."

The old man gestured to the northeast, "Well, son, that hat is the cap the Atlanta Braves wear up in the big city. They are a baseball team."

This excited Diaz. He loved baseball almost as much as football and flashed a toothy smile, "Is that so?" he responded, "Perfect." He paid for the gas and bid the old fellow goodbye.

As he started the car he smiled once again as he glanced at the rearview and saw the car parked off to the side of the building. *Yep*, he thought, *still there, let's go gentlemen.* It was a non-descript, run of the mill brown undercover Ford Crown Victoria and inside, underneath caps of their own, pulled down to the sunglasses covering their eyes, rested the two DEA agents that had called on RB. Diaz put the car in drive and headed towards the coast, watching the undercover pull in behind him.

Chapter 11

The pool at RB's hotel bustled with activity, though few dared to swim. Unlike the day before, the Florida air was cooler than usual, but that didn't stop guests from lounging poolside in their bathing suits, soaking up the sun as it beamed down on them.

The Biloxi detective was no exception. He was sipping a cocktail, enjoying the view, when a shadow fell over him. His eyes were closed and his instincts kicked in. The detective's adrenaline started pumping. Perhaps Burt, always kinda paranoid, might be tired of his old friend.

He slowly opened his eyes and hoped for the best. He smiled and admonished himself when the figure of a hotel worker came into focus informing him of a call for him in the lobby. He gulped down the rest of his drink and reluctantly wrapped a towel around his lower half and followed the white-jacketed attendant inside.

"Brown," he said into the telephone as he sat down in a plush chair surrounded by green ferns. He glanced around; happy the lobby was nearly deserted.

"Good afternoon, Mr. Brown, we *met* back in Biloxi." RB recalled the familiar voice as the DEA agent he referred to as Shaggy.

Strange, he thought, *these guys don't even want to put their name out over a telephone.* "I remember," he replied, "I checked in with your office yesterday. I contacted the individual and everything is easing into place."

"Change of plans," the agent said matter-of-factly, "that particular *individual* is not a main priority right now. We need to get him to introduce you to a friend of his."

RB chewed his tongue and thought about his words for a second before responding, "This individual knows what I do for a living. We usually work together on *some* things, but there are boundaries, you know."

RB thought he heard the agent chuckle into the phone, "RB, we have the highest confidence that you can get this job done. All we need is for you to contact one of his business associates."

RB pursed his lips and grimaced, "I'm already working on getting some information about the gentleman we discussed," he responded carefully.

Shaggy's voice tightened even further, "We need you to contact the *other* gentleman." RB knew he was talking about the Columbian and Shaggy continued, "We need you to meet him. That's it for right now. Get the introduction. Once that is done, we'll contact you. Remember, all the confidence in the world in you. You're our guy."

The phone line went dead and began beeping loudly into RB's ear. He didn't like the way this was headed. Burt trusted him because he never lied to him. He was sure the favor wasn't reciprocated but he certainly didn't want to push that boundary.

He ran his fingers along a long branch of the fern planted next to his chair and wondered what the agents wanted with Mateo Diaz. He wasn't the target when he agreed to come down to West Palm, the Confederado was. He smiled at a scantily clad young lady that sauntered by him, watching her slip through the door to the pool area. As he admired her, he had to remind himself that this wasn't a vacation.

Instead of enjoying the pool, RB went back to his room. He waited a little while and called Burt to set up a meeting for the next morning. When he hung up the phone he pulled the blinds back and peered from the window. He wondered just how deep Burt had burrowed into this mess. Burt Williams was a criminal, but also a friend. Maybe he could save his old friend from going any deeper. But to do that he would have to sink deeper than he wanted. He liked Burt but *loved* himself.

It was unusual for Burt to arrive at the Clark Building any earlier than noon and those were the days on which he actually showed up. Those days were becoming exceedingly rare. This day was an exception as RB wanted to meet at eight in the morning. On most days, Burt was already deep into his daily ritual. A ritual that now included the white powder from South America and bourbon from Kentucky. This morning, however, he hadn't touched either one. He wanted his mind to remain clear when he met with his old friend from Mississippi. He only drank one beer with his breakfast. His still held cobwebs from the days and nights before, but he was as clear as he'd been in days.

RB walked into Burt's office with his usual smile while Burt, already feeling the call of his vices, savagely chewed on a cigar. The gangster wasn't sitting behind the desk but in a small chair facing the window. "What in the hell do you mean getting me here this early RB?" he asked only half-joking. Burt shook his head slightly but noticeably.

The detective eased closer to his friend, angling himself to get a better look at his face. He noticed it was slightly more swollen than usual, his typically chubby features now puffier, as if something had been gnawing at him. Burt pretended the bright rays of the sun blinded him, turning his back to the window. "You need to get up earlier, bud. This place is making you soft, you old crook," RB said with a slight chuckle.

Burt attempted a smile and rolled his cigar to the other side of his mouth, "What do you want?" RB sensed agitation within his voice and coupled with the swollen face, figured out pretty quickly that his friend was partaking of more than just a daily drink. He clapped his hands together, mostly to make sure Burt was paying attention, but the wily old gangster didn't move a muscle.

"I'll get right with it. I'm falling in love with this place, man. The women, the sun, and the *sin*. I bet someone with my *skills* could get set for life down here," RB said. He didn't try to hide anything in his voice as he knew Burt, even sauced, would spot deception.

Burt didn't move or react. He chewed on his cigar, holding his gaze on the sun hovering over the Atlantic. The only sound in the room emanated from the ancient clock on the wall. With each loud tick, the detective's nervousness grew.

"Who are you working for RB?" Burt asked, turning to look his friend in the eye, "As long as I've known you, you've kept it pretty straight. You've wandered into *iffy* territory once or twice but always snapped back before going too far..." Burt paused, stood up and moved face to face RB. It was the detective's turn not to flinch, "So, you're working *something*. You can't tell me you ain't." Burt turned and moved slowly towards the desk; his back turned to RB. "Our friendship extends you *certain* courtesies, but you know that. I don't want to have to draw down on you, but you know I will." The hair on RB's arm stiffened. Burt had never threatened him before. Burt turned quickly, with a wide smile and the cigar dangling from the edge of his lips, "And you know I'll win."

"Even *I* have a point where I'm tired of just making a living, Burt. I see what you got down here. I want in." RB tapped a finger on the window, pointing towards the beach that was slowly filling with people. "I'll shoot you straight, my friend, the DEA did come to me. Wanted me to come down and get some info on the Confederados. That's it." RB felt the cold steel of a pistol touch the back of his neck and he slowly turned to find that Burt, even with his bulk, had snuck up behind him. Burt locked eyes with his old friend and eased the gun down to his side. RB watched every movement, noticing the gun still pointing towards the detective. He didn't want to attract unwanted attention as the office staff began to trickle in. His sultry secretary usually got to work around this time.

Burt flung the cigar near a trash can but missed it badly and sucked his teeth. "We are going to walk outside and down to the beach. I'm going to put this up, but you know I'll use it." RB nodded in acknowledgement and the two walked out of the building and down to the ocean. As they walked RB wiggled his leg to make sure his weapon was still there. He knew it was, but he couldn't help but to double check. He glanced over at Burt as he struggled in the sand. RB, quite sure Burt knew he had a gun, and he knew the reason his old friend didn't take it from him. If it came down to it, the old gangster intended to at least give RB a fighting chance. That was a promise they made long ago.

Fearing for his life at the hands of Burt never really crossed RB's mind before this morning, but as he stared out over the blue waters of the Atlantic, fear crept into the back of his mind. Burt hadn't pulled his pistol again, so RB took that as a good sign.

As they walked, Burt stared out across the water as if watching a distant ship, but the horizon was completely empty. There were no birds bobbing in and out of the water and the water itself barely moved as though it was tired from the wind the past few days. Even though they weren't alone, RB had never felt such isolation before in his life.

Suddenly, Burt stopped and pulled RB to face him by the collar of his shirt, "RB, right now you tell me the absolute damned truth and you *might* walk off this beach." The two old friends were so close that RB smelled the previous day's whiskey seeping through his pores. Burt stared into RB's eyes, "What's going on?" he asked, almost pleading.

RB's eyes narrowed as he matched Burt's stare, "You know I ain't never lied to you Burt. I always shot you straight. I told you, DEA wants Jefferson Black, and they asked me to come down and get some info from you." RB kicked at the sand, "Now I seen what *you* got, and I want a piece. I'm tired of scrounging in Biloxi and I can help you, and honestly buddy, you need it." RB sniffed around his friend, "I know that smell. Smelled it a million times. I know you are on the sauce really bad. I can smell it on *you*. When was your last drink? Yesterday? It's in your system, your pores reek of it. God knows what else you got going on." RB shook his head and turned, slapping Burt's hand away, "You and me both know you can't mix that shit with what you got going on. You ain't got no friends down here *except* me, buddy, and only I can help."

Burt took a step back, his focus returned to the gently pulsating Atlantic. The gangster thought about telling RB that he did in fact have another friend here. One of his most loyal but decided not to mention Dell. He learned long ago to never reveal an ace until it was absolutely necessary. He spit in the water as a wave slowly receded, saliva mixing with the flotsam and jetsam that had washed up in the previous days, "I got some *family* problems I need help with RB. You help me with *that*."

RB jumped at the opening, "You got it, my friend. What is it?"

"Susie's boy, Cliff, he is obsessed with getting his uncle out of prison. Believes the sonofabitch when he says he innocent. Not only that but he still believes his father is alive somewhere. The kid's got problems. Susie went and met with old Mac Tate, you heard of him, right?" RB said he remembered the name. "Well," Burt continued, "He found out Rof, the kid's dad, is most likely dead and the boy still don't believe it. Keeps on digging."

RB, ran his hand across the stubble on his chin and looked at Burt, eyes furrowed, "What can I do?"

Burt didn't take his eyes from the water, "Help him. You're a detective, go and *detect*." Burt finally looked back at his friend. RB didn't have to be a detective to sense the concern dripping from Burt's voice.

In his mind RB questioned whether the concern was really for the boy or something *else*? He got his answer quickly. "I was snooping around, looked this notebook of his and a couple names I *knew* were in there. Chatom and Kendrick. Get with him, find out what he knows about those two and help him get to a point where he gives up on all this shit."

RB nodded along but knew there was more to this than what Burt was telling him, but if this was the job that put him on the inside, he would do it. If he helped the kid out with this, then maybe Burt would let him in a little farther. It did surprise RB, though, that Burt let him in so quickly in the first place.

RB knew the old gangster was nobody's fool and he had to be careful, "When do you want me to get started on all this?" RB asked.

Burt felt his shirt pocket for a cigar, finding one last stogie, he responded, "Tonight. Come over to eat with us. I'll make sure everyone's there, and I'll get the conversation started. You act interested and *offer* to help."

RB stuck his hand out and Burt grabbed it, squeezing it tightly he pulled RB in close enough to whisper, "If you are lying, you know what I *have* to do."

RB felt the hairs stand up on his neck, "I know," he whispered back.

Burt picked up the phone as soon as he got back into his office and dialed home. Susie picked up on the sixth ring. He reminded himself to make sure she remembered *when* to pick up the phone. The Dixie Mafia used subtle things to send code. Little things like picking up a ringing phone after a certain number of rings to let the caller know everything was clear. He feared Susie's new life of leisure in West Palm had caused her to forget those little things. His conversation with RB made him recognize they both were slipping. They would discuss it later as now wasn't the time.

"Hey," he greeted her, "make sure the boys are home for supper. We got company coming."

Susie sighed. The last thing she wanted right now was to entertain but she swallowed her reluctance and complaint, "Sure. Who?"

Burt rolled the cigar around his mouth as his blonde secretary came in and placed a coffee cup on his desk, bending over just a little too far, as usual, and Burt winked at her. He remembered that he was on the phone with his wife and quickly focused on the conversation, "Just RB. Nothing fancy."

There was a short pause before she replied. "May take some *doing* to get Cliff home for dinner. He's planning on going to the library after school and you know he stays until they run him out."

Burt's mood, already tense, craving both whiskey and powder, caused him to lose his cool very quickly, "Get his ass there."

Susie didn't hide her sarcasm when she replied, "Yes, sir" and slammed the phone down.

Burt's day, already starting out badly, grew worse with each interaction and he grumbled under his breath. He eased the pistol out of his belt and placed it gently on the desk in front of him. He didn't try to hide it when the secretary walked back in the door. She pretended like she didn't notice it, but Burt saw her eying it with trepidation.

He threw her a crooked smile, "Got here early, always bring it in when I'm the first one in," he said, trying to ease her mind. She winked playfully and put some papers down on his desk. Burt couldn't help but stare as she bent down to place the papers in front of him.

"Appreciate it," he told her as he caught a whiff of her perfume. She walked back to her desk and curled her legs around the chair, easing to her seat. Burt licked his lips and whistled just loud enough for her to hear. His jaw dropped open when she turned back to him with the tip of her tongue between her teeth and slightly parted lips.

He reached his sweaty palm under the desk, feeling around for the little bag of powder he kept taped there for emergencies. Burt reached in and put a little bit on the end of his finger and bowed his head to partake. The rush wasn't immediate as usual, but he instantly felt better and stood up and followed the secretary to her desk, sitting down on the edge. "Honey, let me take you out to lunch today. Get your things and meet me down at my car," he said, blowing her a small kiss with his lips. She didn't reply but nodded, running her finger down her blouse, pausing on the first button that was actually in use. Burt strolled away, whistling with each step.

Susie tried cooking but it just didn't work out. She spent about an hour or so gathering what she needed and just when she was ready to start, found one key ingredient missing. The shrimp. She sent the housekeeper out to a local seafood market to pick up some steamed shrimp. Burt didn't like shrimp. It was her intention to show him that she didn't like the way he spoke to her on the phone. It was just a little dig, but she enjoyed little digs at him. Especially lately. It was never something that would make him terribly angry, just something that would annoy him. She smiled slyly as she placed silverware on her beautiful dining room table.

Cliff sat atop the kitchen bar flipping through his notebook when his mother walked back into the kitchen. Through clenched teeth he grumbled, "This is stupid! Why do I have to be here? Burt doesn't like me anyway. Let his little *pet* Casey show off for his hoodlum friends."

Susie shook her head and pointed her long finger at him, "Baby, this isn't a hoodlum. This man is a detective and a *friend* from Biloxi."

Cliff cocked his head to one side and asked, "Detective *and* friend? Burt? That don't make sense, mom." Susie couldn't help but smile at her son. Her heart quivered when he used the word, "Mom".

"Burt and RB go way back. They *worked* together here and there. He's down here on vacation and we *will* treat him like family," she told her son.

He laughed and said sarcastically, "Family."

Susie sucked in her bottom lip, bit down slightly, and said with as much tenderness as she could muster, "Cliff, please try. I know Vern has filled your head with a bunch of stuff about Burt. But deep down, son, he's got a good heart. You just gotta get to know him."

Cliff's hand drifted to the lingering bruise on his chest, a dull ache lingering from Burt's kick two days earlier. *If she only knew*, he thought, but said nothing. He jumped down from the counter and wrapped his arms around his mother, kissed her gently on the cheek and said, "I'll try, Mom." Susie's heart skipped a beat once more.

When the five of them sat down at the table to eat, Burt sniffed the air and glared at Susie. She smiled back at him sarcastically and knew she had gotten under his skin with the shrimp. RB dove right into the pot of steamed shrimp and peeled ten of them and gulped them down before he realized Burt wasn't eating.

"Damn, excuse me y'all. I love shrimp. Loved them since I was a boy but we didn't get them much, When I get them now, I just eat until I'm full," he laughed as he finished the sentence.

Burt didn't laugh as he picked up a pile of french fries with his hand and plopped them down on his plate, "I hate the damn things." Cliff shot a sideways smile at his mother. She wrinkled her nose back at him. Casey already had a pile of shrimp peels piled up on his plate with the resulting juice dripping down his chin.

Susie looked at RB and nodded, "Glad you like them." Burt mocked her as he dipped a fry in ketchup and slammed it in his mouth.

Burt, remembering why he set this dinner up, suddenly changed his expression from a grimace to a forced smile and turned to Cliff. Cliff's smile vanished and his eyebrow arched. He always felt uncomfortable when Burt directed his attention to him.

"Son," Burt said, and Cliff raised his eyebrow further as Burt had never called him that, "RB here is a detective. He's on vacation but I asked him to help you. He can probably help you with the Vern *stuff*."

Cliff's expression didn't change as he slowly turned to look at a smiling RB. Just a few days ago, Burt ridiculed and laughed at him for trying to help his uncle.

"What the hell Burt?" he asked before he realized it and his mother kicked him under the table causing him to flinch noticeably.

Burt scanned him from the corner of his eye, forcing himself to continue as if Cliff never spoke, "RB, do you mind?"

RB, with a smile still on his face, told Cliff, "I'd be happy to help you young man."

Cliff tried to change the expression on his face but couldn't asking, "How could you help?"

RB folded his hands together, intertwining his fingers and said, "Son, I've been on a lot of murder cases. Been a detective for a long time. Maybe we can take this beyond the library and do some real police work. It may not amount to anything, but we can try."

Burt nodded, giving his blessing. Cliff didn't respond and continued focusing on RB. He felt certain that this was some kind of angle Burt was playing. He couldn't turn down this kind of opportunity, though. "Thank you, Mr. RB." RB smiled, waving his hand and told him, "It's just RB."

After the uncomfortable dinner ended, Cliff went to his room and Casey followed him in, uninvited. He fell onto Cliff's bed, sprung up grinning and said "So, Burt's not such a bad guy after all, huh?"

Cliff shot him a sideways glance and said, "He's up to something. I'm not a fool."

Casey laughed and said, "You're damn right he's up to something. Trying to get you to realize my father is a cold-blooded killer..." he paused for a second before staring at the floor and continuing, "...and he had something to do with my mom. I damn sure hope you find *that* out and they fry the bastard."

Cliff shook his head, "Case, you're too young to remember. Unc is not like that at all, and I'll prove it. I promise you I will." Casey mumbled something under his breath that Cliff couldn't understand and sprang out the door, slamming it behind him. Cliff threw his notebook on the desk, starting a letter to his uncle. Even though Vern instructed him not to write to him again he had to write. He finally had good news, and he had to tell him. He looked up, stared at the ceiling. With this detective's help, there was hope after all. He hadn't built that last castle just yet.

Chapter 12

"Ain't you supposed to be in school, boy?" Dell Phillips asked Casey when he walked out the back door of the surf shop and noticed him leaning against the brick wall with the other juvenile delinquents. Casey shrugged and grinned.

"I'm *home* schooled," he laughed.

The greasy-haired Mississippian reached into his shirt pocket and pulled out a pack of cigarettes. He lit one, tossing the pack to Casey. He plucked one from the pack, lit the end, taking a long drag and coughing a little as he exhaled. Dell chuckled, "Easy there Hoss," then he turned more serious, "Burt know you here?"

Casey kicked the dirt and said, "He don't care."

For a while now, Dell had wanted to get Casey alone and talk about a few things. Even though he faked ignorance most of the time, Dell knew the kid held the key to Burt's new fortune. It was Casey's mother who had most of the money, and with her gone and his old man in jail, Casey had become one of the richest people in Florida. Details like that never slipped past Dell. He always knew which angles to play.

It was that kind of foresight that propelled him up the ranks in the Organization—along with the protection of Burt Williams. In fact, it was that very instinct, that sharp ability to see opportunities before anyone else, that had first caught Burt Williams' attention.

Dell motioned towards the building and said, "Come on into my office, Case. We need to talk about some things kid." Casey threw down what was left of the cigarette and stomped it out. More than half of it was unsmoked and Dell smirked a little. He looked at the kid's face and saw it was turning a little green and then he couldn't control his laughter, "Easy there kid."

He slapped Casey on the shoulder as they stepped through the back door and into his office, tucked away in the corner of the board shop. Inside, a couple of guys were busy shaping and sanding boogie boards—smaller, more compact versions of surfboards designed to ride the surf right at the water's edge. On Florida's east coast, there were far more days suited for that kind of ride than for tackling the elusive big waves.

They sneered at Dell as he walked past. To them he was a poser and knew nothing about surfing. He was just there to sell marijuana. When he walked past, Casey glanced back, noticing two dusty fingers defiantly in the air. He wanted to confront them, but Dell motioned with his finger for Casey to sit down across the ramshackle desk. He reluctantly obliged as he wanted to be back out with his friends.

Dell sat there. Silent, for a minute before he finally motioned around the building with his hands, "This is all yours, you know."

Casey looked around, shook his head in agreement and realized he hadn't given it much thought. A thirteen-year-old living in paradise usually has other things on his mind and he was no exception, "Yeah, I mean, I guess. My *father*," he rolled his eyes as he said it, "signed it all over to Burt and Susie until me and Cliff get old enough. Ain't *really* mine."

Dell ran his fingers through his long, greasy hair, leaning towards him so he could talk quietly but still be heard over the ongoing work in the shop, "*Your* family's got all the money. The Clark's. Everybody knows that. Vern Bruce didn't have shit." Dell leaned back and fell silent once again, watching the guys working for a second before continuing, "Son, when I was fourteen, I was stealing for a living, knocking over convenience stores, barely surviving. Fell in with Burt and some other boys and now here I am living by the beach. It ain't gonna be that *hard* for you."

Casey trained his eyes on Dell and the hoodlum coked his head to one side, "I'm going to give you a little *free* advice right here. Take what's yours, kid. Damn sure don't let others take it from ya." He winked at the teenager.

Casey stood up, nodded, and told Dell he was heading out back to hang out. "You hang around here long enough kid and I'm going to put your ass to work," he said, mimicking smoking a rolled joint. A devious smile flashed across Casey's face. He snapped his fingers in Dell's direction as he walked out.

As Casey strutted through the shop towards the exit, he noticed a hammer resting in a toolbox. He grabbed it as he strode by and without stopping he swung the hammer in the air, crashing it into the boogie board, destroying the workers' hard work. The two jumped back and for a split second looked as though they were going to attack, but Casey just extended his middle finger and raised an eyebrow. The men froze in their tracks, lowering their eyes to the ground. Casey laughed uncontrollably as he made his way out the back door.

The kid took his place against the brick wall, lighting another cigarette. The guys hanging around the surf shop were all from the rough side of town near the area of Royal Palm. It was a long trip for them to the surf shop, and none of them owned any type of transportation so they hitchhiked or just hoofed it to the shop every day. All kept their hair long, stringy and wore tattered t-shirts. They were poor and most of their families came from the other poor southeastern states hoping for a better life in Florida but ended up even more destitute than when they arrived.

Casey didn't feel that he was better than these guys, in fact, he felt closer to them than he did his own cousin. He exhaled smoke. This time he didn't cough. He thought about Cliff.

When the two of them were younger, they were inseparable, but now, when they speak, something always led to an argument. Cliff had become so enveloped in the hope that one day his father and uncle would be home, and they all would be a family, that he was blinded to everything else, even him.

Casey held no such hope. His father was dead to him. He had never cared about whether Cliff's father was alive or dead. Burt had become his family and to a lesser extent, Susie. She was nice and seemed to care about him, but he knew Cliff would always come first to her. He understood that and had long accepted that truth.

These guys were different. If they called him Ritchie because of the television show about the kid with all the money, he knew it was out of respect, or jealousy, for what he had. They respected him for the power in which he was attached. To them, Burt Williams was God and Casey was Jesus Christ.

"Ritchie, we was just talking about you," a short, pudgy kid said as he noticed him walk up.

"What's that supposed to mean?" Casey asked as he took another long drag from his cigarette but didn't look back at him.

The pudgy kid nudged a taller, but younger kid beside him and grinned, "We're going down to the strip tonight…" he narrowed his eyes towards Casey, "…and make some money."

Casey looked confused, his brow furrowing as the pudgy kid let out another laugh. With a grin, he pulled a small bag from his pocket, the plastic crinkling as he gave it a shake, revealing a generous stash of weed.

"You in?" he asked, eyes gleaming with mischief.

Casey, the cigarette dangling from his lips, smiled. "Where's mine?" All the guys laughed, affirming his acceptance to the criminal side of the group.

Dell, perched just inside the door, listened to the conversation outside. He took a joint from his pants pocket and lit up, ignoring the two workers, who were spooked from their

encounter with Casey. He took a long drag, eased back to his
makeshift office, picked up the phone and started dialing.

"Yeah, man," he said into the phone, "All set."

Casey didn't go home that afternoon as usual. As the sun
dipped below the horizon, painting the sky in warm hues, he and
his friends hopped into the back of an old pickup that had stopped
by the shop, hitching a ride down to the strip.

Most outsiders who found their way to West Palm Beach
came chasing the glamour—the pristine beaches, the high-end
hotels, the promise of a lavish lifestyle. But for the local teens, the
reality was different. There weren't many places for them to go, so
they spent their nights wandering the beaches, lingering in malls,
and loitering in empty parking lots.

Tonight, the mall was the destination for Casey and his
surf buddies, a familiar haunt where they could kill time and see
who else was out looking for trouble—or trying to avoid it.

Not wanting to seem timid, desperate to impress his
friends, Casey promised himself to do whatever they asked. It was
the first time they allowed him to go with them to sell and Casey
wasn't about to wimp out. His palms became sweaty, wiping the
perspiration on his torn blue jeans. The pudgy kid noticed and
laughed just a little but nodded towards Casey, trying to pass
along some confidence. One of them handed him a small bag and
motioned to a guy standing over by one of the storefronts. "That

guy's bought before," the pudgy kid said, "Should be an easy one to break you in."

The mall, crowded with locals and tourists, seemed to grow even busier with the bag of weed in his pocket. He hadn't taken his hand off it and just as he did, he noticed a uniformed cop stroll by, casting an accusing eye towards the boys. Pudgy just smiled as he passed and nodded towards the guy waiting for the sale.

He sensed hesitation in Casey and eased over and whispered in his ear, "That shit happens, man, get used to it and get it done."

The rush of adrenaline started to make its way through Casey's body. His adolescent mind and thoughts, that had been a flurry of activity and worry since the police officer walked by, became more focused. He was ready. His already sweaty hands began to quiver just so slightly, and he could feel beads of sweat starting to form on his forehead. He couldn't feel his legs in motion until he was halfway where the man stood. The guy looked at him, nodding. Casey eased his way through the slight crowd, finally standing next to him.

"Holding?" the guy asked him quietly. Without looking at him, Casey tried to answer but his mouth made no sound. He could only shake his head affirmatively. The guy held the money for the bag in the palm of his hand and tilted it so Casey could see. The kid reached into his pocket and pulled out the bag, holding it tightly in his hand so nobody could see. As the exchange was made, the sweat from Casey's hands made the bag slippery and he almost dropped it when the two went to swap but caught it between two fingers and made the swap clean.

Casey, his head high and his chest poked out slightly, strutted back to the group of teen boys. Each one was laughing heartily and slapping each other on the back. Casey held up his palms. The young teenager had awkwardly taken his first step into the criminal world. He wiped the sweat from his forehead and wiped it again on his jeans. He high fived the boys and couldn't wait to get home and tell Burt.

When he arrived home, he found Susie waiting for him in the living room. It was nearly one in the morning, and she hadn't heard from him, or Burt and she had gotten worried and thought the worst. She was used to Burt not showing up until the wee hours of the morning, but this behavior wasn't something that Casey had ever flirted with. Not until now, at least.

She jumped to her feet, "Where have you been?" she asked angrily as Casey brushed past her into the kitchen. Casey ignored her as he opened the refrigerator and took a swig of milk from the carton. Susie glared at him, her anger rising with each word, "I'm talking to you!"

Casey replaced the milk carton and turned slowly, smiling at her. His voice cold when he finally spoke, "Who the hell do you think you are? I own all this shit." His wide smile seemed to glow from the refrigerator's dim light.

Susie stood frozen, her mouth slightly open, struggling to find the right words. Casey had never spoken to her like that before—never taken such an attitude. The sharpness in his tone lingered in the air, unsettling and unfamiliar.

Without another glance, he casually eased the refrigerator door shut and headed up the stairs, whistling as he went. His carefree tune echoed down the hallway until he disappeared from sight, leaving Susie alone with the weight of what had just happened. She said a slight prayer to herself and went to bed.

The sun shining through the window caused Susie to stir. She was only half asleep as she still had not heard from Burt. She eased along the steps and down to the kitchen. She poured a cup of black coffee and sank into a chair, burying her face in her hands. She wanted to cry, but the years she'd spent surviving on the streets had drained nearly all her tears.

A car door slammed. Her resolve stiffened as she prepared to confront her husband. She took a long sip from the cup, waiting for the door to open. She knew better than to meddle in his business, but she was growing tired of not knowing where he was. She had also noticed he was often cold to Cliff and that was something else she was going to put a stop to.

Looking out the kitchen window she caught a glimpse of the car as it sat at the corner of the house. It was not where Burt usually parked and it was the wrong color, a bright yellow. It had to be a cab. She figured Burt either wrecked his car or was too drunk to drive home, but when a tall, slender man stepped up to the front door, she realized it wasn't Burt. She at once recognized Colonel Duy, the man who delivered the letter from Rof.

"Colonel Duy, it's been a while," she said as he stood stoically at the front door.

The former Vietnamese Army officer, once again well-dressed complete with a jacket and tie, extended his hand, smiled, and replied, "It has Mrs. Williams. I hope you and your family are well. If you don't mind, the taxi will wait for me if we may step inside." Susie gestured towards the living room and asked him to come in.

The Colonel sat down in a chair opposite Susie and crinkled his eyes, "I suppose the news reached you about the camp?" he asked. Susie noticed his accent wasn't nearly as pronounced as before.

She nodded and her eyes began to water once more, perhaps the street hadn't taken all her tears away, "I was told Rof is *probably* gone."

Duy leaned towards her and with his long arm and lanky fingers, wiped the single tear escaping her eye, "My dear child, I bring *good* news. My sources, back home, tell me just the opposite. The camp was removed, that is true. However, two prisoners survived. Those two men, as it was told to me, *escaped*."

Susie put her hand over her mouth, feeling faint, "I was told that there wasn't much hope Rof survived; said it was too long a period of time." Her tears flowed like they hadn't in a long time, breaking through the walls she had spent years building. A sob escaped her lips as she choked out, "I can't take this. I can't take it. Is he, or isn't he?"

She shot up from her chair, pacing toward the window, her breath shaky. She gripped the window's frame as if steadying herself against the weight of uncertainty.

"I can't."

Duy sprinted to where she stood and put his hand on her shoulder, "Whoever told you that, didn't know the *timeline* of events," Duy replied, "I do and I certainly do not want to give you false hope, but," he put his hand under her chin and turned it slowly to face him, "I know *he is alive and* I *feel* he is trying to get back to you and your son."

Susie shook her head, tears still flowing, "I just can't take this much more, I, we, have to know!"

Duy looked outside, staring at the water in the background, "I am working with a man that can get him home. My wager is he *is* alive. You must not give up hope." He turned and took Susie in his arms.

Both were startled when the front door burst open, and there stood Burt, his clothes wrinkled, and from across the room, Susie could already smell the stink of bourbon. He glared at Duy who still embraced his wife, "Who the fuck are you?" he growled.

Duy, still startled but gathering himself, walked towards Burt with his hand extended. Burt was in no mood to shake hands. Susie knew her husband well and hurried between the two men.

"Burt, this is General Duy. The man who was with Rof in Vietnam."

Burt pushed past Susie, nearly shoving her to the ground and grabbed Duy by throat, "You're the bastard that keeps the damned idea of Rof Bruce alive in her head!" With what seemed like one motion, Duy's right hand swatted Burt's hand away from this throat and his other hand threw Burt to the ground, pinning the larger man to the floor with his foot to the gangster's throat.

"No need for violence, Mr. Williams. I am leaving," Duy told him as he eased the pressure from Burt's neck. Burt, still drunk from the night before, tried to regain his composure, pushed his bulk up from the floor but stumbled back with a resounding thud.

Susie knelt, removing the pistol from Burt's belt. "I'm so sorry Colonel," she said as she stood up and ushered him out the door. Duy's eyes narrowed in concern, but Susie nodded that she would be ok. Reluctantly, he bid her farewell, quickly entering the taxi, motioning the driver to leave.

Susie slowly closed the door, turning around to face her husband while he still lay on his back, "You're sorry for him?" Burt managed, "I'm the one on the god damned floor in my own house!"

Susie didn't reply, her tears almost completely gone, but her eyes were red and puffy. She didn't speak as she left him there to sleep off whatever he drank the night before. He was snoring by the time she sat back down at the kitchen counter.

The coffee she had poured before Duy arrived sat on the counter, cold. She poured it down the sink, filled another cup and walked through the double doors onto the deck. The Atlantic was furious today as a strong wind blew from the east, pushing the waves higher than usual and she noticed a couple adventurous people perched upon surfboards bobbing in and out of sight as if they were corks attached to a fishing line.

Her sore eyes squinted in the brilliant sunshine. Slowly she sipped her coffee, wishing to be anywhere but here. She missed Mississippi. Their old lives in Biloxi were never this complicated. She was married to a powerful man who adored her, and she held only *fond* memories of Rof. Back then her only hope was one day easing back into her son's life. She never wanted to interfere with his life, though, as it was free of the grief and heartbreak that she had endured for most of hers.

Now, here they were, she thought as she looked around. The house and everything that came along with it wasn't theirs and Burt wasn't the same man she married, even though she tried to convince herself otherwise. He was a drunk and she suspected him of *other* vices.

She feared that Cliff's life was being wasted on the impossible notion that he could fix everything for everyone. His relentless pursuit of justice, of setting things right, was pulling him into battles he might never win.

And then there was Casey—the boy she was starting to love like a son. She could see him slipping, morphing into another

Burt. But not the Burt she once knew, the one who had pulled her from the streets and given her a chance at something better. No, Casey was becoming the new Burt—cold, hardened, and dangerous. They had everything. Yet, somehow, they had nothing.

She took another sip, and her thoughts turned to Rof. She watched one of the surfers brave the high waves and her motherly instincts wondered if he was hurt when he crashed from his board. Those same instincts told her she shouldn't tell Cliff about Duy's visit.

Until there was some kind of tangible proof, either way, that his father was alive, she would keep it to herself. She placed the coffee cup on the stand beside her and put her hands in her pockets. She felt something there—small, solid, unexpected. Her fingers tightened instinctively around it as she pulled her hand back, clutching whatever it was, her pulse quickening with uncertainty. She held it up and recognized the square shape of a business card. Duy must have slipped it into her pocket as he was leaving. Handwritten on the card was Duy's name and a phone number. She recognized the area code. It was a New Orleans number. She worked there for a while before ending up in Biloxi and remembered the prefixes. Maybe a trip to the Big Easy was just what she needed, not only to find out more, but just to get away. But first, she was going to have a conversation with her husband about his protégé' Casey Bruce and it wasn't going to be pleasant for either of them.

Chapter 13

The Barges seemed like they were barely moving, fighting upstream against the muddy waters of the Mississippi River. Veck Baxter wondered at their sheer size, bigger than most buildings, and pondered how they even remained afloat. It was on one of these massive ships that he made his escape from Vietnam, but he couldn't think about that right now.

Growing weary of his seclusion in the dimly lit hotel room, only catching a glimpse of the mighty river from a few blocks away, he decided it was time to venture out. His body, not completely healed, but finally he felt strong enough for a stroll. The short walk seemed to help his weary bones and the sunshine warming his skin reminded him of home. Just the scent of the river—polluted or not—lifted his spirits, stirring something familiar and grounding within him.

Jeff Black sensed the joy in his friend as he quietly made his way to the bench overlooking the silty water, easing onto the opposite side. Usually, it was nearly impossible to sneak up on Veck Baxter, but today, with the Mississippi distracting him, he accomplished the feat, causing both to smile.

Pointing over the turbulent water, Black said, "Reminds me of the Amazon. Except for the lack of forests but I'm told the forests are further north."

Beck didn't take his eyes off the river, "I never saw much of the Amazon. As soon as I was well enough and we had our plan, I came here." Baxter broke his gaze from the river, turning to look at Black, "Diaz in line?"

Black rubbed his chin, "Williams will not die at this moment." Baxter nodded but didn't change his expression. He hated working with Columbians. While in Brazil he read about the cartels and their brutality. It reminded him of the same brutality of his captors. When he returned to his home country, he had learned about the epidemic their white powder caused.

Baxter sighed deeply, "I despise what we are doing," disgust replacing the joy he felt only moments earlier, "It's a dangerous game with these guys," he said, "But we have to become *part* of the problem to reach the solution."

Black nodded in agreement but motioned behind him, towards the heart of the city, "The biggest part of the problem stems from *our* homeland."

Baxter returned his attention to the water, "I never gave it much thought until I made it to Brazil but y'all opened my eyes." The two men didn't say anything for a few minutes, soaking in the view, contemplating tasks laying before them. When they did speak again, the subject changed to Vern Bruce.

"Vern hasn't asked about his *benefactor*?" Baxter asked, staring at the ground before turning his gaze to the people strolling past them. People meandering along the riverwalk, seemingly without a care in the world. Sometimes he envied those people.

Black shook his head, "Not since Calley first met with him. Strange. From what we know about him, his inquisitive nature, I expected him to want to know from the start," he replied. Baxter, leaning on a cane, slowly stood up and motioned for his friend to follow him down the winding path along the river. The men didn't speak as they walked.

Baxter glanced around making sure they were alone. Only a couple of pigeons pecked at the ground near them. Baxter stopped, propping himself with the sidewalk's railing. "It's time to tell him who we are." Black raised an eyebrow, surprised by his friend's words.

"It was my understanding that would come later," he confusedly replied. Baxter didn't respond but eased himself from the railing and started down the sidewalk again. A group of tourists stopped near them and this conversation needed to remain as private as possible. The two walked down the path a little further, shooing away pigeons pecking at the ground for lost crumbs.

Hobbling along, Baxter glanced back and found enough room between the group of people to start the conversation back up, "We have to feed him information and control what he learns. We don't want him finding out on his own, investigating. Control information and you, in turn, control the mind," he said, closing his eyes.

Black stopped and stared into the water, "What about his nephew? He is investigating on *his* own and I hear the black detective from Biloxi is helping him now."

Baxter switched his cane to the other hand, reached out and placed newly freed hand on Black's shoulder, "You learn that when your life is truly at stake, plans change quickly, my friend." Black nodded and noticed the broad scar on the back of Baxter's hand. This was a man that meticulously planned an escape from a Vietnamese prison camp for *years*. The Brazilian reminded himself that he too must show patience. Black held complete faith in the man and his plan.

Black lowered his head and nodded, "Of course, you are right. I want my people *home* and I have faith in *you* to make that happen."

Baxter spotted a bench and crept over to take a seat. His back pain enhancing with each breath, begging for its medication. His foray outside confirmed that even though his body was healing, he could only stand and walk for a limited amount of time. His body was that of an old, crippled man more than twice his actual age. In fact, Jeff Black was older than Baxter, but you could never tell by looking at the two of them together. The years of brutality he suffered as a prisoner displayed on his skin. His scars ran deep, etched not just into his skin but into his very bones. Black had to assist his friend back to the hotel room, holding him under his shoulder.

When they finally arrived back in the room it was nearly dark, but Baxter didn't need light to find his pills and whiskey bottle. He quickly swallowed down two pain pills with a swig of bourbon and fell asleep quickly. Black left him snoring as he quietly closed the door and left.

Black didn't waste time leaving New Orleans as he had begun to dislike the city itself, along with most of its inhabitants. He felt the allure of Mobile calling him and he loved that city more than the stinking streets of the so called "Big Easy." Also, Mobile was within easy reach of the Florida Panhandle and the prison holding Vernon Bruce in Georgia. He admired the skyline of Mobile growing in the distance, and, for some reason, his thoughts turned to his great-grandmother. It caught him slightly off guard since it had been a while since he thought of her.

Her name was Elmira, but he called her Boa Mae. It was the Portuguese version of the words Good Mamma in English. He didn't know for sure, but he suspected it was because her first grandchild couldn't pronounce Grandmother and that's how it came out. At that time English was still the main language spoken amongst his people, but it gradually faded away with only remnants of their native tongue combining with Portugues. The nickname slowly transformed from the English version, sticking with every succeeding grandchild and great-grandchild until her death at ninety years old in 1957. He only knew her for the first ten years of his life, but her impact lasted a lifetime.

Boa Mae, born in a time of strife for their southern homeland, only remembered fragments of her childhood before Brazil. When she was a young child, the Confederate States burst into existence in a flame of war. The only thing she knew was conflict. Even though few battles were waged on her home soil of Alabama and only limited skirmishes materialized in the southeastern part of the state she called home, she knew the famine plaguing her people from the broader conflict. She always remembered the impoverished conditions during the war as her family contributed everything they had to help the South. What little remained dried up quickly and no new supplies made their way to her part of the world.

Before the war they were considered wealthy by local standards. They held slaves, planted cotton, and reaped the rewards. Her life changed drastically when war broke out between the states. Her father, commissioned a colonel in the 1st Alabama Infantry Regiment and assigned to a company known as the Perote Guards, left home early in the war. He was severely injured in a battle far from their home and remained with a limp for the rest of his life and a ferocious hate of *Yankees*.

After the war finally ended, their lives were left in shambles. They held no power, had no money and they were governed by the United States Military. Her father decided to take his family to the port in Mobile on her tenth birthday and sail for a better life in Brazil. Black remembered as his great-grandmother rocked in a chair on the front porch of her modest home overlooking one of the many Amazonian tributaries and told him stories of her youth in Alabama. He learned from her the country's beauty and how much she missed it. He couldn't get the vision of her weathered face from his mind as he drove into the darkness of the George Wallace Tunnel and under Mobile Bay. He smiled and wished she could see the changes in her beloved homeland.

This time, though, he couldn't stay very long in Mobile as he rushed to visit Vernon Bruce in his prison home. He stopped and picked up a few things from the small home he rented overlooking the river near the smaller town of Spanish Fort. It wasn't exactly Mobile, but, located across the bridge from the larger city he felt at home. He chose this location for two reasons. First, being along a river whose surrounding area looked more like the thick rainforests, made it feel like home. Second was the Confederate Park within walking distance of his adopted home.

The Old Confederacy seemed like a fairytale in Brazil but here it was everywhere, in the memories, monuments and language and he loved it. He always saluted the substantial number of statues he passed that were dedicated to the fallen heroes of the South. Even though the park near his home housed no statue, he saluted just the same as he drove past and headed to Atlanta.

To gain entrance into the prison's death row, Ryan Calley set Jeff Black up as a paralegal. Black, his status in the States illegal, produced fake documents to the lawyer and Calley knew better than to challenge them. After a little wrangling, Black was allowed to accompany the lawyer into the prison.

The Brazilian marveled at the cleanliness and factory-like atmosphere of the American prison. The floors were spotless, and

it even smelled clean, like a doctor's office. Inside, the walls were
relatively clean, and a chemical smell permeated the air because
of the bleach used to hold down infections. It was a sharp contrast
to the prisons in Brazil. Most of the prisons of his home country
didn't even have bedding as the prisoners were expected to
provide their own. Upon entrance of those places, the smell of
feces invaded his nose. No matter what he did, he couldn't get rid
of the smell for months. His clothes stank of the wretched
facilities even after a couple of washings. *How lucky these men
were*, he thought.

Calley noticed his new paralegal inspecting his
surroundings and remarked, "Terrible conditions, huh?"

Black didn't know how to respond as he never saw such
wonderful facilities built to house such vile men. He nodded in
compliance as he didn't want the lawyer to know too much of his
background. The two men made their way into the small meeting
room and took their seats opposite the lone chair across the table.

Their wait wasn't long as the door opened and an
unshaven, unkempt Vernon Bruce walked through in his faded
orange jumpsuit. Black noticed Vern's number printed on the front
and thought how lucky he was not to have it tattooed onto his
skin. Brazilian prisoners never escaped their prison, even when
released.

Vern Bruce no longer looked like a man who had once
lived a life of luxury. To Black, he was just another beaten, broken
soul, indistinguishable from the rest. As he studied the prisoner, he

couldn't fathom why Veck Baxter had invested so much in this frail, defeated man.

Vern glanced at him before taking his seat, showing little interest while the guard shackled his arms and legs to the floor and desk. He didn't show any of the inquisitiveness that Baxter had described to him, only a weak passiveness. Perhaps his friend was misinformed about this man.

Calley didn't just see a broken man across the table. He knew Vern's real nature and put his hand over the prisoner's, "Vern you have to take care of yourself in here," he said, shaking his head.

In the few weeks that passed since their last meeting, Vern seemed to admit defeat in every way possible. The prisoner only chuckled, holding is focus upon the tables, "Appeal still on track?" he asked weakly.

Calley shook his hands, trying to jar Vern from this fugue state. He eagerly told him everything looked good, and that he expected the sentence to change to life in prison. He was open and honest when he pointedly told Vern that that he didn't feel any chance of the conviction being overturned. Calley then turned and motioned to Black, leaned towards Vern and said in near whisper, "The reason we're here today Vern is for this gentleman to explain to you why he is *helping* you."

Vern snapped to attention, finally lifting his gaze from the table, peering at the face of Jeff Black through his narrow eyes.

The Brazilian tried to look Vern in the eye but found them guarded by the prisoner's stringy hair.

Black bowed his head as he began to speak, "Mr. Bruce, it is a pleasure to finally meet you. I've been told a lot about you. My name is Jefferson Black."

Black couldn't hide his accent but tried to sound as "southern" as he possibly could. Vern recognized an accent but couldn't quite place it. To him, though, it didn't really matter where this man came from, it was his motive where his concern lay. Vern's inquisitive nature betrayed him, however, "Where are you from, *Jefferson Black*?" Vern asked.

Black smiled and told him he hailed from the country of Brazil. Vern's eyebrows furrowed as he tried to remember if had any dealings with anyone from Brazil, but none came to mind.

Black noticed the prisoner's confusion and dismissed it quickly, "If I may continue?" Black asked him, and Vern nodded in approval. "My family comes from the town of Americana. Have you ever heard of it?" Vern thought for a moment, running his fingers along the cold steel edge of the table and told him that he didn't think that he had. "Very well, Mr. Bruce. That is a shame as it's home to *your* people."

Vern's eyebrow raised and he pursed his lips for a moment before replying, "What do you mean, *my* people?"

Black placed his hands on the table and then folded them together, each long finger intertwined with another, "It's an exceedingly long story but right after the War a band of

Confederates made their way to Brazil seeking a new life. Boarding a ship in Mobile, they made the long, grueling journey to a new home. Over time some left, some went back home to America, some unfortunately died, but my family survived. They prospered for a while, but here we are a little over a hundred years later with nothing and we want to come *home*."

Vern leaned back as far as his chains would allow and he reached for his beard but the chains binding his hands to the desk forced him to give up that notion, "I've never heard of this. Hasn't been in any history course I ever took, and I love history, soaked it up all my life, and it seems like I would've heard about this."

Black grinned, "I've read a great many of *your* history books and apparently the migration wasn't recorded. The Union won and as I've been told, history is written by the victors. I assure you we are there and that's why I'm here," Black's voice was sharp as steel as he spoke. He was proud of his Confederate heritage and the stories passed down from generation to generation.

"Ok," Vern said and tilted his head to the side, "What has this got to do with *me*?"

Black's grin widened into a smile, "You *are* my family, Mr. Bruce. We share certain ancestors and frankly we need your help bringing *our* family home."

Vern's jaw dropped, his eyes widening enough that Black caught a glimpse of them through the thick shroud of hair. His mind, already skeptical by nature and hardened by the deception and misplaced loyalty that put him in this prison, rejected the notion off hand, "Of course, you know I'm kind of skeptical. That is some story and I'm sure you got *proof*."

Black's expression hardened, "What kind of proof do you need, Mr. Bruce?"

Vern waved his shackled hands back and forth, "We can get around to that. You've got money, I can *see* that." He then pointed a finger at Calley, "What kind of *help* do you need from me?"

Black held up his palms, "Yes, we have money. Yes, we are funding your appeals. But, for now," Black looked around to see if anyone was listening and finally lowering his voice to a whisper, "I need to know *why* you killed those men."

Calley leaned over to the Brazilian and told him that this room was not bugged, and nobody was allowed to eavesdrop. In the United States situations such as these were covered by attorney-client privilege. Black nodded an understanding, "What a country," he marveled, returning his attention to Vern.

Black pointed his long finger back at Vern, "Now, Mr. Bruce. If I may have an answer." Vern smiled through the thick beard and repeated the same story he told Calley in their first meeting. Black didn't blink as Vern spoke. After Vern finished, both men locked eyes for what seemed like an eternity. "Well," Black finally responded, "Who *did* kill them?"

He watched Vern's face for any slight change in expression, flinch or tell, but got nothing. "*You* need to find that out and get me out of here," Vern commanded.

Black nodded and replied, "Surely, Mr. Bruce, we are doing all that can be done and the proof you seek of our relation will come soon. We will see each other again." With that, the Brazilian stood to leave but before he walked away, he placed *his* hands on top of Vern's. Vern tried to pull away, but his bound hands wouldn't move. Black said a quick prayer, removed his hands and he and the lawyer turned to leave the room.

Vern shook his head, "What was that for?" he asked.

Black turned around slowly and simply replied, "Guidance."

When the two men were in Calley's car and they knew truly nothing they said could be heard by others, Calley hesitated to turn the ignition and asked, "Why didn't tell me you two were *family?*"

Black looked at the lawyer, a sly smile emblazoned on his face, "The ties that bound our families are *long* since forgotten. *Family* we are not, we only share blood, and that blood has long since thinned." The Brazilian looked skyward to the thick deck of clouds obscuring the sun, "He is of no importance to *me,* but to my *friend*. The one that plans all of this has his own reasons for Vernon Bruce's inclusion."

Calley shrugged his shoulders, not understanding and at this point, he really didn't care. He had his own motivation that was much more than mere money. The prestige that would follow by freeing such a high-profile client as Vernon Bruce would be nice, but, as he laughed to himself, that too wasn't the real reason he took this job. As he started the engine, he wished his father was still alive to see what was about to come.

Chapter 14

With the bright sun reflecting off the blue water, Mateo Diaz watched the boats tied up in the harbor, bobbing with the steady rhythm of the tide. He stood behind a blue-and-white payphone booth, the salty breeze brushing past him as he admired the view, his voice steady as he spoke into the receiver.

"I will see you soon Phillipe' and I love you very much," he said to the person on the other end of the line as he gently hung up the phone.

His eyes locked on the gently rocking vessels moored near the booth. A wide smile spread across his face because at times like this, he was at his happiest. Soon he and Phillipe' would be together again, but first he had a job to complete. As he left the confines of the booth, his smile vanished. Business, once more, was at hand.

Between the luxurious yachts of West Palm Harbor and the towering structures of Cape Kennedy lay a small, secluded private harbor. It extended from a sprawling warehouse, once bustling with workers packaging and shipping oranges, now repurposed into something far more discreet.

Diaz rented it from one of the many front companies established by Old Man Clark. Most of the time, the warehouse sat empty, its vast interior collecting dust, but on days like this, it served its true purpose—hosting meetings away from prying eyes.

The local police were well compensated to overlook the characterless building and the figures who came and went.

Standing outside the square, unremarkable structure, isolated in the middle of nowhere, Diaz found himself wondering why Old Man Clark hadn't taken full control of the entire operation. *Probably not willing to kill,* the Colombian told himself.

Before entering the building, Diaz' thoughts shifted quickly to his beloved Phillipe' and the smile momentarily returned from their conversation earlier. Opening the door and stepping forward, however, the smile faded once again.

Along with a couple of Diaz' own men, stood Dell Phillips. A cigarette dangling from his lips and for a second Diaz thought he could see it quiver as the disheveled figure took a puff. The hoodlum was severely outnumbered, looking out of place among the Columbians except for a single figure seated in a chair in the middle of the room. The building was starkly lit as there were very few lights and those were placed high in the rafters. A skylight provided limited illumination and since his phone call with Phillipe', the afternoon clouds had begun to build, obscuring what was once brilliant sunshine.

"Where is Williams?" Diaz asked Dell as he finally reached the middle of the vacant building where the long-haired man stood. Dell shook his head and said, "Can't find him."

Diaz's face hardened, his nostrils flaring as he fought to keep his temper in check. He wanted to lash out, to let the man feel the full weight of his anger, but he held back. Instead, his voice was cold and cutting as he said, "A meeting like this, and he can't be bothered to attend?" The Colombian smacked his lips, "bad for business, especially since this *concerns* his own man." As he spoke, he turned his attention away from Dell, narrowing his focus on the figure sitting silently in the chair. Dell simply shook his head and for once had no words.

Diaz took a couple of steps towards forward, motioning for one of his men to flip on the rafter lighting. "Mr. Kennedy," he started, "How unfortunate that our first meeting had to be in a place such as this. I do wish your boss was here."

Kennedy had worked for the Clark Family since he was a teenager, ferrying tourists to the fishing grounds off the Atlantic Coast. His skin, deeply tanned and leathery, his bright blonde hair glowing in the faint light contrasted against the dark Southern Americans hovering over him. He shook visibly but the old sailor still had at least a little fight left in him.

"My boss is Vernon Bruce and the Clarks before him. I don't work for that asshole Burt Williams," he said defiantly. Diaz laughed to himself. He and this rough old guy held the same opinion of Williams, but, again, business first.

"You did agree to perform a *service*, no?" Diaz asked. Kennedy's eyes turned downward, staring at the concrete floor. He hadn't wanted to agree to help Burt that one time, but he needed the money. He spent too much time in the back room of the store at the West Palm Harbor. As his gambling debts began to mount, and he could no longer afford to pay them with a skipper's pay, he agreed, reluctantly, to run out to international waters for one job. He messed it up.

He was to run out beyond the reach of the local police and make a drop, but before he reached the sanctity of international waters, another vessel began following him and he became paranoid. Kennedy wasn't a smuggler; he was just a simple fisherman. He dumped the package prematurely and turned for land. He hadn't even attached the float or the beacon to the package and it quickly sunk to the bottom of the Atlantic.

When he turned back, Kennedy watched the other vessel continue out to sea and realized it was only another fishing boat. When his mind cleared of the paranoia, he remembered all the locals followed the same path out. The old sailor realized that in the excitement of his first foray into crime, he jumped the gun. Knowing if the Colombians didn't kill him for his mistake, Burt Williams surely would. He made it back to the harbor, tied up the boat quickly and fled. He made it as far as Jacksonville before one of Burt's contacts with the state police caught up with him. Now, here he was, face to face with the Columbian drug smuggler himself. His only hope lay in Burt Williams, and the bastard had abandoned him. He tasted sweat beading on his upper lip.

Kennedy pushed his hat back on his head scratching his forehead. Slowly he looked back up at his captor, "Look, I made a mistake and I'm sorry. I don't even know what was in that box, don't want to know," he lied, "But I can make it up to you."

Diaz, tightening his lips, turned slowly to face Kennedy. He took a few steps before spinning around and returning his gaze to the skipper, "How do you *propose* to make this right, Mr. Kennedy?"

Kennedy's hands, still shaking slightly, his voice quivering with each syllable answered, "Whatever you need." When making eye contact with Diaz, the Columbian recognized the fear burning within his eyes. He felt a pang of sorrow for the man, but his face remained as unyielding as stone, betraying nothing to the weathered sailor before him.

Diaz gave a subtle nod to the man standing beside Dell. Before the Mississippian could even register what was happening, the Colombian henchman slipped a silenced pistol from his belt and fired a single shot at point-blank range. The muffled pop barely registered before the opposite side of Dell's head erupted in a violent burst of blood, hair, and shattered bone.

His body crumpled instantly, his eyes still wide, as if frozen in the last flicker of consciousness before his life was snuffed out. When his skull struck the hard floor, it cracked open with a sickening thud, splattering what little blood remained onto the cold concrete. The room fell silent, save for the faint echo of death settling into the space.

Kennedy sat frozen, his muscles seizing in absolute terror. He braced himself for the end of his own life, clenching his fists. When his muscles finally relaxed he made the sign of the cross and began praying loudly to the Virgin Mary.

Diaz smiled and his head inclined to its side, "Catholic?" he asked with a smile.

Kennedy unable to answer nodded slightly affirmatively. Diaz eased to Kenndy's side, placing his hand on his captive's shoulder. He leaned down to one knee, directly in front of him, leaning in close enough he could feel Kennedy's rapid breath on his face and said coldly, "Old man, you've got one chance to walk out of here alive. Diaz pointed to the metal door at the other side of the room, "You don't work for Burt Williams any longer. You work for me now. You will continue to do as Williams' *asks*, but you will report to me."

Kennedy stared at Dell's lifeless body; his face unreadable as he gave a slow nod. But in his mind, the thought of running surfaced once again, creeping in like a whisper he could no longer ignore.

Diaz, his face somber, stood and walked over to the killer. He held out his hand and the man placed the pistol into his palm. Unnoticed, he had slipped a pair of gloves on his hands during the commotion and now held the pistol carefully in one hand while he removed tape covering the handle and trigger with the other.

He bellowed Kennedy's name, snapping the sailor out of his daze just as the Colombian tossed the gun in his direction. On instinct, Kennedy caught it—his fingers wrapping around the cold steel before his mind caught up with his actions.

Realization struck like a bolt of lightning, and he immediately let the weapon drop, his breath hitching. But it was too late. Diaz, calm and deliberate, motioned for the real killer to pick it back up—this time with a cloth.

"I won't kill you," he said quietly, "but I *will* alert the police as to who killed Dell Phillips if you dare cross me."

The old sailor dropped his head, any thoughts of running dissolving. He watched as the Colombian henchman walked away with the pistol, secured in the cloth, and out the door.

Diaz motioned towards the door, "You are free to go, Mr. Kennedy but you should expect my call. I will *then* tell you what I need from you. If you go to the police, you die. If you go to Burt Williams, you die. The only way you live is to become my *friend*," he said, his voice calm and soothing. Kennedy looked into the Colombian's dark eyes, realizing his life was all but over. From this day forward imprisoned in his own skin.

Kennedy stood briskly, hustling towards the door, not looking back. Diaz turned to the body of Dell Phillips, scowling. He hadn't wanted to kill the man, but there was no way he could use him against Burt Williams. Phillips, loyal to the bone, looked on Williams as a father, a mentor. Diaz, dealing with those types for a long time knew this was the only way to properly handle them. He shook his head in disgust but once again reminded himself that all of this was merely a means to an end.

The boat skipper, however, wasn't loyal—a fact made clear when he turned on Williams without much provocation. But what he lacked in loyalty, he made up for in survival instincts. That much had been obvious from the start.

Now, with the pieces shifting in his favor, he saw his chance—perhaps his only real opportunity—to win the game for good.

For some unknown reason, the Brazilians protected the redneck gangster. If they wouldn't allow *him* to remove the liability from the situation now, he would use Kennedy to get his South American neighbors on his side. Williams' psyche deteriorated by the day from the alcohol and cocaine, and it was only a matter of time before the man broke and made a fatal mistake. When he did, Diaz wouldn't hesitate.

Diaz pointed to a couple of armed men near the body and told them, "Put the body where *Williams* will find it," and he walked towards the same exit Kennedy used moments before. The hard bottoms of his shoes thundered throughout the building.

The rays of sun felt refreshing. When he stepped out of the warehouse, the sun once again shone brightly. The air was thick and heavy, saturated with moisture. A shower had passed through while he was inside, and now the humidity crashed down on him like a weight, clinging to his skin as sweat beaded on his brow.

When he finally made it to his car, he cranked up the air conditioner and sat. The only sound was the gentle hum of the idling engine. He hated this part of the business, the killing. He always made sure it was absolutely necessary and then only about business. If he wanted to bring Phillipe' to this country, start anew, *things* like this had to be done.

He had seen pure joy in others' eyes as they killed, but for him, the faces of those unfortunate souls never faded from the back of his mind. Each death by his order weighed on him, and though he felt absolute sympathy for every life taken, he buried it deep where no one could see.

Empathy was a tool most ignored, discarded as a weakness. But he refused to let it slip away entirely. Others may have lost their humanity—but he vowed he wouldn't. Not completely, anyway.

After the incident with Duy and the disastrous way his drunken assault on the Colonel had ended, Burt couldn't bring himself to face his wife. When he woke up on the cold floor, his body ached with the weight of regret. Dried blood crusted around his nose where Duy had forced him down, and a sticky pool of bloody drool had gathered beside his mouth. The taste of iron lingered on his tongue, a bitter reminder of his failure.

When he finally stumbled to his feet, the house was empty. Susie had left without leaving a note nor any sign of where she went. Burt was in no shape to hunt her down nor did he want to at that moment. His head throbbed violently, each pulse feeling as if it might split his skull in two. Every little sound reverberated through his mind like a sledgehammer, amplifying his misery.

He needed tomato juice—fast. Stumbling to the pantry, he rummaged through the shelves until his fingers landed on a couple of cans. With shaking hands, he cracked them open and quickly slurped them down, the thick, acidic liquid offering the slightest relief from the wreckage of his hangover.

When he fell onto the bed, he didn't know how much time had passed since groggily awakening. He wore the same clothes, and he, wincing, could smell the stink of himself. If the boys had been in the house, he never knew it and they didn't bother him. As far as he could tell, nobody had checked on him, not even the staff. *That was their ass*, he thought, *I'm going to fire every damned one of 'em.*

Burt still didn't know what day it was when the phone rang on the kitchen wall right next to his ear. He regretted his choice of seating as he slurped black coffee before reluctantly picking it up.

Susie's voice was on the other side informing Burt she was calling from New Orleans. His wife confessed that Duy told her about a person in the city that could help find out if Rof was *truly* dead. She didn't take the jet; she wanted to drive. The conversation didn't go smoothly as Burt told her that Rof was dead, and she would be better off to believe that fact than to keep chasing ghosts. Once again, an argument erupted between them, voices rising until the inevitable end. Burt winced as she slammed the phone down, the abrupt dial tone blaring in his still-throbbing head like a piercing siren. Grimacing, he closed his eyes, exhaling sharply—another battle lost, another wound that wouldn't quite heal.

For the next few days, his nose stayed buried in powder, and his hand rarely left the neck of a whiskey bottle. His world shrank to a sun-bleached haze, the crash of waves distant and meaningless.

A battered beach chair, planted under the relentless Florida sun with no shade in sight, became his refuge—or his prison. And that's exactly where Casey found him—stoned out of his mind, his skin burned a blistering beet red, a ghost of the man he used to be.

"Burt, you awake?" Casey shouted as he approached Burt's chair. The gangster's head was tilted back, sunglasses hiding his drunken eyes from the sun, with no shirt and rolled up blue jeans. His feet were bare, and they, along with his upper body, burned bright red. He had been out in the sun for a while, oblivious to the world around him, jumping when he heard Casey's voice.

"What the hell do you want?" He snarled at Casey and the boy stopped dead in his tracks.

"Well, uh...," Casey paused, and Burt whipped his head around to face him. "Well, boy? What hell is it?" he asked, his anger swelling with each word. Casey cautiously took the last few steps to the beach chair but stopped just out of Burt's reach.

"Just came from the surf shop" Casey told him, "Dell hasn't been there in a couple days. The guys back in the board shop couldn't get in. They pissed Dell off; he took their keys and now they're locked out. The guys say *nobody's* been around." He talked so fast that he almost ran out of breath.

Burt leaned his bulk forward in the chair and groaned loudly, lifting his burnt arms slightly, flinching in pain. White stripes separated patches of red, the same pattern as his chair, telling the story of how long he had been there.

Burt took off his sunglasses and squinted, "Stupid bastard is shacked up somewhere. How long he been gone?" he asked.

"Two days. Tuesday was the last day he was at the shop," the kid responded.

Burt sneered and said something under his breath about giving Casey a key. At least the kid was dependable. Dell was always messing up like this. Dependability was not in his DNA. His one redeeming quality was loyalty, however. He would take a bullet for Burt and that was the only reason the gangster kept him around.

"Give me a minute, kid, and I'll be up at the house," he growled. Casey nodded and began walking towards the mansion, glancing back occasionally, to see if Burt followed. The old gangster gingerly rose to his feet, stumbling behind him. The combination of powder and liquor held sway over his body and mind. He staggered more than walked. Casey turned around, watching Burt fall face first into the sand. To Burt it felt more like concrete than sand and he was stuck. He couldn't move. Casey ran back to help him to the house. As Casey struggled to get Burt's heavy frame to his feet, he said "Thanks, kid. Looks like you the only one I can count on around here," he said, halfway genuinely. Casey smiled as he bore Burt's weight on his narrow shoulder.

While Burt took a shower and tried to make himself presentable, Casey made him a pot of coffee. Burt emerged from upstairs and quickly drank two cups of the sobering, hot liquid and the two left for the surf shop. Burt instinctively jumped behind the wheel but thought about it for a second and looked over at Casey and said, "Kid, you drive." That excited Casey as this was the first time anyone ever let him drive. When the thirteen-year-old put the car in drive and it began to roll, Burt put his head on the rest behind him and said, "On your own, bud." Once again, without regret, Casey broke the law while Burt snored.

Even with Casey slamming the brakes each time he needed the car to stop, Burt never moved, his deafening snoring betraying his condition. The novice driver hit the curb when he turned into the surf shop's parking lot and the car shook violently before screeching to a stop. Burt picked up his head, looking around halfway caring and said, "Damn son, nice job."

The employees had long since given up and left. Only a couple of kids were leaning against the wall in the back. When he got out of the car, Burt pointed at them and then moved his stubby finger towards the road. They all left without a word. Casey stood tall. He was Burt's boy, picking his chin up as they passed.

"Go back there and make sure everybody's gone," he told Casey, and the kid walked around back while Burt entered the front door. He didn't turn on any lights, easing a pistol from his belt. He peeked around the corner, straining his eyes to see anything out of order. He tried to shake what was left of the cobwebs clouding his mind and he noticed a light on in Dell's tiny office. Someone was there. Despite the darkness he could make out a figure, its head back, unaware of his presence, perched in the chair behind the desk. He began to grin as he was about to catch Dell either strung out and dead asleep or in the company of what he was certain was one of the trashy girls he was known to frequent.

He eased a little closer and opened his mouth wide, about to yell and scare his old friend when Casey ran up behind him. Burt wheeled and pointed the gun at him before he realized it.

Casey's voice echoed through the shop yelling, "It's me!"

Burt shook his head and pointed his short, stubby finger at Casey, throwing the kid an angry look, motioning for him to hang behind. He reached the chair and eased it around, so that the front was facing him, what he saw made his already queasy stomach erupt and he vomited uncontrollably. He tried to stay in between the chair and Casey until he could contain himself and the situation. He was usually immune to something like this but today he wasn't on his game. Even though he tried to shield Casey from the sight, the boy had already positioned himself to see Dell's lifeless body. Casey made no sound, he just stared, his eyes wide and his mouth agape.

Burt had seen a lot of dead bodies in his life, and he usually didn't feel much in the way of pain or sorrow as this was the price of doing business, but he had known this kid most of his life. He had raised him in this life and looked after him. At first Burt felt sorrow, but anger soon outweighed his grief. He saw the shock displayed on Casey's face and knew this was a decisive moment with the kid. He had never killed someone as young as Casey, and he didn't want to start now, but everything hinged on the boy's reaction.

He knelt, every inch of his body still screaming in pain, "Son, you all right?" he asked Casey.

The kid finally turned his eyes, slowly, from the corpse to meet Burt's. "What happened to him?" was all Casey could manage.

Burt decided to shoot straight with the kid, "He got himself shot, Case. But..." he paused. He slowly put his hands on Casey's shoulders, both hands inches from his neck, "we can't have the cops here. You know what *really* goes on."

Casey nodded, still locking eyes with Burt, his heavy breath falling upon Burt's sunburned face.

His shock began to wear off and Casey's body trembled with fear. Tears began flowing as he asked, his voice low and nearly inaudible, "You going to kill me, Burt?"

Burt's finger inched closer to Casey's throat, and he narrowed his eyes, preparing himself for the worst, "Son, today your life starts over, I ain't going to kill you but you are going to help me get rid of this and say nothing about it. EVER."

Burt locked eyes with Casey, his glare unwavering as he waited for a response. Without hesitation, Casey met his stare, his expression steady. He gave a firm nod and said, "Yes, sir."

Chapter 15

Burt wrapped Dell's body in some packer paper, tied it up with string and stood over his friend for a few moments. He had sent Casey to watch for anyone coming around, but, thankfully, nobody came. Casey walked out to the car, stood next to it for a couple minutes, as instructed, ensured no one was around, and popped open the truck. He scooted back inside to help Burt load Dell's limp body. Burt found a chain and a couple of cinder blocks lying around the workshop and placed them next to the corpse.

He eased the trunk closed, propping his bulk on it and staring at Casey asked him, "You still with me, Kid?"

Casey returned his gaze, grimacing, "I sure could use one of those cigars," pointing at Burt's shirt pocket. The gangster gritted his teeth, pulled one out, lit it and held it out to the kid. He took one for himself, unlit, and slapped it in the corner of his mouth, patting the kid on the head.

The drive to the harbor was short and quiet, neither uttering a word. When they arrived, they parked on top of the hill and waited. Even though the air was sticky, it was still winter, even in Florida, and it got dark early. As the last rays of light faded over the peninsula, most fishing boats had made their way in and filled just about every slip in the harbor. Burt, perched like a hawk on the hill, watched until he was sure everybody was gone.

In winter even the store closed early, and Burt carefully made his way to each security camera, disabled them, and cursed the technology as he worked. Casey watched from the car. He was amazed a man of Burt's size could move so quickly.

Burt returned to the car and asked if Casey had seen anyone. The scared kid reported that he hadn't. The two of them carefully made their way to the *Daddy's Girl* with Dell's body. Burt handled most of the load as Casey struggled to keep up. Burt didn't admonish him, only whispering words of encouragement. Once they had the body onboard, Casey returned to the car and retrieved the chain and cinder blocks. He dropped the chain, and something rattled in bush. His heart stopped. Frozen, he glared into the dense vegetation and finally made eye contact with a racoon that was nearly as frighted as he was. Casey shook his head, began breathing again and made his way to the boat, dragging the heavy chain behind him.

They both made one more visual sweep of the area. Satisfied nobody saw them, Burt steered the boat into the narrow pass leading through a jetty and out into open water. The harbor faded from view. Unknowingly, Casey watched as his own innocence slipped away, vanishing like a shadow at dusk.

Their sweep of the property didn't include the back room of the store where Kennedy had called home since his run in with Mateo Diaz. Peeping through the bottom of the room's only window, he saw Burt Williams and Casey Bruce drag the wrapped body to the boat and take off. He had been asleep but jumped to his feet at the sound of the chain crashing to the earth as it slipped from Casey's hand. Now, he was *really* in trouble. If Burt found out what he saw, *he* would be the next to take a final ride out to sea. The old sailor once again wanted to run, maybe down to the Keys or even try for the islands, but he understood he'd never be safe. He did have some friends down there, but he also knew the Columbian's reach would follow him wherever he went. He'd spend the rest of his life with his head on a swivel. He clutched the pistol in his hand, realizing he only had one choice.

RB banged his fist on the front door after repeatedly ringing the doorbell with no result. Finally, after a few minutes, Burt cracked open the door, squinting when sunlight hit his eyes.

"Let me guess, little lady's not at home?" RB asked with a smirk, but Burt didn't return the humor,. He stood glaring at his old friend while the fog rolled through his head. Finally, he just left the door open and walked away.

"What damn time is it?" Burt asked as RB scooted past him.

"Six thirty, you getting soft out here paradise?"

Burt managed a slight grin. These days he usually lay in bed until ten or so, but he didn't want RB to know that.

Walking into the kitchen, RB motioned around and asked sarcastically, "No breakfast and coffee?"

"Everything's in the cabinet, make some," Burt grunted, pointing to the kitchen cabinets.

"I ain't making breakfast, but I'll put on some coffee. You look like you could use it," RB responded, "Rough night?"

Burt reached for his pocket but realized his cigars were in the living room. He just smiled awkwardly as he thought about last night. When he and Casey finally arrived home, they sat down for a long talk about loyalty—the unspoken rules that bound them—and the one commandment of the Dixie Mafia: Thou shall not snitch to the cops.

Burt had been even younger than Casey when he was first introduced to this way of life. He had learned fast, adapted, and survived. Casey would be just fine, he assured himself.

"Yeah, pretty rough. Business," was all he offered, and RB knew to leave it at that. For the moment at least.

The coffee maker gurgled and the last remnants from the brew basket dripped into the pot. RB poured himself a steaming cup, savored the rich aroma for a second before offering a cup to his friend. Burt sighed after he drank it down and let it settle into his stomach.

"Damn good," he complimented RB, and the detective nodded in appreciation. Burt placed his cup on the tabletop and leaned over to RB, "Listen. You and Cliff are getting started today, right?" RB told him that was the plan. "Good," Burt continued, "first thing I want you to do is find out what he knows about those two names in his book, Chatom and Kendrick. Help him, string him along, but don't get serious with it, RB. I know how you are. Just keep him busy is all I need." Burt found a stray cigar on the counter, his eyes curling back in their sockets when it found his lips.

"Sure thing," he said as he sipped his coffee, but Burt's interest in those two names brought out the detective in him. He had to know more.

As the two old friends spoke in the kitchen, Cliff had awakened and made his way down the back stairs, overhearing their conversation. He shook his head. He knew RB was just a Burt Williams crony. He had hoped the detective was different but, in reality, expected nothing less than what he had just heard. It didn't really matter, though, Cliff had plans of his own. He stepped into the kitchen, the two men barely noticing him. Burt didn't turn his attention from the coffee and cigar while RB only nodded.

"Heard you and Casey come in early this morning," Cliff grinned at Burt as he spoke.

Burt still focused on his coffee, grunted, "None of your damn business, kid. Don't you and RB have a big day today?"

RB, noticing the tension between the two offered, "Why don't we take that coffee to go? Surely there is a cup around here." RB fumbled around the kitchen and found a supply of Styrofoam cups with lids. He motioned for Cliff to come with him, leaving Burt alone with his coffee and groggy thoughts. Cliff poured some coffee in the cup, slapped the gangster on the back as he passed, "See you later, *dad*."

Burt said something under his breath, but Cliff knew he had gotten under his skin and smartly left it at that.

"I would leave old Burt alone this morning," RB warned him nodding back to the house, "I know the guy and this, kid, this ain't the morning." Before they got to RB's car, he glanced back and saw Burt peeking out of the kitchen window. RB nodded as if the plan was in motion and Burt held up his coffee cup in salute.

When they were on their way, Cliff became curious, "Where are we going?"

RB kept his eyes on the road as he responded, "How long was you listening this morning?" He cut his eyes over to the passenger and Cliff saw a slight smile.

"You knew I was there?"

RB cocked his head towards him, cutting his eyes at Cliff, grinning, "You don't stay alive in Biloxi without knowing who's around at *all* times, son."

Cliff didn't like being called *son* but didn't protest. "So, are you going to just babysit me like Burt wants?" he asked, watching the row of pines lining the road whizz by, each single tree becoming a blur of brown and green.

RB turned his attention back to the road, "That's what we are going to *tell* him." Cliff bit his bottom lip, wanting to believe RB, but as Unc told him, trust is *earned*.

"First," he told Cliff, "We dig into those names. One, it will help pacify Burt and two, you may have something there."

RB rubbed the stubble on his chin, "What do you know about them?"

Cliff shrugged, "Only what was in the papers."

RB continued rubbing his chin while his other hand remained on the wheel, "Well, the first thing we will do is go to Kendrick's family and friends. Turn over some rocks, see what we find."

"Do we know where they live?" Cliff asked.

RB reached into his pocket, pulling out his Biloxi PD badge, "I may not be a cop here but I'm *still* a cop."

The two DEA agents had already pulled some strings and provided RB information on the Kendrick family. The West Palm police and the county Sheriff's Office were purposely kept unaware of the Mississippi detective and his assignment. One reason was that Burt held sway over many cops in the area and there were whispers they *helped* put Vern Bruce in prison. Second, the Mississippi detective understood early on that it was all about plausible deniability—a necessity in a world where trust was a liability. RB could take no chances. If Burt ever discovered he was working for the DEA, old friendship wouldn't matter. He wouldn't hesitate.

He'd put a bullet in RB's skull without a second thought. "Already found out they live out in Royal Palms. Shouldn't be too hard to find. Probably one of the few black families out that way," RB gestured along his arm, "probably don't hurt." They both grinned at that and continued down the road, heading inland.

RB and Casey drove slowly down the street looking for the right address before finally arriving at the Kendrick home. Most of the lawns and driveways surrounding the modest wood frame houses were filled with boats of differing types but the only vehicle in the Kendrick driveway was an older Dodge pickup that had obviously seen its better days. Eyeing the car suspiciously from the front porch swing was a slender older Black lady with graying hair. She pulled her reading glasses to the end of her nose when they pulled into the driveway. Her suspicion turned more into curiosity when RB, flashing a bright smile, opened his door and stepped out. He told Cliff to remain in the car until he motioned for him. He knew from his *own* experience that his people were timid of law enforcement.

RB kept his smile and made eye contact with her as he walked up the short concrete path to the front porch. It wasn't much of a porch. The house was newer, and concrete was used instead of wood for more of a patio than a porch. Concrete didn't blow away in hurricanes.

"Mrs. Kendrick?" RB asked as he approached the lady and somehow his smile seemed to widen.

"Yes," she answered in a thick country accent, a little out of place in West Palm. Inside, RB celebrated. These were his people. He could identify a Mississippi accent when he heard one and she was definitely from the Delta.

RB took off his cap as he stepped onto the porch, "My name is Ramsay Brown. I'm a detective out of Biloxi..." he paused to gage any reaction, but saw none, "I want to ask you a few questions about your son, Marcus." A direct approach always seemed to serve well with Delta folks. They had no time to waste—most of it was spent simply trying to survive the sweltering heat and unforgiving conditions near the Mississippi River.

Mrs. Kendrick sat her Bible on the swing beside her, careful to bookmark her place, "You don't mind showing me a badge do you, Mr. Brown?" she asked. RB smiled, pulling his badge from his pocket and handed it to her. She held it at the end of her nose, where her reading glasses were still perched, looking over it. With a surprised look on her face, she handed it back to him. "Don't see many *Black* detectives out of Mississippi," she said.

RB shook his head, raised his eyebrows, responding, "No ma'am you don't. Worked hard and went through a lot to get that." He waved the badge in the air.

A slow smile crept onto her face as she said, "I'm sure you did. Now, tell me—what can I do to help you, Detective? And what does my son's murder have to do with a Biloxi cop?"

As RB suspected, she got right to the point and he did the same, "I'll be honest with you, Mrs. Kendrick, I'm not here in an *official* capacity. You see that kid in the car? His uncle is Vernon Bruce, you heard of him, right?"

Mrs. Kendrick removed her glasses, squinting in the bright sunshine and nodded, "The rich white guy that killed some people up north?" she asked.

"That's the one," RB responded, "I'm a friend of the family and we think there is more to it than what's been said." RB grimaced, "Your son found a body and died a while after, correct?"

Mrs. Kendrick fought back a tear, her voice quivering slightly responded, "Yes sir, he was murdered. Ain't found who done it. They asked a few questions and that's all I heard. The case is still open. I call every week."

The tear she struggled to hold back finally slipped over her cheekbone, tracing a silent path down her face.

RB had noticed her features the moment he approached— high cheekbones, deep-set eyes. A Black woman from the Delta, no doubt, but something else lingered in her lineage. Choctaw, maybe. The resemblance struck him, a quiet connection he wasn't sure she'd recognize. He filed it away. He might need it later.

He glanced towards the ground, out of respect, before returning eye contact, "We need to know anything your son said to you about the body and *anything* that happened in the days after. Anyone following him, people he didn't know coming up to him? Anything out of normal."

Mrs. Kendrick turned her attention back to Cliff, still sitting in the seat with his seatbelt buckled, "He thinks his uncle didn't do it, right?" RB nodded yes. "Too many poor people get caught up in mess like this, I don't feel *too* sorry for rich ones that it happens to."

RB angled his head again, responding, "Rich or poor, getting death row for something you didn't do is bad for us *all*. Especially the Christian folk." RB knew how to turn the tide in discussions like this as he had done a million times. If one thing white and black people from Mississippi all had in common, it was religion. They may practice it in separate ways, but it all counted the same.

She sighed loudly, "Son you are so right. Shouldn't matter, we are all the same in God's eyes." She pointed and told RB, "Bring that baby up here. From what I read, that child's been through a lot."

RB figured she read about Casey rather than Cliff but he would have to use what he could to get her to talk a little. "Yes, ma'am he has," RB responded as a concerned look swept over his face. He motioned for Cliff to step out of the car and join them on the porch.

Mrs. Kendrick took Cliff by the hand and asked him to sit in the swing next to her. Her smile reminded him of his mother's and the tone of her voice matched Susie's when she spoke to him, "Baby, what makes you think your uncle *didn't* do what they say he did?" She was once again blunt and direct, and Cliff, like RB, appreciated it.

Cliff took a deep breath, "I know him, *that's* it. I just know him." He looked Mrs. Kendrick in the eye as he spoke, "He took me in as a little boy, when my father's plane went down, and my mom couldn't raise me. She was living on the streets. *He* helped her. He didn't have to. He didn't have to take me into his home, but he did. I promise you there is not a mean bone in his body," He squeezed Mrs. Kenrick's hand, "I promise you that."

Mrs. Kendrick never took her eyes off him as he spoke, her gaze unwavering, as if she were looking straight into his soul, searching for the truth hidden beneath his words. When he finished, she leaned in, put her hands on his cheeks and kissed him on the forehead. Even though they were vastly different, something about Cliff reminded her of own son when he was that age. Perhaps it was his boyish innocence, but there was something there and her heart went out to him. She looked back to RB, "I'll help you all I can. Just promise me, you let Marcus rest in peace. Find who took my baby's life."

"Thank you and I will, Mrs. Kendrick. That's a promise," he said, "I know this isn't the kind of question you want to answer, but was Marcus involved with any type of activity he *shouldn't* have been?" He tried to ask the question as gently as possible, but somehow, each time he had to ask it, it always came out a way he didn't intend.

She didn't flinch and she appeared to sit up straighter. It was clear she had been asked that question in the past, probably more than once. "I'll tell you like I told *our* police. Marcus was as straight as they came. All he wanted to do was work and fish. Poor child, it was fishing that got him killed." RB nodded and tried to convey an apology by gesture, not words, and Mrs. Kendrick seemed to understand.

She stood up from the swing and stood over the chair in which RB sat, "Look Mr. Brown, Marcus had a good job and had applied to the University up in Gainesville." She picked up her Bible and slid a piece of paper from inside. "This is his acceptance letter. It came a week after we buried him," she told the detective and handed the paper to him. RB noticed her lone tear had dried. No others followed. She probably cried about this at some point every day, but she wanted to show strength.

"Any other children," he asked her, and she shook her head. "It's just me and my husband now."

Cliff stood and put his arms around her, "I know how it is to feel alone. I got a feeling that, somehow, Marcus's death is connected to my uncle's problems."

She patted the teenager on the back and asked, "How could you possibly know that?"

Cliff shook his head and looked up at the cloudless sky and said, "I don't understand it. I just *know*."

Mrs. Kendrick sighed again, looked at the ground and then turned her attention back to RB, "I didn't tell the police this. I didn't want them to try and make Marcus out to be something he was not," Her voice softened as she spoke, the edges of her words gentler now, carrying a weight of emotion she could no longer conceal, "A man *did* come up to him right after he found that body. He was kind of a big man that chewed on a cigar. Marcus told *me*, no one else. He was scared."

Unconsciously RB eased to the edge of his seat, as close to her as he could get without touching, and asked "What did he want?"

Mrs. Kendrick looked back at the ground, her eyes blinking uncontrollably, holding back tears, "He offered him money to testify that he saw a white man dump his body. Gave him a description to give the police and everything."

Cliff looked at RB and the detective shook his head slightly, telling the young man to keep calm and let him do the talking. Cliff understood the gesture, easing back into the swing.

In RB's mind, he was shouting at the woman, frustrated by her mistake. But on the surface, his demeanor remained calm, his voice steady as he asked, "Did he tell him what description of the man to to use?"

She looked him in the eye and said, "White guy, black hair with a little gray mixed in on the sides, wearing glasses," she thought for a second, "and slender."

Cliff took his wallet from his pant pocket, took out a picture of his uncle and showed it to both. RB nodded. That description fit him all the way down to the gray showing up in his hair.

"Your uncle?" Mrs. Kendrick asked, closing her eyes with the realization that she had played a part in sending Vern Bruce to death row with her silence.

"What did Marcus tell this man?" RB asked gently.

Mrs. Kendrick stood up and walked to the door, "He told him to get lost." She opened the screen door, stepped inside, and said through the screen, "I don't want to talk about it anymore. You gentlemen have a good day." She started to close the wooden door but glanced back at Cliff, still holding the picture of his uncle, "Baby, I do hope you find truth."

Cliff stood, rushing over to her, slinging the door open, wrapping his arms around her again, this time so tightly RB heard her exhale. For a second her eyes widened with surprise, but she embraced him back and kissed him on the cheek. Before she disappeared into her home, RB handed her the acceptance letter back and told her thank you. He also gave her his card and asked her to call him if she ever needed anything.

Cliff smiled through his tears when the detective took his seat next to him in the car. RB knew better than to show any type of optimism as he'd been burnt too many times. Cliff, on the other hand, couldn't hold back his enthusiasm. "I told you," Cliff exclaimed as RB started the engine. The icy air from the air conditioning washing over their faces.

RB held up a finger, "Easy, son. This only means that there is a *little* more to this story than we've been told. We don't know if he meant Vern Bruce. Hell, that could be any white man within two hundred miles."

Cliff didn't care and he couldn't hide his smile. He took his shirt and wiped away the remains of the earlier tears. This was the first step to finding the people that put his uncle in prison, making him a free man and putting away his stepfather for good. He looked out the window and thought about his mother. Soon, he would free her of Burt Williams.

While optimism flowed through Cliff, RB's mind filled with dread. The detective in him already knew that there was a lot more to all of this than was made public and today solidified his suspicions. His mandate from Burt was to occupy the kid's time, but now, his already smoldering desire for truth had turned into a blazing inferno. At that moment he knew he was going to have to lie to Burt. That frightened him to his core. Burt was good at spotting liars and RB was going to have to walk a fine line with his old buddy.

He put the car in reverse but didn't back into the street. The engine idled with his foot on the brake. "Not a word of this to anyone, Cliff. Not Susie, not your cousin, and damn sure not Burt," he told the kid. Cliff nodded affirmatively but RB was going to need more than that. "I need to *hear* the words, kid."

Cliff nodded again and offered, "Not a word. All I ask, RB, is that you just stay honest with me." The two shook hands and RB eased onto the busy street. They headed back towards the Atlantic.

Chapter 16

New Orleans hadn't changed much in the years since Susie worked there. She didn't miss the place. She had stayed away, mostly to avoid the smell that clung to the city like a second skin. To her, New Orleans always reeked of liquor and body odor—a stench that lingered in her memory long after she'd left. The French Quarter—the most famous part of the weathered old city—was always filthy and reeking from the endless string of nightly parties. She kept her distance, avoiding the tourist trap as much as possible, wanting no part of its chaos or the stale scent of spilled booze and sweat.

Just across the Pontchartrain Bridge was a little motel she frequented back in her working days and as she looked out of the tiny room's window overlooking the sprawling lake, it was as far as she was going into the city until she absolutely had no other choice.

Susie arrived late the night before and as soon as day broke, she called the number on the card and Duy answered on the third ring. He invited her to a small office within the Warehouse District. The district was close to the Quarter but still far enough that she didn't have to smell its stench.

Duy asked her to stop by that afternoon and she eagerly agreed. The address he provided led her to a large, bland building that blended well into the other warehouses and buildings near its location.

He met Susie at a large door near the front and the two walked through a mass of people crammed into the small space. Most of the people working there were of Asian descent and didn't even look up as they packaged indistinguishable items into boxes. She guessed they were probably Vietnamese, like Duy.

"Mrs. Williams, I didn't expect to see you so soon," Duy said as he pointed to a chair across from his desk in the cramped space of his office. There were boxes stacked everywhere, and Susie had to squeeze into the chair opposite him between two stacks of cardboard containers. "I apologize for the mess. We are very busy here."

Susie flashed a quick smile and got right to it. "I have to know more, Mr. Duy. I have to know for my son's sake whether Rof is alive or not," she said, her voice low and mouselike.

Duy's shoulders slumped, a shadow of a frown tugging at the corners of his mouth, the weight of his forthcoming words settling heavily on him.

"I'm afraid I told you all *I* know, Mrs. Williams." He thought for a second, contemplating his words before continuing, "However, I want to put you in contact with someone here in New Orleans that might have information." Duy leaned in, "His name is Jeff Black. He is the man that helped me escape from Vietnam to Brazil and eventually here, to America."

Susie's eyebrows narrowed, her expression tightening with suspicion—or maybe concern—as she tried to read between the lines as she asked, "What would he know?"

Duy took a deep breath and put his hand on Susie's, "He is in the shipping business," he motioned around the warehouse, "As are we. But sometimes he ships other things. Things that were left behind." Susie shook her head and looked quizzically at Duy. "People, Mrs. Williams, people like me.... and also, prisoners that make it from the camp to his ships."

"Did he ever mention Rof?" Susie asked quietly.

Duy wagged his finger, "No. We never discuss that type of business. But, perhaps, he will talk to *you*."

"Why in the world would he talk to me?" Susie asked, tears swelling in her eyes.

"I can say nothing further," he responded, "I will give him your number. If he calls, and it could take a couple days for him to do so, he will help. If he doesn't, well, I'm sorry. I truly am sorry."

Susie nodded and stood to leave. As she squeezed through the narrow gap between the stacked boxes, she paused and looked back at Duy, who had turned in his chair to face the wall.

"When you talk to him," she said softly, "please tell him I can't take much more of this. I have to know."

Duy didn't turn around. His silence lingered in the air as Susie slowly turned and walked out, the weight of her words following her into the hallway.

"I will tell him," Duy said, staring into nothing.

Duy quietly walked behind Susie as she left and after he watched the taxi disappear into the bustling city, went back to his office, quickly phoning Veck Baxter. Baxter was expecting the call and picked it up as soon as it rang. He hesitated briefly to gather his thoughts and words before speaking as he both dreaded and was excited by this part of the plan.

Finally, he spoke, "Good morning, Colonel."

"She is expecting Black's call."

There was a long silence, the only sound the faint hum of the phone line filling the space. Then, finally, Duy spoke again, his voice low and measured, "My duty to you is done, my friend. I will not continue to pull at the strings of this sweet lady's heart."

Duy couldn't see Baxter's smile on the other end. "I appreciate your help, Colonel. Our indebtedness to each other ends here. Just know that she will soon have peace. Your work, while it brings her pain now, sets the stage for her happiness," Baxter replied.

"Goodbye and good fortune," Duy said, and the line went dead. Veck replaced the handset in its place, easing back in his chair. He reached for the bottle of pills on the nightstand but stopped halfway, deciding today was not a day to drift away from reality. He would finally get a chance to see her. He pictured her in his mind's eye so many times that it was the first image he saw when he went to sleep and the first when he opened his eyes. He opened the drawer under the nightstand and pulled out the faded picture he carried all the way from Vietnam. She was young in that picture and that is how he saw her, young, pretty, and full of life. He knew the picture was taken over fifteen years ago. He also knew the pretty girl in the picture had grown into a life-hardened woman, but still, at her core, beautiful. He shook his head in the darkness, called Jeff Black and set him in motion.

After Susie flagged down the taxi outside the building, she asked the driver to take the long route—through the French Quarter—on the way back to her hotel. As they rolled through the crowded, chaotic streets, she lowered her window, letting in the sour, familiar blend of liquor, sweat, and old memories. She breathed it in deeply, one last time, and silently vowed never to return.

As the cab crossed the seemingly endless bridge stretching over the vast, shallow lake that separated New Orleans from the eastern shore, she inhaled the brackish air, the scent of open water and salt-heavy wind filling her lungs. She made another promise to herself then: if Rof was truly gone, she would leave his ghost here, too. A broad smile crept across her face as the tires hummed against the concrete, carrying her forward.

Since arriving back at the motel, she hadn't strayed more than a few feet from the bedside phone. She stared at it, wanting it to scream out, to give her something, anything, but all that met her ears was a deafening silence that pressed in from all sides.

She didn't dare leave the room forsaking food and fresh air. She sat on the edge of the bed, her eyes fixed on the shimmering expanse of Lake Pontchartrain. The waning light danced on the water as her thoughts strayed elsewhere. Slowly, her gaze shifted from the view to the phone beside her, its silence louder than any sound.

Her bathroom visits were as short as possible, leaving the door open when she just couldn't hold it any longer. Her resolve waned a couple of times and she cried for a while but suddenly her tears turned to joy as her mind flashed back to happy times of her youth, before her parents disowned her. She remembered days spent on the white, sugar-like sands of the Panama City beaches with Rof. She remembered his piercing blue eyes and that broad, easy smile—the one that always made her feel seen, cherished, and wanted in a way no one else ever had.

They never *really* dated, but they were always together. She knew about Rof's flings with the tourist girls—brief adventures that never lasted. They always left. But she was the one who stayed. She was always there. She was there the day he received his draft card—the same day their son was conceived. She hadn't realized it then, not fully, but she loved that blonde-haired, blue-eyed beach bum with more of herself than she ever meant to give.

The phone's sudden, loud ring shattered the moment, jolting her back to reality. She just stared at the ringing phone for a few seconds before picking it up, "Hello," she said quietly.

"Mrs. Williams?" Jeff Black asked in his strange accent. She replied affirmatively with tears beginning to form in the corner of her dark eyes. If this *was* Jeff Black, that meant there was still hope that Rof was alive.

Black spoke slowly, ensuring Susie understood his words, mindful of his accent, "My name is Jefferson Black, Mrs. Williams. I am an associate of Colonel Duy. I would like to meet you, in person, to discuss our mutual friend."

"Where? I'm in a motel across the lake," Susie replied, barely waiting for his voice to finish on the other end, her words rushing out, flushed with urgency.

Black told her to meet him at Jackson Square right in front of the famous general's statue the following day. She quickly agreed. The conversation was short and didn't provide a whole lot of information, but she couldn't contain her joy. Hope filled her soul that the next day would bring the news she waited so long for.

Her stomach growled, startling her. Realizing she hadn't eaten since the night before, she decided to visit the little mom and pop café near the motel she had spotted from the taxi earlier. It was close enough that she could walk. Taking a deep breath, the stale air of the room flooded her lungs, and she looked forward to some fresh air. Peeking out the window, Susie saw the sign just down the narrow country road. She clicked open her suitcase, reaching for a brand-new pair of tennis shoes. They were so new and white they almost glowed, catching the last traces of sunlight that struggled to filter into the dimming room.

Her mind filled with visions of a reunion between her, Cliff and Rof as she walked. She hadn't been this happy since her reunion with her son. She remembered how Cliff kept his distance for the first couple of meetings. The first time she hugged him, and finally feeling his arms tighten around her, it had filled her heart with an emotion she couldn't quite explain—something deep, unexpected, and impossibly real.

That was my happiest moment, she thought to herself. She walked with a lightness in her step, a soft smile playing on her lips, as her thoughts wandered toward the future—still uncertain, but at last, filled with hope and possibility.

Chapter 17

Another fight with his wife behind him, Adam Lowell jumped into his car, slammed the door shut, and tore off, leaving a cloud of smoke hanging over the spot where his tires had scorched the asphalt. The acrid scent of burnt rubber lingered in the air long after his car vanished down the road, and his wife's furious slam of the screen door echoed in the stillness. He had already downed a six-pack, and the half-empty bottle of whiskey riding shotgun was next.

"Damn her," he muttered aloud, reaching for the whiskey. But as his hand wrapped around the bottle's neck, a sudden flash of movement in the rearview mirror caught his eye.

He jumped, heart skipping, thinking for a split second it was his daughter. But it wasn't—it was her teddy bear, slumped against the seat, its glassy eyes staring blankly ahead. She must've left it there when he picked her up from school that afternoon.

A heavy sigh escaped him, laced with anger and regret. If things kept unraveling like this, her mother would be gone soon— and she'd take his little girl with her.

Not if I stop her first, he thought, a dangerous edge in his mind.

His little angel was the only good thing he had left in this world. And he wasn't going to lose her. Not without a fight.

He turned up the bottle, again thinking to himself, *this rotten damned life got worse at every turn.* Each time he saw her sweet face, though, life seemed to brighten for him, if just for a minute or two. He reached for the bear in the backseat, turning his back to the wheel long enough for the car to veer off the road. When he felt the steering wheel begin to shake, he wheeled around just in time to see the woman's face before the front bumper made its initial contact with her body and sent her flying over the hood and into the windshield. Her body slammed into the glass and as he slammed on brakes, rolled down the hood and onto the gravel lining the narrow road. Adam couldn't move, his body paralyzed in fear. *Oh my god*, he thought, *what have I done?*

The impact, over in a split second, resounded through the small neighborhood. People flooded from the cafe and the houses surrounding it, hands over their mouths, unable to speak or scream.

Susie's thoughts never strayed from the happiness she had felt just moments before, even as her lifeless body tumbled from the windshield and onto the pavement. The life she had imagined with Rof and their son vanished in an instant—gone in the blink of an eye.

When the paramedics gently turned her head to face them, they recoiled slightly. She was smiling. Susie took that smile to her grave, a final trace of joy frozen in time.

And on the crumpled hood of Adam Lowell's mangled car, one pristine, glowing white shoe remained—untouched, a haunting symbol of what was lost.

Jeff Black watched the crowds file by, admiring the giant statue of Andrew Jackson. He studied each face, hoping it belonged to Susie Williams. His concern grew when she was an hour late and decided to make his way across the bridge and find out why Susie hadn't made the trip.

When he neared the motel, the flashing lights of emergency vehicles greeted him. Yellow tape lined the highway and Adam Lowell's car, the windshield shattered and a small dent on the hood, hadn't been moved. His heart sank and he already feared the worst. Black didn't stop and continued on to the nearest hospital. He slipped an emergency room attendant twenty and his fear became reality.

He settled on a bench outside of the emergency room facing a four-way stop. Cars came and went through the stop signs for a couple of hours while he sat, collecting his thoughts. Black didn't know Susie personally, but through his work with Burt Williams he got to know her from afar. In his mind, she was just a sweet young lady that didn't belong with a gangster like Williams. She was a loving mother and made choices she felt were in the best interest of her son, not herself. Now he had to go tell his old friend Veck Baxter the unwelcome news. He needed a drink first and headed to the nearest bar to gather liquid courage to carry out his unfortunate assignment.

Black didn't open the door with his key but knocked. Baxter opened the door quickly and appeared to be in a good mood for the first time in a long while. His pain had subsided, an exceedingly rare occurrence, and he smiled when his friend entered the room. He motioned for Black to enter and looked behind him, half expecting Susie in tow, but saw no one. When Black sat down next to him, Baxter noticed that his friend had yet to look him in the eye. Something was wrong.

Baxter put his hand on Black's, making sure to make eye contact, "You did meet her?" Baxter asked, hope still permeating from his voice.

Black chewed at his bottom lip and looked at the floor. After a moment he said, "She's gone, my friend. Gone in a horrible accident." Baxter's mouth fell open, stunned into silence, but before he could form a single word, Black began to speak, his tone calm and deliberate, "She took a walk from her motel and..." Black paused. His trembling voice unable to say the words.

Baxter had never seen his friend in such grief. He blinked several times before continuing, holding back rare tears, "Some drunk swerved off the road and hit her. She never felt it."

Baxter snapped his head to the side and grabbed the bottle of whiskey resting untouched on the table between them. But instead of uncorking it, he hurled it across the room. The bottle exploded against the bathroom door, whiskey splattering across the wood and pooling on the floor as shards of glass scattered like shrapnel.

He turned back to Black, his eyes dry but burning, narrowed beneath furrowed brows twisted with rage and something deeper. Pain, maybe.

Black swallowed hard, slowly raising his hands in the air, a silent gesture of caution.

"Easy, my friend," the Brazilian begged of him, "It was a dream not meant to be."

"It's easy for you to say that!" Baxter's voice thundered, "It wasn't *your* dream." He pulled the faded picture from the drawer, crumpled it in his hand, held it to his forehead before tossing it in the trash.

The Brazilian closed his eyes, trying to find words, "Yes, of course you are right," Black tried to console him, "but you must remember, we *all* have lost dreams but, my friend, we can't stray from our righteous path."

The anger inside Baxter intensified and with what energy he could muster, leaped from his chair standing over his friend, his fierce blue eyes staring through him, "This only makes my focus *clearer*. I'm tired of this damn place. I'm tired of these damned walls."

Baxter flicked the light switch and with the room fully illuminated, Black saw the cold, emotionless stare that first he saw long ago in Vietnam. A chill ran down his spine.

Baxter continued, "I'm going home. Not the way I wanted to go, but *everything* is clear now." Baxter turned quickly, almost losing his balance but caught the edge of the table. He looked over the river in the distance and asked coldly, "Does the boy know?"

Black shook his head, "I don't think so. I don't think the news has reached that far just yet." Black grimaced, "When it does, I do fear for his safety. Burt Williams is not a parent for *this* child. Without his mother, I don't know what will happen to him."

Baxter turned again to face him. His expression still showing no trace of emotion, his eyes narrow and focused, he pointed a crooked finger towards Black, "I made a promise a long time ago..." His stony expression fading and his eyes swelling with moisture, "...that I intend to keep." Suddenly, Baxter's voice became as strong as ever and his tears vanished as quickly as they appeared and said, "Make the arrangements. Call Calley. Tell him its time."

Black nodded gently, leaving Baxter alone in his room. The pain, hidden by adrenaline, suddenly flooded his body and Baxter nearly fell as he stumbled towards the bed and collapsed on the mattress. He reached for the bottle of pills, carefully swallowed two and washed it down with a gulp from the fresh bottle of whiskey hidden beside his bed. He put the bottle to his lips, repeating the motion several times. His pain slowly receded and as he drifted away, he focused on the ceiling, but all he could see was Susie's young, smiling face.

Burt grinned when he saw his blonde secretary bouncing towards his door. He remembered their lunch from the other day. Unconsciously, he began licking his lips in anticipation of another *working lunch*. The sweet, seductive smell of her perfume filled his nostrils before she opened the door.

"Mr. Williams," she said seriously, cracking the door just enough to slip her head through, "there's an officer here to speak with you."

Burt shifted the cigar to the other side of his mouth as he glanced out his office window, spotting the uniformed state trooper standing next to her desk. *Damnit man*, he yelled in his mind. He slipped. Used to be, nobody could sneak up on Burt Williams.

The thought of getting rid of the distraction that was his secretary flickered through his mind—briefly. But it vanished just as quickly when she perched on the edge of her desk, leaning forward and thrusting her chest toward the cop. His sly grin returned, curling at the corners of his mouth.

Most of the time, it was detectives who came to see him— not uniformed cops. The break in protocol felt like an insult. With a sigh, he set his cigar in the ashtray resting on his old, antique wooden desk and gave a slight nod. "Send him in," he said, his tone clipped but composed.

"Mr. Burton Williams?" the officer asked.

Burt nodded, "How can I help you hoss?"

The officer handed him a piece of paper Burt hadn't noticed he was holding—*another slip-up,* Burt thought, his eyes narrowing as he took it.

"I regret to inform you sir, your wife, Susan Brannon Williams, was killed in an accident in New Orleans. On this card you will find the detective in charge of the investigation's name and number. He is expecting your call." The officer's voice nor face held any emotion as he spoke.

Burt started to ask him to repeat his words but felt his knees weaken and didn't feel it at all when they buckled. One of his knees hit the floor but he caught himself with his hand before his entire body dropped. The trooper didn't move but the secretary rushed through the door, supporting Burt with her arms.

"There's got to be some kind of goddamned mistake!" he roared, his face flushing deep red with fury and disbelief.

The officer, numb to scenes like this from countless repetitions, responded in a flat, practiced tone, confirming that it was indeed true. He offered his condolences before quietly stepping away, but Burt didn't hear a word of it.

His ears rang, a piercing hum like church bells clanging too close, and his vision darkened at the edges, the room closing in around him.

He tried regaining his footing but failed and his head buried into the arms of his secretary and the seasoned old gangster sobbed uncontrollably. In his shock, he hadn't even asked *how* she died.

Death had hovered around Burt so often that, over time, numbness had taken the place of grief in his psyche. But this time was different—grief surged through him, raw and unrelenting, if only for a fleeting moment.

Then, slowly, his mind began to clear. He drew a long breath, forcing the emotion back down, steadying himself as he wrestled his tears into submission.

Finally, he was able to stand. He rushed the secretary out of the room. She knew better than to protest, but before leaving, closed all the blinds, and shut the door behind her.

Burt stumbled to his desk and reached underneath, pulling out the hidden bag of powder he kept stashed away for moments just like this. With trembling hands, he laid out a couple of lines, leaned in, and inhaled sharply. The fine powder disappeared up his nose, and a delayed rush surged through his body, sending him collapsing back into his chair.

He sat there, eyes glassy and unfocused, staring into nothing. For the first time he could remember, he felt something real. He felt true sorrow.

Chapter 18

Casey sat in his darkened room, the lights off, his body still as he held the curtain open just enough to peer out. Through the narrow gap, he watched the street in the near distance, his eyes sharp, waiting for something—or someone. He hadn't left home since the night he and Burt discovered Dell's body. Around Burt and Cliff, he acted like the same egotistical teenager, but every time the phone rang or a car drove down the street that he didn't recognize, he envisioned police surrounding the house and dragging him away in handcuffs. It never happened and with each passing car Casey felt better, if only slightly.

For the past two days Cliff and RB conducted their investigation, leaving him home alone as Burt was hardly ever home, but this Saturday was different. Cliff slept in and RB hadn't come around. Burt didn't come home at all the night before but, again, that was nothing unusual these days. Casey, sure the SWAT team wasn't preparing to raid his home, made his way downstairs and put a Pop-Tart in the toaster. For some reason he didn't notice the car pulling slowly down the driveway. When he finally saw it, the car had already stopped and there stood RB, staring off at the Atlantic.

Casey opened the kitchen door, motioning for the detective to come in, but RB didn't move.

The toaster let out a sharp *ding*, cutting through the silence.

"Hey, RB, you coming in, man?" Casey called out.

RB jolted, clearly startled, and after a brief pause, gave a stiff nod before stepping forward.

RB eased his way into the house and put his hand on Casey's shoulder. Casey wasn't used to affection like that from RB and he cut his eyes at him.

"Hey Case, Cliff awake?" RB asked as he patted the boy's shoulder and Casey shook his head no and pointed upstairs.

"Go on up there and wake his ass up. I got a Pop-Tart cooking in the kitchen."

RB placed a hand on Casey's head, giving it a light, reassuring pat before starting up the stairs. As he mounted the first step, he paused, looked back over his shoulder, and asked, "You know how to make coffee?"

The young boy smirked. RB smiled back and said, "Go ahead and put some on. We're gonna need it." Casey, sensing something bad was coming, didn't say anything else and did as asked.

RB eased the bedroom door open, finding Cliff lying on top of the covers, snoring loudly. Gently he perched on the edge of the bed and sat there quietly for a few minutes before he awakened the teenager with a slight shake.

Cliff, shocked to see RB sitting there, groggily asked him what was going on. In his line of work, RB had informed countless family members about loved ones losing their lives, but this was the first time he had to tell someone he knew and cared about. Cliff rubbed his eyes and RB just looked at the floor. He couldn't imagine how this news was going to affect this young kid. First, he loses his father before he is born, then finds out he *could* be alive, then his uncle goes to prison for murder and now his sweet mother loses her life so tragically. *Damn*, he thought, *that's more than most go through in a lifetime.*

RB knew that it was best just to get it out of the way, so he cleared his throat and started relaying the story. "Kid got some bad news," he said quietly.

Cliff cut him off, "Unc?"

RB shook his head. "Your mom, kid..." he took a deep breath, "...she's gone," he said, trying to keep his emotions together, "She was walking down the sidewalk in New Orleans from her motel. Drunk guy swerved and..." RB hesitated and could barely speak, ".... she's just gone, son."

Cliff didn't react. No tears, no words, just a blank expression frozen on his face. He stared at RB for a few long seconds, eyes hollow, before he slowly began to shake his head, barely perceptible at first.

RB could feel it—the tension coiling, the rage rising like a storm behind calm eyes. Then it erupted. All at once. An explosion of grief, fury, and helplessness pouring out of the young man's body like it had nowhere else to go.

The kid jumped to his feet, "You're lying! Burt made you do this! You're lying!" he yelled as he tried to strike at RB, but moved quickly to block the blow, throwing his muscular arms around Cliff and held him tightly as he fought to free himself. "Your lying," the kid kept saying as tears flooded from his dark blue eyes.

RB felt the struggle stop suddenly and Cliff's body went limp in his embrace. He whispered in Cliff's ear, "I wish I was son."

"Where's Burt?" Cliff managed after the few minutes of uncontrolled emotion.

"Wish I knew kid, wish I knew," he said, a single tear rolling down his cheek.

Casey had positioned himself outside the door and overheard the two inside. Susie wasn't his mother, but she had taken him in, making sure he felt loved. His eyes began to swell when he heard the front door slam. He ran back to the staircase, heart pounding, and cautiously peeked around the corner to see who had just burst into the house.

Out of the corner of his eye, he saw Burt stumble in. Hours had passed since his body and mind were taken over by the combination of cocaine and whiskey. In those hours his tears had turned to pure unadulterated rage. He bumped into one of the antique chairs, cursed, grabbed it, and smashed it into the hardwood floor, shattering the hundred-year-old treasure into countless fragments.

Casey, watching the scene unfold, and for the second time, he feared facing his mentor. He ran into his room, clicking the door locked, but knew if Burt really wanted to get in, a locked door wouldn't stop him. He collapsed onto the bed, stuffing his head under pillows.

Burt shouted for the boys and RB rushed from Cliff's room. Cliff was still in shock, resting in his bed.

"What the hell you doing Burt?" he asked from the top stair and motioned for the drunk to calm down.

Burt looked up at his friend, eyes narrowed, and asked, "What the hell are you doing here?"

As the words left his mouth, another priceless chair met its end—splintering into pieces that scattered across the floor like fallen debris from a war zone.

"I found out through the local cops. I'm *still* a cop, you know, and I couldn't find you. Somebody had to tell the kid. You sure as hell ain't in shape to do it," RB scolded him as he made his way down the stairs and tried to help Burt keep his balance.

Burt laughed under his breath, "Little bastards got nobody now." RB's flinched from not only the smell of liquor but Burt's unbathed sweaty body.

RB grabbed the larger man by the collar and shook him, "What the hells the matter with you? How can you say that? He's Susie's kid!"

Burt patted his pockets for a cigar but came up empty. Scowling, he muttered, then said louder, "Hope his uncle fries." The words hung in the air, sharp and deliberate.

Cliff, having regained his composure, stood at the bottom of the stairs, yelled back "You go to hell!"

RB whirled to face him, still holding onto the drunken Burt, "Cliff, man, get back up there!" and he pointed to the stairs, "Let me handle him."

Burt laughed, "Handle me? I'm goddamn Burt Williams, you going to *handle* me?" RB had enough, grabbing his pistol from the hidden holster inside his wind breaker, and in one motion crashed the butt down on Burt's head, spilling him onto the hardwood floor, his crumpled bulk falling among the splintered wood.

As Burt toppled to the floor, Cliff sneered as he walked up the staircase, "Hope you killed him."

RB pointed again, his eyebrows furrowed, nose flaring pointed again. Cliff, realizing RB had enough, obliged. The detective looked down at Burt and shook his head, "The things I get myself into," he said under his breath as he reached down for his old friend.

Days melted into months and soon the long, hot, humid Georgia summer came. Taped to the flaking, gray wall, hanging precariously, was a small calendar. It was the only reason Vern knew what day it was, much less what month. Death Row had no windows, nor was any other comfort considered in its design. It was a place built for waiting, not for living. Most of his time was occupied by reading whatever he could get his hands on, but the pickings on the reading cart, brought by his cell once a week, were slim.

Visits from his new lawyer had slowed since he met Jeff Black. In that time Calley had made only one visit and called him just once. The rest of his time, he merely lay on his back staring at the faded paint on the ceiling, wondering how he let things get so far out of control.

Calley's last phone call had sparked a flicker of hope, but that had been a couple of months ago, and now Vern had grown more worried with each passing day. Today, however, held a special privilege for the death row inmates. It was shaving day. It only came once every few weeks and Vern looked forward to each time the day rolled around. An old barber was brought in, and the inmates, usually limited to interacting with the guards and very rarely each other, got to talk with him. The old man told jokes and for those precious few minutes as he lathered him up, everything seemed normal. Each time, after the grey bearded barber completed the shave and a guard led Vern back to his lonely, cramped, damp cell, he would stare at the ceiling for the rest of the day, thinking about the old-fashioned razor he used. The old man conducted his business old school. He used shaving equipment that was considered obsolete by today's standards.

The device he used, an old safety razor, held a double-sided, thin razor blade and the bottom part of the handle turned to open the razor blade compartment. Vern liked it as he preferred it to those new disposable razors. The barber also used old-fashioned, hot lathered shaving soap that felt warm and comforting in contrast to the cold foam from a can. It was the same way Pops shaved and the way his father had taught Rof and himself to shave.

Quieter times like this, alone in his cell, he thought a lot about his father and his brother. Pops entered his mind often these past few days and weeks. Vern thought back to the times they spent together in his youth.

At one point, the three of them fished every day Pops didn't work during the summer. Even if Rof had baseball practice, they got up early, before daylight, making their way into either the bays along the Gulf or Holmes Creek. The creek flowed more like a small river than a creek and it was wide and deep enough for small, gas-powered Jon boats to carefully navigate the dark water.

The old man loved to target the elusive sucker fish. They were large, bony fish with mouths placed on the bottom of their heads, making them extremely difficult to hook. You had to bait them with potato sacks full of cornmeal—otherwise, finding more than one scattered sucker was a rare thing. Thinking back, Vern realized that his father loved preparing his favorite spots more than the catch itself.

They weren't that great to eat but they fought ferociously and that was what Pops loved. When Vern closed his eyes, he could see his father fighting one of the mighty creek fish and the smile that always appeared after he landed one of the dark colored monsters.

The small family rarely visited the famous Panama City Beach Strip together, but one memory from that place stuck with

Vern—a moment etched into his childhood, vivid and unshakable. The Miracle Strip, a stretch of Highway Ninety-Eight that paralleled the beach, was home to the tourist town's motels, hotels, restaurants, and plentiful tourist traps. One such trap left that moment etched in his memory.

In that memory, Vern, Rof, and their father cruised down the Panama City Beach Strip, passing by the towering castle facade of the local wax museum. They'd never actually gone inside—just driven past it now and then on the way to dinner. Outside the castle, actors dressed as Frankenstein's monster or Dracula wandered near the entrance, trying to lure tourists in for a fee.

Vern vividly remembered one time when Rof, still small enough to stand between them on the old truck's bench seat, spotted Frankenstein lurching toward the truck. The moment the creature moved, Rof let out a piercing scream and clawed at their father in terror, trying to scramble into his arms.

The image of his brother's panicked face flashed in Vern's mind, and he burst into laughter—loud, uncontrollable, echoing off the concrete walls of his tiny cell.

Moments later, a guard appeared, walking down the row to investigate the sudden outburst.

The guard barked at him to shut up, dragging his baton along the bars before making his way back to his seat and continued reading his magazine.

Vern's thoughts returned to the present and to his son and nephew. He had found out Susie died a few weeks after the funeral. With no visitors or phone calls except to immediate family, nobody was in a big hurry to let him know. Cliff wrote him a letter dated the day after the accident, but it had taken weeks to reach him.

In the letter, Cliff wrote that he wouldn't stop trying to free him—and that Burt was either high, drunk, or both nearly all the time now.

As Vern finished reading, his heart sank. Susie was gone. She was no longer there to protect either of them. Now, Burt was free to do whatever he pleased—and that terrified him more than anything.

He wrote a letter asking Calley to intervene somehow, but no reply had come. Some days, thoughts of escape crept into Vern's mind—but they vanished just as quickly as they appeared, chased off by the weight of reality. He pressed his fingers against the cold concrete wall; even in the heat of summer, it remained chilled, unforgiving.

He was stuck here.

Little hope remained in his soul for ever getting out of this miserable place. And with every waking hour, it wasn't his own fate that haunted him, it was the fate of his boys.

He wished he could hold onto good memories—like the one of the castle on the strip—but sleep never came at night. Instead, his mind raced, consumed by the thought of Cliff and

Casey, alone in the world with Burt Williams. It haunted him, every moment of every day, a constant weight pressing down on whatever was left of his peace.

Most nights held the same thing for him, sleeplessness and the worst thoughts penetrating his mind. Prison life was monotonous. The hard mat filling in for a mattress felt more like small, sharp knives stabbing him in the back, reminding him that his situation was indeed hopeless. Sleep was a luxury he could no longer afford. Even when he did manage to fall into a shallow, weak sleep, the quiet sounds of the night were deafening. The click-clack of the guard's shoes bore into his mind like a drill. The snoring inmates and their cries of anguish pierced his ears.

Burning in hell would be preferable to this, he often told himself and thoughts of ending it all crept in during the worst nights, beckoning like a warm fire on a cold winter's night.

After another long, sleepless night, the guard finally appeared and told him he had a visitor. Vern sprang up from the hard mattress without hesitation, arms already extended, ready for the shackles.

The guard chuckled, shaking his head. "You're gettin' institutionalized, Bruce."

But Vern didn't care. He didn't even respond. He just wanted to see who had come. And maybe—for a moment—feel like a human being again.

Ryan Calley, already seated at the metal table in the small, windowless room, rose to his feet as the door opened. As

Vern was led inside, Calley extended his hand, a faint, steady smile on his face. The guard shackled him to the floor and table but Vern couldn't erase the smile on his face, catching the lawyer off guard. The last time they met, Vern never even looked him in the eye.

Before Calley could speak Vern asked eagerly, "Any news from my boys?"

Calley shook his head, acknowledged the letter Vern had sent him, informing the inmate it would be a lengthy process to have them removed from the home they shared with Burt Williams. It was, after all, Vern who signed over custody,

He leaned in, quietly asking Vern "Where would they go? Does Susie have any family left?"

Vern rubbed his hands together as he told him her parents were dead, no siblings and her mother and father were only children. Her family was a dead end.

Calley raised his eyebrows, "I do bring good news, however. A motion to vacate has been reviewed to get you off death row. The judge reviewing the case decided that most of the evidence was circumstantial and indicated he would throw out the death penalty, lowering it to life without parole if you just plead guilty."

Vern jabbed a finger toward the lawyer, his voice edged with frustration. "I didn't do this—are we forgetting that?" he snapped, the agitation clear in his tone, his eyes burning with the weight of being unheard.

Calley locked eyes with his client, "Are we forgetting that they are going to *execute* you? Are we forgetting that this is Georgia, and they are just itching to kill you? I'm forgetting nothing, Mr. Bruce. I'm trying to save your life."

What little color holding on drained from Vern's face and he felt sick. Sometimes he forgot this game ended with him in the gas chamber or worse, the electric chair. He looked skyward only to see the same faded ceiling as in his cell, "What happens if I plead guilty and we find a way to prove my innocence?" he asked.

Calley grinned and said, "Henry Alford."

Vern shot the lawyer a perplexed look, "Who the hell is Henry Alford?"

"Henry Alford plead guilty to murder but maintained his innocence. It hasn't been used in Georgia, but it does give us a precedent. It went all the way to the Supreme Court, and it allowed him to plead guilty and if evidence ever came up that exonerated him, it would *have* to be allowed. That is, of course, if his lawyer were held to be competent. I think we have that covered." Calley leaned back in his chair, enormously proud of himself.

Vern, unconvinced but willing to try anything, rubbed his hands together again, "How long will all of this take?" he asked, trying not to inflate his hopes.

"Give me a month and you'll be in general population." he boasted. Vern was still hesitant and asked about Jeff Black's funding. "All paid for. My fees are paid directly from Jefferson Black through a couple of back channels, of course."

It was the only course of action Vern could see that didn't end up with him buried next to Patty Lee in West Palm. That thought reminded him that he needed to change his will. He wanted to be buried next to Pops and beside Rof's empty casket. He asked Calley if he could take care of that, and the lawyer indicated he could.

Vern gave him his blessing to begin the process of his pleading guilty, and just like that, the meeting was over.

Back in his cell, he sat in the stillness and began to think. If he could get off Death Row, he'd have regular visitors, access to a phone, and most importantly, the prison library. That alone could open doors—new possibilities, new strategies, maybe even a real chance at freedom. But the thought unsettled him.

He was placing his hope in someone he didn't know… and didn't trust. And that bothered him more than he cared to admit. There had to be something behind this beyond the flimsy story of Jefferson Black. He didn't believe for a second the two of them were related. He did believe, however, that Black wanted something. The only moment that Black was truthful in their meeting was when he said it was related to Vern's money.

Patty Lee left her entire fortune to Casey and when he got out of this prison, he would be in control of everything until Casey was twenty-one. He snapped his fingers. First things first, he told himself. He would ride this as far as Calley took him and worry about crossing that bridge when he came to it.

Chapter 19

With his spine tingling and the hair on his arms stiff, Kennedy walked through the empty warehouse. He wanted to vomit as he walked past the very spot where he watched another man's life extinguished by a sudden gunshot to the head. Mateo Diaz sat in a worn chair in what looked like an old breakroom, watching a flickering television mounted in the far corner. The only light in the small, cramped space came from the screen, casting a dim, bluish glow that danced across the walls and flickered across his face.

The Colombian didn't take his eyes from the glowing screen as he spoke, "Hello, my friend," Mateo said, cheerfully, "Baseball is one of my true loves. We love playing the game in Columbia, but nobody offers our boys a chance because, you know, *Columbia.*" Mateo shrugged, turning his attention to his guest. "Tell me, Mr. Kennedy. How is fishing?"

Surprised the Columbian asked about fishing, the old sailor stumbled across a few words about the Cobia run up on the northern Gulf Coast coming up in a few months. Mateo grinned, narrowing his focus on Kennedy, seemingly genuinely interested. He slid a shot glass filled to the rim with rum towards Kennedy and offered him a seat. The sailor quickly accepted and grabbed the glass.

"No, Mr. Kennedy," he said as Kennedy consumed the alcohol with a large gulp, "The *other* fishing you've been doing."

Kennedy took a deep breath, wiping his lips, and said with a quivering voice, "No problems, Mr. Diaz..."

Diaz quickly cut him off, "Please, Mr. Kennedy, DIE-AZ not the Hispanic corruption DEE-AZ. My family arrived in Columbia via Spain only a few decades ago. We are more Spanish than Columbian." Diaz motioned for him to continue.

"Sorry, Mr. DI-az," Kennedy corrected his pronunciation and the Columbian nodded, "Just like you told me. We take out a group, just like normal and make the drop while on the run. Most of the time the clients are either puking in the bathroom below deck or stone drunk by then." Diaz cocked his head to the side, a silent cue laced with meaning. Kennedy saw it and nodded in response, understanding exactly what was being asked without a single word exchanged.

"If they are on deck, I distract them with some bullshit about dolphins or something."

Diaz smiled, "Burt Williams?"

Kennedy shook his head, "He ain't no hands-on boss like Old Man Clark, I'll tell you that. But since the guy lost his wife, I ain't seen him."

"Yes," Diaz said with a hint of regret in his voice, "I have heard this. I tried to send him word of colendiencia but he doesn't consider me a friend." Diaz stood and extended his hand to Kennedy and the sailor meekly shook it. "Keep up the good work, my friend. I have a little bonus for you." Diaz motioned towards the darkened door and a tall, slender man in a tan suit appeared with a bag and placed it on Kennedy's lap. The zipper on the bag lay open halfway and Kennedy's eyes widened when he saw a stack of bills hanging out.

"Th, Thank You, Mr. Diaz," Kennedy managed.

Diaz shook his hand feverishly, "Of course. I take care of my *friends*. You've told no one of what occurred here or on the docks?" he asked, turning his attention to the baseball game still playing on the television. Kennedy once again stumbled across some words and finally satisfied his host with a long-winded no. Diaz nodded and motioned towards the door.

"Thank you, Wallace," Diaz said coldly.

As he began to stand, Kennedy froze for a second. He hadn't heard his first name in a long time. His mother was the last person to use it before she passed. As he got to his feet he nodded again to Diaz and made his way out the door. The sweat he hadn't noticed forming on his forehead dripped into his eyes. He wiped the sweat away and picked up the pace.

Diaz focused on the ballgame. His mind, however, wandered elsewhere. Kennedy was a scared man. Scared men were useful if they feared the right things, but it wouldn't be long before the DEA caught wind of the sailor's dealings with Burt Williams and, eventually, himself. His fear could then possibly lead the old sailor in the wrong direction. Diaz cursed under his breath as the pitcher gave up a three-run homer. The distraction was only momentary as he couldn't shake the bad feeling he had about his new business partner.

Diaz genuinely liked Kennedy and deep down didn't want to end his life. But, in this business, he learned long ago that you couldn't put personal feelings ahead of business. People died for that more than any other reason. His predecessor got caught up in things he shouldn't have. Eventually everything caught up with him. His bosses *knew* about Phillipe' because he was honest with them from the start.

Diaz knew that Phillipe' was a nerve that could be exposed, so he took the possibility out the equation. The bosses protected him—under the condition that Diaz would take over operations in Florida. It was part of the deal, and Diaz had agreed. But he wasn't naïve. He knew their protection came with strings. They weren't just shielding him for his benefit, they were protecting themselves. If he ever betrayed them, all it would take was a single phone call, a quiet signal, and both his life and Kennedy's would be over in an instant. Diaz wasn't going to let that happen. Not now. Not ever.

Burt Williams was quickly becoming another exposed nerve. He was unpredictable, volatile, and dangerous. If his downward spiral had begun with the death of his wife, Diaz could have accepted that. He might've even found a way to help the man claw his way back. But the truth was harder to ignore.

This decline had started well before that tragedy, and it was accelerating. Burt wasn't just grieving, he was unraveling. A redneck, want-to-be player trying to act like a kingpin in a game far beyond his control. And that kind of liability couldn't be ignored. Diaz wasn't about to risk his life, or Phillipe's, on a man like Williams.

With a quiet breath, he clicked off the television, the room falling into darkness. He sat motionless, his thoughts circling like vultures, until finally he snapped his fingers. A second later, the man in the tan suit appeared silently in the doorway, waiting for instruction.

The sunlight streaming through the skylight high above the floor illuminated the man just enough that Diaz made sure he looked into his eyes when he spoke. "Do you know the current location of Williams?" he asked, and the man nodded. "Retrieve him and bring him here," he paused for a second, "If he resists, you may employ whatever tactic you need."

The man in the suit tilted his head as if he wanted to ask a question, but didn't dare. Diaz, sensing his man's hesitation, put his mind at ease, "You let *me* worry about the Brazilian and his American *master*."

The man tipped his cap, his mind at ease, set off without hesitation to fulfill his mission. Alone once again, Diaz clicked on the television to find the game over and some dumb American show had replaced it. He didn't care. He just wanted the screen's glow to think help him think in the darkness. *Burt Williams doesn't have long to live the rest of his life,* he thought.

Diaz remembered his trip to that beautiful city in Alabama and his journey through the countryside afterwards. The Columbian laughed aloud as he remembered pulling away from the gas station parking lot and watching the DEA agents pull in behind him. He finished his laughter and picked up the phone.

Burt was in the middle of taking another long swig of tomato juice when RB rushed through the kitchen door.

"RB, what a nice surprise," Burt said sarcastically.

RB took off his ball cap, placed it on the rack beside the door and glared at Burt as he entered. "Good to see you too, buddy," RB replied through a scowl.

The two glared at each other. Both men emanating disdain for the other as RB asked if Cliff was upstairs.

Burt sighed deeply, the weight of it heavy in his chest, and pointed toward the deck. "Out there," he muttered, his voice low and tired.

"No school again today?" RB asked, already knowing the answer.

"Both of them went homeschool, buddy, you know that." Burt shot his old friend a sideways grin.

RB shook his head, replying, "*Bullshit* school. Where is Case?"

Burt shrugged his shoulders and said "Probably down at the Surf Shop. Kid is pretty much running things down there now."

Once again RB just shook his head, "God knows what he's *running* over there."

Burt smiled sarcastically, raising the glass of thick, red juice to his lips. "Parenting, huh?" he scoffed, then laughed as he finished it off in one long swallow.

RB didn't respond. He just shook his head and walked past Burt, leaving the bitterness behind him.

Out on the deck, he found Cliff sitting silently in a chair, eyes fixed on the horizon, watching the waves roll onto the beach in a steady, soothing rhythm.

RB patted his chest as he inhaled a deep, salty breath, "Morning, bud," he said as he approached. Cliff didn't move, holding his gaze upon the blue waters of the Atlantic.

"Hey RB. The water is kinda rough today, huh?"

RB looked out over the water and saw the waves were higher than usual. "Guess Casey and his buddies down at the shop are having a ball today."

Cliff laughed and RB turned back to him, one of his eyebrows raised above the other. Cliff finally looked up from the water, "They don't give a crap about surfing RB. You know what goes on down there. Unc would be losing his mind if he knew."

RB tightened his lips, his eyebrow still resting high on his forehead. He nodded in agreement. "Speaking of Vern, *we* still need to get working on that. The Row takes a while, but each day we ain't working is another day closer..." RB took a seat next to Cliff, "To you know..."

"I just can't get her off my mind, RB." Even with sunglasses covering his eyes, RB could tell Cliff was already near tears. "We lost so much time. Now we're never gonna get it back. NEVER!"

RB took another deep breath of sea air and pulled up a chair next to the young man. He gently put his hand on his arm.

"Son," RB said, looking up at the sky, "I lost my parents when I was young too. Different circumstances, but it *hurt* just the same. I lost a lot of time thinking about them, sitting around, just like you.

Cliff shook his head and told him, "Monday. I promise, RB."

RB patted Cliff's shoulder, "I'll be ready early. You be too." The detective rose and started back towards the kitchen door when he heard the thud and breaking glass. He instinctively reached for his gun.

When he swung the door open, Cliff followed behind him, but RB shooed him back. Burt, lying on the floor, the glass shattered in a thousand pieces, moaned loudly. The man in the tan suit stood over him, pistol drawn but backwards in his hand.

"Hands!" RB yelled. The man complied and placed his weapon on the countertop. "Who the hell are you and what the hell is going on here?" RB yelled, still holding Cliff outside with the palm of his free hand.

"Mr. Ramsay Brown?" the man in the suit asked, his voice heavily accented but calm.

"Yeah, again, who the hell are you?" RB his voice loud, but still in control. The detective shook his pistol slightly to remind his opponent it was still aimed at his torso.

The man in the suit raised his hands slowly in surrender and said, "My *name* is not important." The man, his voice still calm continued, "Who I *work* for is extremely important and what happens in the next couple of minutes will impact all of our lives." He tilted his head towards the window indicating the other gentleman, unseen by RB and Cliff as he snuck up behind them. RB turned his head, and the other man lifted his shirt as sunlight reflected off the white handle of the revolver tucked into his waist.

"My employer, Mateo Diaz, needs to speak with Mr. Williams. *Quite* urgently. He didn't want to comply with my instructions and..." he paused, choosing his words carefully. "Mr. Diaz simply stated that I do what was necessary to bring this man to him." He paused for a moment for his words to sink in before continuing, "Now, Mr. Brown. I know who you *are*. Biloxi detective, moonlighting as a private investigator, old friend of the family. You are a long way from Mississippi, my friend."

RB didn't lower his pistol, but his demeanor eased a bit, "Vacation."

The man in the suit smiled, nodded, and said, "If you don't mind my associate and your young friend joining us, *please*." He made a gesture to lower the weapon and this time RB complied. Cliff and the other man entered the room. Cliff's eyes wide, his hands shaking as he looked at RB.

RB gave Cliff a slight grin, hoping to put the teenager at ease.

"Just Burt Williams business," he said calmly. "Go on upstairs—I'll see you Monday."

He motioned toward the stairs, and without a word, Cliff took off, his footsteps quick and light. RB listened as the boy reached the top, the door closed with a quiet thud, and the soft *click* of the lock followed.

"I'm coming with you." RB demanded. The man rubbed his chin and sighed. "Excuse me if I hesitate, Mr. Brown. You *are* a police officer and your presence at my employer's place of business may not be welcome."

RB shrugged and replied, "*I'll* deal with that."

"As you wish. But I warn you," the man in the suit told him, "Mr. Diaz does not take well to surprises."

RB knelt beside his friend, gently lifting him to his feet and wrapping an arm around his shoulder for support. Together, they moved slowly toward the waiting car.

Burt glanced up and let out a dry chuckle when he saw it.

"Same piece of shit Diaz came in last time," he muttered, a crooked smile tugging at his lips.

The man in the suit joined him in his laughter, "It's a classic."

Burt snickered again, "Classic POS," and passed back out.

RB drug him the rest of the way, shoving him into the back seat. "Ain't easy being a friend to this asshole." Both Colombians laughed a little as they got in the front, leaving RB with his passed-out, bleeding friend in the back.

Burt's condition improved during the drive and RB tried to clean the blood from the top of his friend's head but succeeded in only smearing it, making the mess worse. Burt protested each time he touched the tender spot with his handkerchief, so RB gave up and said, "Just look like a fool then."

The man in the tan suit's friend hadn't spoken since revealing himself in the doorway but leaned over to his friend and said "Como un matrimonio de ancianos."

RB knew very little spanish, but Burt had picked up some during his time in Florida and held up his middle finger to the two men in the front seat. They both laughed and RB shot a confused look towards Burt. "Like a married couple," Burt grunted.

RB laughed and held up his hand, "Well..."

Both men occupying the front seat turned deadly serious as the warehouse came into view and once again RB's detective instincts kicked in and his level of nervousness increased. He wondered what Burt had done to warrant such treatment. *Probably Burt being Burt*, he thought.

RB's body tensed as they were led to the small break room. and he felt for his gun, feeling naked without it. As they entered, the man in the suit flicked the light switch revealing Mateo Diaz but keeping the two Americans in the dark.

"Mr. Brown, I was not expecting *you*," Diaz said as he gazed intently at the man in the suit. The man in the suit's companion had not followed them in and right then the man wished he hadn't either. A smile brushed across Diaz' face and the man relaxed and exhaled silently, leaving the room. "Please gentlemen, have a seat," he said politely as he pointed to a couple of empty chairs across from his. Diaz turned slightly in his chair so he could face them.

"Mr. DIE-az, I apologize, but I couldn't let my friend leave in this shape," Burt hadn't said a word, but he was quickly sobering up and rubbing the top of his head.

"Our meeting was inevitable, Mr. Brown, and I appreciate your *correct* pronunciation of my family's name. Your reputation as a renowned detective holds true," Diaz responded, and RB nodded.

Diaz pointed to the door. "But I must ask you to wait in the room with *my* friends. Burt, Mr. Williams, and I have business to discuss, and you could listen in, but then I would have to kill you," Diaz said coldly. RB froze until a broad, toothy smile appeared on the Columbian's face, "Just a little American humor, Mr. Brown," he said as he again pointed outside. "Show Mr. Brown our best hospitality," he said calmly.

As if summoned by the words, the man stepped out of the darkness, just as swiftly and silently as he had vanished into it earlier—his presence sudden, deliberate, and unmistakable.

RB left the room, glancing back to Burt and the gangster gave him a thumbs up. Diaz turned his attention to Burt. He stood, opened a cabinet and pulled out a towel and a bandage. "For your injury. I had hoped it wouldn't come to that, Mr. Williams."

Burt grabbed the towel and began wiping what he could of the dried blood but handed the bandage back to Diaz, "I'll live," he growled.

Diaz shrugged and sat down next to Burt. "I'll get right to it, Mr. Williams. You wouldn't allow it before but since we are in each other's company let me offer my condolences for your wife." Burt just nodded as Diaz moved on, "Business then. Our operations with Mr. Clark and to a lesser extent, his daughter for her fleeting time, ran smoothly because there was someone visible to those that worked for us." Diaz leaned in, snapping his fingers to keep Burt alert enough to listen, "The operation was small and the boats he provided helped tremendously. Now we only need the boats to get our money safely out of the country." Burt's eyes closed but reopened rapidly a of couple times. Unfazed, Diaz continued, "The Brazilians help us with product up through Mexico. *Your* end of that operation ended yet we continue to pay you the same amount for less risk. That was to show you respect as you assumed control." Diaz stopped abruptly, stood up and walked a couple of steps in front of Burt, his anger steadily increasing, "Now, you disappear for months? Your own people don't know where you go or who they answer to? This is how you run your end? WAKE UP estupido!"

Burt leaned forward, trying to stand, but his head felt like it was splitting open from the wound and pain shot through his whole body as he eased back into the chair. He looked up at Diaz smiling, "I *am* an asshole. You got that part right. But if you ever talk down to me again you son-of-a-bitch I'll kill you where you stand. I ain't afraid of your Columbian ass. If you *could* touch me, I'd be dead already. So shut the hell up and take me home. I'll run this shit the way I want to." Burt grinned as he finished, looking up at Diaz. He asked politely, "You got a Goody Powder?"

Diaz took a knee in front of Burt, their noses almost touching. "Your Brazilian friends won't protect you if you screw up Williams. You think Black gives a shit about you?" The Colombian grinned, "You are a loose end, my friend. You have enemies not only in Columbia but here and in Mississippi also. Not *everyone* agreed with what happened with Lopez. Be careful and do your damned job!"

Burt licked the small amount of blood that had dripped to the corner of his mouth and smiled, "You may take us home now." He reached into his pocket and rolled what was left of a cigar between his fingers before putting it in the corner of his mouth.

"Take them home," was all Diaz said, his voice cold and final as he motioned toward the door. Then he turned his back on them and walked away, saying nothing more, the sound of his footsteps fading into silence.

Burt laughed as he rejoined RB, winked his eye at the detective and sneered, "Nothing to worry about hoss."

As RB walked toward the exit, something made him glance back.

He spotted Diaz, standing motionless, his eyes locked onto them with a gaze so cold and piercing it felt like it burned straight through his soul.

"Uh-huh," RB muttered, more to himself than anyone else, and kept walking.

Chapter 20

Casey had been avoiding home as much as possible in recent days and weeks. His baptism into Burt's world had shaken him to the core, and every instinct told him to keep his distance.

Instead, he threw himself into the only place that still felt somewhat his own—the surf shop. He spent nearly all his time with the crew that lingered there, a ragtag bunch who had once kept to the shadows out back. But ever since Dell's disappearance, things had shifted.

Despite barely being a teenager, Casey now ran the place. He called the shots, and no one questioned it. He had become the de facto leader of their small, unruly band. Even the employees— older, more experienced—had started showing him a level of respect that surprised him. And he liked it.

Casey held up his hands in disbelief when his older cousin walked through the door, "Well, well if ain't Cliff. Want to learn to surf, cuz?" he asked him sarcastically.

Cliff pointed to the back and said forcefully, "We need to talk. Now." The guys lining the wall all turned to look at Casey, their faces a mix of shock and confusion—one or two with jaws dropped wide open.

They weren't used to anyone talking to Casey like that. Even if they didn't fear *him*, they sure as hell feared *Burt*, and that fear carried weight. That respect—earned or not—had trickled down to Casey. And everyone in the room knew it.

Casey lifted an eyebrow but didn't protest, motioning for Cliff to lead the way. Casey shut the door behind the two, his face red and his anger growing.

"Don't talk like that in front of my friends again," Casey warned his cousin. Cliff grunted, shrugged his shoulders and pointed his finger at his cousin.

"Look," Cliff said, "something went down at home this morning. A couple of guys came by and *took* Burt with them. But you know Burt, he didn't go quietly. They knocked him unconscious. RB was there and went with them to look after him but when they got back, neither said nothing about where they went or what happened. RB told me to keep quiet."

Casey shook his head, "Ain't no telling what he's gotten into. None of my, or your, business."

"Yes, it is your business, Casey. You and Burt are tight ain't you? *You* need to find out what's going on before we all get killed."

The images of Dell's lifeless body, weighted down by blocks, sinking into the dark water of the Atlantic rushed into Casey's thoughts and he said, "I ain't getting involved." Casey looked and pointed a finger at his cousin, "And if you had any sense, you wouldn't either. Let all this shit go, Cliff. My dad, your dad, live your life man. We're rich. Don't you realize that? We can do what we want and get away with it."

Cliff grimaced, gently putting his hand on Casey's shoulder, "We're better than *that*. Unc taught us better than *that*."

Casey snatched away from Cliff, his face glowing red, and he put his finger in Cliff's chest, "He's in prison for murder, Cliff! He killed two people and I bet he had something to do with *my* mom's murder." Casey paused for a second as he peered into this cousin's eyes and said coldly, "Probably your mother's too."

Cliff took a deep breath. "Maybe we are cursed, Case."

Casey's anger turned to laughter, "Cursed with millions."

Cliff spun on his heel and stormed through the door, the force of it swinging wide behind him as he disappeared from view, anger radiating off him like heat.

Casey followed him, saw his friends still looking at him and yelled, "Next time I'll kick your ass!" He glanced at his entourage, chin held high, a wry smile spread confidently across his face. But deep in the recesses of his mind, the scared young kid still lurked—silent, desperate, screaming for his cousin's help.

No one could hear him. Not even Cliff.

Cliff fell into the seat, slamming the car door and turning the key. He revved the engine, taking off leaving traces of rubber and a whisp of black smoke as his tires found the highway. He intended to go straight back home but found himself headed north on A1A, hugging the coast.

He drove with his windows down, letting the cool ocean breeze flow through his hair and didn't stop until he saw a sign reading Titusville. He eased the car to a stop in a sandy spot just beside the highway. The wide waters of the Indian River flowed in front of him and from this spot he could see the unmistakable

Vehicle Assembly Building on the horizon. The massive building, standing proud on the grounds of the Cape, could be seen for miles. Cliff sat, the sun beaming down from above, lost in his thoughts. Since he earned his driver's license, this was the place he often came to get away from Casey, Burt and even, sometimes, RB.

As he sat, staring at the colossal building, he thought of what little family he had left. Now there was only Casey and his uncle. He shuddered when he thought about how he was losing them too. RB had become like family to him, more of a father figure than that deadbeat Burt, but he wasn't blood.

He missed his mother more with each passing day. From the day she came back into his life, she asked him for nothing but a second chance. She was genuine, kind and she loved him unconditionally. Cliff felt she was the only *pure* soul that he ever knew. He had learned about her background and the choices she had to make as a teenager, back when she was completely alone with a child she couldn't take care of. Cliff never blamed her for leaving him with his uncle. It was the only choice the young girl had.

Now she, too, was gone. He closed his eyes, and her smiling face emerged in the swirling kaleidoscope of color and shadow behind his eyelids. The wind whispered through the open window of the car, and for a fleeting moment, he heard her voice—soft, familiar, impossibly close. She was everywhere. And nowhere all at once.

He leaned his head back, his eyes still closed, running his hand slowly across his face. RB was right. He had to start working on his uncle's case again. He had to get his mind back on track. He had to get away from problems that seemingly crashed upon him at every turn. He had to get back in school. His mother would want that. She wanted him to make something out of himself and he envisioned her, standing outside the car, smiling at him but her hands locked on her hips with *that* look. The look that told him that sitting there, feeling sorry for himself, wasn't going to cut it.

A voice startled him from his car's open window. He jumped to attention, trying to catch his breath. His attention had been so intently focused on his thoughts he hadn't noticed the young girl walking up beside him.

"What are you doing?" she asked in a giggle.

He didn't know how long she had been watching him, and he didn't know what to say but managed, "Just thinking."

Her head tilted slightly to the side, and a crooked little smile played across her pretty face. "Most people use this area for other things," she giggled again, her eyes twinkling with mischief.

Cliff, momentarily mesmerized by the way her curly brown hair danced in the wind, took a breath and pulled himself together. "Well, I'm not from here," he said, his voice steadying. "Drove up from West Palm—just needed a place to park and think."

He pointed toward the building in the distance, a faint smile tugging at his lips.

"Plus, I like the view."

The girl's crooked little grin widened into a full, toothy smile. She looked to be about the same age as Cliff, maybe a year younger, her eyes bright with curiosity and something playful just beneath the surface. He noticed she held a pair of shoes in her hands. Glancing down, he noticed her toes wiggling playfully in the sand.

"I'm Cliff," he said awkwardly as he stuck his hand through the window, waiting for her response.

She shifted the pair of shoes from one hand to the other, looked out at the river and then back at him, "Katrin," she replied, "but everybody calls me Katie." She placed her hand in his, and Cliff—doing his best not to seem too eager—shook it gently, noting the softness of her touch. It lingered with him, subtle but unmistakable.

When he finally released her hand, he noticed she ran her finger along the top of his as she let go. He pointed to her bare feet, "What are you doing out here?" he asked.

She looked back across the river and said, "Waiting on my dad. He works over there. At the Cape. I usually walk by the river in the afternoons waiting for him. I volunteer over at the rec center as a lifeguard during the summer and he picks me up."

Cliff couldn't contain his excitement, "He works for NASA?"

The young brunette grinned, her teeth sparkling in the sun's waning glow, "He's an engineer over there," she paused for a second and looked towards the road, "There he comes. I better walk towards him. Don't think he'll like me standing here talking to a *stranger*."

Cliff scrambled to find a scrap of paper, quickly finding an old receipt and a pencil in the console. "How about your number, Katie?"

She smiled, grabbing the scrap paper, quickly jotting it down. "Call me," she said as she handed it back to him, her smile still glowing in the faint sunlight. With one more quick smile, she started walking down the road to meet her father.

Before she had taken but a couple of steps, Cliff said, "I don't even know your last name."

"I don't know yours either *daydreamer*," she responded mischievously.

"Bruce," he said simply.

She turned her head slightly, her expression unreadable, and for a moment, Cliff couldn't tell if the name meant anything to her or if she was just being polite.

"Call me and find out," she said, laughing as she turned to meet her father.

Casey didn't linger around the surf shop for too long that afternoon. The rest of the guys went out to sell but he went home. He found Burt sitting on the deck, in what had become his usual chair, with a glass of whiskey in his hand. Beside him on the small table was a mirror. Burt scrambled to put it away, but Casey noticed it anyway.

"Rough day?" Casey asked as he reached for the whiskey bottle and refilled Burt's glass.

"Ain't been seeing much of you lately, kid. You been hiding?" Burt sneered.

Casey took off his sunglasses, shifting his eyes between Burt and the wooden boards under his feet. The frightened kid emerging once again, "I ain't used to doing what we did, Burt. I ain't proud of it and I'm scared."

Burt reached into his shirt pocket and pulled out a cigar, then offered one to Casey, but he declined. The gangster stuck his in the corner of his mouth while he spoke. "Well, you better *get* used to it kid. We're about to be in a war."

Casey took a step back, his eyes wide, "What the hell you talking about?" he asked sheepishly.

Burt reached over, picked up a box of matches, struck one and lit his cigar, letting the match burn down to his fat fingers. He smiled and looked Casey in the eye. "We're fixing to take over *everything* around here, kid. Get rid of some Columbian monkeys and make a lot of money."

Sometimes Burt forgot that Casey was only about to be fourteen, but when he did, he reminded himself that he was younger than the boy the first time he put a bullet in a man's brain. "Don't worry kid, we got help coming. I called up to Biloxi this afternoon," he laughed, "The calvary's coming." He leaned over, pulling Casey in. The kid felt like throwing up when the smell of Burt's breath hit him, but he tried not to wince. "I only got one job for you," Burt said, "Make sure your damned cousin and RB stay out of the way."

Casey stared at his shoes, trying not to smell Burt's odor. "I told him this morning to stay out of that shit. Enjoy life," Casey said meekly.

Burt reached and grabbed the boy by the collar, "Well you un-tell him that! Tell him that he needs to keep working on it. Keep him busy. That'll keep RB out of it too." He shook the boy slightly, "Got it?"

Casey trembled as he tried to speak. All he could do was just nod. The gangster, his already bulky body swelling even more with the alcohol and cocaine, took a long swig from his full whiskey glass, drinking all but what covered the very bottom of the glass. He shook the small amount and said under his breath, "This ain't going to take long."

When the sun rose over the Atlantic Ocean the next morning, Casey, not wanting to tangle with Burt or Cliff, was already out of the house and at the surf shop. The shop wasn't open on Sundays, but his buddies always showed up to hang around and see what kind of trouble they could get into. Before any of them arrived, however, Casey saw an old, beat-up car ease into the parking lot.

Casey felt uneasy, not only because he didn't recognize the car, but also what Burt told him the day before. "Damn, I need to keep a gun around," he said aloud to himself.

Casey watched as a chubby—not fat, but just chubby enough to notice—Hispanic man climbed out of the beat-up jalopy. The stranger glanced around for a moment before making his way toward the building.

He didn't try the door. Instead, he knocked gently on the glass and stood there patiently, smiling into the dim interior. Casey hesitated, unsure. But something about the man's calm demeanor told him this visit wasn't random. He probably *knew* Casey was inside. With a cautious breath, Casey reached over and unlocked the door.

"We're closed on Sundays, sir," Casey said as sternly as he could manage, "Come back tomorrow."

The man respectfully took a step back, asking, "Casey Bruce?"

Casey, his eyes wide, waiting for a gun, knife, or something, felt his muscles tighten, adrenaline surging through his body, "That's right," he responded, ready to slam the door and flee at the first hint of danger.

"Well, then. You're the *man* I wanted to meet today." the man responded, his smile broad, "My name is Mateo Diaz, a friend of the family you might say. Let's talk," Diaz eased past Casey welcoming himself inside the shop. "Let's use the office in the back." As he brushed by the kid, he purposely ran his arm along Casey's, feeling the boy's tension.

"Don't worry young man," he told Casey in a soothing voice, "I'm a *friend*." Trying to calm his young host's nerves, he complimented the shop as he walked towards the back, gesturing for Casey to follow. "But lock the door before you do," he commanded, "We don't need any of your little weed dealer friends interrupting us."

"Yes, sir," Casey said instinctively, immediately regretting it because if Burt taught him anything it was to not bow down to anyone. Diaz, recognizing the mistake, smiled back at Casey. The two sat down in a couple of chairs on the same side of the small desk in the confined office. The building was dim, shadows stretching across the walls, but enough light filtered in through the front windows for them to see each other's expressions—subtle, cautious, and searching. Diaz, still sensing the kid's apprehension in Casey's body language, tried to keep the boy at ease by reveling at the surf boards on the wall, but there was *business* at hand.

"Young Casey Bruce, son of the infamous Vernon Bruce," Diaz started, "Ward of Burt Williams."

Casey's eyebrows lifted in confusion, his eyes narrowing slightly as he tried to make sense of the unexpected visitor standing in front of him. "I guess that would be me," he said in as deep a voice as possible, trying to act as tough as his nerves would allow.

Diaz didn't break his smile, his confident demeanor radiating from every inch of him as he spoke.

"I've been wanting to meet the man with the real power in the Bruce family." His tone was smooth, almost playful—but laced with something unmistakably serious beneath the charm.

"I don't know what the hell you mean, Mr. Diaz," he said, his voice edged with a mix of confusion and caution.

Diaz put his finger to his mouth, carefully orchestrating his own body language. "Your guardian, Burt Williams, holds no *real* power over you. He only holds sway over you now because of your age." The Colombian stood up, walked to the door, slowly turned, and asked, "What has he told you of our business together?"

Diaz slowly pulled a small pistol from his pocket and set it on the desk beside him with deliberate ease. Casey tensed instantly, his body stiffening, and Diaz knew the move had served its purpose. He had the young man's full attention now—but he also wanted to keep him calm.

Resting a finger lightly on the weapon's handle, Diaz smiled and said smoothly, "It was just bothering me, my young friend—poking me in the ribs. Pay it no attention."

Casey couldn't take his eyes off the pistol as he responded, "I don't even know who you are, Mr. Diaz. That's the truth."

Diaz ran his fingers though his dark hair, "He didn't have a conversation with you yesterday about his plans?" Casey froze, not knowing how to respond. His mouth opened, but no words came out—just a shallow breath, caught somewhere between confusion and fear.

Diaz nodded, "Rest assured, I know his plans, young Mr. Bruce. I know what he *intends* to do. Your silence reveals the truth," Diaz said coldly. Casey once again tried to speak, but, again, he couldn't. He couldn't produce any sound, let alone form words. His throat tightened, and all that emerged was silence, thick and heavy.

Diaz continued, "I only tell you this because I don't want you or your cousin hurt. He walked back to where Casey was seated, "You can help me with that." He knelt in front of the kid, "Burt Williams is an evil man, my young friend, an evil man with evil plans." The Colombian reached up and put his hands on Casey's shoulders, "I know what he made you do."

Casey's eyes dropped to the floor, his apprehension melting into shame. "I can help you, if you let me." Diaz patted Casey on the shoulder as he stood up to leave pausing to smile once again at the kid, repeating, "If you let me."

Diaz said nothing more. The Colombian didn't look back as he made his way from the building. Casey didn't move. He didn't know what to do. If this man *knew*, that meant *he* was the one who killed Dell. The thought terrified him—gripping his chest like a vice, cold and unrelenting, as it settled deep in his gut.

When he was sure the car had pulled away, he sprinted from the office, locking the door and throwing a glance in every direction.

As much as he had tried to stop it, the emotions crashed over him, unstoppable and suffocating. He turned his back to the door, sliding down the cool glass until he hit the floor. With his elbows on his knees, he buried his face in his hands. And then the tears came—silent at first, then harder, as the weight he'd been carrying finally broke him open.

Diaz' smile vanished from his face as he started the engine and sped down the road, leaving a hazy layer of smoke behind him. He banged his fist on the steering wheel and cursed. He hated using children like this. He hated doing it in his native Columbia and he hated that he had to resort to it in this country.

Diaz could hardly remember his childhood. Those early years were little more than shadows now. His life before the one he lived now felt like a distant dream, blurred and unreachable, long since buried beneath the weight of everything he'd become.

His own childhood tale was all too common in the harsh reality of Columbia. The only thing he remembered about his mother and father was the fear that spread across their faces as he and his brother were dragged away. He could remember the anguish emanating from their bodies as they limply collapsed to the ground, knowing they could do nothing to save their children. He often thought about them. That one last glance at their faces seared into his memory. He presumed they died a long time ago, perhaps that fateful day was their last on Earth. He would never know for sure.

Everything he did from that day to now was merely a means to an end. Every evil thing he was forced to do was performed in the hope that one day he and Phillipe' would be free. That day was finally in sight. He pulled into an empty parking lot, as most stores were closed on Sunday, and pulled up next to a car with two occupants. He simply waved as he passed by. The car began moving and so did his plan.

Chapter 21

"They're trying to make this beach as beautiful as the ones in Alabama and Florida," Veck Baxter said, his tone dry as he stared out the windshield at the shoreline. "But somehow, it just doesn't work."

He sat beside Jeff Black in the parked car, both men watching the slow rhythm of the waves as tourists wandered the sand, unaware of the conversation unfolding just across the street.

Black looked out across the water noticing the color wasn't emerald-green but a darker shade of blue. "Reminds me of the Atlantic side in Florida," he returned.

Baxter grinned, "Brown sand there too, but here, at least, they try to make it look *inviting*."

A stiff breeze blew in from the Gulf causing the palm trees scattered about to sway. Baxter enjoyed watching the scene around him unfold. Families with kids, and a whole bunch of different types of people making their way to the beach across the road put a smile on his face. The sun, high and warm on this summer morning made the midday air hot, humid but the breeze blowing in from the water made sitting in the car tolerable. At least for a while.

Baxter turned to his friend, "Well, how did it go?"

Black pulled the ballcap over his eyes and leaned back in his seat. He tilted his head towards the window, catching the breeze on his face. "Williams has made a lot of enemies in this town lately. The gentleman I talked to says a lot of people that considered him a friend, feel *slighted* and left out of his Florida enterprises."

Baxter tapped his cane on the floorboard, "So, they are wanting to play ball?" he asked. Black raised an eyebrow, rubbing his chin. Baxter laughed when he clarified, "I mean do they want to *work* with us?"

Black, catching his friend's meaning, grinned and gave a slow nod. He appreciated the layers hidden in Southern speech— the way a simple sentence could carry a dozen meanings. He loved the complexities the Southern version of the English language offered, where tone, timing, and context said just as much as the words themselves. He remembered Bao Mae always used phrases such as that. The thought of her made him impatient. He couldn't wait to get the rest of his family back to this place to their ancestral homeland. The place they *belonged*.

"Let's get going then," Baxter commanded.

Black started the engine, pulling onto the highway leading to the interstate just north of the beach. A long time had passed since Baxter had found his way back to Alabama. The drive to Montgomery was also the first time he had been out of New Orleans since returning to America.

As Black drove, the pair remained silent. Baxter's thoughts turned back to everything he had endured since that fateful day he received his draft card. He found it peculiar that all the men in the POW camp with him had all been southern and all were drafted.

Abandoned in that hell, they bonded while some of the others, from other parts of the country, were released and went home. At least Baxter hoped they went home.

At first, Baxter thought it was all a coincidence. The officers left first and then the enlisted guys from up North. In the end, just the guys from below the Mason-Dixon Line and the captives from the South Vietnamese Army were left. As time passed, the Rebs, as they began to call themselves, drew into each other and became a tight-knit group with only one thing on their mind. Escape. They plotted daily but the only way any of them left the camp was death. One by one they died off from starvation, disease. Some were beaten to death and a couple took their own lives. In the end, there were only two. Two that were so similar they could be mistaken for brothers.

The Vietnamese guards were even more brutal towards their South Vietnamese counterparts. They endured torture endlessly and mercilessly. What they endured was something Baxter tried to shut out but resurfaced each time he closed his eyes. The North Vietnamese soldiers looked down upon the South Vietnamese as traitors to their own people. At least the Americans, in their eyes, were *true* soldiers.

Miles passed. Neither had said a word since leaving Biloxi. Black broke the silence as they neared the tunnel in Mobile. The friendship between the two men strengthened the more they were in each other's company and Black could tell when his friend's pain reached a zenith.

"Back *there*, my friend?" Black asked and Baxter shrugged his shoulders.

"I'm always there," Baxter replied, his voice low and steady. "That place never leaves me. Tell me, did y'all hear of us when your ship came into port over there? Rumors? Anything?"

Black didn't answer right away. He knew exactly where this was going. Baxter had hinted at it before, circling around the thought like it was too painful to speak outright. He wanted to know if their captivity had been an open secret. If sailors coming into port had heard the rumors, then the American government had to have known. And if they *knew*—that meant they didn't care. That was the part that haunted Baxter the most.

Baxter found out that Rafael Demingo, the dead DEA agent, had used Rof Bruce's situation to worm into the Clark Family's dealings with the Columbians. A fact Black discovered quickly in his association with Burt Williams. If the DEA knew, the Government and Army would have to know. Deep in his heart, he knew, but for some reason, never wanted to believe it.

Baxter noticed his friend's silence. His focus had been on the passing cars of the interstate and now on the growing Mobile skyline quickly advancing in front of them, but he turned his intense gaze to Black.

The Brazilian knew he had to offer some kind of answer, and sighed. He didn't turn his attention from the road and said, "You know we did."

Baxter shook his head, his voice rising with frustration. "This damned country hasn't given a shit about us since our war, Jeff. I get it now—I really do—why your family left."

He tapped his cane sharply on the floorboard, the hollow thud echoing in the confined space of the car. His agitation needed somewhere to go, and the cane bore the brunt of it.

"We're going to make it right," he said, more to himself than to Black, but with a conviction that left no room for doubt.

The car rolled eastward along Interstate 10, the hum of the tires steady beneath them. Soon, the Wallace Tunnel came into view—its arched entrance yawning open, ready to swallow them beneath the waters of Mobile Bay. They could've bypassed the tunnel entirely, taking I-65 north toward Montgomery. But Black had made a choice.

He wanted Baxter to see it—the engineering, the progress, the quiet power of this country. He wanted his friend to witness firsthand what their homeland had built, what it was still capable of. Even in its flaws, there was something worth seeing. Something worth remembering.

"It opened in the mid-seventies, *after* you left," he told Baxter. When he realized they were below the water of the bay, Baxter turned his attention to the tunnel's lights and said once again, "We are going to make it right."

The small boarding house rested upon a bluff overlooking the Alabama River just outside of Montgomery. Baxter insisted he stay near water if for no other reason than the view of a river or ocean often calmed him when he became agitated. Those episodes had become fewer lately, but they still bubbled up, again, mostly at night as he slept.

The Alabama River's ancient, swift water, that in days before dams, flowed freely was more of a muddy, slow-moving lake now. The dam down river, not generating electricity when they arrived, made the water motionless and stagnant looking. The only evident movement was from large barges slowly creeping by ferrying goods from factories in the capital city towards the port in Mobile, leaving gently rolling wake behind them.

Every now and again Baxter watched a fishing boat float by. He wished he could join them. He heard of the spotted bass inhabiting this part of the river and wished he could spend one more day with his father, fishing. At this moment, however, all he could do was watch and remember.

"I take it this will do, meu amigo?" Black asked as he sat down next to him.

"Perfect," he replied, "This place smells so much better than New Orleans." Baxter inhaled a deep breath and exhaled just as hard. "The smell is *closer* to home, but it still holds the aroma of a city." Baxter put his hand on Black's knee, "You better leave now if you want to get to West Palm before the sun comes up." He leaned in close, "Keep your thumb on those guys from Biloxi. Use them but don't trust them. They are loyal only to money."

Black nodded in agreement and asked how quickly he should get in touch with Diaz? "Quickly," Baxter replied,

"Alliances don't hold. Williams can't *see* next week, only what's in front of him at the time." Black nodded once again, and the two men said their goodbyes.

Baxter didn't go back inside the boarding house after Black left. He continued enjoying the sights and sounds of the mighty river, resting in the rocking chair on the bluff's overlook. He smiled sheepishly as he thought about Burt Williams. The buffoon, busy making his plans, ignorant to the fact he and his friend were always going to be one step ahead. He laughed loudly, the sound sharp and full, echoing off the water below, bouncing back like a voice from another time.

Black pulled into the parking lot of the Clark Building as the sun peeked over the Atlantic. He and Burt had arranged to meet before anyone else came into the building and he expected to see his car when he arrived, but the lot was bare. Black sat, alone, for an hour while the sun grew higher in the sky and right when he was about to start the engine, Burt's car turned the corner, almost hitting his parked car, before slamming his car's transmission into park inches from his own vehicle.

Burt's window was down, and Black could already smell liquor oozing from Burt's pores while he sat in the car staring at him with a scowl. When the two men exited their cars, Black didn't smell the stench of booze on the gangster's breath. He knew what that meant. Burt's intake of alcohol had intensified to the point that it was always in his system, a sure-fire sign of an alcoholic. The Brazilian wondered just what *else* was in his system.

Black managed a smile, sticking his hand out, "Good to see you again, Mr. Williams."

Burt just sneered at him, "With as much as we been though, *Jeff*, I figure you just call me Burt."

Black bowed his head slightly, "I'll continue with *Mr. Williams*."

"Suit yourself," Burt replied, raising an eyebrow, and motioned to the building.

Black took a seat in Burt's office, expecting the gangster to do the same but Burt excused himself to the bathroom. When he returned, he noticed a minute white speck on the end of Burt's nose. Black shook his head slightly, catching himself, and stopped quickly, hoping Burt didn't notice. Burt, however, didn't seem to mind if his counterpart noticed or not. Finally, after a few moments of silence, the two men just staring at each other, Burt wiped his nose with his hand erasing the evidence.

Frustrated, Black's fake smile had long since vanished and his face hardened, "So, you're mad the Columbians roughed you up a bit," he stated.

Burt's eyes narrowed and he pulled a cigar out of his pocket, "This is all business. They didn't *rough* me up, they sucker punched me."

Black chuckled to himself, "I heard you were already drunk and stoned and didn't want to cooperate."

Burt leaped to his feet and growled, "I'm Burt Williams. If I don't want to do something, I don't. These fucking Columbians think they own this place. They don't."

Black shook his head slowly, "So you want to go to war, correct? You've already called your pals in Mississippi."

Burt eased back into his chair, "How in the hell do you know that?"

"I didn't for sure, but *now* I do," Black told him, the veins in his neck pulsing, "You really don't know how to conduct business do you?" He paused, gently rising to his feet, standing over the gangster, "But, Mr. Williams, you have luck on your side. You have us."

Black turned his back to Burt, "Our business with the Columbians is, in fact, almost complete. But we aren't going to rush into anything. That is not good business. It is Mateo Diaz that you have trouble with, no?"

Burt spun in his chair, facing the window, "If we get rid of that bastard, they'll just send someone else."

Black agreed adding, "Possibly someone worse. Have you considered that, Mr. Williams? Or has your rage blinded you?" Black's voice remained calm even though his words bore a crushing weight. "We do things the *right* way. The Columbians can never know what we do or what we agree to here." Black looked at his reflection in the door's glass and his voice became icy cold, "When our business is finished, we will send them back to their god-forsaken land and rid this country of their scourge."

Burt, still facing the window said sternly, "I don't give a shit about your ideals. I'm a crook. Always have been and always will be. That's what I know. In my eyes, if a man crosses you, you take care of it. Business be damned."

Both men turned to face each other, locking eyes, "That is why you fail," the Brazilian told him.

Burt burst out in boisterous laughter, waving his arms around the building, "What do you call this?"

Black didn't hesitate, "Luck." Burt's laughter still echoed throughout the empty office building as Black strode towards the front door, not looking back.

The Brazilian made his way back to his hotel, fuming as he drove. He looped around several times, making sure nobody followed him. That was a favorite tactic of the Dixie Mafia. It was stupid and predictable, just as the confederation of criminals itself. At first Black didn't feel that way about Burt Williams, but in his mind, now, there was no doubt. Burt's drinking and new habit amplified his stupidity. Before, he'd masked it well. He was cool, composed, always in control. But now, the gangster couldn't hide it. The rage was there, plain on his face, bleeding through the cracks in his hardened exterior.

"Just like we thought," he said into the payphone just down the street from his hotel.

Baxter, on the other end, replied, "Damned redneck idiot. Can't see past his hand. All the same though. He was going to be dealt with at some point, just coming sooner than I figured. But, Jeff," Baxter's voice became worried, "We can't let the *kid* get hurt in all this."

"I'll make sure he isn't. The other boy is already...." Black paused, "...wrapped up in it. Already helped Williams with a *disposal* job."

Silence hung in the air, heavy and unbroken, the only sound the labored breathing of the man on the other end. Then, at last, Baxter spoke, his voice rough with disbelief.

"Damn Vernon Bruce," he said. "His own son."

Black responded, "é o que é".

"Damn Portuguese," Baxter protested, "what the hell does that mean?"

"Is what it is," Black told him.

Baxter thought to himself, *that's easy for him to say. Black hadn't made the promises that he had.* He bit his tongue and didn't say the words aloud.

Instead, Baxter told his friend, "Get with Diaz tomorrow. Enjoy the night. Tomorrow, hell is upon us."

Burt didn't linger in the office after Black left. He didn't go home either. He stopped by the surf shop and shooed all of Casey's guys out the door and locked it behind him. Casey didn't expect to see Burt as he never came by the shop, especially after he found his friend dead in the office.

"What are you doing here, Burt?" Casey asked as Burt brushed past him into the office, wagging a finger calling him to follow.

"Kid..." Burt told him, looking around to make sure they were alone, "...came to tell you what we talked about before is about to hit the fan." Casey felt a chill run down his spine. He didn't know what to think or say, so he stayed quiet and let Burt do the talking.

"Met with a guy today," he said confidently, "His outfit is going to help us. My boys from Biloxi are coming down too. Don't know what these guys I met with today are planning, but it's going to be bloody." Burt propped his boots on the desk, "You up for that, kid?"

Color drained from Casey's face as he grabbed the pack of cigarettes on the desk, lit one, slowly exhaling the smoke, "Damn, Burt. What do you want me to do?" He was afraid to ask but he had to know what Burt expected out of him. His mind flashed back to his encounter with Diaz, and for a brief moment, a chill ran through him—what if Burt knew? What if this was a setup? But the thought dissolved just as quickly as it came. No, that wasn't it. Not yet.

Burt continued, "Guy named Diaz, a Columbian. He's the one that had them come to the house the other morning." The gangster took his feet off the desk and leaned towards Casey, "He dies for that. Nobody does that to *our* family." Burt had never called Casey family before, and his color slowly returned.

"I'm family?" he asked sheepishly.

"Hell, yeah you are. You're like a *son* to me, Casey. More than your damned cousin."

Casey, shaking his head replied, "We're just different, Burt. Cliff's family too. He's just been through a lot. Cut him some slack." As soon as the words left his mouth, he regretted them.

"So have you!" Burt's voice and anger escalated. "Your damn no good father killed two people. Left you to rot in that hell up in the Panhandle. If it wasn't for me, you'd died there!"

Casey looked at the floor and said lowly, "What do you want me to do?" Burt stood, smiling, put his arm around Casey and the two of them walked outside.

Chapter 22

Peering out of a window at the police station, Shaggy watched cars motoring up and down the busy street below. Mateo Diaz sat on a couch, alone, and noticed Shaggy's partner, the one he met in Gulf Shores with the crew cut after they followed him from Mobile, wasn't in the room. He was glad. The military man reminded him of the corrupt soldiers back in Columbia. The ones that snatched him from his family so many years ago.

"I've been watching. Nobody tailed you," the agent told the Colombian, slowly turning to face him.

"Nobody tails me," Diaz replied, "I'm the boss."

Shaggy smirked, thinking to himself, *OK bossman.*

"So," Diaz said, "You want Burt Willaims."

The agent turned his attention back to the window, speaking slowly, "I want Burt Williams dead."

Diaz cocked his head to one side, an eyebrow arching with quiet suspicion. Shaggy caught the look and quickly held up a hand, his voice low and steady.

"It's clean," he said. "This room's tight. Whatever we say in here doesn't go anywhere. Stays between us."

Diaz didn't respond right away, but the concern in his eyes lingered a moment longer before he finally nodded.

"I must ask you," The Colombian paused, tilting his head in the opposite direction, "I apologize, I do not know your name."

Shaggy said, "Guess you can just call me Shaggy, everybody else does."

"Well, *Shaggy*," Diaz chuckled boyishly as he said the name, "Seems like you'd want a buffoon like Williams to be leading the way. Sooner or later a fool like him will talk."

The agent shook his head, "No sir. Mr. Williams is a loose cannon. He gave up my former partner a while back, caused him to get fitted with some concrete shoes, or that's what the consensus is around here. Never found his body."

Diaz thought for a moment, grinned, and asked "Rafael Demingo?" Shaggy nodded in affirmative. "So, it's revenge you're after," the Colombian said coldly, adding "Or maybe just some kind of reckoning." Diaz stood, "Demingo was also a *loose cannon*, as you say. He wanted to shut us down at all costs. By me being here with you, today, I take it you don't share his commitment to our demise."

Shaggy, still watching traffic through the window replied, "Oh, don't get me wrong. I *hate* what you do. I despise it. But I know that your business is here to stay. No matter what we do, we will never *stop* you. I'm not getting into that with you, right now, Mr. Diaz. Just know that Williams is going. Soon. You help us, we help you. Details come later. First *Williams*."

The Colombian walked over to the window, "You want *me* to take him out, don't you?"

"Nothing you ain't already planning to do anyway," Shaggy told him. Diaz noticed the corners of his mouth upturned in a smile. The agent, somehow, had gotten wind of the discontent between his group and Burt Williams.

"How can you help?" Diaz asked.

"My partner, you met him up in Alabama, is with the chief of police right now clearing your path with the locals. I'll give you the location in a few days," Shaggy told him.

"That doesn't give me much to go on and just what does my organization *gain* from this?" Diaz asked, gritting his teeth.

The agent scratched his head, turned, and looked Diaz directly in the eyes for the first time, "We aren't helping your *organization.* We are helping *Phillipe'*."

Diaz froze, broke eye contact, and said in a whisper, "You know I can't betray my people. Only death would follow."

Shaggy walked over to the door, slowly turned the knob, and cracked it open. He leaned out, scanning the hallway.

It was empty.

No footsteps, no voices—just silence and the lingering smell of stale smoke clinging to the air like a warning that someone had been there not long ago. Satisfied, he shut the door and turned back to Diaz.

The agent eased the door shut, "I'll be square with you, Mr. Diaz. This is what we offer. Phillipe' in *this* country. The two of you starting over. Safely far away from this mess."

The offer took Diaz by surprise but also sparked hope in his mind, but the reality of the situation crashed upon him.

"Phillipe' is not easily hidden. The reach of my organization is far greater than yours. You offer a death sentence, only *delayed*."

Shaggy again locked eyes with the Colombian, "There is risk, I'm not going to lie to you, but, what if there is a chance. That's what I offer, a *chance*." The agent walked over to the desk, took a file, and flopped it down on the couch, "I've done my research, Mateo, I know you only do this as a means to an end. An end with you and Phillipe *safe* here in the States. That only happens with us." He sat down, offering Diaz the seat next to him and the Colombian accepted. "I'm assured that people within this administration know what a *win* is. It isn't necessarily an absolute victory and sometimes there is room to compromise."

Diaz stared at the floor. This was his first real chance at freedom since childhood. Real freedom. He picked his eyes up from the floor and noticed the American flag waving in the stiff breeze. Its bright colors glowed in the Florida sun and Diaz, at that very moment, made up his mind.

Diaz extended his hand, and the agent grabbed it tightly, "But don't forget, Mr. Diaz. You screw me, I'll put a bullet in you myself."

Diaz increased his grip, matching the agent, "Likewise." Diaz left and Shaggy watched him from the window until he cleared the parking lot.

The agent with the military buzz cut cracked open the door, sticking his head in and asked, "Did he buy the crap about Demingo?"

Shaggy shrugged his shoulders, "Doesn't really matter. When I dangled the bait in front of him, he bit."

The agent widened the door, came into the room, and sat down in the chair Mateo occupied just a few minutes ago, "They all got a pressure point. Just got to find it and squeeze."

Shaggy locked eyes with his partner and said, "You do know *how* he intends to take Williams out, don't you?"

"Nothing different than what those gangs out on the coast are doing. Keep their hands clean using kids," he responded, flipping through the file Shaggy had thrown on the couch. He slid on his reading glasses. He hated them, but his age was catching up. As he flipped pages, he saw pictures of Burt Williams, Vernon Bruce, and Ramsay Brown. Young Casey Bruce had a page in the file, but no picture. "Just think, after this is over, with Williams out of the way and another Bruce on the hook, *we* will run this state."

"Flip back over to Brown," Shaggy said, and his partner flipped a couple of pages backwards. "We brought him down here to do a job and then we kinda just let him go." Both agents looked at each other and Shaggy finally finished, "Let's just send him home. Turns out he is pretty much useless to us."

His partner tapped his finger on Casey's page file and flipped back to the pictures of Cliff and RB. He looked up at his partner standing above him, "Maybe, not," he said, "Dial him up," he told Shaggy. The agent leaned back in his chair, a slow smile spreading across his face—calm, confident, and just a little too knowing.

The phone rang a couple times and RB picked up on the other end. "Mr. Brown," Shaggy said into the phone, "This is your *friend* from Biloxi."

"You ain't gotta introduce yourself, *Shaggy*, I know voices. It's my job, you know," RB said sarcastically. "Now, what can I do for you?"

Shaggy fanned himself with the file, "Just passing on a little information for you. It's about the Patty Lee Bruce murder," he said, "I know you and the boy are working the other two, Beck and the guy from Mississippi," the agent paused for effect and shot a wry smile at his partner before finishing, "Lucky Clay."

"Vern Bruce's wife. I'm trying to stay out of that one," the detective replied.

"Yeah, I know you don't want nothing to do with it, but I thought you'd like to know about this. Just call it professional courtesy," Shaggy said, the smile still on his face as he spoke.

"Watcha got?" RB asked, his curiosity overriding his instincts.

Shaggy tossed the file on the desk and a picture slid from the corner. He picked it up, showing it to his partner and the other agent nodded. "I'm holding a picture of what looks to be a soaking wet Burt Williams hustling, if you can call it that, off a beach. Tourist that took it didn't know what she had. We just *happened* to come across it. Thing is," he paused again for effect,

"It was taken the evening Patty Lee Bruce's throat was sliced. Lady said the cat in picture got off an inflatable boat with another man, but they went separate ways."

"Circumstantial, they coulda been fishing. Ol' Burt loves to fish," RB told him.

Already knowing it was circumstantial, but willing to play along with the detective, "Yeah, that's why *I'm* not doing anything with it. Just thought you might want to know. I know you're tight with the Bruce boys and thought they may want to know."

The line went silent for a few seconds before RB's deep voice responded, "I'll check it out. Any way I can get a copy?"

Shaggy gave his partner a thumbs up and winked, "Anything for a fellow officer of the law."

The drive to the police station was short, and RB arrived not long after receiving the call. Both agents were already waiting in the lobby, hands outstretched in greeting as the Biloxi detective walked in. After a brief exchange of pleasantries—tight smiles and firm handshakes—Shaggy reached into his jacket and casually tossed a photo to RB. It landed in his hands with a weight that felt heavier than paper.

RB held the picture in front of him, shaking his head. "Kinda looks like Burt but it's blurry. Nobody could ID him from this picture and if they could, like I said, circumstantial."

Both Shaggy and the other agent nodded in agreement and Shaggy shot his partner a quick glance. "Except for the lady that *took* the picture. She picked Burt out from an old mugshot."

RB sat down, placing the photo next to him on the couch. He interlocked his fingers, looked up at the agents and asked, "If you can't do nothing with this, why you showing it to me?"

Shaggy took the seat next to RB, placed his hand on the detective's shoulder and used his most sincere voice, "Because if my mentor killed my mother, I'd want to know." Shaggy took a deep breath, "You know that kid is going down a dark path with Burt Williams. Maybe you can use this to save his life."

RB jumped to his feet, pointing his long finger down at Shaggy, "So now you two are concerned about Casey Bruce? Son of a convicted murderer, protégé' of a known member of the Dixie Mafia, and soon to be tied in with the Columbian Cartel?" he asked loudly.

Shaggy's partner put his palms in the air, "Look, take the picture with you. Use it, don't use it, I, we, have no control over what you do with it, but I will tell you this, if you don't, you'll regret it."

RB took the picture and put it in his shirt pocket. "Tell me what you guys are up to. I know you don't care about these boys. I know you only care about scoring points and this ain't no damn game. These are good boys. Casey might have gone a little off track, but they both *can* be saved. Tell me right now what game you are playing or I walk."

Shaggy's partner shook his head, "Mr. Ramsay, you aren't walking away from *anything*. You just told me in your own words that you care about these boys. You ain't going to leave them high and dry. Even if you did, who gives a shit? You ain't even done what you're supposed to be doing down here," he paused, "Mateo Diaz? How close are you to him right now? Just met him, right?" He motioned to shaggy, "Just let him go back to Biloxi where he belongs. Let *real* cops handle this."

RB's face flashed with anger, his jaw tightening and eyes narrowing—but just as quickly, he forced himself to calm down. This was a game. And he knew their kind. They didn't care about justice, or people—they cared about control. About winning.

"Fine," he growled, his voice low and clipped. "You handle it. I'm out."

He turned on his heel, already walking away, not waiting for a response.

RB flung the door open and stormed out without another word. The two agents stood in silence for a few seconds before smiles came over both of their faces. "That went according to plan," Shaggy said. His partner nodded.

"All of the pieces are in place," he responded, "And, if this works, we take care of Diaz, Williams, and set us up with the Bruce boy for life."

"What about Black and his bunch? We just going to let them take over the Northern Gulf?" Shaggy asked.

"Why not? We know what to expect out of that bunch. They want to use what's left of the Dixie Mafia, which ain't much, to start another war and they're damn well welcome to try." He pointed towards the door, "We send that guy back up there and *he* watches it for us. He's a cop. A real cop. We play him right and he does exactly what we need."

"What about that other guy. The one in Montgomery?" Shaggy asked.

"That guy is just a cripple. He thinks he's planning all of this, but..." the agent said, putting his finger to his forehead "... he ain't. I am."

RB pulled into the first parking lot he saw. He needed a moment to think. RB pulled out the picture and cursed. Now he *knew*. Burt, somehow, had a hand in killing that boy's mother. The image may be blurry, but there was no mistaking it. That was Burt Williams. The thought of burning the picture crossed his mind but knew it wouldn't do any good. If there was one, there was more. He ran his finger along his mustache and closed his eyes. He thought about praying, but it'd been so long since he talked to God, he figured he wouldn't listen anyway.

Shaking his head, looking out of the window, he watched traffic hurrying down the busy street and cursed again. Not only had Burt killed that woman, which was something he probably didn't even think twice about, but he had the stones to try and raise her son as his own. Only a monster could do something like that. RB had always considered Burt Williams to be a friend. They were on opposite sides of the law, but friends regardless. There were lines they didn't cross, and one often helped the other. Right then, RB felt the weight of guilt crushing him. The question in his mind burned like acid in his mouth, *Did I get all of this started?*

He remembered the day, so long ago it seemed, when Burt came to him needing information on Christian Lopez. He did as his friend asked and helped put all of this into motion. Could he have told him no and perhaps things might have been different? Maybe not. Burt had other contacts in the Biloxi Police. But ultimately, the blame rested on *his* shoulders.

The guilt inside him swelled, heavy and relentless. He hadn't cried in a long time—hadn't *let* himself. And now, when he wanted the tears to come, to wash some of it away, they wouldn't.

Not now.

This was his chance—maybe the only one he'd get—to make up for even a fraction of the pain he'd helped cause. Because whether through action or indifference, the Bruce family had suffered. And much of that suffering traced back to one thing: his friendship with Burt Williams.

He channeled his rage into his fist, slamming it against the steering wheel again and again, each hit echoing through the car like a drumbeat of frustration. Breathing heavily, he looked at the picture one more time—his jaw clenched, eyes burning—before slipping it back into his pocket.

He ran his fingers across his face, trying to steady himself. If he fell apart now, he'd be no good to anyone. If Burt did this, and with this picture, there was no doubt in his mind that he did, Burt had to have been the one to set up Vernon Bruce. But why? He couldn't have known that Vern would turn his son over to him. There was absolutely no way he could've known that. If Vern exited the picture, Cliff wouldn't get a penny so that was no avenue for Burt.

RB shook his head. Pure luck was the only way to explain it. Burt Williams, always the luckiest bastard he knew, lucked into it all. The money, the power, everything.

Although he tried his best to fight it, a tear formed and worked its way slowly down RB's cheek. He wiped it away and during the motion, his mind cleared, his decision firm. Cliff was older than his years and this was something he could handle. Casey, explosive and unpredictable couldn't.

He turned the ignition, and the engine screeched loudly. He shook his head; he never turned the engine off, and the starter tried to engage an already running machine. He put the car in gear and sped out of the parking lot and headed to the Clark house and a conversation he didn't want to have. "Damn you, Burt," he yelled, catching another gear.

Chapter 23

Light pulsed through the thin motel curtain, a steady rhythm of red and white radiating from the flickering neon sign just outside. Burt sat motionless, eyes fixed on the glowing word VACANCY as it blinked on and off, casting shadows that danced across the walls like ghosts he couldn't escape.

He leaned over the table, plunging his nose into the white powder, inhaling it all in one deep breath. His body trembling as the narcotic entered his bloodstream. After the initial rush wore off, he put the bottle of whiskey to his lips, drinking down what was left in the bottle. He reached beside him and ran his fingers through his secretary's blonde hair and a finger from the other hand ran down the side of her naked body.

They had checked in the day before and now the sun was setting over the peninsula. The only sound came from the air conditioner humming away, trying in vain to cancel out the hot, humid, Florida air.

"Let's go out," the secretary cooed.

Burt sighed and pointed to the door, "There's the door. Go."

If this guy wasn't so rich, she thought to herself, *she would do just that,* but she leaned back onto the pillow and lit a cigarette.

The desk phone rang, and Burt picked it up at once as he was too strung out to follow the rules. "What took you so damn long?" he yelled into the phone. The answer from the other end infuriated him even more and he slammed the receiver on the table before returning it to his ear. "Get y'all's ass down here by tomorrow. We are going to end this shit." This time Burt hung up the phone and took the cigarette from the blonde. He was out of his cigars and needed nicotine.

He tried to sit up and swing his feet to the floor, but the room tilted beneath him—whether from the powder, the whiskey, or both, it didn't matter. His body gave out, and he collapsed back onto the bed with a grunt.

After a few clumsy attempts, he finally managed to sit upright, hunched on the edge of the bed like a man twice his age. Reaching for the phone, he picked up the receiver and began pressing the buttons. Each one let out a sharp squeal in his ear, the high-pitched tones slicing through his pounding head. He liked the ease of it—just pushing buttons. But somewhere deep in his mind, he missed the slow, deliberate spin of a rotary dial. The sound it made. The patience it required. A different time. A different man.

Jeff Black, with his unmistakable accent, answered at the other end. "Black, we need to talk. I'm out here at the Breeze, room 18, first floor. Get here as soon as you can." He hung up, not waiting for an answer. Easing back onto the bed, he and the blonde went at it again.

Jeff Black held the phone to his ear, the dial tone still ringing in his ear. His face reddened. He slowly placed the receiver back onto the hook as his hand shook slightly. He was thrilled that soon he would never have to hear that voice again. *Burt Williams must've descended from the lower classes of old Southern society*, he thought to himself, *if not a carpetbagger.*

Boa Mae had told him when he was young about the people that inhabited her homeland. They came from a strong, sophisticated stock. They were the high class of southern society, holding most of the money and power. Their mansions were beautiful creations, often nestled in the heart of sprawling pecan or oak orchards. The grand homes stood in quiet elegance, framed by trees that whispered with age and southern history.

She told him stories of the lifestyle they enjoyed before the Yankees ripped it all away. When he closed his eyes, visions of how he imagined those days rushed upon him, always making him feel better about himself and his place in the world. He would be the one to get all of that back. Maybe not in the form she would recognize, but something similar—something modern, reshaped by time yet still echoing the past.

Bao Mae also told him about the lower classes of white people in the old Confederacy. The ones that worked as slave drivers. To her, they were the lowest of the low and she considered them lower than the slaves themselves. Some would beat a slave just for the enjoyment of it. They would torture a slave until their devilish lust for hurting the defenseless waned. Even though she was incredibly young, she remembered such an occurrence and the look on the slave driver's face. As he beat the slave, salvia dripped from his foamy mouth and his eyes seemed to glow red. The vision, burned into her memory, repulsed her each time she thought about it. She saw so much pain inflicted by these men as a child and she held her head high when she told him that her father eventually forbade them on her family's plantation.

He was sure those types of people were the ancestors of men like Burt Williams. People who liked to inflict pain just because they could. Evil men, not like his genteel forefathers.

Black shook his head. People like Burt Williams should be purged from the *new* southland he envisioned. When the Confederados finally took over the Dixie Mafia, that would be one of his priorities. The Burt Williams types of the *new* South would meet their fate. You could be *enterprising* without being cruel.

He called Veck Baxter, and his friend greeted him warmly, "Hello my friend, I suppose that you're calling with news of some sort."

"Burt Williams wants me to come to his motel over on the coast. By the sound and urgency in his voice, I believe he wants to strike at Diaz. Now rather than later," Black told his friend.

"Yes, I suppose the time *has* come. I spoke to our friends in Biloxi and they're playing *ball.*" He waited for a second to make sure the reference hit home with the Brazilian this time, heard no protest and smiled, "They are *supposed* to meet y'all at the dock tomorrow. Be prepared. It will happen quickly. Diaz will put the final touches on his end tomorrow morning. The *others* did their job today. But..." Baxter paused and chose his words carefully, "If the plan goes awry, Williams doesn't leave alive. No matter what happens."

"I know, my friend," Black responded. "I'll take care of it *myself* if need be." Black hesitated but he had to ask, "What about Vern Bruce? Is that business taken care of?" He waited for Baxter's response but for only a second.

"Calley tells him today and my visit comes after everything plays out tomorrow," Baxter said quickly.

Black released a deep breath, "I know you are ready to put that business to rest. Finally, you can keep your promise to your friend."

"It's driven me to this point, Jefferson," Baxter replied, "When I finally see this man, eye to eye, everything we've worked for will be done." He wanted to tell him more but now was not the time. He had burdened and relied on Jeff Black for so long, he didn't want to burden his friend any further. "Good luck, irmão," he said as he hung up the phone.

Black scribbled quickly on a notepad provided by the hotel, each stroke of the pen deliberate. He wrote in Portuguese, a habit born of caution. If anyone happened to find the note, they'd be none the wiser.

He pulled the closet door open, the same dark suit of clothing he wore the night of Patty Lee Bruce and Christian Lopez' deaths folded delicately in the back. He put them on. In his right pocket he placed a pistol and the left already contained his knife. He hoped he wouldn't have to use either of them.

Calley, pointing to the line along the bottom of the page, told Vern "Here, sign right there."

Vern held the pen in his hand, hesitating, looked up at his lawyer and asked, "Just to be clear, If I plead guilty, that doesn't mean that I AM guilty."

Calley nodded patiently, though inside he was screaming with frustration.

Across from him, Vern moved slowly, deliberately, the pen shaking slightly in his hand as he lowered it to the page. After a long pause, he signed his name. When it was done, he let out a deep breath, as if the weight of the moment had been resting on his chest.

"The judge has informed me that upon your signature and within a few days you are to be moved from Death Row to general population." Calley shook Vern's hand as best he could with Vern still shackled to the table, "Congratulations, Mr. Bruce. You are not going to die, well..." he laughed, "by the hand of the State of Georgia, anyway." Vern tried to smile at the joke but both men knew the slight grin wasn't authentic.

"One thing though, and we talked about this, no more appeals. What is done is done," Calley informed him.

Vern nodded. "Traded my life for the chance to see my boys again. When can they visit?" he asked eagerly.

Calley glanced at the ceiling, thinking for a second before responding, "Within a few weeks. But, Mr. Bruce, I've been told your son doesn't want to see you."

Vern knew from what he had read in a letter from Cliff that Casey's hate for him not only remained but had grown, fueled by his belief that his father was somehow responsible for his mother's death.

Vern lowered his head onto the table, the cool surface pressing against his forehead as the silence wrapped around him. He may not have killed his wife—but the guilt of letting their marriage, and their family, deteriorate to the point it had, festered deep within his soul. After a long pause, his voice came out low and heavy.

"If I can talk to Cliff… he'll get through to Casey."

The attorney dropped his head, "Mr. Bruce this isn't my place to say, but from information I've gathered, your son is getting in pretty deep with Burt Williams and his *dealings*. The guy he hired to run the front company, some kind of surf shop, is missing and your son has taken over the day to day of the business."

Vern lifted an eyebrow and asked, "Front company? What's the front for? Running it? He's only a kid!"

Calley raised his hands, "All I know is that it is not good," he told him and stood up to leave. He knocked on the door, letting the guard know he was ready to go.

"Get Cliff here as soon as you can. It ain't too late," Vern pleaded, his voice shaking and Calley nodded as he walked out the door.

The usual despair didn't set in when the guard locked him into his tiny cell. He knew it was only temporary this time and his thoughts focused not on himself, but his son. He heard the guard murmur something about "lucky rich bastard" as the iron door slammed shut. His happiness didn't last long, however, as his thoughts drifted from his son to his father.

He remembered a day when it was just the two of them down on Holmes Creek near the tiny town of Vernon. The tiny town was infamous because some of the residents were accused of cutting off limbs in order to collect insurance money. Some guy in Hollywood even caught wind of the story, came to town to shoot a documentary he wanted to call "Nub City, USA." The townspeople wouldn't have it and according to legend threatened to drown him in the black water of Holmes Creek if he continued with the movie he wanted to make. Eventually the film focused on small town life and some of the more *interesting* people that lived there. Vern chuckled to himself when he thought about the old story.

Vern and his father didn't care about the town's reputation, all they cared about was the baited sucker hole they fished. It was there, on a tiny boat powered by a small gasoline engine that his father taught him about honesty.

Vern couldn't remember how old he was, but he did remember not having a driver's license yet, so he was probably around fourteen or fifteen, just a little older than Casey was now.

The two of them had stopped at a small store just a few feet from the bridge leading into town, spanning the creek. While his father pumped gas, young Vern wandered ahead into the store, the bell over the door jingling as he stepped inside. He made his way to the cooler; its glass fogged slightly from the cold inside and stared at the rows of soft drinks stacked neatly behind it, filled with bright labels and fizzing promises waiting to be chosen.

It was one of the old-style drink coolers, not upright but like a chest that you had to open from the top. Right on the top edge of the cooler, sat several open containers of candy bars. Pops didn't like his boys eating candy bars. The rush of sugar always made them hyper as little kids, so he never bought them, even when they grew to be teenagers.

Instead, he always bought little round cans of "Viennees" as he called them, small sausages pre-cooked and ready to eat. That was their fishing meal. Vern wanted one of the candy bars so badly that he couldn't take his eyes off them. Before he knew it, he reached up in a catlike manner, took one and stuffed it in his jacket pocket right as Pops was opening the door and walking up to him. He was sure he was caught, but Pops said nothing. Vern grinned as he had gotten away with it.

A little while later they launched the small boat and made their way down the narrow creek, through the moss-covered limbs that hung over the water to their secret fishing spot. Pops had been quiet on the way down the creek as he concentrated on keeping the boat near the middle, dodging shallow obstacles that hid in the opaque water, known to sink even the sturdiest boats.

They set up their fishing lines and waited in silence for the tips of the long bamboo poles to arc towards the water, indicating one of the mighty fish had taken the bait. Vern sat quietly, the earthy scent of the slowly flowing water filling his lungs, surrounded by the soft rustle of leaves and the distant call of birds. It was peaceful. It was the kind of peace he rarely felt.

It took him a while to notice the gaze, but eventually, he caught sight of Pops watching him from the corner of his eye. His heart sank into his stomach. The calm of the moment shattered, replaced by the weight of something unspoken—something he knew was coming.

"Mr. Eli, the old blind man that owns the store back in town, you know anything about him?" Pops asked, his voice calm. Vern shook his head no and kept his eyes focused on the end of his fishing pole, not wanting to make eye contact with his father.

"He lost his sight in World War One. He volunteered to fight, went to France and next thing he knew he was in this long hole in the ground, praying he wouldn't die."

Vern nodded as he remembered what his father was talking about from history class, "Trenches. They were called trenches, Pops."

Pops squinted his eyes, continuing with the story, "Yeah, I guess that's what they called them, anyway, he lost his sight when they sprayed him with some kind of chemical and he couldn't get his mask on. Really, he's lucky to be alive. Been running that store ever since. Refused a government check once, and said that's not what he fought for. One of the most honest men I've ever known in my life. He'd give you the shirt of his back or the shoes off his feet." Pops' voice never wavered, steady and controlled, each word deliberate. He didn't show a flicker of emotion as he spoke—his face unreadable, like it had been carved from stone.

Vern still didn't move his eyes from his fishing pole as his father kept talking, "When we get finished here, son, this is what you are going to do. You are going to go back into that store, alone, and tell Mr. Eli exactly what you did. You are going to stand in front of him and tell that blind veteran, that went to war to keep you free, what you did. I'm not going with you," he paused and looked at his son until Vern reluctantly turned to look at his father's eyes, "And I'm not going to interfere if he calls the law, and he probably will. I damn sure would." Pops put his weathered, work-worn hand on Vern's shoulder, "Do you understand me?"

Vern could say nothing, even if he wanted, only nodding his head. Pops told him to put his pole in the boat and get ready to head back to the boat landing. It hurt Vern even more because he knew how much Pops loved to fish and had looked forward to this trip. Now he had ruined it, not only for himself, but for his father.

Pops' demeanor didn't change. Without a word, he calmly and deliberately reeled in his line and began tidying up the boat, prepping it for the slow, treacherous trip back up the narrow creek.

The return was colder than Vern expected. The sucker fish they'd come to catch thrived in the rare deep cold snaps that swept through the usually warm Panhandle. The fish loved it—he did not.

He hadn't noticed the chill on the way down, shielded by the trees and his own excitement. But now, with the wind cutting directly into his face, the cold felt sharp, bitter—like something you'd expect in Chicago or somewhere farther north.

The sky had turned a dull gray, thick clouds hiding the sun. Vern pursed his lips, the chill settling into his bones, the gloomy weather mirroring the weight in his chest.

Pops, true to his word, stayed in the truck as Vern slowly made his way back into the store. When he opened the door, the bell on top chimed and even though only a couple of people were there with the old man, Vern felt a lump swelling in his throat, but chewed it back and stepped in, avoiding eye contact.

The old blind man welcomed him, smiling behind the counter, just as he had the first time. Vern thought to himself that this couldn't get any worse. Surely when this man found out what he had done, he would be furious and call the sheriff. He prepared for the worst.

His voice cracked when he said, "Mr. Eli, I'm Vern Bruce." The old man's smile remained as he nodded. Vern placed the candy bar on the counter in front of him. To Vern's surprise, the old man's smile never faded. It stayed fixed on his wrinkled, whiskery face—calm, knowing, and untouched.

"I know who you are, son, and I *know* why you're here," the old man said through the mustache that fell below his top lip as he ran a finger down the candy bar where Vern placed it. "Your Daddy is a good man. Known him most of his life. He send you in here?"

Vern began to nod but realized Mr. Eli, his sight taken from him long ago, couldn't see him and said "Yes, sir. I'm sorry."

The smile finally left his wrinkled face, and he leaned down across the counter and asked Vern, "Are you *really* son? Or are you doing this because your father told you to?"

Vern's eyes dropped to the floor, shame creeping into his expression. For a split second, he considered lying—but the truth slipped out instead, quiet and honest.

"My dad made me," he said under his breath.

The old man tightened his lips, reaching for an old tobacco pipe next to his money box. He put it between his teeth and his smile returned. "Honesty, son, is something not everyone has. You have it. You could have lied to me, but you told me the stone-cold truth. I respect that." Vern shook his head slightly in disbelief as the old man continued, "Tell you what, I'm going to let you make it up to me. You come down here once a week, sweep my store for month, and we'll call it even."

Vern couldn't hide his broad smile, and he reached up to shake Mr. Eli's hand and to his surprise the old man grabbed it tightly, returning the gesture.

"I left my eyesight in France, but I brought my ears back home with me," he said, laughing.

"Yes, sir." Vern said loudly and ran out of the store. Pops leaned on the hood of his old Ford truck, talking to a passer-by. He didn't smile or say a word. He just nodded and the two of them got in the truck and bumped along the road in silence.

Neither spoke of the incident again. Vern not only kept his end of the bargain but worked for Mr. Eli throughout his high school years and only bade goodbye when he left for Tallahassee and college. Mr. Eli passed away the same week he left. He hadn't thought about him for a long time and tonight, from a prison cell, he remembered the lesson learned from an old blind man.

Vern knew the moment he lied that he sacrificed the honesty those men had once seen in him. And when he signed that guilty plea, it was like putting his name on a version of himself he didn't recognize. He could pretend he did it for the chance to see his boys, to be close to them in any way he could. But deep down, he knew better. If Pops and his Mr. Eli could see him now—see what he had become—they'd be disappointed. Deeply. Painfully.

Tears began to form in his eyes, but he fought them back. He remembered the last thing Mr. Eli told him, "Son, your word is your bond." Vern could hear the old man's voice in his mind and he couldn't hold back the tears any longer. They streamed down his face. He squirmed on the hard mattress, closing his eyes,

knowing it was going to be another sleepless night.

Chapter 24

Cliff sat perched on the sandy beach, the warmth of the sun kissing his face, but his thoughts were miles away. No matter how hard he tried, he couldn't shake Katie's pretty face from his mind. It lingered there; soft, smiling, and impossibly distracting.

For the first time in a while, his morning didn't start with thoughts of his uncle or father. It didn't fill him with warmth like the sun on his face, though. He couldn't help but feel a little selfish. It didn't feel right thinking about his own happiness when Unc was still in prison and his father's fate unknown felt wrong, but he couldn't get her face out of his mind. The sand felt course as he wiggled toes. He missed the sugar white, soft sands of the Panhandle where he and Casey played as young kids.

He glanced down at the small sheet of paper held delicately between two fingers, its edges fluttering slightly in the breeze. The allure of her phone number was overwhelming. Teenage thoughts consumed him. Just for once, he wanted to call this young lady. He so wanted to live a life he hadn't allowed for himself for so long, but he couldn't shake the feeling that in doing so he was pushing his family to the side. He stared into the bright sunshine, squinting, trying to figure out what to do. Out of the corner of his eye, he saw RB walking across the sand.

Cliff held up his hand as RB approached, "RB, I don't think I want to go today. I've got something else I need to do."

"Son, we need to talk." RB looked around, "Just you and me. Where's Casey?" Cliff shrugged his shoulders and told the detective he hadn't seen his younger cousin today and he was probably at the surf shop. "Let's go to the house," RB said, looking around and nodded his head towards the mansion beyond the swaying vegetation on the dunes.

The pair sat at the small breakfast table in the corner, RB eyes down towards the floor and said lowly, "Now, son, I need you to promise me you won't get riled up over what I'm about to show you and tell you." RB looked up at the teenager and waited for a response.

Cliff smiled at him, trying to put him to ease and nodded, "RB, whatever it is, you know me."

The detective eased the picture out of his pocket and placed it on the table in front of Cliff. Cliff reached out, slid the picture over to him and picked it up. He peered at it for several seconds and said, confused, "Looks like Burt on a beach."

RB took a deep breath, "That's exactly what it is." He looked at the palm dancing in the wind outside, trying to find the words, "The place and time is what's important."

Cliff tilted his head, his gaze breaking from the picture as he turned to face RB. "What's the deal RB?" he asked, his voice starting to show concern. RB took another deep breath. He had passed the point of no return, and he had to tell Cliff the truth.

RB took the picture from Cliff's hand, pointed to the image of Burt, and said, "That was taken on the beach near the

West Palm Marina..." he paused, "...Same night Patty Lee Bruce was murdered." RB waited for Cliff's reaction before continuing, but Cliff only sat there in silence, so the detective went ahead, "Lady took the picture because the guy startled her in the dark and the flash caught him right in the face. It's blurry, but it's him. Burt Williams, in the vicinity, when she was killed," RB paused again, "It ain't just a hell of a coincidence." He looked toward the heavens, "As bad as I wish it were."

Cliff's stonelike face stared back at RB and the detective couldn't tell if Cliff grasped exactly what he had told him.

RB decided to tell the kid the cold truth. He leaned in, matching Cliff's expression and put his hand on the kid's shoulder. "Burt is a stone-cold killer, kid, always has been. I've waited on the day he would turn on me and if he finds out about this, today would probably be that day."

Cliff's eyebrows furrowed, "All right, but why tell *me*? This has more to do with Casey. That was *his* mom," Cliff asked.

RB shook his head. "You want Casey to live, don't you? You know he would go after Burt and what would happen, Cliff? What would Burt do?" Cliff thought about what RB said for a moment, realizing RB was right. He shook his head in agreement. Casey couldn't know about this, not for now, at least.

Cliff stood up, "What do we do RB?" he asked.

RB scratched the stubble on his chin and took yet another deep breath. "*I* confront Burt with this, consequences be damned and try to get him to tell me the truth. Maybe, just maybe, I can get the truth about your uncle out of him. We both know that he was involved in that, and I think *you* were the reason."

Cliff closed his eyes as tears began to fall, "I've always known. All of this was *my* fault. My fault for being born. My fault for causing Unc and Patty Lee to grow apart. My fault for loving my uncle more than anyone. I should've just stayed with my mother." Cliff stopped his tears, but the color drained from his face, "She might still be alive, too, if I hadn't have...."

RB jumped up, put his arms around Cliff, "Son, ain't none of this your fault. Not a damn bit. You've been dealt a bad hand since you got put on this earth." He squeezed Cliff tightly, "I know that your mother loved you son. She loved you so much that she let you go. She loved you so much that she wasn't going to take you away from the life you had." RB took Cliff's head in his hands, "Burt Williams, son. Burt Williams is the bad guy here. You did nothing wrong."

Cliff buried his head in RB's arms, no longer holding back tears. He cried for what seemed like hours before and, in between sobs, he asked RB to let him go when the detective confronted Burt.

The detective shook his head, "I'm going to wear a wire, son. If he finds it or even thinks I'm betraying him, the game is over. I can't put you in that position."

"You can't do this without me, RB, and you know it," Cliff told him, wiping the tears from his eyes, "At the very least, I owe it to Casey to find out the truth about his mother. She may have not given a damn about me, but Case was closer to *her* than his dad. I'm *going*, RB."

Keeping Cliff safe had to be his highest priority and the only way to do that was to keep the kid close. RB relented, "You go, but you stay in the background, hidden." He said, pointing his long finger at Cliff, "If it goes bad, you stay hid. You wait. You wait for hours if you have to, make sure he's not watching, and you go to this man in Biloxi." RB handed Cliff a card with the name *Stacy Rose – Biloxi Police* printed on it along with a telephone number and address. "Get in a car and go." He put both his hands on Cliff's shoulders, "I trust this man with my life, son. You promise me that you will." Cliff nodded and promised RB he would do exactly as instructed.

"How do we do this," Cliff asked.

RB sat back down and leaned back, his hand nervously rubbing his chin, "We tail him. Tomorrow night, we tail him. He'll probably still be shacked up with that secretary of his and we do it there. Corner him up a little bit. If it does go south, confined space could give me the advantage and son, if it does go bad, and I live, you know what that means."

Cliff bit his lip, "It means you gotta get out of here. No more help with Unc."

RB saw the hurt in the kid's eyes, "Head up kid. I'm from Biloxi, Mississippi. I've gambled all my life and here I am." RB beat his chest. They both smiled. Just a little. But behind those faint expressions, a shared sense of dread crept quietly into their minds. Neither said it aloud, but they both felt it. Something was coming—inevitable, heavy, and close. And no matter how faint or forced, neither smile could hold it back. Not now. Not anymore.

"What happens if it goes bad and you have to *kill* Burt?" Cliff asked, his voice cracking slightly.

"We may never know what happened," he said, looking into Cliff's eyes. RB shrugged his shoulders and said, "Son, that's a gamble we're taking. This is an all or nothing move here. But, if something happens, and either Burt's gone or I am, start with Kendrick. There's something more there. I know it."

The surf shop was unusually busy for a change. Since Dell's disappearance, Cliff's friends had taken over the inside of the shop, chasing away business. Most times, tourists came in but quickly left when they saw the weed dealers hanging around. Casey didn't mind. He didn't want customers anyway. This was just the place he came, hung out and smoked weed when he wanted to get away from Cliff and Burt. The summer, however, was winding down and the tourists came in looking for stuff to take home. They filled every corner of the shop and Casey couldn't wait until they were gone so he could light up.

He looked up from a Penthouse magazine just in time to see Mateo Diaz walk through the door. The Columbian wasn't smiling and seemed to bulldoze his way through the tourists, actually pushing one aside with his shoulder. Stopping in the middle of the show floor, he yelled, "Sorry my good people, but the store is closing!" With that announcement, a couple more of his men entered the store and began herding the crowd out, locking the door as the last one scurried out the door.

Diaz, the floor empty as even Casey's friends got the message and left with the tourists, turned his attention to the young teenager and gestured in his direction. Casey eased the magazine under the counter and felt for the gun he hid there after his first encounter with Diaz. Diaz moved his finger back and forth and Casey slowly put his hand back on the counter, the gun remaining hidden away.

"Young, Mr. Bruce. Hello," Diaz tipped his cap as he spoke, "I apologize for the interference in your *commerce,* but we really needed to speak alone."

Casey's hands began sweating, but, remembering what Burt had told him about weaknesses, he didn't want Diaz to notice. "Sure, Mr. Diaz. Let me stick my head in the shop and tell those guys to clear out."

He hoped Diaz would comply and if he did the young teenager decided he would make a run for it. Diaz stomped those thoughts into the ground when he replied, "No need, young Mr. Bruce. Some of my men told them you were closing early and therefore to leave." Casey felt a knot form in his throat. He was trapped. He could try and get to the gun again, but there were two men already standing on opposing sides of Diaz. He saw their hands inside their thin sports jackets.

Diaz pointed to the small office and as they walked inside, Diaz' companions took up stations on either side of the doorway. As they sat down, Diaz reached into his pocket. Casey flinched visibly. "No, no, no Mr. Bruce. There is no need to be afraid." Diaz said, looking around as if to inspect the shop making sure no tourists remained. "I am here once again, as your friend." A sideways grin appeared on his face as he spoke, and his voice gentle and calm.

His voice didn't calm Casey's nerves in the least, and he felt beads of sweat forming on his forehead. "Do you have anything cold to drink, perhaps a Dr. Pepper?" Casey told him there was a drink machine near the shop doors in the back. Diaz motioned and the two guards left. "They will retrieve us some refreshment. While they are gone, I want you to see this." Diaz placed a photograph on the desk in front of the kid and the wry smile turned upside down. Diaz repositioned the desk lamp so that it illuminated the picture. "Do you know who this is?" he asked, speaking as though he soothed a crying baby.

Casey held the picture under the light. "Looks like Burt but it's a really bad picture."

Mateo nodded slightly, but noticeably and held his frown as he replied, "It is *indeed* Mr. Williams. A picture taken by a frightened woman. Poor soul was too frightened to bring it to the police, but someone finally convinced her to do so."

"Burt was probably doing her, right?" Casey tried to laugh but it came out more of a slight nervous chuckle.

Diaz shook his head, "You shouldn't think of such things, my friend. You are too young." he scolded Casey.

The teenager raised an eyebrow. The urge to run became overtaken by the urge to fight. He tilted his chin back, grinned at the Colombian asking, "What the hell does this have to do with me?"

Diaz glanced around the room again, more for effect than surveillance, moving his face closer to Casey's, "The evening this picture was taken was the night your mother died, my friend." He stared at Casey for a second before continuing, "The location was the beach near the marina in which you and your mother sailed." Diaz motioned with his hands as if to say, there you go.

At first Casey didn't realize the importance of Diaz' words, but, slowly, his adolescent brain began to process the information. As the realization of what he told him sank into his mind, his face reddened. "What the fuck are you saying? Burt had something to do with my mom?" he asked, anger dripping from his words.

Diaz rubbed his hands together, "I'm afraid, my young friend, that is *exactly* what I'm saying. There is no other reason for Burt Williams to be there. None. He was there with an associate of mine. They were there to kill Christian Lopez, but Williams took your mother's life without pause," he told him coldly.

Casey burst from his chair, "But why? Why would Burt kill my mother?" he asked, shaking his head.

The Colombian stood, took a couple of steps towards the wall with his back to Casey, "Think about it. Long ago, he was tasked with taking Cliff away from his uncle for familial reasons that I won't go into now. He saw an opportunity to take *you*. Take you and your money and power also. He took it. Gambled with *your* life and won." Diaz paused and asked Casey if he understood what he was telling him, and Casey shook his head yes, but the Colombian knew that it couldn't be making sense in his youthful mind but continued, "*He* made it so that you would be taken to Dozier. *He* knew your father couldn't allow that. Vernon Bruce made a deal with the devil and put the soul of his only son in peril, *hoping* you would be safe until he worked things out, but Burt Williams made sure that didn't happen."

Casey's face held no emotion, almost as if a stone wall formed right before Diaz' eyes. "Mr. Bruce, Casey, I tell you this so that you will *know*. What you do with it, is entirely up to you," Diaz said. The Columbian reached into his pocket once more and this time, Casey didn't flinch. It was like the child, in shock, became impassive and unreactive. Diaz shook his head slightly and for the first time hesitated to move forward, but he knew he had little choice.

In his hand, he held a pistol, its weight steady and deliberate. Without a word, he placed it directly on the picture still lying on the table. The chrome plating caught the glow of the desk lamp, casting sharp reflections across the surface—cold, bright, and unmistakable.

Diaz pointed towards the weapon, "This gun is not traceable. It has no markings and no numbers." He pushed the weapon towards Casey and said, "Do with it what you must." Casey didn't move and Diaz whistled. The guards returned holding no refreshments in their hands. "One more thing, Casey, your cousin *knows*." The kid's stone face melted away instantly, "What do you mean he *knows*?"

"Your cousin received this same information today. The detective told him. Perhaps you should talk with him." Diaz said nothing else. He left, along with the two guards, got into his old car and left. The driver Diaz had sent to shoo away the workers in the back had long since started the engine, waiting for the rest of the party to return.

Casey fell into a chair. He sat there alone in the dark and in silence. He put his head in his hands, trying to understand everything he was told. He needed to talk to Cliff. Together they would figure out what to do about Burt Williams. *Cliff will know what to do*, he thought, *he had to*.

Casey's emotions were in turmoil. The anger he felt mixed with guilt. Guilted over the fact that he let that monster into his life and let the asshole manipulate him like this. Guilt that he helped Burt get rid of Dell's body overwhelmed him. He thought he had fought through it, but now, knowing that Burt had worked him, it swelled to the top of his very soul. He screamed in the silence and thought about the monster he had become.

Casey's only hope lay in his cousin. Cliff and RB probably were already planning to do the right thing and do it by the law. Casey opened the top drawer of the filing cabinet beside the office door and a bottle rolled back and forth. He grabbed it before it could roll to the back once more. He twisted open the top and turned the bottle towards the sky. The alcohol burnt his throat as it made its way into his stomach. He repeated the motion several times, pushing himself past the edge, until his young system couldn't take any more. Finally, he collapsed back into the chair, breath shallow, his head spinning like the room was tilting beneath him.

The alcohol pulsing though his veins and with his young mind burning for revenge, he yelled, "To hell with Cliff." He took another swing and said in a whisper, "*I'll* take care of this."

Chapter 25

The motel room was dark. The secretary had long since left to return to her own family, her tryst with Burt Williams over. Burt sat in a chair facing the window with the curtain pulled back so he could see the flashing neon light. A bottle of bourbon sat empty on the table beside him. He glanced back at the old-style alarm clock between the beds, realizing dawn was near.

Through the gently swaying palms and the glow of the sign, he watched Jeff Black's car ease into the parking lot. The tall, lanky Brazilian parked far as he could from Burt's room and walked slowly towards the door, his head forward, but his eyes were darting back and forth, on surveillance. Both men knew all too well that the quiet times were the ones that demanded the most vigilance. When everything seemed still, that's when trouble usually crept in.

He watched as Black carefully approached the door, his steps slow and measured. But before he could knock, Burt swung it open, already expecting him.

Black gave a short nod and stepped inside, only to pause for a moment as the smell hit him. The aroma of stale liquor, sweat, and something else he couldn't quite place filled the room. He winced, the reaction unmissable, but said nothing.

"Do you even take baths anymore?" Black asked.

Burt just shrugged, shifting his weight, "No point, really."

Black took a couple of shallow breaths, continuing into the room. He sat on the unmade bed that held empty bottles and an ash tray laying on its side, clinging to the wrinkled sheet.

The Brazilian shot a glance towards the ceiling, gathering his thoughts before he spoke, "Mr. Williams, tonight we will meet with Diaz and his people at his warehouse. Don't you think you need to sober up before that happens?"

Burt smiled as he slowly sat back down and resumed looking out the window. In a low tone of voice he said, "For what we have to do, I *want* to be stoned." He reached into the shirt lying on the floor beside him and took out a small bag, shaking the contents onto the table. With a razor blade, he shaped the powder into a straight, precise line. Without hesitation, he leaned down, planted his nose, and inhaled the entire thing in one sharp, practiced motion. When he finished, he lifted his head slowly and looked back at Black. A dusting of powder clung to the tip of his nose, his pupils dilated, eyes momentarily rolling back before settling. A wide, crooked smile spread across his face—euphoric, wild, and unsettling.

Black shook his head in disgust. There was no use in any further discussion with Burt Williams and at this point, he was disgusted and didn't really care.

"Boys in Biloxi said they would be here, should be enough," Burt told him, trying to focus his eyes, and then he turned to face the Brazilian, "What about *your* people?"

Black replied sternly, "My people are few, but what they do is what is *important*."

"Just make sure they are there." Burt said, still trying to focus.

"My people are dependable," Black responded, "I trust them with my life."

Burt snickered, widening his eyes to look at the sun slowly illuminating the water across the street. "I trust *nobody* with my life," he said under his breath.

Black turned his head slightly but not enough that Burt could see his expression, "Is that not what you are doing tonight?"

Burt wheeled the chair around, spinning it on one leg. When it stopped he leaned as close to Black as he could, the unmade bed separating them. "I always have an ace in the hole."

Black smiled, humoring the stoned gangster, "And what would that be?"

Burt stood up, opened a drawer from the nightstand and pulled out a long, sharpened hunting knife. "If I told you, it wouldn't be an ace." Burt placed the knife back into the drawer, gently sliding it shut. Black sank deep in thought as Burt sat back down and fumbled around for the full, unopened bottle.

Hopefully, Burt would either pass out from the drink or the powder for a while so he could contact Baxter. Every plan they had put in place could be thwarted by some wildcard that Burt Williams pulled from his pocket. Unfortunately for Black, Burt didn't pass out. He didn't use any more powder, but his drinking didn't stop. His system had long since grown used to the abuse and it refused to shut down. For hours they sat. Burt grew drunker and angrier while Black grew more apprehensive.

He caught a break volunteering to go to vending machines in the lobby to grab them something to eat. He couldn't leave Burt for very long, but he had to get some food into him to soak up some of the poison flowing through his body.

When he walked in, he noticed a pay phone in the corner and nodded to the clerk behind the desk. He didn't want to seem out of place and tried his best to be unnoticeable. He took great care for the clerk not to hear his conversation as his accent was noticeable to most.

"What news?" Baxter asked, his voice low and rough on the other end of the line.

Like Black, he hadn't slept much in recent days. He had been up since before the first hint of daylight. His body, still broken and slowly healing from years of captivity, ached with a relentless, familiar pain that seemed to live in every muscle, every joint. Even the pills barely touched it anymore.

"Burt Williams is high and extremely drunk. He told me his people are on their way from Mississippi. Everything is working out. But there is one thing," he said carefully, "Williams feels he holds some kind of *ace*, as he calls it. He will not tell me what it is."

"That ace is the son of Vernon Bruce. But..." Baxter paused, "Diaz holds *that* card, and he will play it tonight. Just be sure we have the backup plan in place. Just in case."

"It is my experience that nothing ever goes *according* to plans. I am always prepared," Black assured him. "We just need to make sure that Williams' ace is indeed what we think."

"It is. If it isn't just take care of it *yourself*," Baxter replied and wished his friend good luck before hanging up the phone.

Black placed the phone on the hook but stood there with his hand on it for several seconds before he realized the clerk stared at him from behind the desk. He flashed a toothy grin in the clerk's direction before selecting some candy from the machine and scurrying out the door. He studied each person, every car and every movement, no matter how slight, on his way back to Burt's room. When he opened the door, Burt's deep guttural snoring reverberated throughout the room. Black laughed to himself and thought, *now he sleeps*. He sat back down on the unmade bed, pulled his shoes off and threw his feet onto the sheets. Before long, his snoring joined Burt's.

While Burt and Jeff Black snored in the hotel room, Casey was just getting out of bed. Surprisingly, he slept well even as the words of Mateo Diaz echoed inside his mind the entire night. Before he fell into the deep sleep, no doubt aided by the intoxicating liquor he drank before leaving the surf shop, all he could picture was Burt Williams, knife in hand, taking his mother's life. As he opened his groggy eyes, he felt the throbbing in his head and contemplated drifting back to sleep but didn't. He forced himself out of bed and after he put on some clothes, he stumbled out of his room looking for Cliff.

The search didn't last long as he found Cliff in the living room with his notebook in his lap. He wrote furiously on one of the pages as Casey sat down next to him. Immediately, Cliff closed his notebook. It had become a diary of sorts and Casey didn't need to know what he wrote.

"What are you hiding?" Casey snapped as he eyed Cliff. Cliff shook his head and just said it was a note to a girl he met a couple of weeks ago. Casey nodded but didn't believe him. He looked at his cousin and asked, "What was you and RB up to yesterday? You figure out the mystery?" He wanted to ask Cliff, point blank, about what he learned about Burt, but the old gangster did teach him some things and one of the most important was not to tip his hand too quickly. Instead, he probed gently and hoped Cliff would give up something on his own.

"We just looked into some stuff, nothing major. He's coming by in a little bit and we are going to check some more things out. Why are you so interested all of a sudden?" Cliff asked, raising an eyebrow.

"He is *my* dad," Casey replied matter of factly.

Cliff responded curtly, "You never cared before."

Casey slowed down his thoughts, choosing his words carefully, "Well, I've been thinking about him..." he paused,

"...and my mother. One is never coming back, the other, well, there *is* still hope."

Cliff tilted his head to one side, hawkishly staring at his cousin's face trying to figure out his angle, "If I find out anything, I'll fill you in."

Casey raised his palms, accepting the answer, even though he knew it wasn't the whole truth. He nodded to Cliff and went into the kitchen, leaving the older cousin alone with his notebook.

Casey sank into the corner nook, his anger swelling. Cliff had the opportunity to tell him the truth, the whole truth, at that moment, and he didn't do it. Casey didn't feel betrayed, he merely felt alone. Burt had been the only person in his life who seemed to care—especially after Cliff's mother died. But now, with everything unraveling, that connection felt distant, frayed. For the first time, Cliff felt completely alone—like he was the only person left on the planet.

He gathered himself, opened the refrigerator, and drank milk straight out of the carton. There was nobody around to tell him not to. It was like he and Cliff were on their own and they pretty much were. Burt had disappeared and neither had heard from him for days now. Casey was happy about that. Right now, he didn't want to hear Burt's voice.

Cliff walked in and pulled a glass out of the cabinet and placed it next to the carton. "We ain't gonna live like animals," he told his cousin. Casey wanted to start a fight, telling Cliff to mind his own damned business, but bit his tongue. He decided to play along and poured the milk into the glass, throwing a facetious grin in his cousin's direction.

"Where are you and RB going?" he asked, still probing.

"I honestly don't know. RB just said he had a lead on something, all I know," he lied, and Casey knew that he was lying. Cliff's voice always gave it away. Casey didn't know exactly what changed in Cliff's voice, but somehow, he could tell.

"Burt ever come up in y'all's snooping around?"

Cliff shot Casey a confused look, "Why would Burt come up?"

Now it was Cliff turn to poke around for information from his younger cousin. "Well, I mean, he *is* what he *is*," Casey told him, trying to keep his words vague.

Cliff nodded confusedly and said, "I'm glad you're finally realizing that Burt Williams may not be the best role model."

Casey laughed, "I've always known that, but you do what you have to do."

"We agree on something," Cliff said with a smile and slapped Casey on the back. Even though both cousins were speaking as though they agreed, they both eyed each other suspiciously, toying with the truth. Cliff went back to the living room, picking up where he left off in his notebook and Casey called one of his buddies to come by and pick him up. He didn't have to wait long and as soon as he arrived, they left for the surf shop.

Cliff sat on the couch, staring blankly at the sheet of paper in front of him, a pencil resting loosely in his hand. He didn't want to write anything more. The small spark of connection he thought he might've made with Casey was something he desperately wanted to grow, but the lie he'd told was already gnawing at his soul. He hated lying. Always had. Probably why he was so bad at it. But this one had felt necessary.

If he told Casey what he'd found out the day before, his cousin wouldn't be able to hold his temper. Cliff knew it. And if that happened, things would spiral out of control—and fast.

His mind turned, however, to why Casey asked the questions he did. He wondered why Casey, for the first time, had shown interest. When RB got there, he would tell him about Casey's questions and see what the detective thought. It could be nothing, but then again, he couldn't take chances. His family was at stake.

Mateo Diaz waited in the parking lot of the surf shop. He had been there, baking in the Florida sun for hours expecting Casey to show up. As he was just about to give up and make his way to the Clark House, he saw young Casey in the passenger seat of a newer model Mustang pull into the parking lot. The weed business amongst these young guys thrived and Diaz thought about the future when these same guys fell under the control of the cartels. The day the rednecks were gone, with the Brazilians taking over their enterprises up north.

The deal worked out between all the parties involved finally would allow for a sort of peace and an end to the violence surrounding the game they all played. He also thought of the day when Phillipe' lived in America with him. He smiled and held his hand out of the window. He still drove the old jalopy but figured Casey was young and dumb enough to try to ignore him.

When Casey saw Diaz waving from his old car, he thought about telling his buddy to pull back out onto the highway and head out of town, but youthful curiosity set in. He pointed and they pulled up next to the Columbian.

"Mr. Bruce," he said, "Just wanted to give you a little whisper." Diaz nodded towards the driver and Casey got out and told him to take off. The guy in the car didn't hesitate and sped away as quickly as he could.

"What's up?" Casey asked, wiping his long brown bangs out of his eyes so he could look Diaz in the eye.

"Tonight, my friend, Mr. Williams will come to my warehouse. He thinks he is going to kill me and take over my business..." he bowed his head so that he could lock eyes with Casey without taking off his sunglasses, "...as he did yours."

The blank expression Casey had worn the night before was gone. Now, emotion bled through—his jaw tightened, and a flush crept up his neck, coloring his face with rising anger.

"Where is your warehouse?" he asked, his voice sharp, clipped, and full of barely restrained fury.

Diaz didn't smile and his face, also, showed no emotion, "I will send a car for you. You be *here* in a couple of hours. Do you still have the *item* I gave you?" Casey nodded and a smile spread across Diaz' face, "Good. Be here."

Diaz drove away but Casey didn't go into the surf shop. He walked across the street, sat down on the sand, and watched waves crashing onto the beach. He watched the seagulls as they floated on the breeze above him, hoping for a piece of bread or scrap of a doughnut. As soon as they discovered nothing was coming their way, they flew away searching elsewhere for their next meal. He reached into his pocket and pulled out a small cassette player and put the headphones over his ears. He pushed the play button and Ronnie Van Zant's voice sang about flying away, free as a bird. Right then, Casey wished he *was* one of those seagulls floating on the breeze. Flying away to a different life.

Chapter 26

For once, the warehouse wasn't dark. Diaz had made sure
of that. Fluorescent lights buzzed overhead, casting a sterile glow
across the massive, empty space. He sat alone in the corner office,
glass walls giving him a full view of the cavernous interior.

Loud popping sounds echoed through the emptiness as the
metal structure expanded and contracted in the sweltering Florida
heat and thick humidity. They reminded him of gunshots—distant,
muffled, but unmistakable. The sound was burned into his
memory.

As a child, he hadn't feared the crack of gunfire—*not at
first.* But the ricochets, the wild, unpredictable whine of bullets
bouncing off trees—that's when fear set in. That's when danger
became real.

He remembered how his mother would rush them into the
floor, lifting the loose plank that covered a hole in their
ramshackle home, guiding them into the crawlspace like she'd
done it a hundred times. When he closed his eyes now, he could
almost see her thin frame crouched over them, shielding them
with her body.But when he opened his eyes again, she was gone.
Just another ghost, fading into the fog of memory.

The years were few before he went from hiding under his
mother's care to ending a man's life. There was no fear, no hatred,
no feelings at all when he first pulled the trigger. There was only a
job to be done and being the child he was, he didn't know what he

should feel so he felt nothing. The feeling of numbness accompanied him each time he took a life. *Now*, he thought, *I'm going to do the same to another child.* A chill ran down his spine and the hairs stood to attention on his arms. The door swung open on the far end of the warehouse and his focus on the task at hand returned.

Two men appeared and with the bright lights shining down from the ceiling, he could see that it was Burt Williams and Jeff Black. Their guns drawn and both seemed confused as they stepped into the brightly lit space. Diaz smiled because the men expected darkness, so he flicked a switch on the wall and gave it to them. Diaz began walking towards them, his weapon safely tucked into the back of his pants.

"Gentlemen, welcome," Diaz said as they met in the middle of the building, "What brings you here on this night?" The only light now coming from the office behind Diaz, giving him the advantage.

Burt snickered some words he couldn't quite make out, and Diaz could tell he wasn't quite sober. The Colombian realized, however, he had enough of his wits about him to be dangerous. "Just thought we might have a little talk about *business*," Burt said, this time there was no mistaking the gangster's words. As he spoke, Burt positioned his pistol so that the cold steel pointed directly at Diaz' torso. Black held his weapon by his side.

"Mr. Williams, just what are your intentions?" Diaz asked as he nodded at the pistol in Burt's hand. Burt listened intently to the darkness before speaking. A heavy rain began to pound the warehouse's metal roof, each drop landing with a sharp, echoing clang that quickly built into a near-deafening roar. Diaz didn't flinch. He just sat there, letting the sound wash over him; loud, relentless, and oddly familiar. Like the chaos he'd grown up with. Like home.

"Where's your *friends*, Diaz?" Burt questioned the Columbian.

"Oh, they have the night off." he replied.

Lifting his pistol, Burt noticed the smile on his opponent's face "I'm just going to put a bullet in your grinning ass and be done."

Mateo's smile widened, "Aren't you afraid of what would happen not only to *you*, but your family, Mr. Williams if you do such a thing?"

Burt returned the Columbian's smile, "What damn family? I ain't got none."

"What about your boys Mr. Williams, what are their names, Cliff and Casey?" he asked, still smiling.

"Those are just little bastards with nowhere else to go. One's a pussy and the other is a loser. Y'all won't get *me*. I'll make off with every penny. You see..." Burt continued, waving his gun up and down, "...when that boy of Vern Bruce is dead or in prison, I'm going to get it all." Burt leaned towards him and said, "Kill him right now and you'd be doing me a favor."

Black, silent as the two men confronted each other, took a step away from Burt, slowly raising his weapon, aiming it at the gangster. "I kinda figured that," Burt said and let out a whistle that was barely audible over the rain beating down on the roof. The door opened once again, and a single figure appeared.

Burt yelled, "Where's the rest?" There was no reply as the figure walked slowly towards them. Burt asked again and still there was no reply. Burt hadn't noticed Black moving away and when he reached the wall, the lights once again flashed on, nearly blinding everyone for a split second. When Burt's eyes regained focus, the slight frame of Casey Bruce began to emerge in his vision. He held a silver-plated gun in his right hand, while his other hand balled into a fist.

Out of the corner of his eye, Burt saw Diaz had pulled his weapon, trained it on him, and suddenly sweat began to form from every pore in his bulbous body. He held his smile, however, and said, "Son, I don't know what he's told you, but..." Burt felt the floor first, not the initial impact of the handle of Diaz' weapon. He quickly scrambled back to his knees, fury surging through him as his pale skin flushed crimson.

"You bastards!" he roared, voice cracking with rage. "Just wait until my boys get here—none of you will see tomorrow!" The threat echoed off the warehouse walls, sharp and wild, filled with a desperation that couldn't be masked.

Jeff Black finally spoke as he stepped back towards the three, "Nobody's coming, Mr. Williams. It seems you've crossed too many people in your beloved *Biloxi*. When I reached out, they didn't hesitate to abandon you. They wasted no time in agreeing to *our* deal."

Burt just glared at him. A small stream of blood trickled down his forehead. He cursed the traitors back home to himself, "Son of a bitch," was all he said aloud, his mind burning with thoughts of vengeance. *It ain't gonna end like this*, he thought.

"This, Mr. Williams, is where we say adios," Diaz said coldly and motioned to Black. The two men started walking away. Burt looked at Casey and smiled, "You think this *kid* is going to put a bullet in me?" Burt laughed loudly and winked at Casey. "You motherfuckers are dead! you just don't know it yet!" Burt yelled.

The two men didn't turn around, walking out the door, not closing it completely. Casey and Burt were alone. Burt tried to get up, but the teenager took a step towards him and pulled the hammer back on the pistol. The rain pounded harder against the metal building, a relentless drumbeat that swallowed every other sound. It filled the space completely, drowning out even the faintest noise. He didn't hear the soft click of the pistol being cocked. It was as if the world had gone silent in every way that mattered. It was as if he had become deaf to everything but the storm above.

"Son..." Burt started but Casey cut him off.

"Don't you call me that. I heard *everything,* Burt. Diaz put the phone on speaker in the office. I was on the other end. I heard.

You want my money. *Kill him*, you said." Burt's smile disappeared instantly. He began nervously stumbling over his words. His confidence dissipated as sweat beading on his forehead began pouring down his face like a crimson river, mixing with blood.

"Listen, kid, remember what I told you," Burt pleaded, hoping he could talk his way out of the situation, "When someone has a gun to your head, you do what you got to do to survive."

The expression on the kid's face eased as Burt sensed his confusion. "You are like a *son* to me Casey. I got plans for you kid, big plans, but first, you got to lower that gun." He held up his hand and motioned for Casey to lower the weapon. The other hand eased behind his back and felt the handle of his grandfather's knife. No one had noticed the knife stuffed in the small of his back.

Casey's breathing intensified. He blinked continuously, trying to regain his composure. His right hand began to tremble, and the pistol felt like a hunk of lead, growing heavier in his grip.

"Would your *mother* want you to do this?" Burt asked. Suddenly the revolver felt lighter and the tremble that overtook his hand steadied. Casey moved the weapon back towards Burt's forehead.

"*You* killed my mother, you bastard!" he yelled.

Burt didn't flinch and said calmly, "*Those* people killed your mother, son." Casey's anger only grew as he reached into his pocket and took the picture of Burt and tossed it on the floor in front of the prostrated figure.

"You killed her and now it's your turn," he returned just as calmly. Burt, for the first time, saw real resolve in his eyes. He didn't really believe it before, but now he thought the boy just might actually do it.

While Burt tried to talk his way out of death, Diaz and Black sat in the parked car, waiting for young Casey to pull the trigger. The thin metal siding wouldn't muffle the sound very much, even in the pouring rain. Diaz kept his window rolled down. It didn't matter if the old car got wet on the inside or not. They had to hear. If the kid didn't get it done, they had the front covered and his most trusted men had the back.

Suddenly, car lights popped up around the corner and the Columbian threw a glance to Black. He shook his head, indicating he didn't expect visitors either. Diaz didn't want to leave with the issue still in doubt, but he had no choice but to back away from the warehouse and hide the car, and themselves, in the thick undergrowth.

He started the engine and quickly, without turning on his headlights, backed the car into a small space between a couple of swamp palmettos. The other vehicle pulled up beside Burt's parked car, turning off its lights. When two occupants stepped out, through the blinding rain, Diaz recognized Cliff Bruce and the detective from Mississippi. He motioned for Black to remain quiet.

"You sure they went in there?" Cliff asked. RB nodded.

The detective grimaced. This was something he hadn't counted on, and he looked at Cliff. He couldn't leave the boy alone, so he pointed a finger at the boy's chest.

"Stick close to me..." RB said slowly as he took a deep breath, "...I don't know what we are going to find in there."

Cliff only nodded, unable to speak. The two cautiously made their way to the door. The rain finally started to subside when RB placed his hand on the door knob. He eased it open, glancing around quickly before closing it. In that quick scan of the building, he saw two figures standing in the middle of the expansive floor. One held a gun on the other. The detective closed his eyes and said a quick prayer under his breath. The thought of telling Cliff to hold back crossed his mind, but knew the kid would be safer with him.

He eased the door open and saw the two were so concentrated on each other, they didn't notice the door. He opened it enough to step in and Cliff held tight behind him.

He assessed the situation, recognizing Casey and Burt and the realization hit him. Casey Bruce was about to kill Burt Williams. He tried to keep Cliff behind him, but the kid realized what was happening at the same time as RB, darting past the detective who had assumed a defensive position with his gun pointed in Casey's direction.

"Casey! No!" Cliff shouted as he sprinted towards his younger cousin, hoping to stop him from pulling the trigger. Cliff knew that in taking Burt's life, his cousin would end his own. He couldn't let that happen.

Casey, startled, jumped back. Burt took full advantage, getting his bulky frame to his feet as quickly as he could. He made a motion to reach for Casey's weapon, but RB had already drawn a bead on his old friend.

"No Burt! Don't move!" RB yelled and Burt took a step back.

"Buddy, am I glad to see you!" Burt said, his familiar smile returning. Cliff reached Casey, his gun still trained on Burt and knocked it out of his hand. It slid across the slick floor, far away from anyone's reach. Casey stumbled sideways and finally caught himself before he hit the floor behind Burt.

He turned and glared at his cousin, eyes blazing with pain and fury. "He killed my mother, Cliff!" he shouted, his voice raw, the words cutting slicing through the tension.

Cliff gained his own balance, "I know Case. I didn't want to tell you. I knew how you'd react." He pointed at Burt, "We are going to do this the *right* way."

Casey shook his head, tears flowing from in his eyes, "There's only *one* way."

Burt kept his eyes trained on RB and said, holding his hands in front of his body, "Whoa, RB. I didn't kill that boy's momma."

With his pistol trained on his friend, he nodded his head slightly, "Yes you did, Burt. I've seen the picture. You're going down for this one."

Burt replied, "Fuck that picture, RB. After all we been through?" Burt wagged his finger at RB, "You know I got shit on you, my friend. I go down, you go down, and as for you, jackass..." he said, turning his gaze to Cliff, "I'm going to finally get rid of you." He pointed his stubby finger at Cliff, "RB this kid ain't nothing. He's got nothing and you know it. We are supposed to work the other one," he tilted his head towards Casey, "Millions."

Cliff threw the detective a confused look and shook his head, "I knew you were just working me."

"Cliff, this goes deeper than you know. I've been working *all* of you. For the DEA, kid. I truly want to help," RB told him, "But right now, you gotta trust me." Cliff took a deep breath, nodding in agreement.

RB turned his attention back to Burt. "These boys are just that, Burt, boys. Children. I ain't like you and I don't give a shit what you *have* on me. I'll deal with that, and I'll pay my penance but you gotta go down," RB told his old partner. He reached in his jean's pocket, taking out a set of handcuffs and tossed them to Cliff, "Put them on him and then go in that office and call the cops." Cliff plucked them out of the air and headed towards Burt.

Burt turned his attention to Cliff and said, "You little shit. You are supposed to be my *son*. Fuck you. Should've took you out with your damned uncle. Maybe your mother would still be alive!" RB and Cliff snapped to attention. They looked at each other intensely.

"What the hell do you mean, Burt?" RB asked, taking a step towards him, motioning for Cliff to stay where he was. Burt smiled. He eased his hand into his shirt pocket, gently removing a cigar and just as slowly placed it in the corner of this mouth.

"I'm the only man on earth who knows what really happened with *all* that," Burt said, rolling the cigar around to the other corner of his mouth.

Cliff struggling to keep his composure yelled, "What do you know?"

With the cigar clenched between his teeth, Burt said, "You really want to know who killed Lucky Clay? What's the first rule of assassinations, kid?"

RB cocked his head to one side and said under his breath, "*Kill* the assassin."

Burt smiled, the cigar dangling from the corner of his mouth replied, "Sounds about right."

RB shook his head slightly, "So Beck killed Lucky."

Burt continued to roll the cigar in his mouth, "You got that right."

RB looked at Cliff, "That'll clear your uncle of one of the murders, kid." Burt looked back at his stepson. His demeanor changed. The old gangster couldn't help himself. He wanted to inflict as much pain on the kid as he could. Burt, grinning, said "And *I* killed the cop, but you'll never prove it."

RB stood in stunned silence as Cliff lunged towards Burt. The gangster shoved him to the side using the weight of his massive bulk. Cliff slid across the floor while Casey took a step towards Burt. In the same motion, Burt lunged for RB, but the detective was ready and pushed him backwards. Burt stumbled but didn't fall, regaining his balance.

"Stupid move, Burt." RB said as he pulled a tape recorder from his inside jacket pocket and replayed the confession.

Burt reached skyward with his hands, "Alright, you sneaky bastard, you got me. Now, let's make a deal." He continued chewing on his cigar as he spoke and said, "I know you got contacts. You'll make me a deal and I'll give you Diaz and those fucking Confederados."

RB shook his head, "That probably ain't going to be possible, Burt." RB slid the recorder back into his pocket, motioning for Cliff, who had regained his composure, to put the handcuffs he still held on Burt's wrists.

As Cliff took a step, Burt sneered, "Go ahead, you little bastard. Do it. As for you, you mother-fucking-ni..."

Before Burt could finish his sentence, a blade burst through the front of his throat, silencing him instantly. While the others argued, Casey had moved—slowly, quietly, deliberately. No one noticed as he slipped the blade from its sheath, each step calculated, fueled by rage and something far colder. And then, with one precise motion, he drove it through the back of Burt's neck.

The cigar slipped from Burt's mouth and hit the floor with a soft thud, rolling slightly before coming to a stop. In its place, a red-tinted bubble began to form within the gaping hollow of his mouth, expanding with each desperate breath. Blood poured from the wound as Casey pulled the knife back through, smooth and deliberate. Burt slowly turned, his eyes wide with disbelief as he faced his killer.

He tried to speak—tried to make sense of what was happening—but the bubble grew larger, trembled, then burst with a quiet *pop*.

Burt Williams collapsed to the ground. One final breath rattled from his lungs as his arm twitched, fingers stretching weakly toward Casey's pistol lying on the floor. He reached for it, his eyes locked in a last flicker of defiance. But the strength never came. And then, nothing.

RB and Cliff stumbled backward, their mouths agape, frozen in disbelief. The weight of what had just happened pressed down on all of them like a collapsing roof.

Casey stood motionless, his chest heaving, staring at them with a steely, unreadable gaze. But then, without warning, the dam broke. The tears he'd buried for so long came pouring down his face, raw and uncontrollable.

He opened his trembling hand, and the bloodstained knife clattered to the concrete floor. No one spoke. No one could.

Casey dropped to his knees, the flood of emotion finally overtaking him. Cliff followed, falling beside him and wrapping his arms around his younger cousin, holding him tightly as if to anchor him in the storm.

RB moved toward Burt's body, kneeling beside the lifeless figure. With a heavy breath, he turned the gangster's massive frame onto its back. The wound in his neck was still oozing, blood pooling beneath him, creeping outward in a slow, red tide. RB stared at the wound for a long moment, then reached up and gently closed Burt's cold, unblinking eyes.

"Stupid bastard," he muttered.

Chapter 27

Mateo Diaz and Jeff Black waited for the gunshot that never came. All they heard was faint shouting inside the building and rain pounding the roof of the car. Rain that began as a tropical downpour now dropped lightly from the starless sky. Diaz glanced at his companion in the passenger seat and said, "This is not going as planned. We may have to finish what we started." Black continued staring off into the dense undergrowth, contemplating their next move. Finally, he nodded in agreement and the two men slowly made their way back into the building, forcing their way through the thick swamp palmettos that had hid their presence.

They made their way through the side entrance to the building as quietly as possible and through a narrow hallway ending with a doorway into the warehouse. Burt Williams, lying in a pool of blood, caught their immediate attention. Casey, Cliff, and RB stood over the motionless figure, silently, even as they noticed Diaz and Black staring at the scene. Cliff and RB watched the South Americans as they slowly made their way to Burt's lifeless body, guns drawn, but at their side.

Diaz knelt beside the body, his sharp eyes narrowing as he peered into the jagged wound left by Casey's fatal strike. He studied it for a moment, calm, clinical, then looked back at Black and gave a single, solemn nod. It hadn't gone the way they planned. It hadn't been clean or quiet, but the deed was done. Burt Williams lay dead at their feet.

Black stared down at the body for a moment, then nudged the knife with the toe of his shoe. The blade, slick with blood, was already beginning to dry, its edge still glinting faintly under the warehouse lights.

Diaz stood, saw the blood on Casey's hand and put his hand on the kid's shoulder, "You did what was necessary, my friend. There is no shame in that. This man killed your mother."

Before he said more, RB stepped in-between them, "No more," he told the Columbian, standing nose to nose with him.

Diaz knew when he needed to back off and he moved a couple of steps backwards. Black asked what happened and RB looked at him suspiciously.

"Maybe I should ask you the same question," RB barked at him, noticing both men still held their weapons. He eased his hand into his pocket, fingers brushing against the cold, familiar steel of his revolver.

"We gave this man information you would not," Black said matter-of-factly, "He needed to know who killed his mother."

"This is a child," RB said, pulling his revolver from his pocket. He didn't aim the weapon, but like the other two, held it at his side, ready in an instant. "How do you know who killed his mother? That picture wasn't evidence enough." RB looked at Casey, "That's why I *didn't* want you to know," he pointed to Cliff, "and why *he* didn't want you to know. Not until we knew for sure, anyway."

Black stood at attention, looking at Casey with his dark, piercing eyes, "I was there. I saw this man put the knife into her." He gestured at Burt, "I was with him." Casey's hand and fingers turned into a fist. RB saw the boy tense and stepped in front of him. He reached behind and put his hand on Casey's shoulder.

"You were there?" RB asked and Black nodded, "I was there to kill the Columbian. That was all. Williams was there to assist me with that task and only that task," he looked at Casey, "He killed your mother without orders to do so."

Casey stood silent. He hadn't spoken since he buried the knife into Burt's flesh. RB watched the kid's reaction, feeling his tension ease. RB glanced over at Cliff and the teenager stood with his hands on his head, absorbing everything that happened.

The detective realized they had to figure out what to do with the mess at their feet. He looked at Diaz and said, "We have to figure out what *happened* here."

Diaz shook his head in agreement and replied, "The boy cannot take the fall." RB pushed the knife, still laying where Casey dropped it, with his foot. He noticed the gun laying on the floor and he also noticed Burt's dead hand still reaching in vain. RB leaned down, picked the weapon up and began wiping any fingerprints it may hold away. When he was confident in his work, he placed the gun in Burt's rapidly cooling fingers and wrapped his chubby finger around the trigger. He then picked up the knife and repeated the process but this time when he finished, he held the knife in his own hand.

RB gathered everyone closer and said, "Burt had the boys under the gun. Somehow, I don't remember how, I got around him and I took him out with his own knife. I'll keep it vague. The fewer the lies, the less we gotta remember. The prints will match the story." RB could see the murder playing out in his mind as he spoke. *I'm getting too good at lying*, he thought to himself.

"There are no cameras here, nor outside," Mateo said gesturing to the building, "The story could work, but..." he paused and looked at each person individually, "...only if we agree to this story. There can be no loose ends."

All eyes turned to the two teenage boys. Casey was already nodding in agreement and RB looked at Cliff. "You gotta go along with this, son. For him." RB pointed at Casey. "I hate lying as much as you do, but we have to."

Cliff grimaced but said, "I'll do whatever it takes for *my* family." RB tried to smile at him, but it came out more of a frown. "All right, it's settled. One thing though. Where do you two fit in?" RB motioned towards Diaz and Black.

"Mr. Black and I came to check on my warehouse. We found the situation and I called the matter to the police," Diaz told the group. All nodded and Diaz started walking towards the office, but RB stopped him.

RB's eyes cut to Diaz, a flicker of concern tightening his jaw, "The two of you together? There will be questions." Diaz shrugged and told the detective he would take care of it and not to worry.

RB accepted him at his word. He already knew that Diaz held connections within the DEA, and he wondered if Diaz knew the same about him.

The first call Diaz made was not to the local police but to the DEA. He gave Shaggy a quick rundown of what had transpired. He also informed him of their plan to cover it up. The agent replied they would be there soon, but not before the local police got to the scene. Shaggy instructed him to hang up the phone, call the police and follow through with the plan. They would back him up. Mateo agreed and hung up.

The wait for the police turned out to be brief. Sirens broke the silence not long after the call was made, and soon the warehouse was swarming with local officers. Within minutes, the detectives had separated everyone, each seated apart to give their version of what had happened.

Each account matched, no deviations, no contradictions. But early in the questioning, one of the detectives learned that RB had delivered the fatal blow, or so they were told, and he was quietly placed in the back of a black-and-white squad car, taken to the station for further questioning. Out of respect for a fellow officer, they didn't cuff him. They didn't have to. RB sat silently, knowing how the game worked and that his answers would matter more now than ever before.

As soon as the locals removed RB from the scene, Shaggy and his clean-cut partner showed up. They pulled rank on the police and before long they had the South Americans in their custody. Cliff and Casey were taken to child services. The scene had cleared. The flashing lights were gone, the questions silenced. All that remained was the lifeless body of Burt Williams, lying still in the vast emptiness of the warehouse with only a few cops and technicians around. Forensics wouldn't be complete until the next morning. Until then, the body stayed where it was, alone, untouched, and surrounded by the quiet echoes of everything that had just unraveled.

Upon arrival back at one of the DEA safehouses, Black called Ryan Calley and told him about the Bruce children's predicament. He informed the lawyer that he needed to board a plane and get to West Palm before daylight. The children would not hold up well under questioning and he, especially, feared the oldest was most likely to crack and confess the truth.

The next call he made was to Veck Baxter. He didn't explain in detail the events of the evening but informed him he would be in Montgomery as soon as he could. He did tell his friend Burt Williams was in fact dead but didn't elaborate any further.

After hanging up the phone, he walked back into the conference room where Shaggy and his partner sat with Mateo Diaz. All had steaming cups of coffee. Diaz was finishing up his story. The real story. He informed the agents every detail of what happened. The agents, happy with the results, were dismayed that there were so many loose ends. The unexpected arrival of RB and

Cliff Bruce changed everything, and they had to improvise on the fly, Diaz informed them.

"Improvise, adapt, overcome," the clean-cut agent said aloud, and the South Americans looked at the agent, obvious confusion on their faces.

Shaggy grinned, "A saying in the United States Marine Corp." He pulled up his sleeve revealing a tattoo of the Marine motto "Semper Fidelis". Diaz hadn't figured this man was ex-military by his appearance. The long hair, unruly hair must serve as a deception. The Colombian filed it in his memory. He always liked knowing little tidbits about his friends, and even more his enemies.

"We will make sure the local police buy the *other* story," Shaggy told the men sternly, "You get up with that lawyer? Those boys need to be out *tomorrow*."

Black nodded and said, returning the agents tone, "They will be home before lunch."

"Perhaps we can help with that too." Shaggy looked at his partner and motioned to the door. The clean-cut agent gave his partner a thumbs-up and walked out the door and picked up the telephone.

Since he was a sworn officer and carried a private investigator license in Florida, RB's weapon was allowed to keep all his belongings with the exception of his gun, which he handed over when the police first arrived. He wasn't under arrest nor was he officially detained. The detective informed them right away that he intended to cooperate fully. As another professional courtesy, he hadn't been patted down, so the recorder concealed in his jacket pocket remained hidden. He meant to keep it that way, at least until he found the right person in which to disclose the information. RB hoped it wouldn't take long.

To RB's relief, that person walked into the room a couple of minutes after the Mississippi detective sat down. They didn't take him to the small room in which they usually interrogated criminals, but to a comfortable conference room. If this conference room was like the one back home, it probably wouldn't be bugged. RB grinned as he thought about how cops are very protective of what they say amongst themselves.

The detective assigned to dig into Burt's death was probably the oldest one on the job in West Palm and more than likely the closest to retirement. His hair bore none of the color that it once did and looked like it turned completely grey a long time ago. He wore glasses as thick as RB had ever seen and he could tell he wanted to treat this as a mere formality. He was all business and that was what RB needed right now.

The old man sat down directly across from RB, pulled his glasses to the end of his nose, and stuck his hand across the table, "Mr. Brown, I'm Detective Rick Shirley. I just need to get your statement on what happened and after that, you will more than likely be released to go."

RB nodded, then casually traced a slow circle in the air with his finger. Shirley understood the signal immediately. RB watched the breath leave the older man's chest, his shoulders sagging under the weight of what that simple gesture meant. What should have been a straightforward process had just turned into a mess, and they both knew it. With a reluctant sigh, Shirley gave a slight nod of agreement, an unspoken acknowledgment that things were about to get complicated.

RB grabbed his hand, shook it vigorously, but didn't immediately let go, "Look, I hate to drag you into this, but we've really got a mess on our hands," RB warned him. "Burt's death went down like I said, but there are other things at play, and it goes deep, real deep. You've heard of Vernon Bruce I assume."

Shirley closed his eyes and let out another deep sigh, "I know that one of those kids at the scene was his son and the other a nephew. Stepfather dead at their feet." Shirly snatched his hand away from RB, "You telling me this is a *family* thing?"

RB stood up, walked around the table, taking the chair next to Shirley, and said in a hushed voice, "It's a hell of a lot more than just a family thing. You got a lot of..." RB paused, looking for the right words, "...*stuff* going on right under your nose." RB put his hand on Shirley's shoulder and the old man closed his eyes. RB continued, "But first, we got to clear an innocent man." Shirley reopened his eyes, leaned closer to RB, "You mean Vernon Bruce, don't you?"

356 Last Castle in the Sky

"The man didn't do what they accused him of. It's all right here," RB said as he pulled the recorder out of his pocket and placed it gently on the table. He played the tape and Burt once again gave his confession.

The older man pursed his lips and raised an eyebrow, "We are going to do this by the book. I mean, BY THE BOOK." He hit the desk with his palm, got up and started for the door. RB reached out and grabbed him, "Be careful who you talk to. DEA is neck deep in this too. Working *both* sides." The gray-haired man let out another sigh as he walked out of the room. Before he walked three or four steps, he turned around and stuck his head back in the door. "Those two agents that took the two South Americans?" he asked.

RB simply said "Yes."

Shirley stood there for a second before turning to leave once more. This time he walked out of RB's sight. The Biloxi detective sat there, the fluorescent light flickering above his head and the only sound he could hear was the unceasing buzzing coming from the same light. He wondered if he made the right decision about trusting Detective Shirley. He didn't even know the man. He relied on his instincts as a detective. Instincts that told him if someone lingered as long as Shirley had on the job it was because either he genuinely cared about doing it the right way, or he needed the money. If he needed the money, RB felt that it wouldn't take long to find out.

The sun's first rays of the day sparkled across the water as Ryan Calley's plane began its descent into the airport. It had been a while since he landed here. The last time it was with his family on a long-needed vacation. This time, it was to rescue two kids who had seen way too much at their youthful ages. As the tires scrubbed onto the runway, he thought about the damage done to those two young men, one barely old enough to drive and the other *just* becoming a teenager. They reminded him of his own sons, and he silently hoped his boys would never have to face what these two kids faced, or the future being played out before them.

At least his sons had him.

Tate had gone most of his life without knowing his own father—his *real* father. But now, as he sat surrounded by the quiet hum of luxury, the soft leather beneath him and the muted clink of ice in his glass, he couldn't help but feel grateful. Grateful that the old man had found him. Grateful that he'd been set on this path.

He picked up the shot glass, a small pool of whiskey still clinging to the bottom and raised it with a quiet reverence.

"Thanks, old man," he said, tilting it back. "Rest in peace."

That afternoon, Cliff and Casey Bruce, released into his custody, were safely back home at the Clark Mansion. As they entered the house, Calley let out a whistle, admiring the architecture and decor. The housekeeper met them at the door and both boys went directly to their room. Neither spoke very much since he picked them up and he didn't blame them. Calley introduced himself, sat down on the couch, picked up the phone and dialed the number Black had given him to use when all was completed.

"The boys are home," Calley said into the phone and Black thanked him for getting there so quickly. Calley added, "It shouldn't have been as easy as it was to get them released to me."

"We've got some help down here. All I can say." The receiver went to a dial tone as Black hung up on the other end. Calley thought it was kind of funny that Black didn't ask about Vernon Bruce. Perhaps, he thought, he didn't know. Black also didn't know that Detective Shirley from West Palm had called him to let him know that RB had evidence that would probably clear his famous client in Georgia. That would be the first conversation he would have tomorrow.

Calley sank back into the couch, letting the oversized cushions swallow him up as he rubbed his forehead, trying to ease the weight of everything pressing down on him.

Tomorrow, the process to secure Vernon Bruce's release will begin, something that had once felt impossible, now suddenly within reach. But tomorrow also meant Black would have a decision to make, whether to keep RB close… or cut him loose for good.

Calley let his gaze drift across the expansive living room, the quiet opulence surrounding him, and then toward the large bay windows where the Atlantic shimmered under the fading light. A slow, knowing smile crept across his face. One way or another, everything was about to change.

Chapter 28

"That's going to change things," Jeff Black said, shaking his head slowly as the weight of the news settled in. Ryan Calley sat quietly across from him, the silence stretching between them.

Black stood, the chair creaking behind him, and walked to the hotel window. He parted the curtain with one hand, staring out at the distant horizon as he took a sip from his coffee. The steam rose into the morning light, but his thoughts were already racing ahead. Everything was shifting now.

"I wanted you to know before I started the petition. It might take a few weeks for everything to go through, but Vernon Bruce is more than likely going to go free," Calley said as he took a step towards the door. Black extended his hand, and the men shook, "Thank you, Mr. Calley for your loyalty. We will not forget it."

As the lawyer closed the door behind him, Black knew he was going to have to call Veck Baxter. He took a deep breath and decided to take a walk before he made the call. It was early morning, and the gulls were out in full force. They scavenged local parking lots in search of a morning meal. Black stopped, took a seat on a bench overlooking one such expansive lot, taking note of his surroundings.

It was empty. Most of the tourists had packed up and returned home, their summer vacations now fading memories.

A slight crispness hung in the air, left behind by the cold front that had blown through with heavy rain two nights earlier. In South Florida, this was how fall made its quiet entrance. Not with changing leaves or chilly mornings, but with a brief breath of cool air, quickly chased away by the return of heat and humidity. It was subtle. Fleeting. But it was the only sign the seasons had shifted.

Black sat quietly, staring at the gulls above him, his thoughts racing about everything that had happened the past few days. Burt Williams was now out of the way, but Vern Bruce coming back complicated matters. They needed his money to bring more of his people from Brazil and now it looked like the boy wouldn't get a dime for a long time, if at all.

The core of Baxter's plan hinged on getting their hands on that fortune, but now that seemed like a longshot at best. Black sighed. Casey Bruce would have been easy to manipulate. But now, all bets were off. He *had* to make the phone call. He eased to his feet, rubbing his temples, and started back.

Back in his hotel room, Black stood in silence for a moment, staring at the bottles of whiskey Burt had left behind. He hesitated, the weight of what had happened clinging to the room like a shadow. Pouring a drink felt wrong, *drinking a dead man's liquor*, but he needed the jolt. Just enough courage to make the call.

He unscrewed the cap, poured a generous shot, and turned it up in one swift motion. The burn hit immediately, sharp and unwelcome. He wiped his lips with the back of his hand, grimacing. He'd never liked the taste of American bourbon.

The line began to ring. On the other end, Veck Baxter answered. Black began without pleasantries, "Burt Williams is dead. The boy, Vernon Bruce's son, killed him but the black detective took the blame..."

Baxter cut him off before he could finish, "Wonderful, great news."

Black took a breath before continuing, "There is more. Before he died, Williams confessed to killing Beck and he told of how he set Lucky Clay up to be killed by the officer. The detective got it all on tape and now, the police here know." The line fell silent for a moment before Baxter finally replied.

"Well, that complicates things just a little bit."

"Indeed," Black replied, "How do we get our hands on the Clark money now?"

"There was a marine in the camp for a while. He died there." Baxter closed his eyes, and he could see the young marine's face once again, but he quickly put it out of his mind and focused on the task at hand, "He had a saying, improvise, adapt, overcome. That is what we'll do. Leave everything to me, I'll handle Vernon Bruce *and* his son."

A smile crept across Black's face as he listened to the voice on the other end. He wondered why he had ever doubted Veck Baxter.

When Baxter arrived in Brazil, he was a shell of a man. His body was broken, his mind hanging on by threads. But even in that shattered state, Black had seen something rare in him. A fight. A fire. The kind of resilience few men carried after living through the kind of hell Baxter had endured in Vietnam. And Baxter hadn't just survived, he had rebuilt. Slowly, piece by piece, he clawed his way back to something resembling his former self.

He had given everything to help the Confederados, never once asking for anything in return. It was his way of repaying the debt, for their help, for his escape, for his second chance. Jeff Black now held a rare thing in his world: complete trust and unwavering faith in another man. And that man was Veck Baxter.

"Yes, my friend," he answered, "Just tell me what I need to do."

"I will, but first, I must meet Vernon Bruce. Face to face," Baxter told him. Black explained that Ryan Calley was on a flight to Atlanta as they spoke. He was to notify Vernon Bruce of his impending freedom, and the lawyer would keep him informed of Bruce's reaction. The two old friends said their goodbyes, ending the phone call.

After ending the call, Baxter set the phone down with quiet purpose and stepped outside. For the first time in what felt like ages, he didn't use the walker. The cane was still in his hand—he wasn't quite free of it yet—but his stride had weight, balance, purpose. His legs, once frail and uncertain, were growing stronger with each passing day.

He stood alone at the riverbank, the humid breeze brushing against his face as he watched the muddy waters roll steadily by. They moved with the same quiet determination he felt stirring in his own chest; slow, relentless, unstoppable.

The Alabama River flowed swiftly as the rain that pummeled West Palm a few days before tore through Montgomery a day or so earlier. The river was swollen, its muddy surface churning with urgency. Entire trees, uprooted but still intact, raced past, carried swiftly by the current like driftwood in a flood.

Baxter watched them go, silent witnesses to something far bigger than themselves, and he couldn't help but feel the weight of it. The river was moving fast. And so was everything else.

The old building he now called home sat safely perched on a high bluff, overlooking the raging river below. From this vantage point, he watched the swollen waters rush past, powerful and unyielding. He thought about how this same current would continue on—winding its way through the land until it emptied into Mobile Bay, then into the Gulf of Mexico.

Home.

The word settled in his chest like an anchor. He could almost smell the salt air, feel the Southern heat on his skin. He wasn't there yet, but soon. Soon he would be.

His legs and back, even though he felt better and the pain not quite as intense, began their all too familiar ache and Baxter sought refuge in a nearby chair. He closed his eyes and took a deep breath as he settled into the chair's comforting frame. His mind turning to the changes in his plan. He repeated the words, *improvise, adapt, overcome* to himself.

His mind, clearer than it had been in a long while—freed from the fog of painkillers he no longer needed as much—drifted to thoughts he hadn't revisited in some time.

He had once intended to isolate young Casey Bruce from his family, to sever the ties before they could root too deep. It was a calculated decision, one made in the name of control, of molding the boy into something… useful. But now, with the haze lifted and the weight of everything that had happened settling on his shoulders, he found himself questioning that plan. Maybe he already had.

If they separated *him*, they also separated the money. Baxter banged his fist on the arm of the chair. It would've been easy since friction *already* existed between the two cousins and Vern, locked away, wasn't able to help his family. Getting Vern free from death row and into general population where he could be manipulated was also gone. All because Burt Williams couldn't keep his mouth shut, even confronted with death. Baxter cursed his name.

He hadn't planned on meeting Vern face to face—not yet. Before all of this, he couldn't see how it would help. Confrontation seemed unnecessary, even counterproductive. But now, things had shifted. Now, it was inevitable.

The Bruce family couldn't be allowed to unite. Not in peace. Baxter knew too well the danger that kind of unity posed. If Vern was released and managed to reconcile with his son and nephew, everything Baxter had worked for could unravel in an instant. He couldn't let that happen.

If he didn't face Vern soon, look him in the eye, there was a real chance the pieces of that fractured family might come back together. And if they did, all would be lost.

It wasn't about the money to him. Money was secondary but he would never admit that to Jeff Black. Black was like family to him. He was trusted, loyal, and closer than most blood relatives had ever been. But Baxter had been betrayed by family before. That kind of wound never fully healed. It lingered beneath the surface, reminding him that trust was always a gamble… and loyalty had its limits.

Trust and betrayal were just something that happened in life. He had resigned himself to the fact long ago. He had to keep the promise he made, so many years ago, in that vile prison camp in Vietnam. Once he did that, he could finally go home. He could rest.

Calley waited in the same small, cramped, dark room in which he had met with Vernon Bruce several times before. This time the room seemed brighter. Even the smell didn't seem quite as bad. Maybe it was because, for the first time, he was there with good news.

He knew little about the benefactor. He had met only Jeff Black, and even then, barely knew the man. Their interaction had been brief, professional. Detached. His job had been clear: get Vern off death row. Not free him entirely. Just keep him alive.

Still, whatever news had shaken Black so badly, he hoped it wouldn't have the same effect on the guy pulling the strings. Chaos at the top always trickled down.

The snapping lock on the door brought him back to reality, turning his attention to the guard opening the door, leading a shackled Vern Bruce in his bright orange jumpsuit to the table. The guard locked his feet and hands to the table and left the room, nodding to Calley as he did.

"You here to get me to sign another lie to save my ass?" Vern asked, staring into the cinder block wall.

Calley shook his head, a faint smile tugging at the corner of his mouth. "No, Vern," he said calmly. "I'm here to tell you a story. A story that ends with the death of one Burt Williams."

His words hung in the air, heavy with finality, like a door creaking open on the past, and slamming shut on everything that came before.

Vern's jaw dropped, "Somebody finally killed that fat bastard, huh?" The joy hearing about Burt's death overtook his thoughts for a split second before the fact dawned on him that his boys were now all alone.

"My boys?" Vern asked frantically.

Calley calmed in with his hands, "They are fine. In fact, they were there, when Williams died." Calley leaned towards him, "Do you know a detective from Biloxi, Ramsay Brown that everyone calls RB?"

Vern thought for a second, replying "He the one helping Cliff on my case?" Calley responded that he was and then relayed the story of Burt Williams' last moments.

Vern put his head on the table, "My God. What else do my boys have to go through?" he mumbled, but loud enough for Calley to hear.

The lawyer reached out to put his hands on top of Vern's. He felt the cold steel of the cuffs as he did. "I thought the same thing, Vern," Calley shook Vern's hands, "But I do have good news." Vern looked up at Calley with intense, narrow eyes, saying nothing. *What kind of good news could possibly come from all of this*, he asked himself.

"Vern, Burt Williams *confessed* to Beck killing Lucky Clay before he died," he paused as Vern raised his head from the table, "And he confessed to *personally* killing Beck. Detective Brown recorded the whole thing. I'm filing, today, a petition for your release."

Vern shook his head slowly, confusion etched deep into his features. He opened his mouth to speak, but no words came—just silence and the growing weight of disbelief. What little color remained in his face, faded from years without sunlight, drained completely. His mouth hung open, eyes searching Calley for any hint that this was some kind of sick joke. It took several moments, and every ounce of strength he could muster, before he finally managed to speak. His voice cracked, barely more than a whisper.

"But… the confession," he said, his throat tightening around the words. "The one I signed… admitting guilt…?"

His question trailed off, but the pain behind it lingered. Raw, haunted, and desperate for a truth he wasn't sure he could bear.

"Remember Henry Alford?" the lawyer asked.

Vern nodded, "Of course. I just hope you know what you're doing, and this works out."

Calley laughed, "*Full confidence*, Vern. You'll be out of here in time for Christmas with your boys." he returned.

Hope amplified inside Vern, replacing the shock. His thoughts cleared, questions flooding from his mouth, "How long before I get out? Can I make calls in the meantime? Do I have to go back to death row? Can I see my boys?"

"I'm going to withdraw the confession. You'll still be on death row, but it should only be a couple weeks. You'll go from there directly to freedom, my friend. But, until then, all rules of death row still apply. Just hang in there."

Vern pursed his lips, "Easy for you to say." He picked up his shackled hand as far as he could and stuck his finger in the lawyer's direction, "Just make sure somebody makes copies of that tape. I've heard tales of things like that going missing," Vern instructed.

Calley smiled once again, "Way ahead of you. My source already has a copy waiting on my desk. RB is soon to be released and I'm going to make sure he doesn't go anywhere. We will need his testimony, along with the tape."

"From what I hear, RB is a standup guy, he ain't going anywhere." Vern told him.

Calley shook his head, "That's not what I'm worried about," the lawyer replied, "There are more factors at play than you realize. I can't tell you right now just what I'm talking about, but just know that your boys are safe, and I'll make sure RB is too."

"Thank you, Mr. Calley. When all of this is done, I'll owe you." Vern said appreciatively. It was the first time Vern seemed genuine in his interactions with Calley, and the lawyer nodded.

"When you get out and find out everything that I'm talking about, you may just *hate* me." Calley told him as he stood, shook Vern's hand, nodded once more, and left the room. The guard didn't at once storm in and take him back to death row and Vern figured Calley must have bribed him. Bribed him for a few moments so Vern could process everything. He appreciated the extra time. He sat there, with only the faint light coming from the single bulb and in quiet. He couldn't even hear the noise of gen pop just through the wall from where he sat. He contemplated the last words Calley told him. What could possibly make him *hate* the lawyer that played such a large part in clearing his name and going home to Cliff and Casey?

So many thoughts raced through Vern's mind that when the door finally swung open, he jumped. His hands and feet caught on the iron restraints and his wrist began bleeding slightly. The guard slapped him on the back of his head, slamming his head on the desk, sending his vision spinning.

"Now I got to take you to the infirmary, asshole." The guard unlocked his restraints, reaching under Vern's arms to help him to his feet. He dragged him along the corridor more than he helped him walk, Vern's feet barely cooperating beneath him. The pain surged through his skull in relentless waves, crashing and receding like the tide, each one worse than the last. He tried to focus, to stay conscious, but the agony blurred everything. The corridor stretched endlessly ahead, and all Vern could do was cling to what little strength he had left.

When they finally made it to the infirmary, he dropped Vern harshly onto an open bed and placed him in restraints. His head hurt not only from the slap on the back of the head, but from the intense glow from the fluorescent lights in the room. He stared at the light, trying to focus and for a second, he thought he saw his wife, Patty Lee. Before he drifted into darkness, he could have sworn he heard the words "I'm sorry."

He awoke groggily, blinking against the dim light, to find a smiling, beautiful face hovering over him. For a moment, he wasn't sure where he was, only that the pain in his head still pulsed like a distant drumbeat. But he felt more grounded now, more like himself.

It had to be the shock of Calley's words... and the blow to the back of his head. The two had collided, dragging him down into that dark, confused state. Now, slowly, he was surfacing.

"I'm sorry," the nurse repeated, "The guard didn't tell me what happened, but I got a feeling." During his time on death row, Vern learned not to snitch on other prisoners or the guards. Nothing good ever came from either.

"I don't remember," Vern lied, managing a slight smile. The nurse didn't return the smile as concern spread over her face.

"If you guys don't ever tell me what happened, I can't help." He recognized the sincerity in her voice, but it didn't change his mind. She realized Vern, like most prisoners, wasn't going to say anything, so she leaned down and whispered into his ear, "My name is Doctor Marceaux. I'm here nearly every day if you happen to *remember*." Shame overwhelmed him and his face turned red as he assumed she was a nurse because she was a woman.

"Thank you, Doc," Vern managed, as she walked away. He watched her every move as she walked and noticed when she glanced back at him. He could tell she didn't wear perfume at work, but as she leaned over him, he caught a faint trace of something soft and floral, the lingering scent of the weekend or maybe her last day off. It was subtle, almost gone, but it clung to her like a memory she hadn't meant to bring with her.

After being confined in that tiny death row cell for so long, any smell that pleasant, *that human*, was enough to etch itself permanently into his memory. Even if he was strapped to the bed like an animal. He lay still, the throbbing in his head gradually dulling to a manageable ache, eyes fixed on the overhead light as it buzzed faintly. Voices drifted in and out, soft and muffled. He asked himself, *Was that Patty Lee's voice or the doctor's he heard?*

For a few moments, his mind wasn't focused on the problems at hand, only Dr. Marceaux's face. *Marceaux*, he thought, *Cajun?* He ran her voice back through his mind, realizing there was a bit of an accent. He looked around for her, wanting to call out, but she had disappeared.

The brief moment to himself, and the fleeting thoughts of the doctor, didn't last long. Footsteps echoed in the hallway, growing louder, more purposeful. The quiet was gone, replaced by the familiar rhythm of intrusion. Whatever peace he'd found was already slipping away.

The burly guard that hit him on the back of the head reemerged and began to release his restraints. "Time to go back to your hole, jackass." he mumbled as Vern struggled to his feet.

The guard didn't seem interested in helping Vern this time and he was glad. He wanted to take the bedpan on the table next to his bed and whack the bastard over the head with it, but if he did, he knew what came next. He buried his anger but silently vowed to remember the guard's name. He looked at his shirt and read "Lincoln." Vern repeated the name all the way back to his cell. He promised himself that he would right all the wrongs done to him. When the dust cleared Mr. Lincoln would be first.

The cell door slammed behind him. Vern looked around at his cell. He picked at the peeling paint and closed his eyes. His days there were numbered. He sat down on the hard mattress and tried to think about what his next steps were. He couldn't though.

Doctor Marceaux's perfect face kept floating into his thoughts, uninvited. Her soft voice, laced with that slight Cajun accent, whispered through his ears like a memory he couldn't shake. It was a distraction he didn't need.

He was still a convict and an inmate on death row. Men in his position went mad thinking about things like that, letting their minds wander to dreams that would never come true. Even now, with the faintest glimmer of hope flickering on the horizon, he couldn't afford to let his own thoughts turn against him.

But despite his efforts to stay grounded, as he drifted off into the deepest, most peaceful sleep he'd had since being locked away…

All he could see was her face.

Chapter 29

Cliff opened the door to find RB standing there, ballcap in hand, a somber look etched across his face. With Casey still asleep, the two of them settled in the kitchen, the silence between them stretching long and heavy. Words felt unnecessary or perhaps they were just too difficult.

RB finally broke it, his voice quiet but firm. "Go wake up your cousin. We all need to have a conversation." Cliff sat for a moment, eyes searching RB's face, a thousand questions crowding his mind. But he didn't ask a single one. Instead, he gave a quiet nod, patted his hand against the table, and stood. Then, with a slow breath, he made his way upstairs.

Casey hadn't strayed far from his room since he and Cliff returned home with Ryan Calley. Every time he closed his eyes, the same image met him: Burt's crumpled body, twisted and lifeless, lying in a widening pool of blood on the warehouse's cold, unforgiving floor. And when he did manage to sleep—brief moments stolen from the storm inside—his dreams dragged him right back to that moment. The cold steel sinking into Burt's neck. The resistance of flesh. The sickening *gurgle*. His final, desperate attempt at life.

Each time, Casey jolted awake, heart pounding, the sound still echoing in his ears. He wasn't sure which was worse, being awake with the guilt or asleep with the memories.

When Cliff opened the door, he found Casey lying on his bed, eyes wide open and fixed on the ceiling. The light from the hallway caught the faint shine in his cousin's eyes. His recent tears not fully dried. Cliff stepped in softly, his voice low and careful.

"Hey, Case… RB's down in the kitchen," he said gently, not wanting to press to hard.

"I don't want to see him."

Cliff sat on the edge of the bed, the palms swaying gently outside the window, "We gotta talk to him, Case. We ain't got a choice." Casey finally turned his eyes toward Cliff, the weight of exhaustion and emotion still lingering in his expression. He didn't speak, just giving a slow, silent nod.

The cousins slid into the opposite side of the corner nook across from RB. The detective tried to smile, but they both saw through it and Cliff looked at Casey and then back at RB, "Just get to it," he told him.

RB nodded, "All right guys, here's the deal." he began, "They bought it. Casey, you're in the clear. You boys did a good job. I know it was hard, but you did what you *had* to do."

"What about my uncle?" Cliff asked.

Casey interjected, "Who gives a damn?"

Even if his father's innocence was proven, it didn't matter to him. Blame and hate were the two things Casey held on to since Vern's arrest and conviction. He wasn't going to give them up easily. It would be a long road for the father and son. Cliff knew that much. The pain, the distance, the damage done, it wouldn't vanish overnight. But even so, he held on to hope. Despite everything, they were still family. And sometimes, *that* was enough to start healing.

Cliff's eyebrows furrowed, "We both do Casey. He didn't do what they said. We have proof." Cliff put his hand on Casey's shoulder, "One day, Case, you are going to sit down, face to face. You gotta give him a chance...." he paused and waited for Casey to look at him, "...and forgive him."

Casey shook his head, pushing Cliff out of the nook and sprinted back up the stairs to the sanctuary of his room. RB looked at Cliff sympathetically, "He's got a long way to go. That boy's been through a lot. You both have." Cliff walked to the counter and started a pot of coffee. He hadn't tried the stuff before, but right now he needed a cup.

"You never answered the question, RB. What happens with Unc now?"

RB put his ballcap on, "I don't really know. I'm not a lawyer, Cliff. Calley went up there and he should be letting y'all know. But, if I had to guess, he'll be out. Soon. They ain't no way they can hold him with that confession."

Cliff smiled as the coffee started dripping into the pot. "I guess building castles in the sky worked."

RB looked confused.

Cliff walked over to the window, looking up at the clouds lazily rolling by. "Mom would sit out on the beach a lot and watch the clouds. She would sit out there for hours, watching the sky like a crazy person." Cliff turned to face RB, "One day I asked her why she just stared up there at nothing. She smiled, took my hand, and told me that she was building castles in the sky, in other words, dreaming about what she wanted and seeing it up there, in the clouds. The clouds could be anything you want them to be. It makes sense if you think about it. I always saw Unc back home. I used to look up and stare at the clouds like she did, thinking about it, making it appear, making it happen. I guess that last castle I built up there worked."

RB walked over and patted Cliff on the shoulder, "I guess it did, son. If anyone believed in him, it was you."

"RB, will you go talk to Casey?" Cliff asked, lowering his head, "Don't mention Unc, just talk to him as a *friend*. He hasn't got many friends that are worth anything. He needs one, he needs you." Cliff took the first sip of his coffee, looked up and RB saw the seriousness in the kid's face. RB couldn't turn him down, and nodded, grabbing the coffee Cliff poured for him as he passed.

RB tapped lightly on the door. He heard Casey's muffled voice tell him to come in. He hadn't gone back to bed but was facing the corner window overlooking the palms. RB threw a glance to the other window and wondered why Casey had chosen this one as the other faced the ocean.

"Casey, you mind if we talk for a moment?" RB asked, slipping in behind Casey. The kid didn't look away from the window or speak, staring outside.

RB stood, also watching them through the window, finding solace in the swaying movement of the long, lanky trees. He realized why Casey had chosen this instead of the ocean view.

RB looked through the pane of glass, but what he saw wasn't the present. It was his past, vivid and unrelenting.

Memories stirred behind his eyes, reflections of choices made, people lost, and moments that shaped the man he had become. The world beyond the glass blurred, and for a moment, he wasn't standing there at all. He was back where it all began.

"I lost my mother pretty young, too. Not too much older than you. Beautiful woman. I can picture her in my mind. Every detail of her face comes into view when I close my eyes." RB paused, taking a deep breath and slowly let it out and closed his eyes, picturing his mother's smiling face. He talked lowly as if talking to himself but loud enough for Casey to hear, "1950s Mississippi. Different world back then. Ain't going to go into detail, but she was murdered, just like your precious mother."

The detective lowered to one knee, looking Casey in the eye, "I'm the one who found her." Casey turned his attention from the window and looked sideways at RB as the detective continued, "My anger consumed me, hated everyone; nobody could tell me a damned thing for a long time. Didn't want to hear from nobody, not even my father."

Casey twisted his lips. Tears once again filled his eyes. He had held it in for so long that when he finally let them go, the words didn't come out steady or calm. They came out in a violent scream.

"It ain't fair!" he yelled, the sound raw and cracking as tears streamed down his face. Years of pain, anger, and helplessness poured out in that single moment, leaving him trembling in its wake.

RB put his arms around Casey, "I know, son. Life ain't fair. Never has been, never will be. But it's life. We let it tear us down or we stand against it and fight like hell. I gave up my hate and anger. Had to or I wouldn't be here. I ain't telling you to let it go, it's a damn hard thing to do, but you gotta fight it, with everything you have," RB felt tears forming in his own eyes and fought them back.

Casey couldn't stop his tears, he pulled away from RB's embrace, jumping to his feet, turning his back to the detective. He closed his eyes and between the flashes of light, he saw an image of his mother form. He wanted to call out to her, but when he opened his eyes, the image faded quickly.

He couldn't turn around to face RB when he spoke, "I'm not a good person, RB. I'm not. I done something, with Burt, I..." He couldn't speak—his throat tightened, and his lungs fought to pull in air. Each breath came in short, shallow gasps, as if the weight of everything was pressing down on his chest, stealing the words before they could form.

RB once again reached out to Casey, placing his hand on the child's shoulder, "Don't measure yourself with what Burt *made* you do, son. Whatever it is, it was him." RB turned Casey around to face him, "If you want to tell me, I'm listening," he said as he let Casey go and backed up slightly.

Casey finally caught his breath, as his tears slowed. He thought about it for a second. Visions of Dell's wrapped body slowly sinking into the cold, dark Atlantic filled his mind, with his whole body shaking, told the detective, "I got rid of Dell Phillips."

"What do you mean, Casey?"

Casey peered at the floor, the confession escaping from his mouth slowly, "We found his body in the office at the Surf Shop. I don't think Burt killed him, but he didn't want cops around. We..." he paused and caught his breath once more, "...we wrapped up his body and took it out, tied it to blocks and pushed it into the water."

The more he confessed, the more comfortable he became, and the words flowed easier. His body stopped shaking and the tears stopped completely. Relief spilled over him as he confessed everything.

RB blinked rapidly, his mind wrapping around what the child told him. "Phillips, the thug from Biloxi, right? One of Burt's boys." RB asked, squinting, trying in vain to remember Dell's face. Casey nodded. "Heard of him but never run across him too often back home." RB ran his fingers along the stubble on his chin, "But look Casey, that doesn't make you a bad person. In no way. That was all Burt. He was my friend." RB closed his eyes, "But he *was* a bad person." The detective thought for a moment,

"Anybody else know?" Casey shook his head no and RB rubbed the ballcap across his head and asked, "Where did ya'll take a boat from?"

Casey finally looked back at RB and told him they took the *Daddy's Girl* out of West Palm Harbor. "It was late, nobody around. Burt made sure cameras were off."

RB pursed his lips, "Burt was no idiot so I'm sure he paid attention to detail. That's why nothing ever stuck to him in Biloxi."

"I don't want Burt's life, RB. I don't want to be like that."

RB smiled at the kid and said, "You don't have to be, son, and you won't." the detective looked out the window and back to the swaying palms outside, "For now, don't tell anyone about this, not Cliff, not the cops, nobody. Let *me* take care of it."

Casey felt he could trust RB. Trusting someone, after all that had happened, was something he hadn't done in a while. Suddenly, Casey reached out, put his arms around RB and buried his face in his shoulder, "Thank you," he said quietly.

In that second, RB was reminded that Casey was a child and didn't deserve all the pressure he had been under. He would give his life for these two boys as if they were his own. "You don't ever have to thank me, son," RB whispered, "Ever."

Cliff was grabbing his car keys and heading out the door when RB made it back downstairs. Cliff stopped halfway through the open door and asked, "How'd it go?"

RB smiled, nodded, and said, "Kid's going to be all right. Where you going?"

Cliff smiled slyly, "Gotta make a run up to Cocoa, I met somebody up there and she invited me to see the shuttle on the pad."

RB, confused, asked, "She? Space Shuttle?" He couldn't hide his slight grin.

Cliff replied, "Yeah, her dad is an engineer up there. She can get close to the launch pad."

RB laughed. Relieved that Cliff was trying to lead somewhat of a normal life, said, "I'm sure that's the *only* reason you're going." Cliff smiled as he looked back, running out the door, jingling his keys. RB's smile widened and he said aloud, "Go be a kid."

He heard the car speed away, so he poured himself another cup of coffee and sat down at the counter. He looked around and thought what a fool Burt Williams must really have been to have all of this and lose it the way he did.

As he put the piping hot beverage in his mouth, he thought of Marcus Kendrick. He was just a kid too and didn't deserve to die like he did. He thought of his mother, alone swinging on her front porch, reading her Bible. She raised her son the right way in a place where kids like him seemed to turn down the wrong path on a daily basis. He couldn't get her off his mind while he finished the cup and decided he owed it to the young man's mother to tell her about her son's killer. He slurped down the last drop, placed his cup in the sink, looked around one more time, and cursed Burt's name before leaving.

The old, beaten pickup looked like it hadn't been moved since the day he and Cliff visited as RB pulled into the driveway. Mrs. Kendrick wasn't sitting on the porch, so he walked up and knocked on the door. To RB's surprise, Mr. Kendrick answered the door, and RB took a step back. If he didn't know any better, he would think his own father had answered the door. The only difference would've been the hat. RB's father never wore any type of hat and by the look of Mr. Kendricks old hat, it was probably his favorite, and he had worn it for a long time.

"You must be that detective from back home," Mr. Kendrick said in his slow Mississippi drawl. He opened the screen door and stepped out. Before the door could slam shut, Mrs. Kendrick grabbed the door and followed her husband onto the front porch of their brick home. RB smiled and told her hello. Mr. Kendrick motioned with his hand. RB took a chair and the couple sat down on the front porch swing.

"What brings you back, Mr. Brown?" Mrs. Kendrick asked and tried her best to smile but there was still a vast sadness dwelling within her.

RB sat up in the chair and ran his fingers slowly across his whiskers, "I have some news. News that I thought you might want to know. Figured I owed it to you to come out here and give it to you in person."

"You know who killed my son?" Mr. Kendrick asked before his wife could do so. RB hesitated but he was going to be truthful, no matter how much it hurt, him or the parents that brutally lost their only child.

"I *knew* the day you told me about the man asking Marcus to lie. I *knew* that moment," RB said in a muffled voice but not losing eye contact with Marcus' mother.

Her expression didn't change, and her voice didn't quiver as she responded, "I know, child. I know."

RB looked confused, thrown off. He had expected anger, maybe frustration, anything but the calm, steady grace that met his confession. It unsettled him more than yelling ever could.

"I don't understand," RB said, and Mrs. Kendrick, for the first time, smiled genuinely at the detective.

She reached over and gently placed her hand on RB's, her touch soft but certain. "I saw it in your eyes," she said quietly. "When I gave you that description, I saw your eyes change."

She paused, her gaze steady.

"He was a friend of yours, wasn't he?" she asked, her voice full of compassion, not accusation.

RB felt a chill pass over him, "Yes ma'am, he was. Not the best guy in the world," RB paused, remembering he wanted absolute truth with them, "He was mean, cruel, and a criminal. But he was my *friend*. It's funny how cops and criminals are like that sometimes. I would've busted him in a heartbeat. But, truth be told, I always liked him. I can't explain it." RB shook his head,

"He probably just had me fooled. He was rough but he could lay on the charm if he wanted." RB glanced over at Mr. Kendrick. The older man's eyes stared into the distance, but RB saw the anger underneath his cold stare.

"What was his name?" Mr. Kendrick asked through clenched teeth.

"A man named Burt Williams, from Biloxi. Dixie Mafia." RB told them.

Mr. Kendrick removed his hat and began fanning his face, a slow, thoughtful motion. But the moment RB mentioned the Dixie Mafia, something shifted.

A shadow passed over Kendrick's face, his features tightening, eyes narrowing. The easy expression was gone, replaced by a dark, hardened look that told RB everything he needed to know.

"Dixie Mafia? That's back home, that ain't here," Mr. Kenrick responded.

RB nodded in agreement and replied, "Not a lot. He came down here...you wouldn't believe me if I told you the story. But the kid with me last time, Burt Williams was his stepfather."

RB stopped for a moment, not sure if he wanted to tell the Kendricks everything but again, he promised himself that he would tell these people the absolute truth. He continued, "I was there when he died. I can't give you details..."

Mrs. Kendrick stopped him, "I don't want to know. I wish he were alive. Alive so my boy could get justice." She patted RB's hand. He hadn't even noticed—her soft hands were still resting gently on top of his own.

Her voice was calm, steady. "I see it in your eyes, Mr. Brown. You're a good man. I know you done what you thought you had to." The words settled over him like a blanket, warm, forgiving, and more grace than he felt he deserved.

For the first time in their conversation, RB didn't know if he could hold his emotions in check, "Sometimes I just don't know," he replied, his voice shaking slightly, "I feel like I've gone *too* far, but that boy and his cousin, they don't have anybody right now. I gotta protect them."

She looked towards the sky and RB remembered what Cliff had told him about castles and the sky. "This world is evil, Mr. Brown, but I raised my son to overcome that. We scraped and scrounged to get out of Mississippi, ending up in Miami. So many kids down there killing each other, people using them for drugs and such. I couldn't let my Marcus live like that. Took everything we had to move here, but we did it for *him*. He was going to college..." Mrs. Kendrick couldn't hold back tears of rage, and they streaked down her cheeks as her voice grew louder.

Mr. Kendrick put his arms around his wife and nodded in RB's direction, "Maybe it's time for you to go."

Before he stepped off the patio, RB turned. His voice grew horse as he told the Kendricks he was truly sorry.

Mrs. Kendrick, her tears gone, and her voice calm once more said, "You want to do right by Marcus? Stop this killing! It's the drugs, child. Stop them!"

Her words rang in RB's ears as he got in his car and started the engine. Mr. Kendrick still held his wife as they walked back into their home. RB wiped his eyes. Tears were becoming a common thing for the Mississippi detective. He fought them back once more as he backed into the street and made his way towards the coastline.

As he drove, he thought about what Mrs. Kendrick had said. He couldn't remember noticing any young men walking the street on the drive over, but on the drive home that was all he saw. Kids of every color, hanging out on the corners and RB knew what they were doing.

He tolerated a lot of things in Biloxi. The one thing he didn't was drugs. He hated the effect they had on people, especially his own people. Now, here he was, caught up in the biggest lie of his life and mixed up with the Columbian Cartel of all things, not to mention that bizarrely acting Brazilian.

RB had to keep reminding himself that everything he was doing was for those two boys, but deep down, he felt as guilty as Burt. *He* was the one that gave Burt the information he needed to make his moves. Without that he wouldn't have wormed his way into the Bruce family. He shook his head as he thought about all the lives lost since that first meeting with Burt.

He didn't know Marcus Kendrick—but somehow, he felt like he did. Another innocent life taken. For nothing. He wasn't going to let that happen again, especially not to those boys.

Even if it meant giving his own life to protect them, he'd do it without hesitation. Some debts couldn't be repaid with words. Only with action.

Chapter 30

The cell door slammed shut with an iron thud behind Vern. But this time, he smiled. This time, he was on the *other* side of the cage. It would be the *last* time he'd ever hear that chilling sound.

Calley had promised he'd be home in time for Christmas. For a while, Vern had doubted it. Hope was a dangerous thing for a man behind bars, but today was Christmas Eve, December 24th, and Vernon Bruce, exonerated by the words of a dead man, was walking free.

As he walked down the dim corridor that housed death row, he glanced inside each cell and nodded to each man he passed. Even though most of these men were guilty of taking someone's life, Vern's heart went out to them. None of the prisoners looked back at Vern. They just looked at the wall or the floor. They all wanted what he had. The freedom to walk out of this place. Few that heard those iron bars slam behind them left the way he was leaving today. Nearly all made that walk one last time, meeting their fate. Once Vern walked through the last iron door, his thoughts turned from the prison to Cliff and Casey.

He wanted to get home as quickly as he could and see them with his own eyes. He wanted so desperately to put his arms around them. He wanted to talk with Casey and tell him he was sorry for everything and maybe gain his son's forgiveness. The last time he talked to Cliff, he had told him most of everything that happened but omitted Casey's part in all of it. The kid was smart enough not to talk over a prison phone. Instead, Calley told him in their last meeting before the judge granted him his release. Vern shook his head, wondering about the damage already done to his young son and hoped it was not too late to help him. He needed time and now, thanks to Burt Williams' stupidity and stubbornness, he had that time.

The discharge process went quicker than expected and within an hour, he stood outside, looking back at the prison for the last time. Ryan Calley's car waited for him just outside the gate and Vern was grateful the lawyer came, personally, to give him a ride. He opened the passenger door, and a wave of warmth rushed out to greet him. It wrapped around him like a blanket, a welcome contrast to the biting cold of the frigid Central Georgia air.

"Welcome back to the world of the free," Calley said as Vern took his seat and threw the small number of items he brought from his cell onto the back seat of the Caddy. When he took a breath, he could still smell that the "new" hadn't worn off the lawyer's car. He wondered if his *benefactor* also paid for the car. Vern extended his hand. When Calley reciprocated, Vern gripped it tightly, shaking it vigorously, "Thank you Mr. Calley. Thank you for everything."

Calley nodded, "Things fell into place like I hadn't ever seen before, Vern. You are extremely *lucky* in a sense."

Vern nodded in agreement as he settled into his seat, "Yes sir, I am."

Calley pulled away from the prison, the tires crunching over gravel as they picked up speed—but this time, Vern didn't look back. No glance over the shoulder. No second thoughts. That chapter was closed.

The prison wasn't far from the small airstrip where Calley had told him they'd catch the Clark jet back to West Palm. So, when the car passed the weathered sign pointing toward the runway, Vern noticed.

"Shouldn't we turn back there?" Vern asked pointing back toward the sign.

Calley gritted his teeth for a second and responded, "Mr. Veck Baxter would like to see you."

Vern tilted his head, "Who?"

Calley grinned as he realized that Vern probably thought Jeff Black was the person responsible for his services, "Mr. Veck Baxter is my employer, your *benefactor*. The man who pays the bills."

Vern's eyes narrowed, suspicion creeping into his voice.

"I thought Jeff Black was that man," he interjected, his gaze fixed on Calley, searching for answers behind calm eyes.

Calley looked out the window, watching the open fields pass, "They are partners and friends, but it is Baxter who put all of this in motion."

"What about that bull about us being related?" Vern asked with a crooked smile.

Calley turned his attention from the passing fields to Vern, "I understand that Mr. Baxter will provide you with all the information you desire. He's waiting for us in Atlanta." After what felt like miles of winding back roads and endless stretches of quiet, they finally reached the interstate.

Without a word, Calley merged onto the highway and pointed the car toward downtown, the city skyline slowly rising ahead like a promise, or a warning.

Every time Vern returned to Atlanta he thought back to his childhood. The first time he saw the tall buildings and the airplanes from the highway he felt like he was in some other world. It was so different from the pine trees, rivers, creeks, and swamps of the Florida Panhandle. This time was no different, it was more like the first time than ever before. He felt reborn.

The car traveled south of the downtown area and in the near distance, Vern saw the majestic form of Atlanta Stadium take shape. He, Rof and Pops made the four hour drive a couple of times in the late 1960s to see the Atlanta Braves, formerly of Milwaukee, play baseball. Vern liked baseball and enjoyed the trips, but Rof genuinely loved the game and so did Pops. He figured that's why they were so close, their love for the game.

On Pops' last night on this earth, he was perched atop a worn barstool watching his Braves lose. To Pops, however, it really wasn't the game that mattered. It was the dream he and Rof once shared.

They used to talk about it like it was destiny: Rof out there on that field, wearing the uniform, hearing the crowd chant his name. But when he hurt his knee, that dream disappeared in an instant, fading like the final out under stadium lights. Still, Pops held onto it. Right up until the end.

Vern admired the architecture of the structure as they got closer. The massive white columns, bending a little over halfway from the top, offering a slight bit of shade for those hot, humid Georgia summer day games. He remembered the booming voice over the PA system welcoming everyone and the smell of hot dogs hovering over the place. Vern thought they were going to pass by the stadium and looked at the lawyer with his eyebrows raised in more suspicion than surprise when Calley took the off ramp leading directly to ballfield.

"Why are we going to the stadium?" Vern asked, doing his best to keep his voice steady. But as he rubbed his hands together, he felt the clammy dampness on his palms, his nerves betraying him. They had started to sweat.

Calley pointed to the stadium, "This is where Mr. Baxter wanted to meet. It's empty this time of year, but the outside of the stadium is open. He instructed that he wanted you to meet him in front of the Hank Aarron statue. That's all I know."

Vern began to squirm in his seat and eased his hand along the door handle. After being locked up in such a place as death row, all kinds of wild thoughts ran through his mind. He seriously considered jumping out of the car, but common sense finally caught up to his racing thoughts. If someone wanted to kill him they sure spent a lot of money when they probably could have it done in prison for just a carton of cigarettes. As he eyed his surroundings, his senses were on high alert.

Calley eased the car to a stop in front of the statue and took a deep breath. He didn't say anything. He motioned towards outside.

Vern turned his gaze to the massive bronze statue—and there, beside it, stood a man. He leaned on a cane, his back to Vern, head tilted slightly upward as he stared at the towering white columns that held the stadium in place. The figure didn't move, didn't turn, just stood there as if lost in thought… or waiting.

Vern opened the door slowly, the weight of the moment settling in his chest. He stepped out, one foot on the pavement, eyes locked on the man ahead. It was time for answers.

The frigid wind whipped around the bowl-shaped stadium sending a chill directly to Vern's bones as he slowly walked towards the statue. Atlanta lay perched on top of a plateau in the foothills of the Appalachian Mountains, and it was always a little colder than the surrounding areas. Vern, being a Floridian, didn't like cold and wished he had a thick coat like the man before him wore, but there wasn't time for a shopping trip.

As Vern drew closer, the man remained still, silent, motionless, as if carved from stone. He didn't turn around. He didn't shift his weight. He simply stood there, staring up at the columns, as if whatever he saw in them was more important than the footsteps approaching from behind.

He leaned on his cane and Vern could tell he was entirely dependent on the crutch and would likely fall over without it. Vern stopped a few feet away, looked up at Hank Aaron with his mighty bat in full swing and prepared himself for whatever was to come.

"Mr. Baxter?" Vern asked, his voice straining through the crisp air. Baxter didn't turn around. He just kept staring at the stadium. Vern tried again and this time he spoke louder, "Mr. Baxter? I'm Vernon Bruce."

"I know who you are, Vern. Welcome," Baxter said through a trembling voice. The strength he had gained over the past couple of months waned and he struggled to remain standing, even with the help of his cane. He turned around and gently leaned against the statue's concrete base.

Vern studied the man as he walked closer. His hair dark, but bits of a graying blonde sprung from underneath his fedora. The cap was pulled low, casting a shadow that obscured the man's eyes—but Vern could still see the lines etched deep into his face.

Like cracks of time, weathered and worn, like the bark of an old tree. There was a story there—maybe several—and Vern felt the weight of it pressing in the air between them.

They were deep and made him look a lot older than his true age because looking at the man's hands, they looked young but scared. As he leaned against the concrete, Vern noticed a grimace on the man's face.

Baxter studied Vern's reaction closely, catching the slight wince of pain as he stepped closer.

A faint grin tugged at the corner of his mouth. "Years in a Vietnamese prison camp will rob you of your years, Mr. Bruce," he said, his voice low, weathered, and edged with something between bitterness and pride.

Vern instinctively took a step back, his eyes narrowing as a surge of uncertainty ran through him. There was something about this man. Something in the way he spoke, the weight he carried, that felt familiar. Suddenly, a thought struck him like a jolt: *What if the connection he felt wasn't just his own? What if this man also connected back to Rof?* His mind filled with questions; rapid, urgent, and impossible to ignore. *Could this man finally have answers about Rof's fate?*

"Mr. Baxter," Vern started, "Did you know my brother, Rof Bruce? Is that why you helped me?" Baxter summoned the energy to regain his footing and leaned heavily on his cane as he slowly made his way to where Vern stood. He had to concentrate on every step as each one caused pain to shoot up his legs and into his spine. After a few painful steps, Baxter stood directly in front of Vern, and they stood toe to toe.

"I *knew* your brother," Baxter said as he slowly looked up. When their eyes finally met, Vernon stumbled backwards, and a smile widened over Baxter's face.

"I see *you*, Vern," Baxter said as he began to chuckle. A chuckle lasting just moments until the pain inside his body made him stop.

Vern didn't recognize the broken, scarred body standing before him—age and suffering had reshaped the man into something almost unrecognizable. But the eyes. The *eyes* didn't change.

Piercing, unmistakable blue—the same eyes he had looked into so many years ago, during that final, bitter argument with his brother. When their bond fractured, when everything fell apart. Vern's breath caught in his throat. The weight of realization crashed over him. He wasn't looking at Veck Baxter. He was looking into the eyes of his brother.

No words came out, no matter how hard Vern tried. His lips parted, his throat tightened, but nothing emerged—only silence and the slow, stunned shake of his head as bewilderment washed over him.

Rof's smile vanished in an instant. His jaw tightened, and he began to grit his teeth, the years of pain and anger rising to the surface. His lips curled into a scowl as he hissed through clenched teeth, "Nothing?" The word hung in the air like a challenge, sharp and full of wounded disbelief.

"Well, I got enough to say for the both of us, I imagine," he said as he tried in vain to get comfortable on the concrete, "First let me say, you look old, brother. Looks like that silver spoon you hoped you'd get when you married Patty Lee was filled with salt and rust. It shows." Rof's chuckle began again but didn't last as he motioned towards his broken, scarred body, "Not the same as I left huh? Crash almost killed me, broke my back and it didn't get well in no hospital. Gooks didn't care if I lived or died."

Vern's shock began to fade, and finally he was able to speak, "Bird strikes," he said, barely above a whisper, "Bird strikes took the plane down. That's what they told Pops."

Rof smiled, "Of course they did."

"I never thought I'd see you again, Rof..." Vern's voice cracked as he spoke, the weight of years pressing on each word.

He paused, eyes widening as the realization hit him like a bolt of lightning. "Your son. Cliff." His voice dropped to a whisper, thick with emotion. "Do you know about him?"

Rof's face twisted as if fighting back tears, but his eyes remained dry—too worn, too hollow to weep.

"Yes," he finally said, his voice low and heavy. "I know of him. I know Susie is gone too."

For a moment, the grief softened his features. But just as quickly, it vanished, buried beneath years of bitterness and rage. His posture straightened, his jaw tightened, and when he spoke again, his voice was forged from steel.

"I know you left him with a man like Burt Williams, too."

Each word landed like a blow—sharp, cold, and merciless.

Vern shook his head slightly, "I had no choice."

Rof shook his finger at Vern, "Sure you did. You could've fought the bastard. But I know you brother. You're a damned coward. Always have been." Rof leaned as close as he could to his brother and whispered, "I ain't forgot that it was supposed to be *you*."

"Rof, that was a long time ago. Let's don't bring that back between us..." Rof held up his hand to stop Vern from speaking, "It never left, Vern. Never. You took my life from me, left me there to rot for all those years." Rof shook his head and unconsciously made his fist into a ball. He pointed his free finger in Vern's face, almost touching his nose, "All those years. Nothing but the thought of knowing you were out there living your life. Money, power, women. And then," he retracted his finger and chuckled again, "To find out that you screwed it all up, priceless."

Vern again tried to speak but Rof cut him off, "When I made it to South America, I found out you were up for murder. You. Vernon "Golden Boy" Bruce killed two people. You know, I couldn't help but laugh. I knew you didn't do it but somehow your stupid ass got the rap."

"Why the ruse? Why not come home? Why not come get your son?" Vern finally managed to cut in, jumping to his feet, "Why hide as this Veck Baxter?"

"All in due time, Vern, all in due time," Rof said as he crossed his legs, trying to fight off the pain.

Vern held up his hands, "Why the hell did you help me If you hate me so much?" he asked.

"I wanted you off death row. To torture you. Like I was tortured over there. You're getting out had *nothing* to do with me.

I just wanted you to rot. Like me." Rof gestured towards his broken body.

"Rof," Vern pleaded, "There's no sense in this. I love you. You are the only family I got besides the boys."

"The boys." Rof said, shaking his head, "My son and your son," Rof thew a wry grin towards his brother, "Your son, the murderer."

"He did what he had to do," Vern said, his head dropping, "He did what he had to."

"Keep telling yourself that," Rof said coldly, "Cowards always say they did what they *had* to do."

"So, is this all you wanted, Rof? Just to tell me once again that you hate me? After all these years?" Vern asked.

"Well," Rof said, his voice flat and deliberate, "first thing—you need to understand, my name is *Veck Baxter* now." He stared hard at Vern, his expression unreadable. "Rof Bruce died in Vietnam. He's gone. And what's standing here now—that's Veck Baxter." He let the words hang for a moment, then stepped closer, voice tightening.

"Such a good friend, close as a brother. I couldn't let *him* die, you know…Like you left *me* to die. That ain't what brothers do."

"I ain't going to call you Veck Baxter, Rof. I'll tell the world who you are if I have to."

Rof leaned forward, supported his weight on the concrete and lifted his cane towards Vern, "I ain't going to tell you now why but you ain't going to tell anyone who I am. Only two men know who I am, and they will kill anyone, including you, to keep that secret."

"Why in the hell would they keep your secret, *Rof?* Why would anybody?*"* Vern asked, raising an eyebrow.

"Because if you don't, that son of yours is in a heap of trouble. I know what he and Burt Williams did the night Dell Phillips was killed."

"Who?" Vern asked. He hadn't been told about the incident with Dell Phillips. In fact, he had no clue who Dell Phillips was.

"Let's just say, you don't want to ruin the homecoming you got planned, Vern. Secrets kept brother. You don't tell Cliff that I'm alive. Not now. I've got things to do before I come get *my* son," Rof said, still shaking his cane at Vern.

Vern peered into Rof's crystal blue eyes again and said coldly, "My brother *did* die over there. I don't know this Veck Baxter."

"And you killed him." Rof responded, just as coldly. Vern nodded his head and said, "You come after my boys, Rof, and I'll do what I have to do."

"You didn't have the guts to take your rightful place way back then, you ain't got any now. I'm coming after my son, Vern. Damn sure as I get things ready, I *am* coming."

Rof stood up, leaning on his cane, "Now, Mr. Calley will see you to the airport. Go home, see *our* boys. You just remember, not a word. Live life until I come calling, and I will."

Vern took a few slow steps toward the car, the hum of the engine a low reminder that Calley was still waiting in the driver's seat. He needed distance, space to breathe, to think—but just as he moved, Rof's voice cut through the crisp air behind him.

"Somebody is always watching."

Vern froze. He turned slowly, looking back at Rof, still perched on his cane, steady, unreadable, like a monument to pain and survival.

"I love my brother, *Rof Bruce*, and I'll never stop looking for *him*!" Vern shouted, his voice echoing across the open space, raw and full of pain.

Rof scoffed, the sound bitter and sharp, cutting through the emotion like a knife.

From behind a row of bushes, Jeff Black emerged silently, as if he'd been there all along watching, listening. Without speaking, he moved beside Rof, eased an arm around him, and quietly led him away.

Black gave Vern a single, solemn nod. A signal. An ending. Vern turned back toward the car and walked steadily, his jaw tight, his heart heavy. This time, he didn't look back.

Chapter 31

The small twin-engine jet touched down smoothly, tires whispering against the runway before it glided gracefully toward the private hangar. It was a quiet return, no crowds, no fanfare— just the low hum of engines and the weight of unfinished business waiting beyond the hangar doors.

Vern rubbed his face and scratched at the stubble on his cheeks, relieved that Calley opted for the private runway and not the local airport. The lawyer's informants had tipped him that there were countless reporters waiting for the politician turned murderer and now, newly exonerated, return. Even though his boss didn't exactly tell him to spare Vern such madness, he felt compassion for him.

Calley glanced over at Vern, noticing a slight smile. The lawyer couldn't hide his, not only being proud of his accomplishment, but knowing his father, wherever he was, could be proud also and rest in peace.

As Vern stepped off the plane, the sunlight hit him full in the face, warm and real, although freedom still felt foreign on his skin. He shook Calley's hand one last time, a firm grip exchanged between two men who now had a bond. A bond that had grown deeper as Vern began to respect his attorney.

Then he saw it. Parked beside the hangar was a long, polished Lincoln. Old Man Clark's signature ride. Leaning against it was a man in a sharp suit, dark sunglasses hiding his eyes, arms crossed casually like he'd been waiting all day.

Vern hesitated. But the man offered a small, knowing smile and motioned for him to come closer. Cautiously, he started walking, his steps slow, deliberate. He glanced back once, just as the plane door sealed shut with a metallic snap. Moments later, the engines roared to life, the sound swallowing the silence as the jet prepared to leave him behind. Whatever came next, it was here, waiting.

"Mr. Bruce," RB called out over the noise of the jet as he noticed Vern watching him, slowly making his way to the dark colored Lincoln, "My name is Ramsay Brown. I'm the one that's been kinda helping your boys."

Vern shot RB an inquisitive look, eyebrows raised, searching for some hint of explanation. RB just smiled. Half in amusement, half in reassurance, continuing like he'd been expecting a question, but Vern wasn't quite ready to ask it just yet. There was more to come. Vern could feel it.

"Cliff and Casey are safe at the Clark House, and I'll get you to them, but, right now, on the way, we need to have a conversation."

Vern still silent, the only noise escaping the jet engines as the aircraft returned to the sky, only nodded as he climbed into the back seat. RB slipped in beside him and nodded to the driver. As they steered onto the main road, RB gave him a hard look, examining Vern as he would a suspect before starting an interrogation. He caught himself and forced another smile.

The detective recounted the turbulent events involving Burt Williams, the boys, and the ensuing chaos. Vern listened intently, piecing together fragments of a story that had haunted him during the last days of his imprisonment.

Vern already knew most of it and he had heard RB's name come up several times from Calley, but they had never met. As RB spoke, he also watched the detective closely and after the short conversation, Vern was glad—*grateful*—that his boys had someone like RB to look after them. In a world that had taken so much, knowing they had a steady hand, a loyal heart, gave him a measure of peace he hadn't felt in years.

RB did hold back a little his friendship with Burt, but he did confess they knew each other from Biloxi. In RB's mind, that was a whole other conversation the two of them must have later but, for now, it was best to keep him in the dark about their nefarious past.

The driveway hadn't changed a bit. As the car eased to a stop in front of the house, Vern stared out the window, memories flooding in with every crack in the pavement.

When he stepped out, the stiff ocean breeze hit him like an old friend. He stood still for a moment, letting it wash over him, breathing in the thick, salty air. Vern hadn't realized how much he'd missed it, all of it, until this exact moment. For a moment, he missed Patty Lee.

Vern turned his attention to the sprawling mansion, eyes tracing the familiar lines of the roof, the tall windows, the Atlantic peeking through the shrubbery. It looked exactly the same as it had on that fateful day. The day he left with murder in his heart. The day he set out to kill his wife and Christian Lopez. The day he never made it.

Instead, he was arrested and railroaded for the murders of two people he hadn't even known, victims in someone else's twisted game. He shook his head, as if he could rattle the weight of the past loose.

Let it go, he told himself. *Let it stay buried.* It was time, finally, to start thinking about his future. The memory of Patty Lee faded, and another face slowly replaced it. The doctor's pretty face. Taking a deep breath, he expected his senses to fill with the warm, muggy air of the coast but, instead, he caught a slight wisp of her perfume. *Has she been here?* he asked himself but shook his head. "Dreams," Vern said aloud, "Only dreams."

RB sat quietly in the car, hands resting on the open window, eyes fixed on nothing in particular. He didn't say a word, letting Vern take it all in. The house, the air, the memories that surely weighed heavy as the ocean breeze rolling in. The man deserved his moment alone.

He understood. A man coming back from hell deserved a few minutes to gather himself. And after everything Vern had been through, RB wasn't about to rush him. He'd wait as long as it took.

Just as Vern reached for the car's door handle, the front door of the house burst open with a loud *creak* and a bang. Cliff came flying out. No hesitation, no words. He didn't touch a single step as he leapt from the small patio, his feet barely brushing the ground before he collided with his uncle in a fierce embrace, nearly knocking Vern off balance. Neither of them spoke. They didn't need to.

Tears poured freely as they held on tight, the weight of everything between them dissolved in that single, silent moment.

When Cliff finally pulled back, he stared up at Vern's face, eyes red but bright. They smiled, broken, grateful, overwhelmed, as tears dropped onto the driveway.

Out of the corner of his eye, Vern caught sight of Casey. He was standing in the doorway, watching. But unlike Cliff, there was no emotion etched into his face. No joy, no relief. Just a blank, unreadable stare.

Cliff turned, motioning for his cousin to join them, but Casey turned his back and walked back into the house. Both RB and Cliff had hoped for a different greeting from the young teenager but understood when it didn't happen.

Cliff frowned, his eyes flicking between Vern and Casey, the unspoken tension settling thick in the air. But Vern gave him a look, a subtle nod, a quiet reassurance.

It's okay. He understood. Love and trust weren't given back freely. Not after everything his son had gone through. If he wanted Casey's heart again, he'd have to earn it. Step by step. Word by word. Vern was ready.

The three of them finally made it inside and Vern explored with his eyes. The outside of the house may look the same, but Susie had put her own mark on the furniture and décor. Nothing was the same. The old couch and most of the antiques were gone. The young housewife had replaced them with modern, modular furniture. Vern smiled. It reminded him of the simplicity of Pop's modest home back in the panhandle.

Vern picked up a picture from the coffee table. It was a picture of Susie and Cliff, out on the beach and Cliff had an arm wrapped around his mother. He was happy the young lady that had lived such a harsh life, had at least some time with her son, even if Burt Williams was involved. He was also grateful for the time she took with his own son. He looked up toward the ceiling, eyes glistening, whispering a quiet thanks under his breath.

Cliff put his hand on Vern's shoulder, "Unc, let's go *out* and celebrate. You're home."

Vern shook his head, "I'm home and *this* is where I want to be tonight."

Casey sat quietly on one of the few remaining pieces of old furniture tucked into the corner of the cavernous living room. The emptiness of the space made the distance between them feel even greater as the three of them stepped deeper into the house.

Vern stopped just a few steps away, so close to his son, closer than he'd been in years but they were so far apart. He had imagined this moment so many times, rehearsed what he'd say… but now that it was here, nothing came.

Father and son locked eyes, both frozen, their emotions masked by years of pain and silence. They just stared, both motionless, speechless. It was RB, standing between the two storms, who finally tried to break the silence.

"I'll tell y'all what, why don't I go get us something to eat? Give you guys some time?"

Vern nodded quietly and eased himself down into Old Man Clark's chair, directly across from Casey. The leather creaked beneath him, familiar and unwelcome. He was surprised the chair was still there. Part of him had hoped it was gone, cleared out like the rest of that dark past. But like the Old Man's memory, it lingered. Unmoved. Unshaken.

Vern leaned forward, reached across the coffee table, and gently tried to rest his hand on Casey's knee. Casey flinched, jerking his leg away without a word. The rejection stung, sharp and immediate, but Vern said nothing. He just let his hand fall back into his lap, the silence between them now deeper than before.

He finally found words, "Son, I know it will take time. I know that. I'm so sorry all this happened to you," he looked back at Cliff, still standing, "To both of you." The front door shut, and they heard RB start the engine. They were alone.

Cliff glared at Casey, raising his eyebrow, "Case, you could say *something*," he said.

"You want me to say *something*?" Casey replied coldly, "Ok," he said, pointing his finger at his father, "Did you have *anything* to do with killing my mom?"

Vern clasped his hands together, fingers locking tightly as if holding himself together by sheer will. He brought them up over his face, shielding his eyes from the weight of the moment.

His voice came out just above a whisper, heavy with regret, "Yes, son. I did." The truth hung in the air. The words raw, undeniable, and long overdue.

Cliff took an awkward step back, glaring at his uncle. Casey shook his head, his eyes narrowing and the veins in his neck pulsating. Casey balled his hands into fists as Cliff motioned for him to calm down, but the young teen only sneered at him, ready to attack his father.

"I may not have killed her myself, but I drove her to Lopez. I put her in that situation, son. We were so different. I should've known we were never going to work. She wanted *so* much more than I wanted. I *did* want money and power but not like *she* did."

"So, you saying it was her fault? That what you saying?" Casey screamed as Cliff positioned his body between them.

"No son," Vern replied calmly, "It was mine. Mine alone." He almost said it. He almost told them what his true intentions had been the day he was arrested. The rage. The plan. The dark place he had let himself go. But he stopped. Neither needed to hear that.

Not now. There would be a time for the whole truth. But today was about fragile steps, not shattering confessions.

"You bastard," Casey said under his breath as he took off up the stairs to his room, the slamming door vibrating through the house.

Vern looked at Casey, "That went well."

Cliff shrugged his shoulders, "Unc, Case has been through more than he ever should've. Give him some time. He'll come around." Cliff felt the words burning like acid in his mouth as they escaped his lips. He wanted to believe his words himself, but right now, truthfully, he didn't.

Vern excused himself to take a shower and get cleaned up. He hadn't had a hot, private shower in so long, he didn't know what to do without someone timing him.

As the hot, soothing water cascaded over him, Vern let his eyes close, the steam wrapping around him like a quiet embrace. His thoughts circled one thing. Casey.

How do I reach him?

Maybe, he reasoned, if they all sat down together when RB returned… if they could just share a meal, something simple and human, maybe he could salvage the day. Maybe that would be the start. Maybe.

He let the water splash off his face and when he closed his eyes, he saw Rof, not the broken Veck Baxter, but the youthful, vibrant brother he had known. With everything surrounding his homecoming, his brother's threat had been pushed to the back of his mind, but now it returned, literally staring him in the face each time he closed his eyes.

"I'm always here if you need me."

The words drifted through the steam, soft but clear—familiar. Vern jumped, his eyes snapping open as he spun around, heart racing. But there was nothing. No figure behind the glass. No voice in the hall. Just the steady hiss of the shower and the pounding of his own heartbeat.

He stood there for a moment, frozen. Then, frustration boiling over, he slammed his fist into the cold, unforgiving tiles. The sound echoed in the small space, sharp and hollow, like the ache in his chest. He couldn't think about *her* right now.

"Someone is always watching", he heard his brother's voice say. Vern cursed aloud. He didn't want to start off their new chance at life with a lie, but he would do anything to protect his boys. He wasn't going to tell them about Rof. Not right now.

RB returned with dinner in hand, the smell of warm food filling the quiet house like a welcome home banner no one had to hang. He and Cliff pulled the dusty cover from the long-unused dining room table, the fabric releasing a puff of time into the air.

Cliff took care in setting the table. Each fork, knife, and plate placed with precision, as if royalty were expected to walk through the door. He wanted this night to mean something. His uncle's first night back had to be more than just *free*. It needed to be *peaceful*. Maybe even *happy*. If only for an hour, Cliff wanted

Vern to sit at that table, relax, smile… and forget, just a little, that he'd ever been locked away in that awful prison.

Cliff couldn't help but wonder if Casey was going to join them or stay locked behind that closed door, stewing in silence. But his fears eased when he heard the soft creak of hinges and saw his younger cousin emerge, quietly making his way to the living room, flipping on the television.

Cliff said nothing. He didn't want to push, didn't want to risk sending him retreating again. So, he let it be, pretending not to notice, even as hope flickered quietly in his chest. If Casey could just get comfortable… if he could drop the armor for even a little while… maybe that wall between them would finally begin to crack.

Vern smelled the warm aroma floating from the kitchen food as he stepped out of the shower. He could already taste it, the sear, the seasoning, the warmth. He couldn't wait to sink his teeth into the steak waiting for him, the first real meal in what felt like a lifetime. It wasn't just food. It was freedom on a plate.

He looked down at his bare feet and, for a brief moment, hoped his favorite sneakers might still be tucked away in the closet, untouched by time. But when he opened the door, that hope vanished. The closet was empty. Stripped clean. Nothing remained.

With a quiet sigh, he pulled the same blue jeans and T-shirt he'd worn from prison back on. They felt heavier now, like they carried more than just fabric. They still smelled faintly of that horrid place.

He didn't bother with the shoes. The carpet, warm and soft beneath him, was a small comfort he wasn't ready to let go of. He dug his toes in and crinkled them against the fibers, over and over, grounding himself in the simple joy of being home.

The prison had offered nothing but cold, unforgiving concrete beneath his feet. Hard floors that stole warmth and comfort with every step.

But this old, fluffy shag carpet, faded and worn from the '70s, felt like a luxury. It wrapped around his bare feet like a quiet welcome home, warming him in a way he hadn't realized he missed. He stood there, toes sinking into it, and let the feeling settle.

Tomorrow, he thought, maybe he'd walk out to the beach, even if the cold still lingered in the air. He longed to feel the sand again beneath his feet, to reclaim even the smallest piece of the life he'd lost. It wouldn't be the same. It wouldn't be like the soft, squeaky sand of his Panhandle childhood, but it would be sand. It would be the salty, heavy air and the soft crashing of waves. And right now, that was everything.

When he ventured back downstairs, RB and Cliff were already seated at the table and Vern joined them. RB at once noticed Vern wearing the same clothes and made a mental note to find out where his wardrobe was stashed away first thing the next morning. Cliff sighed and yelled into the living room to Casey that they were ready to eat. The teenager said nothing but raised his middle finger so only Cliff could see and took his time making his way into the room.

He sat down at the far end of the table, separating himself from the others like a silent barrier. Without a word, without a glance, he opened his container and began to eat, his eyes fixed on the food in front of him.

RB looked down the length of the table, chewing slowly, then set his fork down. "Casey," he said gently, "why don't you come sit with us?"

Casey let out a grunt, his expression twisted with annoyance, but after a few seconds, he stood up. With a muttered sigh, he grabbed his Styrofoam container and shuffled down the table, finally settling into the empty seat beside Cliff.

Cliff gave him a warm smile and a quick wink. It wasn't much. But it was a start.

"So, RB, many people in town? I haven't gone out for a couple of days," Cliff asked, just trying to break the ice.

"Not many, most snowbirds have gone back up north for the holidays. Something about Yankees and snow for Christmas," RB replied as he sliced through his steak.

Vern grinned, "I miss Christmas with Pops," He said quietly, "Too bad you boys didn't know him. He loved spending Christmas Eve with us. He worked most of the time but always made sure he was home that *one* day."

Casey sighed once again, rolling his eyes, "Must've been nice to have a dad that cared about you," he said under his breath but loud enough for everyone to hear.

The three of them pretended like they hadn't heard Casey and tore into their food. Vern crinkled his toes on the hardwood floor, wishing it was carpeted like the bedrooms.

"How's that little girl up in Cocoa, Cliff?" RB asked with a smirk pointing towards Cliff.

Cliff, annoyed, but through a fake smile responded, "Awesome. Her dad is going to let us watch the shuttle take off next month, on the cape."

Vern looked confused, "On the cape?"

Cliff smiled, "Her dad is a NASA engineer. Works out on the cape."

Vern sat back and put down his fork, "That's great, Cliff. What's her name?" The conversation between his father and cousin seemed to annoy Casey but remained silent, picking at his food.

"Katrin. Katrin Huber. Everybody calls her Katie, though. They're from Alabama, or at least that's where her dad went to school." Cliff glanced at Casey as he spoke, who was mouthing all of his words back, mocking him. He tried to ignore him, but his blood boiled. As much as he and RB tried to make this a nice meal for Vern, Casey seemed intent on destroying it. He buried the impulse to lash out at his cousin and continued, "She's going to school up there too. Auburn. Got to say, I'm giving it some thought too."

Vern smiled through a mouthful of food, the warmth in his expression unmistakable. "I'm glad, Cliff," he said, nodding gently. "Proud for you."

The words hit Casey like a spark to dry brush, igniting the frustration that had been simmering just beneath the surface. He'd been teetering on the edge for minutes, barely holding himself together, but Vern's quiet pride pushed him over. His mocking smirk twisted into a cold, furious glare.

"What the fuck ever," he snapped, venom lacing his voice. "You ain't going to college. That girl even know who you are? Who *we* are?"

Cliff, his eyebrows raised in irritation. "I told her everything."

Casey snarled, spitting words through a bitter laugh, "Oh, I bet. Bet she ran to tell Daddy that you're the nephew and ward of the *infamous Vernon Bruce*, huh?" His voice dripped with sarcasm. "That your stepfather was the outlaw, *Burt Williams*?"

He paused just long enough to let the sting settle before laughing again, sharp and humorless. "Yeah… I'm *sure* he loved that."

"Casey. Enough," Vern scolded his son, pounding his fist on the table, "You are hell-bent on ruining this and it stops now."

Casey jumped up, sending his chair flying into the wall behind him. "Hell no! You don't get to tell me shit, *convict*."

RB stood quickly, chair scraping against the floor as he tried, vainly, to defuse the situation. His mouth opened, a calming word on the tip of his tongue. But it was too late.

Casey was already up, storming toward the side door. He threw it open and disappeared outside, the storm door slamming behind him as he headed for the beach, rage and pain trailing like a storm cloud.

Cliff pushed back his chair, ready to follow, but RB reached out and placed a firm hand on his shoulder. He shook his head slowly, eyes steady.

Let him go, the gesture said without a word, *Sometimes the fire has to burn out on its own.*

"Give him some space, Cliff," RB said aloud.

"He's more like his uncle—your father—than me," Vern said, shaking his head as he glanced at Cliff. "Rof was impulsive, always flying off the handle. He hasn…"

Vern stopped himself mid-sentence, the word catching in his throat. He had nearly spoken of Rof in the present tense. A flicker of emotion crossed his face as he quickly waved a hand, dismissing his own words.

"Forget it," he said, drawing a breath, steadying himself.

"We've got a long road ahead," he finally managed, the weight of it all settling in his voice.

For the rest of the meal, they ate in silence. After they finished, Cliff volunteered to clean up the mess. Vern thanked him and asked RB to join him on the deck. The detective obliged and the two men made their way outside, sitting in chairs with cushions as they held some semblance of warmth. The breeze blowing in from the ocean seemed colder than Vern remembered. He wished he had put on some shoes.

After they sat in silence for a few minutes, Vern looked over at RB, "Mr. Ramsay, thank you for everything you've done. Without you, *both* of my boys would be lost."

RB held up his hand, "Just call me RB, Vern," he replied, "And I got to be honest with you. When I met your boys, I was supposed to be working *for* Burt, but I was also working for the DEA." RB sat back in the chair and thought for a second, "You got a messed-up family, Vern. DEA, Dixie Mafia, ain't no telling what else," He put his hand on Vern's arm, "*But* you also got a second chance. These two are good boys and they need you. Casey is just a kid. He's still got a chance. You gotta be the one that helps him."

Vern looked up. The stars were bright, shining over the ocean, "Casey is so lost. I just can't imagine what that mad man put him through. I bet on Susie but when she got killed…"

RB interrupted him, "You did what you had to, Vern. I'm from Biloxi, but Dozier is known all along the Gulf Coast. A lot of boys that go there, they never make it out."

Vern sighed and said, "I may have saved his life back then, but I just might've damned it to hell at the same time." Vern sat back in his chair so that he would be able to look RB in the eye. "Look, I got to tell you something, but it can't go no further than me and you." Vern hadn't known this man but a few hours, but he had to take a chance. He couldn't do this alone. Surely, he wasn't the one watching as Rof had warned.

Vern took a deep breath and leaned in closer to the detective, "My brother *is* alive." Vern said, looking around to make sure Cliff hadn't wandered outside. He could see him through the window still working on the remnants of dinner, so he continued in a hushed voice, "He is using the name Veck Baxter. I met with him today, before coming home, up in Atlanta. He's broken, RB. His body and mind are just broken. He still blames me for everything that happened to him." Vern stood up, "He also warned me not to tell Cliff about him and if I did, he said he had information that would send my son to Dozier. It's damned if I do and damned if I don't. I just don't know what to do."

RB, staring at the boards making up the deck, replied "Vern, I don't know this *Baxter*, but I do know his partner, Jeff Black. Brazilian dude calls himself a Confederado. I've looked into his eyes, and they are cold, Vern. Cold as I ever seen. Whatever they got planned, it can't be good."

"I know. I know," Vern said as he ran his fingers through his hair.

Just off the deck, Casey crouched low in the dunes, the tall, wispy sea oats swaying gently in the night breeze, cloaking him in shadow. The crashing waves of the Atlantic echoed behind him, but his focus was fixed on the soft glow of the house, where the two men on the deck talked. They couldn't see him. They didn't know he was there.

He shook his head slowly, a bitter smirk curling at the corner of his mouth. "Daddy's home, Cliffy boy," he whispered, the words cutting through the darkness like a promise. Or a threat.

Chapter 32

Mateo Diaz stood silently, hands in his pockets, watching through the giant glass windows as massive airliners roared into the sky with impossible grace. He rubbed his forehead, both in fatigue and quiet awe, taking in the constant rhythm of flight. One plane after another lifting off or touching down like clockwork.

The sheer volume of people amazed him. So many lives crossing paths, all with destinations, all with stories. The buzz of humanity moving with purpose. Some with joy, others with tension fascinated the Colombian.

His eyes caught a moment that made him pause: a man bolting from the jetway, his eyes scanning the crowd until they landed on her—the woman who had been pacing, glancing at the arrivals board every few seconds. The two collided in a tearful embrace, and for a moment, the chaos of the airport faded around them.

Diaz smiled softly. Then, his eyes shifted upward to the glowing flight board. It was almost time.

He double-checked the board, rolling constantly with updates to flights and saw the flight from Panama was arriving on time. His hands clutched the small briefcase that sat in his lap a little tighter. The time was near, and he scanned the distance, waiting for the jet to glide from the clouds onto the runway. He couldn't remember being this excited before and he couldn't hide the smile on his face.

It wasn't long before Diaz saw the plane touch down, its wheels kissing the runway with practiced ease. Smooth. Controlled. Like everything about this moment was meant to be.

As the aircraft began its slow taxi toward the terminal, Diaz's eyes locked on it, unblinking. *Phillipe was on that airplane.* All the years. All the blood. All the unspeakable acts he'd committed, the loyalty he'd bartered, the silence he'd kept, all of it had led to this. This moment. This arrival. As the plane inched closer, Diaz's jaw tightened ever so slightly. The waiting was over.

The path had been anything but easy. There were nights Diaz thought he wouldn't live to see the next morning. Moments when a single misstep, a single hesitation, could've ended everything. Many times, he believed an act, a hit, a betrayal, a deal gone wrong, would be his last. But somehow, he had survived them all. And now, with that plane rolling in and Phillipe on board, survival didn't feel like luck. It felt like purpose.

Not only did he perform those horrible actions for the cartel, but he also did things he would never speak of again in the name of the United States government, specifically the DEA.

The DEA had no intention of stopping the flow of powder into their country. In fact, they made more money from its sale than the cartels. Since Reagan had come to power, the flow of the most important substance in the world hadn't just increased, it had *raged.*

The powder flowed like the Amazon after a monsoon. Steady and Unrelenting. Flooding every corner of America with white powder, while those in power vowed to destroy it and those who sold it. The great American contradiction.

They waged a war on drugs with cameras rolling and speeches thundering, all while the real war was being lost in the alleys behind boardrooms, and in handshakes too clean to be questioned.

Diaz had seen it all. He watched them preach purity while their own pockets bulged with the profits of the poison they claimed to condemn. Hypocrisy never smelled so sweet.

He stood in the heart of it now, surrounded by men in suits, women in heels, families clutching stuffed animals and carry-ons. Everyone with somewhere to be. He watched them with sharp, knowing eyes and wondered how many of them would sneak into a bathroom stall minutes from now? How many would bend over a piece of glass, nostrils flaring, chasing escape before even claiming their luggage? More than anyone would admit. And far fewer than *he* supplied.

The Reagan Administration had waged a war on drugs, but behind the scenes, they regulated the supply as they could never quell the demand. The American Government used money from cocaine to facilitate their tiny proxy wars around the world. If the American public knew the real purpose of the DEA, they would want Reagan's head on a spike. That little general from Panama he met years ago, in the company of the DEA, turned out to be very adept at not letting that happen. He once again clutched the case sitting on his lap when he turned his attention outside.

Out of the corner of his eye, Diaz spotted the plane, Phillipe's plane, easing into its designated spot just outside the terminal. His heart thudded once, hard. He held his breath as the jet bridge connected, metal and machinery forming the final link in a journey years in the making.

A few moments passed that felt like hours before movement in the glass tunnel caught his attention. There he was.

Agent Shaggy, still a mystery in name but not in role, walking with the same slow, calculated pace Diaz remembered. And then, behind him, no, beside him was Phillipe. Diaz almost lost it right there. *His* Phillipe. Alive and well mere steps from him, holding the agent's hand like all the years of distance and darkness hadn't swallowed them whole.

A lump swelled in his throat, and he blinked quickly, almost letting the tears fall. But not yet. Not here. Not until they were face to face.

A broad smile swept across his face as he saw the premature grey hair sweeping down, nearly covering the thick glasses on Phillipe's face. Phillipe hadn't noticed his brother waiting for him at the gate. Diaz wondered if he even remembered him at all. So many years had passed since the two of them had been together.

That lingering fear, years of doubt, of imagining every possible outcome, vanished in an instant. Phillipe grinned wide, brushing the hair from his eyes with that familiar flick, then tugged eagerly at the agent's hand. His other hand shot forward, finger outstretched, pointing straight at Mateo. The joy on his face was unmistakable.

In a heartbeat, he broke free from Shaggy's grip and sprinted down the terminal walkway, weaving through the crowd, nearly bowling over an elderly couple along the way. The couple, recognizing him from the flight, simply chuckled and stepped aside, their smiles widening as they watched the reunion unfold.

Phillipe' reached his brother, throwing his arms around him with such force that Diaz staggered back a step, breath caught in his throat. Phillipe' held on tight, years of longing poured into one embrace, and Diaz returned it just as fiercely, closing his eyes, letting the moment wash over him like grace. For the first time in a long time, his world felt whole.

"Hermano! Hermano!" Phillipe yelled as he hugged his brother. Diaz kissed him on the cheek and brushed his hair back. Phillipe was tall for someone with Down Syndrome, but Diaz still had to lean down to move his hand to his brother's cheeks and lock eyes with him. Under his thick glasses, tears began to roll down Phillipe's cheeks, "Hermano! ¡Te amo!" he yelled uncontrollably.

In Spanish Diaz replied, "My brother, my blood."

Shaggy caught up with the two, out of breath, and interrupted their reunion. "Here are the tickets," he said as he held the two slips of paper in front Diaz, "business first, though."

Diaz returned to his seat and picked up the case, that in his excitement, he had left behind. He opened it and held it in front of the agent. Shaggy flipped through the papers and found what he wanted. Pictures. Pictures of young Casey Bruce and Burt Williams in the act of dumping Dell Phillips' lifeless body into the *Daddy's Girl*. The pictures were stunningly clear although Phillips wasn't visible, only the sheet encompassing him. Shaggy grinned. He didn't want them to convict, only to coerce.

"Kennedy?" Shaggy asked, his tone casual but knowing.

Diaz nodded, a grin tugging at the corners of his mouth. "When we land," he replied smoothly.

Shaggy returned the grin, nodding in agreement. He reached into his coat pocket and handed over the tickets. Diaz grabbed the two tickets to their freedom, crisp and warm from Shaggy's hand. The men shook hands firmly, the kind of grip that sealed more than a deal.

"Better hurry," Shaggy said, glancing toward the nearest terminal screen. "Plane leaves in thirty minutes." He leaned in just slightly, lowering his voice.

"I'll be expecting your call."

Diaz nodded again, tucking the tickets into his jacket, then turned to find his brother and his future waiting.

Diaz eyed him nervously, "The cartel will leave us be?"

Shaggy put two fingers in the air, closed together, and said, "Scout's honor. All taken care of." As he removed his fingers from the air, he suddenly grabbed Diaz' arm, causing Phillipe to jump.

"Just remember, *Hermano,* you are in service to the United States of America. Congratulations for you and your brother as her newest citizens, but remember too, it comes at a price."

Phillipe' hadn't said a word since his brother had turned his attention to Shaggy and he was visibly nervous. He didn't understand what was going on, but he could read emotions and the conversation frightened him.

Diaz grabbed him by the hand without a word and the two walked away, blending into the crowd. Shaggy closed the case and sat down in the exact seat Diaz occupied moments before. He closed his eyes and thought about the journey that lay ahead. He stood up, elbowed his way through the crowd, making his way to a row of pay phones.

He glanced around the terminal, eyes scanning for a payphone with some privacy. Spotting one tucked near a quiet vending area, he made his way over and picked up the receiver.

No one nearby. Perfect. He dialed the number quickly, letting it ring twice before hanging up. A signal. A test. Then he dialed again.

This time, the line barely made it to the second ring before someone on the other end answered. No greeting. No hesitation. Just breath on the line, waiting. They knew who it was.

In smooth, measured Spanish, he spoke into the receiver,

"General, everything is in place. Your visitors are on their way. Give me a couple months, and we'll be ready."

There was a pause and then a single word came through the line:

"Admitido."

Then the line went dead. Shaggy calmly returned the receiver to the cradle, his face unreadable. He turned, briefcase in hand, and began walking toward the exit of the sprawling airport, the crowd seemed to part around him.

He had a meeting in the heart of the city with Veck Baxter and Jefferson Black. And punctuality, in his world, wasn't just courtesy. It was survival.

Pelham Pugh

The Fractured Horizons Series:

Perfidious Tides

Last Castle in the Sky

Live the Last Day (Fall 2025)

If you enjoyed *Last Castle in the Sky* please leave a review
on Amazon and/or Goodreads.com

Thanks,

Pelham Pugh